THE WAY YOU LOOK TONIGHT

Books by Carlene Thompson

Black for Remembrance
All Fall Down

THE WAY YOU LOOK TONIGHT

Carlene Thompson

Hodder & Stoughton

First published in Great Britain in 1995
by Hodder and Stoughton
A division of Hodder Headline PLC

10 9 8 7 6 5 4 3 2 1

British Library Cataloguing in Publication Data

Thompson, Carlene
Way You Look Tonight
I. Title
813.54 [F]

ISBN 0 340 63262 3

Typeset by Avon Dataset Ltd, Bidford-on-Avon, B50 4JH

Printed and bound in Great Britain by
Mackays of Chatham, Chatham, Kent

Hodder and Stoughton
A division of Hodder Headline PLC
338 Euston Road
London NW1 3BH

In memory of Margie

Thanks to Janice Daniels, Dick Young, Dave Sizemore and George Lucas

Prologue

When he entered the bar at ten, Kelly's was packed, which he guessed was usual for a Saturday night. Every few minutes the door opened, spilling a shaft of light, the blare of the jukebox, a gust of cigarette smoke into the cold, quiet night. That's how all those places were – loud, bright, smoky. He endured several cigarettes, sipped three shots of abysmally bad Scotch diluted with flat soda, diplomatically fended off the attentions of a fiftyish barmaid with a lumpy figure and careworn eyes, and managed to speak briefly to only two other people for over an hour and a half. Then he left.

Outside, a frigid gust of air washed over him. He drew a deep breath. Brisk, clear, clean air, he thought. Pure. Snow fell heavily, veiling the street lights, carpeting the sidewalk, forming small drifts against storefronts. He remembered being eight years old and climbing on to a red sled he'd found abandoned on the sidewalk, waiting for the garbage truck. He'd been too young to care about its chipped paint and bent runner. He was only aware of the sharp air, the lacy snow sparkling in the moonlight on the hill behind his house, the exciting ride ahead . . .

He shook his head slightly, bringing himself back to the matter at hand, lit a cigarette, and focused again on Kelly's. A couple emerged, laughing giddily as the woman slid on the snow. They headed north, away from him. For the next few minutes, no one else came out. As if drawn by a distant, irresistible call, they had abruptly started abandoning the bar half an hour ago. Now the stream of revelers had begun to trail off. It must be near closing time.

Kelly's blue neon sign shone. The sign was what had attracted him to the bar – the blue glow turned spectral by the mystical veil of snow. He had an appreciation of lights, and this one was lovely. He wondered how many other people were sensitive to its impressionistic beauty. Not many.

He'd found most people had exasperatingly dull, prosaic perceptions. He always reminded himself that he shouldn't measure them against himself. After all, he was special – intelligent, sensitive – things people in those pathetic Personal columns claimed to be but probably weren't. However, he couldn't help being constantly aware of his superiority. It was a fact of life.

He was half finished with his cigarette when a woman came out the door. He'd seen her earlier, sitting at the bar, not in one of the booths. She was a regular because the bartender had greeted her by name. Sally? Was that it? It didn't matter. Names gave people an identity, so he didn't like to think about them, not even nicknames.

She stood uncertainly in front of the door, squinting up the street then down, toward him. He was not well concealed, but that wasn't important. She didn't have *his* vision, despite her youth and beauty. He recalled from the bar that her eyes had been large and gentle, her face pure, innocent perfection. She'd reminded him of Olivia Hussey in the movie *Romeo and Juliet*. A rose among thorns. At times like this he always thought of the song 'The Way You Look Tonight'. He sang softly, his words drifting away in the cold wind. 'Some day when I'm awf'ly low/When the world is cold/I will feel a glow just thinking of you/And the way you look tonight.' His mother loved that song.

In the gleam of the blue light, he could see the girl blinking rapidly against the snow peppering her smooth face. The man's heart beat faster as he stared at her, willing her to come his way. Every nerve in his body seemed to ignite as he waited, willing, *willing*. The girl turned north, took two steps, then abruptly turned around.

That was the Power! he thought exultantly. No one was immune to the Power, the power of *his* will, especially not the unformed mind of a young female.

He tossed away his cigarette and slowly, quietly slid down until he was sitting on the snow. She hurried along, then halted when she heard his moan echoing in the alley. 'Miss,' he called feebly. 'Miss!' She tensed, ready to run, but still stared at him. 'Somebody mugged me,' he slurred, pulling a red-stained handkerchief away from the side of his head where the hair grew thick. 'Hit me. Don't think I can walk.' She hesitated as snow fell steadily on her long, shining dark hair. She looked like a frightened child, not sure whether to be friendly or run as fast as she could for home. Then she frowned. 'Do I know you?'

2

'I don't think so,' he said in an instinctive bid for anonymity, then realized his mistake. She wanted to help and vaguely acknowledging an acquaintance would have erased her fear. Now suddenly reversing himself and announcing she *did* know him would sound like a lie and send her scurrying away. Better not to out-think himself. Just play it pitiful. He spoke more clearly, injured innocence throbbing in his voice. 'Miss, please. If you'll just help me up, I'll find a phone and call an ambulance.' He stood, then bent forward. 'Oh, God!'

She was beside him in an instant. A big-city woman wouldn't be so gullible, he thought with amusement. But in a place like Wheeling, West Virginia, they tended to be more trusting. He always counted on that fact. He pulled away the handkerchief and groaned. 'I didn't know there was so much *blood*. Oh well, I'll live, although I'm awfully dizzy,' he mumbled with a feeble laugh, noticing how her dangling gold filigree earrings caught the dim light.

She was all business, suddenly in control. Or so she thought. 'You just put your arm around my neck, mister. We'll get you in that bar down the street and call for help.'

The man's gloved right hand slipped into his coat pocket and closed around something as he smiled at her with carefully practiced gratitude. 'You're an angel, young lady. You'll be rewarded for your goodness.'

TWO

Twenty minutes later what was left of Sally Yates opened her eyes. Pain. It overwhelmed her awareness. Pain and a cruel, suffocating band around her throat. She clawed at it. A rope. A rope with knots. Around the rope, warm slickness.

She reached up and touched her head. The left side felt strange – dented. Blood gushed from it, covering her face, saturating her hair, dripping on her white imitation-wool coat she thought so elegant. Her hand trailed down to an eye-socket puffed shut, a crushed cheek, and further down to the jagged end of a bone sticking out in the jaw area. What in the name of God had he done to her face? Then she remembered – the hammer. She'd seen it after he laughed as he jerked the pierced earrings from her ear-lobes.

The pain was almost unbearable. Dazed, she rolled over, fighting for balance, her mind reeling. 'You got no business goin' out tonight.' Her mother's words rang in her head. 'Jack's gonna skin you alive if he finds out.'

'I'm twenty-two,' Sally had protested. 'He's always gone and he never wants to have any fun. Besides, I'm just going to a movie.'

'Movie, my foot. You're goin' to that bar – that Kelly's. You should stay home and mind your baby.'

Amy. Safe at home with Sally's nagging but loving mother. But what if Sally didn't survive this? Amy would be raised by Jack, who was quick to scream and hit and kick when things didn't go his way.

The thought of her eight-month-old baby flooded Sally with new resolution. Fighting the urge to lie back in the snow and let darkness descend, shutting out the pain and the horror, she forced herself to look up. With her right eye she saw something looming above her. She reached out. Cold metal. A dumpster, she thought, fighting for clarity. He'd pulled her behind a dumpster before he yanked the rope so tight it cut off her air and rendered her half-conscious before the rape and the beating.

She tried to swallow and choked on something in her mouth. She spit up a small wad of . . . of what? Leaves? Twigs? She couldn't see in the dark. More bits floated around in her mouth, lodged near the broken jaw bone, but she didn't have the energy or the tolerance of pain to dig them out with her tongue.

Her breath rasping, trying to force its way past the stricture of the rope, she clambered to her knees and crawled. Her stomach churned with nausea. Her left third finger hurt and hung at an odd angle. It was broken, and her wedding ring was gone. How strange, she thought dimly. The bastard took my wedding ring!

Snow coated her hair and pressed against her bare knees – her panty-hose were in shreds – but she couldn't feel the cold as much as she had when she first opened her eyes. Snow crunched beneath her weight as she dragged herself to the street, the street where people might be, the street where lights glowed, where help lay.

She fell sideways a couple of times, and once she was aware of slithering along, like a snake, her tongue protruding as she fought for air. The nails she'd manicured just that evening broke raggedly as she pulled herself forward, occasionally reaching for the rope around her neck, the rope embedded deep in her young, soft skin. She'd lost her shoes, she realized dreamily. Good shoes. Her very best. Real leather. Have to find them later.

The street. Through her one good eye she surveyed the area. No one around, but she dragged herself on. On and on. Everything whirled and she closed her eye, still pulling herself forward. After an eternity she heard someone shouting, 'What the hell?' Dimly she became aware of people around her. A man turned her over, then muttered, 'Sweet Jesus, no!'

She felt an absurd wave of embarrassment, an irrational desire to cover her ruined face, but her hands wouldn't move any more. 'It's Sally!'

'How can you tell?' a woman quavered.

'The hair. Sally, what happened?'

Hank, the bartender. She tried to talk, but no words emerged. Her throat seemed swollen shut. He worked futilely at the rope.

Sally's body went limp. She'd lived through the strangling, the rape, and the beating, but something was happening in her brain. Her physical sensations were dimming. Brain damage. She knew – she was a nurse. Desperately she fought to regain the pain that indicated continued life and normal brain function.

'Who did this to you?' Hank demanded.

The woman's voice rose eerily. 'Oh, lordy, lordy! Look at her face! She's beaten to a pulp!' She moaned. 'I think I'm gonna faint. I'm goin' down right this instant.'

'Stop worrying about yourself and call for help!' Hank shouted.

'I can't. I'm sick. I'm shakin' like a leaf.'

'Dammit, Belle, stop actin' like a jackass. You're scarin' the hell out of her.'

'*I'm* scarin' her! Listen, she's way past scared. Can't you see she's dyin'?'

Dying, Sally thought in one last, dim flash. I'm dying on a cold, snowy sidewalk, all because a man in an alley asked for help.

1

'Great party, as usual.'

Deborah Robinson looked at Pete Griffin's reddening cheeks and forehead perspiring below thinning brown hair. She'd thought earlier the room was getting a bit stuffy. Pete's condition proved her right. The roaring fire in the fireplace was adding too much heat. 'I'm glad you're enjoying it, Pete,' she said, making a mental note to turn down the thermostat and lower the furnace heat. 'We've never had a party this big.'

'I feel a little out of place with all these attorneys. Am I the only non-lawyer you and Steve know?'

Deborah laughed and started to say, 'Of course not.' Then she glanced around the room. Everyone was either a lawyer or accompanying one. 'It doesn't look like we do, does it? But you know how our Christmas parties usually turn out – gatherings for the people Steve works with in the Prosecutor's office.'

'Well, it was nice of you to invite me anyway.'

'We *always* invite you. You're one of Steve's oldest friends.'

Pete grinned. 'Steve's just hoping I'll start doing his taxes for free.'

'It's always good to have a CPA on your side, particularly one who owns the largest CPA firm in town. By the way, where's your son?'

'At fifteen, Adam considers himself too cool for parties like this. He's at a friend's house listening to brain-rattling heavy-metal music and complaining because I won't get him a car.'

'He doesn't even have a driver's license yet.'

'Adam considers that a moot point,' Pete said, pulling a droll face. 'He thinks we should be planning and saving. He wants a Viper.'

'Just the thing for a new driver.'

'I agree. A fifteen-year-old with a fifty-thousand-dollar sports car. I get dizzy just thinking about it.'

Deborah laughed. She understood why Pete was Steve's closest friend. Aside from sharing memories dating back to when they were children, Pete was intelligent, unassuming, and always there when you needed him. Deborah had always been particularly fond of him, with his diffident manner which hid a dry humor and iron devotion to the son he'd raised alone after his wife left him three years ago, never even trying to get custody of the child and rarely communicating with him. The last she'd heard, Hope Griffin was in Montana, valiantly working at preserving the environment. 'Save the wolves and abandon your own son,' Deborah's husband Steve had said sourly. 'Now there's a woman with her priorities straight.'

'Personally, I think it would be wonderful to be fifteen and have so many hopes and dreams,' Deborah said, trying to put Pete's concerns over his son's grand ambitions back in perspective. 'I remember at that age I thought I was going to be the next Karen Carpenter.'

Pete smiled. 'And I was going to be the next Frank Lloyd Wright.'

'I didn't know you were interested in architecture.'

'I wasn't after I found out being able to do some oil paintings my grandmother gushed over didn't mean I had a talent for building design.'

'I guess our experiences were similar. All it took for me was hearing a tape of myself singing "Rainy Days and Mondays" to do the trick. I was horrified. Still, it was fun for a while to believe anything was possible.'

'Adam is still at that stage. He changes his mind nearly every week about what he wants to do with his life. Last week he saw *Top Gun* again, so now he's going to be a jet pilot. Wait until your little Brian gets to be this age.'

Deborah looked at him in mock horror. 'He's only five. I hope I have a few more peaceful years.'

Pete glanced at his watch. 'I really hate to put a damper on the party, although I don't think I'll be missed, but I told Adam I wanted him home at eleven. I like to be there waiting for him, so I should be going.'

'You could call from here to make sure he's heading home soon.'

'And humiliate him in front of his friends?' Pete shook his head sadly. 'Deborah, you have a lot to learn about teenagers. That would bring on several days of sullen silences and looks full of burning resentment. I don't think I'm up to it. No, I'll just be waiting like a huge mound of conscience when he gets in. If he's not on time, I'll be able to deliver my

7

time-worn speech on trust, responsibility, and the consideration he deserves to give other people, particularly his poor old dad.'

'You're a cruel and heartless man,' Deborah laughed.

'The worst. It's my greatest joy in life.'

Deborah signaled Steve, who was talking to Evan Kincaid. Steve – rangy and earnest-looking although capable of a rare, boyish grin – hurried to her, his light brown hair damp at the hairline, his own color heightened.

'So, how're we doing over here?' he asked easily.

'Pete thinks he should go home to check on Adam.'

'He's not sick, is he?'

'No, just out partying with friends.'

'Is that all? In that case, how about having one drink with me before you go? I think I've got some really good stuff out in the kitchen. Chivas Regal, twelve years old.'

'That's hard to turn down,' Pete said. 'But Adam . . .'

'Hey, cut the kid some slack, will you? Fifteen minutes isn't such a big deal.'

Pete looked torn, then smiled. 'All right, a quick one and then I'm on the road.'

'Can you do without me for a few minutes?' Steve asked Deborah.

'I'll try to muddle through, but don't you two start talking over the good old high-school days and stay in there for ever.'

'We'll try not to,' Steve laughed over his shoulder as the two started toward the kitchen.

No, they certainly wouldn't, Deborah thought. Pete was much too concerned about Adam to linger for long. He was overprotective with the boy, and according to Steve, had been ever since his divorce. He'd lost his wife and he was afraid of losing his son, too, which was unlikely because beneath Adam Griffin's teenage bravado, he was deeply attached to his father. Still, she knew that Steve, meaning to be kind in asking to have a private drink with Pete, was merely making the man more nervous about his delayed arrival home.

Deborah sighed and gazed around her large living room which had once been divided into two smaller rooms whose different functions she had never been able to determine. Steve had resisted taking out the wall between them – too much trouble, he said – but Deborah insisted. Now the two small rooms formed one spacious room made airy by a huge front window instead of the four small, paned windows that were impossible to clean.

Deborah was pleased with the remodeling and thought Steve was, too, although he never said much about her efforts, obviously hoping not to encourage her to make further changes.

The smell of roast duck, candied yams, and mulled wine wafted over her from the buffet table. Her stomach rumbled maddeningly – she'd been so consumed with fixing food for two days it had lost its aesthetic appeal. Empty stomach or not, she didn't feel she could force down a bite. Besides, she was very tired. It seemed every year the party became more elaborate, and she liked to cook everything, not order from a caterer. She now found the parties more exhausting than fun, and the family ended up eating leftovers for days.

She circled around the room, asking if she could freshen drinks, offering cookies and reminding people about all the apple, pumpkin, and mincemeat pie still sitting on the buffet table. One attorney, whose name Deborah could never remember, was holding forth on a case he'd handled last year while his wife interrupted constantly, correcting everything he said, oblivious to the growing coldness of his eyes and tightening of his jaw. The girlfriend of another was talking loudly to a blue-haired matron about a serial killer luridly named 'The Dark Alley Strangler' by a local newspaper. 'It scares me to death to think he struck again just last Saturday night and this time right here in West Virginia,' she was saying. 'That's seven times in three years. And that last girl. Poor thing. She was a nurse with a little kid. She's still hanging on, but they don't expect her to live.'

Deborah cringed. She supposed it was only natural that the serial killer would be mentioned at the party, but this was supposed to be a festive occasion and the discussion of violent death threw a definite pall over the evening. So much for holiday cheer.

Deborah moved on, turning down the thermostat five degrees and seeing that her guests were comfortable. Few were friends of hers. Most of them came from Steve's world, and she sensed a lot of them thought Steve had married beneath himself. Steve told her she was imagining things, but she felt their distance. Part of it was her own fault, though. She wasn't the life of the party or the confident socialite. In fact, she had come to hate the Christmas parties, which had been a pleasant ritual she and Steve started the first year they were married and over the past seven years had turned into an ordeal. Maybe this one would be the last, Deborah mused. Maybe next year she could talk him into having only a few close friends over before Christmas.

She retreated to a corner of the living room, Campari and soda in hand. Light refracted off the layers of smoke. Even the lights on the Christmas tree seemed muted, as if circled by fog. Her eyes stung beneath her contact lenses and although she had given up smoking two years ago, Deborah now felt an overwhelming desire for a cigarette – *anything*, even if it were one of the reduced tar and nicotine brands she used to hate. She would be tempted to smoke again until the room aired out, which would take a couple of days, she thought unhappily. Thank goodness she and Steve had only one party a year. If the house smelled of smoke too often, she'd never control her urge for nicotine.

She knew she should get out there among the guests and socialize, but her head was starting to hurt, she was dead tired after all her cooking, and she was feeling more and more self-conscious in the white wool dress with scoop neck and gold belt that had drawn Steve's look of censure earlier. 'Don't you think that's a little . . . revealing?' he'd asked gently. 'Why not wear the black velvet – the one I bought you just last year?' How could she tell him the black velvet dress felt bunchy and hot, its sleeves too tight, its skirt too long even for her five-foot-eight frame? Still, she would have changed to please him if the doorbell hadn't rung just then with the arrival of their first guests.

Deborah smiled across the room at Barbara Levine, her friend and Steve's associate in the Prosecutor's office. She'd met Barbara the first year she worked as a secretary in the office. One dreary November Sunday they ran into each other in a video store, both looking for *Dr Zhivago*. Barbara had already found the movie and was paying the rental fee when Deborah went to the desk, asking if it were available. The salesgirl told her they had only one copy. 'Oh, I guess I'll look for something else,' she said, disappointed, when Barbara suddenly suggested, 'Why don't you come home with me and watch it?' Stunned at such an invitation from the seemingly all-business, hard-as-nails lawyer who had intimidated her from day one in the office, Deborah had demurred, but Barbara insisted. They watched the movie in Barbara's apartment, eating microwave popcorn ('the only thing I can cook,' Barbara confided) and by the end of the movie they were both in tears when the handsome Zhivago fell dead in the street while chasing his oblivious, beloved Lara. Later they had gone to an Italian restaurant together, and from that day on, Deborah had lost her fear of Barbara. They'd become friends, both with a deep love of animals, romantic movies, and Agatha Christie novels.

10

Barbara crossed the room to her side. 'Has Steve deserted us?'

'He's in the kitchen having a drink with Pete.' Barbara smiled.

'Pete's such a nice guy. I wonder why he never remarried.'

'I suppose because he was so badly burned the first time. And he devotes a lot of time to Adam and the grandmother in Wheeling who raised him after his parents died. She's in her eighties and has a lot of health problems.'

'None of those reasons seem good enough for him to have cut himself off from a social life,' Barbara said. 'He needs a girlfriend, someone with some life who'll make him start acting his age. *And* make him get a new wardrobe. His clothes all look too big, not to mention years out of date. I'm no fashion plate myself, but it seems like he's *trying* to look ten years older than he is.'

'Remarks like that won't earn you a visit from Santa.'

Barbara giggled, her laughter softening her dark, hawk-like features. When she was young, she'd probably been attractive in a chiseled, dramatic way, Deborah often thought. But at thirty-eight, after fifteen years of twelve-hour work days and little in the way of beauty care, she usually looked thin, tense, and slightly weather-beaten with her uncreamed skin and face naked of make-up except for a careless slash of lipstick. Tonight she'd chosen an unflattering bright pink. Right now some of that pink decorated a front tooth, but Deborah had learned how defensive Barbara could be about her appearance.

'By the way, you look great,' Barbara said. 'I knew that dress was for you as soon as we spotted it in the store window.'

'Steve doesn't like it.'

'No, probably not. He's a sweet man, but he wants you to look a dowdy sixty-year-old instead of a sexy twenty-eight-year-old.'

'Oh, Barbara, he doesn't.'

'Yes, he does. He doesn't want you flying the coop into the arms of some other guy.'

'That's hardly likely. Besides, you think Steve's a lot more Machiavellian than he is.'

'Says you. You've been brainwashed into thinking you aren't anything special in the looks department. I, on the other hand, am beginning to resemble my mother, and she *is* in her sixties.' She held up a chocolate almond cookie she'd been munching. 'And these don't help maintain a girlish figure.'

'Barbara, you're thin as a rail.'

'Flabby thin, not taut thin like you.'

'You don't run after five-year-old twins and a dog all day. But in any case you do *not* look like you're in your sixties.'

'Well, I at least look every year of my age plus a few more.'

Yes, she did look every year of her age, Deborah thought with regret. It was no wonder everyone had been surprised when Barbara began dating Evan Kincaid, seven years Barbara's junior and considered the glamour boy of the Prosecutor's office. According to Steve, some of the young secretaries could barely hide their jealousy and constantly made catty remarks behind Barbara's back about the relationship. 'But I understand it,' Steve said. 'Barbara's a brilliant, witty woman. Besides, Evan isn't one to judge by exteriors.'

'He's like you in that respect.'

Steve smiled. 'Sweetheart, you're a very nice-looking woman.'

Nice-looking, Deborah thought dismally. Nice-looking with her long black hair Steve liked to see pulled back in a French braid and serious blue-gray eyes usually hidden behind glasses she wore when working, nice-looking with her tall, slender frame he preferred in simple clothes, nice-looking with her smooth, creamy skin which cosmeticians at the department store make-up counters claimed was more like that of a woman five years younger. Nice-looking, but not a beauty like some of his former girlfriends had been.

'A quarter for your thoughts,' Barbara said.

'A *quarter*?'

'Inflation.'

'I was just thinking about some of the women Steve used to date. Where's my quarter?'

'I don't have my purse with me. And why in the *world* would you be thinking about women Steve used to date?'

'Do you remember the ones who used to come by the office? They were so flashy. I wonder why he picked me.'

'Maybe because they were *all* flash and no substance. I remember giving him a stern talking-to about that one time.'

'I'm sure he appreciated it.'

'He told me to mind my own business. But shortly afterward he started dating you. Smartest move he ever made.'

'Spoken like a true friend. Some of them even had money.'

'Money?' Evan Kincaid said, walking up and putting his arm around

12

Barbara's waist. 'Are you two discussing the root of all evil?'

Barbara made a face. 'He's not only great-looking, he's a mind-reader.'

'No, a lip-reader,' Evan laughed. 'I've been hovering nearby, although you two were too engrossed to notice me.'

'Deborah is torturing herself by wondering why Steve didn't marry some flashy woman with money.'

Evan shook his head. 'Sometimes I think you women look for something to worry about.'

Barbara threw Deborah a wry look. 'Men, of course, never worry.'

Evan laughed. 'Not like you do. In any given day the love of my life here thinks of at least twenty things to fret over.'

'I do *not*!' Barbara protested in offended rage, although she couldn't hide her pleasure at hearing Evan call her the love of his life. They had been seeing each other for nine months, and Barbara had confided that the last two hadn't been smooth. 'He thinks I pull rank on him because I'm older,' Barbara said. 'You do,' Deborah returned frankly. Barbara looked sheepish. 'I know. I hear myself doing it, but I can't seem to stop.'

Now, however, Barbara glowed as she looked adoringly up at the blond, blue-eyed Evan who Deborah thought resembled a young Robert Redford.

The resemblance was even more pronounced than usual tonight. Maybe it was the lighting, or maybe it was that Evan looked more relaxed than he often did. Either he and Barbara were getting along better, or the drinks had erased some tension from his incredibly handsome face.

Evan raised his eyebrows enquiringly, and Deborah realized she was staring at him. 'Can I fix the two of you fresh drinks?' she asked quickly.

'I think I've had my limit,' Evan said, holding up a half-empty glass. 'Barbara?'

'This mulled wine is delicious, but powerful. One more glass and I'll start telling dirty jokes.'

'Cut her off, Deborah,' Evan said abruptly. 'Dirty or clean, she couldn't tell a joke right if her life depended on it.'

'That is not true,' Barbara retorted. 'I heard a hilarious one just today. You see, there was this—'

'Oh, God,' Evan groaned in exaggerated dismay.

'I have to check on things in the kitchen,' Deborah laughed, turning away from them.

'Coward,' Evan muttered.

Steve was closing the back door behind Pete when she walked into the kitchen. 'Everything okay?'

He glanced at her, relief showing in his green eyes which had looked tired and a little bloodshot lately. 'Yeah. I wish the guy would let up on Adam. He acts like some old-maid aunt or something.'

Deborah put her arms around his neck. 'Honey, saying "old maid" is no longer politically correct. And *why* does everyone act like overprotection is the sole domain of women?'

Steve raised an eyebrow at her. 'Mrs Robinson, drink has loosened your tongue. However, I stand corrected.'

'Thank you for allowing me to speak my mind. You're simply too kind,' Deborah said drily.

'No, I'm simply tired to my bones, not to mention a little worried about Pete. I wonder what will happen to him when Adam leaves home and he doesn't have anyone to stew over?'

'Barbara thinks he should find some nice woman.'

'That *would* be a perfect solution. But he's lived alone so long. And he was never a ladies' man, even when we were young. Then there's the fact that he's been very successful. He could get entangled with someone who's just after his money. I guess any romantic pairing is a risk, though.'

'Is that how you felt about our marriage?'

Steve tightened his arms around her waist. 'No. I knew we'd work out.'

Although he smelled strongly of the cigarette smoke that was stirring Deborah's desire for nicotine, she loved his embrace. Steve was not a demonstrative man and if he hadn't recently consumed a few drinks, he probably wouldn't be hugging her in the kitchen with twenty guests in the living room. Knowing this, however, only slightly lessened Deborah's pleasure. She stood on tiptoe and kissed him lightly. 'I'm glad we got married.'

'Are you?' Steve asked.

Deborah pulled back, looking at him. He seemed troubled. 'Of course. Why do you ask?'

'Because sometimes I think you're disappointed in me.'

And sometimes she was, Deborah thought guiltily. Sometimes she wished she'd married a man who loved her passionately instead of caring for her in the steady, distant way that was Steve's. But those kind of dreams should have been left behind in her teenage years, she reminded herself. This was real life, not one of her cherished romantic movies. Steve wasn't the poet Yuri Zhivago and she wasn't the tragic, dazzling Lara. As her father had often told her, she wasn't beautiful, or talented, or especially intelligent. She was just an ordinary woman whose only gift lay in the ability to keep house and cook well. He'd been disapproving when she'd become a secretary in the Prosecutor's office in Charleston instead of marrying Billy Ray Soames, the Baptist preacher back home in southern West Virginia. Later, his anger at her for marrying a man she'd dated for only two months had been totally out of proportion. In fact, he and her mother had visited only twice during her marriage – once when the twins Brian and Kimberly were born, and again last year when they were passing through Charleston on a rare vacation. In return, Deborah had taken the children to visit them only three times. As a result, Brian and Kimberly were barely aware of their grandparents' existence.

'I'm not disappointed in you,' Deborah said, jerking herself out of her thoughts. 'You're a wonderful man.'

Steve's eyes crinkled at the corners as he smiled down at her. 'And you're a wonderful woman.'

Deborah cocked an eyebrow at him. 'We have to stop these torrid exchanges when we have guests.' Steve laughed, and Deborah felt immeasurably relieved that he appeared more at ease. For the last couple of days he'd seemed morose, distracted, irritable. She knew something was wrong, but he wouldn't discuss the problem.

She hugged him fiercely. 'Hey, trying to break my ribs?'

'Sorry.' She released her hold. 'You know I always get emotional at Christmas.'

'You get emotional over every holiday. That enthusiasm is one of your most endearing traits. It's great for the kids, too. You make holidays an event for them.'

'I just remember when I was a child and my father did nothing but complain about the commercialism of holidays and where had people's values gone, and of course there was no Santa Claus and no Easter Bunny, what nonsense, etcetera, etcetera. It ruined everything for Mom and me.'

'Well, no one could accuse your father of getting a real bang out of life.'

'That's putting it mildly.'

The phone rang and Steve reached for the cordless extension on the kitchen counter. 'I'll get it. And right before I came in here, I noticed we were getting low on ice. There's no more left in the freezer.'

15

'There's a bag in the deep freezer in the garage. You take care of the phone and I'll take care of the ice.'

Opening the kitchen door into the garage, Deborah was at first shocked by the difference in temperature. Then she gratefully breathed in the cold, clear air. The heat and smoke and noise inside had been aggravating her dull headache. She flipped on the garage light and glanced at her watch: 11.15. The party would be winding up in about half an hour. Some of the guests had already left. Thank goodness. Although she'd have a ton of food to put away, maybe within a couple of hours she could get her aching feet out of these new and very tight high-heeled shoes and into her bed. She was exhausted and felt like she could sleep until noon tomorrow.

She lifted the heavy freezer lid. Frosty air wafted up, making her gasp. As she leaned over, she spotted something red atop the foil-wrapped meats. Brian's toy fire truck. She pulled it out, alarmed. Obviously the kids had been playing and managed to open the freezer. What if one of them decided to climb in? It wouldn't take long to smother if help didn't arrive immediately, and she couldn't keep her eyes on both children constantly, especially since she did so much clerical work at home. Presently she was typing a would-be author's manuscript which contained grammatical errors in almost every sentence. She spent hours poring over grammar books so she could prove to the defensive author that she wasn't making up rules as she went along. She would put a lock on the freezer, she decided. She'd buy a padlock tomorrow.

She lay the toy truck, coated with a heavy layer of frost, on the floor and lifted the bag of ice. As she was coming back into the kitchen, Steve flashed her a quick, almost apprehensive look. 'Certainly. Thank you for calling,' he said stiffly into the receiver, then hung up. 'Here. Let me help with the ice.'

'Who was on the phone?' Deborah handed him the cold plastic bag. His hands shook slightly.

'Joe.'

'Joe?' Joe Pierce was an investigator with the Prosecutor's office. 'Why is he calling at this hour?'

'News about a case.'

'He's working past eleven o'clock on a Saturday night? Is that why he didn't come to the party?'

'I think he had a hot date.'

'Women are allowed at the party.'

'I don't believe chit-chatting with people from the office is what he had in mind for tonight. Anyway, you know how he is,' Steve said distractedly, setting the bag of ice in the sink. 'He works with us but he's not prone to socializing with us.'

'Well, why was he calling? To give you a bulletin on his date?'

'Hardly. He just thought of something that might help me.'

'And this thought came to him during his hot date? Things can't be going too well,' Deborah joked. Steve didn't answer. His forehead was creased and he tore into the bag of ice with unnecessary aggression. Her smile faded. 'What case are you two working on?'

'I need the ice bucket.' Deborah stared at him, puzzled. Was he paler? Did his eyes look even more troubled than they had for the past couple of days?

'Steve, is something—'

'I said I need the ice bucket. It's in the living room.'

'I heard you. Why are you acting so strange?'

'I'm not acting strange,' Steve snapped. 'This stuff is cold. It's ice, you know. Would you please get me the bucket?'

Deborah bit back a retort. She usually didn't question Steve about cases, but he'd been so edgy lately and something Joe told him had obviously agitated him further. Clearly, though, he had no intention of confiding in her.

It's probably nothing, she told herself as she walked back into the living room to retrieve the ice bucket. He's just been working too hard lately and the strain is beginning to tell. In a couple of weeks, when the holidays are over, everything will be fine and we'll return to our humdrum routine.

Unfortunately, she didn't believe herself for one minute.

2

Tired as she was after the party, Deborah had trouble falling asleep. Steve lay beside her, quietly snoring. After eighteen years of listening to her father's stentorian snores which seemed to shake their cheap little house to the foundation, she had deeply appreciated the quiet she found in her small Charleston apartment. After marrying Steve, she'd been dismayed to find that he, too, snored. But at least he didn't make the window-rattling racket her father did, and she'd soon learned to ignore it.

Tonight, however, the snoring set her nerves on edge. She resisted an urge to give Steve a sharp nudge in the ribs. He would only emit an incomprehensible grumble, then resume the noise within two minutes. Sighing gustily, Deborah turned on her side and pulled the pillow around her head. Very comfortable, she thought sourly. And I can still hear him.

Oh, Deborah, what's really wrong? she wondered, rolling on to her back and releasing the pillow. Are you like the kids, who turn cranky when they're overtired? Or is it something more complicated? Are you resentful because every year you put in so much work on a party for a bunch of people who are mostly strangers to you? Or are you hurt by how completely Steve shut you out after that phone call this evening? Yes, her mind said. It was all three, but mostly the phone call which bothered her.

She didn't expect her husband to confide everything that went on in the Prosecutor's office, but that call was different. That call seemed *personal*, she thought suddenly. And he'd hung up so quickly. The idea of a mistress flashed through her mind, but she quickly dismissed it. She had never for a moment during their marriage doubted Steve's fidelity. No, the call *was* business, just as Steve had said. But it wasn't ordinary business. She'd seen Steve express frustration, even anger over a case, but never the hand-trembling tension she'd witnessed earlier. And although he was sleeping

18

now, he'd drunk more heavily than usual all evening, and even more so after the call. Steve wasn't sleeping the sleep of a peaceful man. He was sleeping the sleep of a drunken man.

Impatiently, Deborah threw back the covers and walked to the window, peeking between the mini-blinds. How cold everything looked in the bleak light of the halogen dusk-to-dawn lamp attached to the back of the garage. Bare deciduous trees loomed over a carpet of frost-stiffened brown grass. The flower garden was an empty plot. The fanciful bird-bath Barbara had given them one summer bore an inch of frozen water. The only things that seemed alive were the evergreens planted along the back fence. She smiled. It had been Steve's idea to buy a living tree every Christmas and plant it in the back yard when the holidays were over. The one they'd bought for the children's first Christmas was the largest, standing tall and green in the far left-hand corner of the yard.

Distantly she could hear the brass wind-chimes she'd hung on the roof of the small back porch. A gentle breeze sent them dancing merrily. Slowly the breeze picked up speed and they jangled, no longer melodious but strident, demanding. She looked back at the evergreens to see their feathery branches waving—

Something moved near the tallest tree. Surprised, Deborah frowned and squinted, reaching for her glasses only inches away on the nightstand. She slipped them on and looked intently. The figure appeared to be just under three feet high. A dog? She couldn't think of any dogs in the neighborhood that tall or with hair thick enough to form such bulk. Actually, since the Vincents down the street had gone to Florida for Christmas and taken their ancient toy poodle Pierre, there were *no* dogs in the neighborhood aside from their own, Scarlett. Besides, the back yard was surrounded by a chain-link fence and last month, after Scarlett had learned to flip open the latch, Deborah had found a strong clip at the hardware store to keep it fastened. The gate couldn't possibly come loose without the use of human hands.

The figure stood up. Deborah drew in her breath. It was a man wearing a billed cap and a bulky jacket. He was watching their house, seeming to stare right back into her eyes.

Light bloomed behind her. 'What's wrong?' Steve mumbled.

Deborah whirled. 'Someone's out there! A man is hiding around the evergreens.'

Steve shot out of bed and within seconds was stampeding down the stairs. Deborah flew along behind him. 'Steve, what are you doing? We should call the police!'

He ignored her, charging ahead like a man possessed. By the time they reached the kitchen, Deborah was winded. 'Steve, we have to call—' She broke off in horror as Steve jerked open the back door. 'He could have a *gun*,' she cried.

Steve didn't stop and, in her shock, she automatically followed. They both exploded out the door in a flurry of instinctive behavior and stood on the back porch, robeless and barefoot. Deborah shivered. 'Steve, this is crazy,' she said tensely, the cold air snapping her back to rational thinking. 'We have two little children upstairs. If we're shot and killed—'

'Go inside,' Steve hissed.

'But—'

'I said to go inside!'

She stepped back into the house, amazed as she watched Steve stalk off the porch back to the evergreens. He went between and behind every one of them, and she thought she heard him saying something. Deborah shuddered, waiting for a burst of gunfire, Steve's scream as a knife plunged into his stomach, or even the sight of his body dropping from a powerful blow to the head. But after a couple of minutes, he emerged and raised his shoulders. 'Nothing out here.'

'But there was,' she insisted.

'Some kind of animal,' Steve said, his arms folded across his chest as he loped back across the lawn, his bare feet obviously suffering the bite of frozen ground.

'It was *not* an animal,' Deborah maintained, stepping out on the porch again, blocking Steve from entering the back door. 'It was a man. He must have run when he saw our bedroom light go on.'

'I doubt that. He'd have to move pretty fast and there's not a sign of anyone having been around the evergreens.'

'You mean he didn't leave the convenient lighter or even his gun?' she asked, her voice turned waspish by Steve's casual attitude. 'And since when do animals stand nearly six feet tall? Or do you think perhaps it was a bear?'

Steve was shifting from foot to foot. 'Deb, don't get nasty. Let's get back inside before we freeze to death and be glad no one was there. Like I said, it was probably just a stray dog.'

She stood her ground, searching his harried face with her own worried, angry eyes. What on earth was wrong with him? she wondered in bewilderment. Then she heard the faint sound of metal clinking against metal. Steve's gaze shot to the gate, and Deborah didn't need him to tell her the gate she'd clipped shut that afternoon was open, swaying back and forth in the freezing night wind.

3

Deborah awakened to find Brian, Kimberly, and their brown, mixed-breed dog on the bed with her. Kim had named the dog Scarlett after seeing *Gone with the Wind* on television last year. Although she didn't understand most of the movie and had the impression it was about the period of time when Mommy and Daddy were little, she was enchanted with the ladies' gowns and the name Scarlett O'Hara. Brian, who was in favor of naming their new puppy Lassie, had acquiesced after a violent squabble with his sister during which she threatened to tell every bad thing she knew about him. Deborah, amused, doubted that the little boy had too many awful secrets, but the threat worked.

'Aren't you *ever* gonna get up?' Brian asked.

Deborah shut her eyes against light streaming through the big bedroom window. 'What time is it?' she mumbled.

'Noon.'

Kimberly always said noon, no matter what time of day it was. Deborah opened her eyes again to smile at the blonde-haired, green-eyed child who looked so much like Steve. Brian had dark brown hair and her serious blue-gray eyes.

'It isn't noon,' Brian said solemnly. 'It's 9.31 a.m.'

Brian was extremely proud of his ability to tell time, an ability Kim did not possess and resented mightily. She stuck out her tongue at him. Scarlett – all fifty-five pounds of her – trampled around the double bed, shook her floppy ears vigorously, then darted up to plant a kiss on Deborah's nose.

'What a way to wake up,' Deborah moaned. 'Where's Daddy?'

'In the kitchen drinkin' coffee,' Brian announced. 'We want French toast. He said he can't make it right. He tried to feed us cereal.'

'But we wouldn't eat it,' Kim added staunchly. 'How come you're in bed so late? Did you get drunk last night?'

Deborah looked at her in astonishment. 'I certainly didn't. Where did you get that idea?'

'Terry says her mommy and daddy always get drunk at parties. What's drunk like?'

Deborah gently pushed dog and children aside and struggled to a sitting position. 'Drunk is when you get all dizzy and silly and usually end up sick.'

'How come people'd want to get drunk?' Brian asked.

'Beats me. But neither your daddy nor I got drunk. We were just up until about one o'clock.'

Brian frowned. 'A.m. or p.m.?'

'A.m.,' Deborah said, smiling. 'A.m. comes after midnight.'

Brian stared off as if he were adding this information to some kind of data file. Kim looked disgusted. 'We want French toast,' she said again.

'Okay. If everyone will clear out, I'll get straightened up here and be down in about ten minutes to fix French toast.'

'Can Scarlett have some, too?' Kim asked.

'She usually manages to have some of whatever we eat, although the veterinarian says she shouldn't.'

Kim wrinkled her nose. 'I bet *he* wouldn't like to eat dog food all the time.'

Brian looked at her disparagingly. 'That's 'cause he's not a dog.'

'Kids, please,' Deborah said. 'Downstairs. Brian, you get out the carton of eggs and the milk from the refrigerator. Kim, you get the bread and cinnamon and nutmeg. Put everything on the kitchen counter.'

The children scrambled off the bed, happy to have been assigned such important duties. With Scarlett racing after them, they tore out of the room and down the stairs.

'Don't run on the stairs!' Deborah called, but her words were drowned out by the pounding of small feet and big paws. She sighed. Less than a week until Christmas and the kids were so excited they ran, jumped, and giggled constantly. Deborah wondered if she'd been such a jubilant child at five. She didn't think so.

She climbed from bed, her feet hitting the carpet she'd never wanted. The house she and Steve bought shortly after their marriage was over a hundred years old. The oak floors were in deplorable condition, and she'd wanted to refinish them. Steve had nixed the idea. 'Too much trouble,' he'd said. 'I don't know anything about refinishing, anyway.'

'I do, and I'd love to work on these floors. They'd be so beautiful.'

'Carpet,' Steve had said in a tone that brooked no argument. 'I gave in about taking out the wall downstairs, but that's it. I don't want to be tiptoeing around sticky varnish for the next year. Besides, there were hardwood floors in my parents' house. I hated them.'

Deborah had felt immediately saddened. Steve seemed to hate anything that had to do with his childhood in Wheeling. But his feelings were understandable considering the way it culminated when he was eighteen. That was when the gardener, Artie Lieber, had raped and beaten Steve's younger sister Emily with a pipe. The sixteen-year-old girl had suffered brain damage and although doctors said the damage was more psychological than organic in nature, Emily was spending the rest of her life in a nursing home. Steve's parents were gone that weekend and Steve had been left in charge, told never to leave his sister Emily unguarded because Lieber had been fired after making advances to the girl just a couple of weeks before.

With teenage carelessness, however, Steve *had* left his sister alone for two hours while he went to his girlfriend's house. When he came back, he saw Lieber bending over Emily, his lips still obscenely pressed against the already unconscious girl's. It was Steve's testimony that put Lieber away for thirty to fifty years for sexual assault with a deadly weapon, but the damage was done. Emily lived in little better than a vegetative state, and Steve's parents were never able to forgive him, although they made an effort and kept in touch with him sporadically. Still, that event had been the turning point in Steve's life. It was responsible for his becoming a prosecuting attorney. It was also responsible for turning him into the good if overly serious man he'd become.

Deborah pushed back her hair and reached for her robe. No sense in going over all that, she thought. Maybe long ago the forgiveness of Steve's parents could have eased his overwhelming sorrow and guilt, but now nothing could – not the children, and certainly not her. She had learned to accept that fact. But she could do her best to make his life as happy as possible, even if the effort was sometimes disappointing. He was a good husband, she loved him dearly as she knew he loved her and the children, and they had a pleasant life, free from infidelities and serious arguments. In fact, compared to the life of shouting and domination her mother endured, Deborah's life was almost perfect.

She washed her face, brushed her teeth and hair, and put on a little lipstick to counteract her morning paleness. Racing outside barefoot in thirty-degree weather hadn't helped her appearance, she thought ruefully. Nor had the fact that she'd been unable to sleep for hours after the incident, puzzling over Steve's strange behavior. But at least the children had been unaware of the activity. They hadn't said a word about it.

When she arrived downstairs, Steve was sitting at the table drinking coffee and reading the morning paper while Brian and Kimberly stood by the counter, beaming.

'We got all the stuff,' Brian said proudly.

'He almost dropped the eggs,' Kim added.

Brian scowled at her, but Deborah smiled. For all their bickering, the two children were devoted to each other and nearly inseparable. When their kindergarten teacher, Miss Hart, made them sit on opposite sides of the room, Kim had cried and Brian arrived home announcing he was going to quit school.

'We'd better get started, then.' She looked at Steve. 'How many pieces do you want, honey?'

He glanced up from his paper with an absent smile. 'Don't think I'm too hungry today.'

'Not hungry!' Kim cried. 'But Daddy, it's *French toast*! And it's almost Christmas.'

Steve opened his mouth and Deborah knew that with his perpetual logic he was about to ask what French toast had to do with Christmas, then thought better of it. 'You're right, Kimmy. I'll have two pieces.'

'I want eight,' Brian said.

'*Eight!*' Deborah exclaimed. 'How about starting with two and going from there?'

'Okay, but I can eat eight.'

While Deborah poured milk into a mixing bowl and began stirring in eggs, Brian asked his father, 'Can we put the train around the tree tonight?'

The tall Christmas tree had been put in place and decorated Friday night, but because they were afraid one of the guests might trip over the model train-set Brian always wanted zipping through a wonderland of cotton and toy villages beneath the limbs, they had delayed setting it up until after the party.

'Okay, son. I'll have to get it down from the attic this afternoon.'

'I'll help,' Brian said.

Deborah shook her head. 'No you won't. Those attic steps are too steep.

25

You're going Christmas shopping with Kim and me this afternoon.'

'But I always get to help set up the train,' Brian protested.

'I didn't say you couldn't help set it up. You just can't carry boxes down from the attic. You tried last year and fell.'

Kim giggled and Brian went crimson at the memory of tumbling down the last five stairs and ending up going to the hospital for six stitches in his scalp. 'Scarlett got in my way,' he said hotly.

'We didn't even have Scarlett then,' Kim argued. 'You're just clumsy.'

'Am not!'

'Are too!'

'Kids!' Steve said sternly. 'Remember that Santa's still watching to see who's naughty and nice. Fighting isn't nice.'

They both hushed instantly, terrified they could ruin their chances for all the gifts 'Santa' always left. Deborah grinned as she sprinkled cinnamon and nutmeg into the milk and egg mixture. Steve might have managed to short-circuit the arguments for at least ten minutes with that dire warning.

'Some guy was hiding in the back yard last night,' Brian suddenly announced, trying to make an airplane out of his paper napkin.

Deborah and Steve glanced at each other apprehensively. 'What makes you think that?' Steve asked.

'Scarlett was growling. She left our room and went into the guest room and looked out the window. I got up and looked, but he ran off. Then I saw you, Daddy. You ran out there and you didn't even have your robe on!'

Kim's face creased in concern. 'Was it a robber gonna steal our Christmas presents?'

'No, honey, it was just someone playing a joke,' Deborah said.

'What kind of joke?' Kim asked.

Deborah hesitated. 'A hiding joke.'

Brian looked perplexed. 'Do grown-ups play hide-and-seek?'

Steve was trying not to grin as she floundered for an answer. 'Sometimes. It's a silly thing to do.' She glared at Steve. 'And Daddy was very silly, too, to go out without his robe. He'll probably catch a cold.'

'Are you sure it wasn't a robber?' Kim queried again. 'Mrs Dillman says there's a Tom Peeper around.'

'A peeping Tom,' Deborah corrected. 'And Mrs Dillman gets mixed up sometimes. It was nothing to worry about.' Kim still looked troubled. Wanting to change the subject, Deborah turned to Steve and asked quickly, 'Want to come to the mall with us? It's going to be lots of fun.'

26

Steve went back to his newspaper with ostentatious casualness. 'I hate the mall scene. About a million people will be there today.'

'That's what makes it fun,' Kim said. 'Lots of people.'

'Maybe for you, sugar, but not for me. I can't stand crowds.'

'Oh.' Deborah glanced around to see Kim looking worried before she asked, 'Did you already buy presents?'

Steve smiled. 'Relax, Kimmy. I did my shopping early.'

'That's good,' Kim said, obviously relieved.

'Will any grandmas and grandpas come this year?' Brian piped up.

Deborah was busy putting dripping pieces of bread into butter sizzling in the skillet, but she could feel Steve stiffen. Sometimes she believed one of the things that had drawn them together was their aloneness – she had no siblings, he had only one who had stopped functioning as a normal person fifteen years ago, and both were almost completely estranged from their parents. The difference was that Deborah had never felt close to her mother and father so she did not suffer over their coldness. Steve, on the other hand, couldn't get over losing the love and respect of his. 'I don't think any grandmas or grandpas will be here this year,' he said with a mixture of discomfort and regret.

'That's okay,' Brian returned. 'Jimmy said his grandma and grandpa always come and cause trouble.'

'They *complain*,' Kim explained, proud of her new word. 'Jimmy says they make every Christmas bad.'

Deborah brought the first batch of French toast to the table. 'Well, we'll have more fun because it'll be just the four of us.'

'Five,' Brian said. 'Don't forget Scarlett.'

The dog was standing by the table wearing her most pitiful look as she gazed up at the platter full of fragrant French toast. 'How could we ever forget Scarlett?' Deborah laughed.

Later that day, when she and the children were bundled up and ready for their trip to the mall, Deborah went into the family room where Steve sat with his eyes fixed on a televised football game. She knew that look, though. He wasn't really watching.

'Steve, what's bothering you?'

'Nothing.' After seven years together, he still won't confide in me, Deborah thought. She also knew he grew testy when she pushed, but she couldn't help it. 'You've been behaving oddly for days. And as for last night, I've never seen you be so reckless.'

27

'It was just a dog.'

Deborah tensed. 'Will you stop this ridiculous insistence that I saw a dog? Don't you think I know the difference between a dog and a man'?'

'It was dark and you're nearsighted.'

'The yard is lit and I was wearing my glasses. Honestly, sometimes you act like I'm one of the kids.'

'I do not.'

'Yes, you *do*. And what about the clip on the gate?'

'I don't know.'

'You *do* know someone was out there. You were expecting it. That's why you took off like you did, running barefoot and weaponless into the yard.'

'Yeah, I'm psychic. I was sure we'd have a prowler last night.' The smile he tossed at her didn't take the edge from his voice. She stared back stonily and his eyes dropped. 'Look, I know I've offended you. I'm sorry. And I did behave like a crazy person last night, but I'd had a lot to drink.'

'Steve, stop talking to me like I'm an idiot.'

He looked at her tiredly. 'Okay, maybe there *was* a prowler, but there's no sense in harping on it. The kids will hear you and be scared to death.'

'But I think we should do something.'

'Such as what? Call the police to say you thought you saw someone in the dark, someone who didn't try to break into the house or leave a trace of their presence? It's useless, honey. This isn't television. They're not going to set up surveillance. You'll just frighten the children. If he shows up again, we'll call, but just drop it for now, okay?'

She could call the police herself, of course, but he was right. She would only alarm Kim and Brian for nothing. 'All right,' she said reluctantly. 'But if I see something tonight . . .'

'We'll call in the cavalry.'

'If you don't, I will.'

She caught a flash of something in his eyes – annoyance, shame, and defeat all at the same time. 'We'll do whatever you want,' he said tonelessly.

'Okay.' Then, to ease some of the tension, she asked, 'Sure you don't want to come with us today?'

'Deb, you know I—'

'Hate crowds. Yes, I know. I just thought the kids would get such a kick out of it if you came with us.'

'Is it absolutely necessary for you to go?'

Deborah stared. 'What?'

'Wouldn't shopping be easier on a weekday?'

'Yes, but all the entertainment is today. You know how the children love it.' She frowned. 'Why don't you want us to go?'

'I didn't say I didn't want you to go.'

Irritation flooded through her. 'You're evading me again. Steve, what in heaven's name is *wrong*?'

'Nothing.'

'Like hell. If you're worried about us for some reason, either tell me why or come with us.'

'I'm not worried.'

'You're also one very poor liar.'

Steve's face tightened. 'Deborah, stop badgering me. I have an appointment this afternoon, but if you're so damned determined to go to the mall, then *go*. I just thought you might enjoy shopping when it's not so crowded.'

Deborah thought of the strange call he'd received last night. 'May I ask with whom you have an appointment?'

'No, you may not.' Deborah's eyes narrowed. 'Don't give me that look. It's about . . . a . . . Christmas surprise, so can we *please* not make a federal case out of it?'

Christmas surprise indeed, Deborah thought angrily, but this conversation was going nowhere. She knew when to throw in the towel. 'All *right*, keep your mysterious appointment. But it would mean a lot to the children if you'd come with us.'

'Maybe another time,' Steve said, as if Christmas rolled around every couple of weeks. 'You have fun.'

'How can I help it when you've set such a joyous mood for the day?' Deborah glared at him, infuriated that he had once again shut her out. Something was troubling him, but he wasn't going to give her any information. Well, fine. Let him keep his secrets. 'We'll be back around five,' she snapped. 'Don't forget to get the train-set out of the attic, that is if it doesn't interfere with your mysterious *appointment*.'

4

Forcing down her anger, Deborah strapped the children into her station wagon, pulled out of the driveway and started down the street. Woodbine Court was always quiet – there were only four houses in the little cul-de-sac. Still, it seemed odd to have the place so deserted. The Vincent family two houses down had gone to California for the holidays, and the O'Donnell house across the street, a lovely two-story brick building with a broad bay window overlooking the front lawn, had been for sale ever since the owner had been transferred three years ago. Deborah believed it hadn't sold because it was a bit large and overpriced for this neighborhood. She'd been curious when the realtor's sign in the front yard disappeared several months ago and lately real estate agents had stopped escorting clients through the house, but so far no one had moved in. Perhaps someday it *would* sell, though hopefully to a family with children the right age to be playmates for Kim and Brian.

As Steve had predicted, the Town Center Mall was packed. Deborah had done most of her shopping earlier, for which she was grateful, but the children had wanted to do all of theirs this weekend.

'Got your money?' she asked cheerfully as they crept through the parking garage behind a long line of cars, their drivers all looking for a space. The smell of exhaust fumes crept in even through the closed windows of the station wagon, and Deborah wished everyone would stop dragging along in search of a choice spot when they were all going to end up on the top two floors anyway.

'I got *my* money,' Kim said, pulling out her small red plastic purse. Deborah had decided that this Christmas she would let the children carry their own money. They were only five, but she would be there to supervise their purchases. 'How much did you say I have, Mommy?'

30

'At last count, eighteen dollars seventy-five.' Throughout the year Deborah paid them in dimes and quarters for little chores they did around the house. 'How about you, Brian?'

'Twenty dollars and ten cents,' he said proudly. 'I worked harder than Kim.'

'You did not!' Kim flared.

'Did, too. I picked up those leaves for Mrs Dillman.'

Deborah grimaced at the memory. Mrs Dillman, their next-door neighbor, ninety-two and senile, one day believed Brian was the seventeen-year-old Vincent boy who lived down the street and, unbeknown to Deborah, hired him to rake her lawn and dispose of the leaves. Deborah soon discovered Brian struggling with a huge, rusty rake as he tried to gather up the thousands of oak leaves covering the woman's big lawn. She went to the door and tried politely to explain that Brian was only a little boy who could fall on the rake and poke out an eye. Mrs Dillman promptly lapsed into a rage, tossed a crumpled dollar bill in Deborah's face, and told her to get the little brat out of her yard. The next day she had forgotten about the affair and delivered a plate of half-baked oatmeal cookies to Deborah's door. Deborah had taken the soggy mess, thanked the woman profusely, and wondered why her family didn't do something about her. She couldn't go on living alone much longer.

Once they were finally in the mall, the children were delighted by the elaborate decorations and the Christmas carols sung by a local school choir. They frowned, however, when they saw the Santa Claus holding children on his lap and asking what they wanted for Christmas. 'He's not real,' Brian announced.

Kim agreed. 'He's not fat enough.'

Still, they stood and watched for ten minutes. Deborah thought they probably both wanted to sit on his lap, just for the fun of it, although neither would admit it. 'At least he laughs,' Brian said. 'The one last year acted like he didn't even *like* kids.'

When they finally got down to shopping, though, the trouble began. Kim couldn't decide whether to get Daddy a set of golf clubs or a new briefcase. When Deborah explained both were out of her price range, she opted for a kitten. 'Kimberly, Daddy doesn't want a kitten,' Deborah told her. 'Anyway, it's better to rescue one from the animal shelter, don't you think?'

'Yeah. Can we go there?'

'Not now. We're at the mall already, so let's pick out something here. How about a nice pen?'

'A pen!' Kim wailed. 'I always get him a pen.'

'Last year you gave him that goofy candle you made in play school,' Brian said.

'It wasn't goofy!'

'It kept fallin' over. Besides, what's Daddy need a candle for? He's got lamps.'

'Then I'll get him a lamp.'

'Kim, a nice lamp costs too much,' Deborah explained.

'Everything costs too much!' The child's eyes filled with tears.

It was going to be a long day, Deborah thought.

The deejay on the car radio announced it was 6.10 when they pulled back into their driveway. Deborah and the children were exhausted, but at least all their presents had been bought amidst two crying spells from Kimberly and one twenty-minute sulk from Brian when she wouldn't let him go off shopping by himself.

The only shopping Deborah managed to do was at Waldenbooks, where the dynamic young manager she'd come to rely on lured her over to the table where a local author was signing her latest mystery. The middle-aged woman looked shy and tired, but cheerfully signed a copy of her book which Deborah intended to give Barbara. As Deborah stood in line waiting to pay for the novel, Brian continually let out exaggerated sighs of boredom while Kim kept retrieving books from around the store and taking them to the author to sign. The woman said she couldn't sign a book she hadn't written. 'Why not? *You're* a writer!' Kim argued. 'But I didn't write *those* books,' the woman patiently explained. Kim didn't understand and started to cry again. Gritting her teeth and still angry with Steve, who could have been such a help today, Deborah realized she hadn't the endurance for any more shopping while dealing with both the restless kids *and* the crowd. She would finish her shopping tomorrow, she decided, when the children were in kindergarten and the mall wasn't so crowded. Right now her big white two-story house with its dark green shutters looked like heaven.

Darkness had already fallen and Deborah was surprised to see that no lights burned inside the house. But then both doors on the double garage were up and Steve's white Chevrolet Cavalier was gone, too. He must have left some time during the afternoon and they'd beaten him home.

32

Where had he gone? she wondered as she unlocked the door leading from the garage into the kitchen. She hoped he'd remembered to bring the train-set down from the attic before he left. Otherwise, there would be another battle with Brian, who would be determined to help his father retrieve the boxes.

Scarlett was anxiously awaiting them. Both children gave her a passionate greeting before the dog ran to the back door. Obviously, she badly needed to be let out, which meant Steve must have left some time ago. Deborah opened the door and Scarlett shot into the fenced back yard.

'Why don't each of you carry your packages up to your rooms for now,' Deborah said, going through the house and turning on lights. 'We'll wrap them later and put them under the tree.'

'We'll need lots of paper and tape,' Kim said.

'Yes, I know. We have plenty. Are either of you hungry?'

'We ate two times at the mall,' Brian said.

You needn't remind me, Deborah thought, still feeling the greasy hamburger she'd had at two o'clock and the heavy burrito she'd eaten at five. The children had been delighted with the food. Deborah felt as if she needed a big dose of antacid.

'Take off your coats and come back down. I'll have some milk and cookies ready.'

'I want a Coke,' Kim said.

'You've had two today. It's milk or nothing.'

Kim groaned. 'Okay, I'll drink milk, but not very much.'

'Half a glass,' Deborah called, then walked back into the kitchen, looking at the small chalkboard beside the wall phone. No note from Steve. Well, that wasn't surprising. She'd never been able to get him to leave notes. In fact, he often didn't call when he was going to be late, a habit that annoyed her, especially when they were waiting dinner for him. 'But you could have it worse, my girl,' she said aloud. 'At least you know he's not getting drunk in a bar or seeing another woman.' Steve's moral rectitude was one of the things that had attracted her to him. He might be unintentionally inconsiderate and neglectful sometimes, but his integrity was unfailing.

A sharp bark and scratch on the door let Deborah know Scarlett was ready to come back in. She opened it and the dog, after a perfunctory lick of her hand, shot upstairs to the children.

Deborah fixed a fresh bowl of water for Scarlett and opened a can of Alpo. Then she set out two glasses of milk and some sugar cookies on the old refectory table in the large kitchen. The table needed refinishing, too, she thought briefly. But then, the whole house needed redecorating. She'd been saving money from her clerical work for redecorating since Steve didn't seem to have much interest in how the house looked as long as it was relatively clean. If left up to him, nothing would be done until the furniture literally fell apart beneath them, another trait of a son whose mother was obsessed with neatness and redecorating. She sympathized, but after all, the whole family couldn't constantly tiptoe around Steve's idiosyncrasies. After Christmas, she would simply take matters into her own hands. All these years with Steve had taught her that although he might complain about changes she wanted to make, he would eventually subside as long as she didn't bother him with details.

Within minutes the children and the dog were back, and all set to eating ravenously. 'I thought you two weren't hungry,' Deborah said.

'We're not,' Brian returned. 'But cookies are different. You make good cookies, not like Mrs Dillman.'

'She's very old,' Deborah said. 'She was probably a good cook when she was younger.'

'She's got *great*-grandchildren,' Kim said between cookies. 'That means her grandkids have kids.'

Deborah smiled. 'Very good. Do you know how many she has?'

'Lots. She's got pictures of them all over.'

'I know.'

'Do our grandparents have great-grandkids?'

'No. They won't until you two have children.'

'Oh. Well, I might never have kids. I'm gonna be a tightrope walker,' Kim informed her.

'Is that right?' Deborah asked, sipping some instant coffee. She hated instant coffee. 'I thought you wanted to be the check-out girl at the grocery store.'

'That was before. Now I want to be a tightrope walker and wear sparkly outfits.'

Brian gulped down the rest of his chocolate milk. 'I'm gonna be a lawyer like Daddy.'

'That takes a lot of school.'

'That's okay. I'm good at school.'

Strange, Deborah thought. Even at five they seemed to have a sense of what they excelled at. For Brian, it was intellectual pursuits; for Kim, it

34

was athletic activities. The little girl had incredible grace and balance, as her dancing teacher had pointed out to Deborah.

After they had eaten, Deborah looked around for the model railroad set and was relieved to find it resting on the couch in the living room, along with the bag of glitter-decorated cotton they used for snow, and another box bearing miniature houses, animals, and trees which provided the countryside for the train to run through. 'When's Daddy comin' home to help us put everything together?' Brian asked, eyeing the boxes with a mixture of joy and anxiety. They had never assembled the train-set without Daddy.

Deborah glanced at her watch. Seven o'clock. It had been dark for well over an hour, Steve had left no note, and Scarlett clearly had not been let out for some time when they arrived home. Angry that he had disappeared for such a long time without leaving any word concerning his destination, Deborah called Evan Kincaid.

'Hi, Deborah. What can I do for you?' Evan asked jauntily.

'I seem to have lost my husband,' she said, fighting to keep her voice even and pleasant. 'The kids are waiting on him to help with the model train. Have you seen him?'

'No. Not today. How long has he been gone?'

'I don't know. The children and I went to the mall. We left around one o'clock and he wasn't here when we got back a little after six. I get the feeling he hasn't been here for quite a while. There are no dirty dishes in the sink – not even a glass. And the dog was desperate to be let out.'

'Didn't he leave a note?'

'No, but then he rarely does.'

Deborah heard Barbara in the background asking what was wrong. Evan put his hand over the mouthpiece as he told her Deborah was looking for Steve. 'I haven't seen him,' Evan said, returning to her, and Deborah sensed a cautious note in his voice. 'Maybe he's Christmas shopping.'

'He did say he had an appointment concerning Christmas.'

'What kind of appointment?'

'I haven't the faintest idea, especially since he said he already had his shopping done, although I don't know where he hid his presents.'

'Probably Pete's. He has lots of room.'

A beat of silence passed and Deborah suddenly felt a quiver of anxiety. 'Evan, something's been bothering Steve for the past couple of days. Do you know what it is?'

'I . . . well, I've noticed he's not quite himself.'

'But you don't know what's wrong?'

Evan took a deep breath. 'Deborah, I'm sure Steve just went out to do some errand – maybe to buy something special for Christmas – and he's running late.'

His voice rang false. What is wrong with him? Deborah thought, her anxiety growing. She felt sure Evan knew something, but he wasn't any more communicative than Steve had been earlier.

'You'll let me know when he gets in, won't you?' Evan asked. There it was again, Deborah thought. Evan wouldn't be so concerned unless he believed something was wrong.

She wanted to ask more questions, but for some reason Evan wasn't talking, so she gave up. 'Sure, Evan. Tell Barbara hello for me. And thanks.'

'For what? I wasn't much help. But you take care and keep your doors and windows locked. Around Christmas there's always a lot of breaking and entering.'

Evan had always been friendly, but never overly concerned or protective. Apprehension fluttered through Deborah. 'Evan, *what* is going on?' she asked, thoroughly frustrated.

'Nothing. Just give me a call in a little while,' he said briskly. 'If Steve's not back, Barb and I'll come over and keep you company.'

Deborah hung up the phone and looked out the window, more troubled than she had been before she called Evan. A heavy cloud cover obliterated the stars and moon. Only the dusk-to-dawn light broke the utter darkness. Then, to her dismay, the light blinked a couple of times and went out. She gasped before reminding herself that the light had been blinking for weeks. The bulb was going and should have been replaced long before this. Still, its dying at this particular time, when she had such a creeping, uneasy feeling about Steve, seemed ominous. But she was not a superstitious woman. The light going out had nothing to do with Steve.

'Did Evan know where Daddy is?' Brian asked, making her jump as his young voice piped up behind her.

'No, honey, he didn't. I think we should go ahead and start unpacking the train. Then when Daddy gets here, we'll have everything ready.'

But by 8.15, when all the train cars, tracks, snow, houses, and tiny animals and trees stood in disarray around the tree, Steve still had not appeared. Angry and worried, Deborah put another album of Christmas carols on the stereo. 'God Rest Ye Merry, Gentlemen' reverberated through the living room.

'I hate that song,' Kim said. 'I want "Jingle Bells".'

'We've listened to that a hundred times,' Brian complained. 'I want MTV.'

Steve didn't like the children watching the often sexually graphic videos on MTV, but tonight she was certain they were too engrossed with the train to really watch. They'd just listen to the rock music. Besides, she thought she'd scream if she heard another Christmas carol.

She turned off the stereo and flipped on the television. Steven Tyler of Aerosmith was singing 'Janie's Got a Gun'. Images of blood and a body being covered by a sheet flashed across the screen. She cringed, but as she'd expected, the children weren't really watching. Brian was pretending to play the guitar while Kim danced around him, her long, fine blonde hair flying. They were so wound up tonight, the activity would probably be good for them, Deborah thought. But what about her? Pretend guitar-playing and dancing weren't going to help. What should her next move be?

Impulsively, she called Mrs Dillman. The old woman's voice sounded feeble at the other end. 'I hope I didn't wake you,' Deborah said.

'I was taking a cat-nap.'

'I see. I'm sorry I disturbed you, Mrs Dillman, but I wondered if you'd seen my husband leave the house this afternoon.'

'Two-thirty.' The woman's voice turned crisp. 'I just happened to be looking out that way and I saw your husband's car leave.' Mrs Dillman was *always* looking out their way when she wasn't asleep.

'Two-thirty. Are you sure?'

'Certainly. I'm not beyond telling the time.' Deborah wasn't sure about that, although Mrs Dillman had bouts when she was as alert and observant as Sherlock Holmes.

'Was my husband alone?'

'Yes. You and the children were gone. Left a good hour ahead of him.'

'We went Christmas shopping.'

'That's what I thought.' Mrs Dillman paused, then asked sympathetically, 'My dear, you don't think your husband has abandoned you, do you?'

Deborah blinked. 'You mean left me? Oh, Mrs Dillman, I don't think so.'

'I only ask because my husband abandoned me. Said he was going out for bread and never came back. That was forty years ago.'

Deborah knew this wasn't true. Alfred Dillman had died eight years previously in a car wreck.

'It caused a terrible scandal,' Mrs Dillman continued, warming to her fantasy. 'Everyone felt so sorry for me. What a foolish man, they all said, leaving a fine woman like you. I tell you, my dear, I don't know how I lived through it, but I have backbone. That's what my mama always said.' She sighed. 'Well, that's men for you. They're all alike.'

Deborah wanted to argue the point, but it was useless. Acquiescence was the key to keeping the woman calm and amiable. 'I suppose you're right.'

'Your husband could be in Las Vegas,' Mrs Dillman added helpfully. 'He could be with my Alfred drinking and gambling and cavorting with tarts.'

In spite of her alarm, Deborah almost laughed at the thought of either the aged Alfred Dillman, a former Presbyterian minister, or Steve slipping into Mrs Dillman's picture of debauchery. 'That's a possibility,' she said kindly. 'I'll certainly check into it.'

'All right. But if you find Alfred, tell him not to come home. I will not have him back, no matter how repentant he is!'

'I'll tell him. And thank you again, Mrs Dillman.'

She hung up the phone and rubbed her temples, which were beginning to throb. That call certainly hadn't gotten her anywhere, and every other house in the cul-de-sac was deserted.

So now what? Deborah thought. If Steve *had* left at 2.30 as Mrs Dillman claimed, he'd been gone six hours. But if he'd left much later . . .

She went back into the living room. Kim and Brian were collapsed on the couch, giggling after their rock and roll performance. 'I want to look like *that*,' Kim said, pointing to an impossibly buxom woman with tousled hair slinking across the screen.

'You're much prettier,' Deborah said absently, then came to herself. Steve would have a fit if he walked in and saw the children watching the video. 'Let's see what else is on.'

She punched buttons on the remote control until she found an innocuous-looking movie on the Disney channel. Both children immediately lost interest in the television. 'Where's Daddy?' Brian asked.

'I'm not sure. Maybe we should start putting the train tracks together. Or would you rather just go to bed?'

'*Bed!*' both children echoed in horrified tones as if Deborah had just asked if they wanted to be burned at the stake. 'Our bedtime is 8.30.' Brian looked at the Regulator clock above the gray-and-maroon-striped couch. 'It's only 8:13,' he announced triumphantly.

'I'm sick of you tellin' the time,' Kim stormed. 'It's *boring*.'

'You're just mad 'cause you can't do it.'

'I can, too. I just don't want to.'

The children were exhausted and cranky after their day in the mall. They needed sleep, but neither was willing to admit defeat and go to bed. Deborah's voice was taut. 'Okay, tonight you can stay up late. Start on the train tracks. Do you know how to put them together?'

'Sure,' Brian said.

'Good. I'm going to make some more calls.'

She listened to the children squabbling in the living room as she retreated to the kitchen where they couldn't hear her. They weren't worried yet – not like she was – only disappointed. She dialed the Prosecutor's office, hoping that maybe Steve had gone in to work on a few things and forgotten the time. No answer.

Frustrated, she fixed another cup of instant coffee, this time something called French Vanilla Café, which was sweet and fragrant. The women who sipped it on television commercials looked well groomed and insouciant, as if they hadn't a care in the world. They certainly wouldn't want me in one of those commercials, Deborah thought as she caught a glimpse of herself in the kitchen mirror. With her lipstick worn off, her hair stringing down from its long braid, and her eyes slightly bloodshot beneath their contacts, she looked tired and messy. And she was dying for a cigarette.

On impulse, she rummaged through a drawer until she found a half-empty pack of Salems. She looked at it for a moment and even sniffed the stale cigarettes inside. 'No, I *won't*,' she said determinedly. She dropped the pack of cigarettes and closed the drawer.

She drummed her fingers on the counter, wondering what to do next. Her eyes fell on the address book beside the phone. She flipped through it and found the number for the nursing home in Wheeling where Steve's sister Emily stayed. The nurse sounded baffled when she introduced herself and asked if Steve were there.

'Why, no. Mr Robinson was just here last weekend. He only comes every couple of months, and he's *never* here on a Sunday night.' The nurse's tone changed to one of curiosity. 'Can't you find him?'

39

Frazzled and worried, Deborah wanted to bark, 'Would I be calling there if I could?' 'No, actually I can't,' she managed with relative calm. 'We seem to have gotten our wires crossed today. I just thought maybe he'd come up to visit Emily one last time before Christmas.'

'I haven't seen him since last Sunday afternoon. But you tell him Emily's doing just fine. She even spoke today.'

'She did?' Deborah asked in amazement.

'Yes indeed. She said "Steve" plain as day.'

'That's wonderful. I didn't know she ever said anything.'

The nurse sounded surprised again. 'Oh, yes, ma'am. Not often, but occasionally. Funny your husband didn't tell you. Most of the time she does it when he's here.'

Deborah had visited Emily with Steve only once, when they were first married. She looked like a young teenager then, not the twenty-three-year-old woman she was. She had mahogany-brown hair, much darker than Steve's, which had been allowed to grow long and glossy. But it was her eyes Deborah remembered the most vividly. Long-lashed and a clear willow-green, they would have been beautiful if they hadn't stared so vacantly directly in front of her. Deborah had asked to visit Emily again, but Steve discouraged her. 'No sense in it,' he'd said. 'She doesn't know you're there.'

'But you go,' Deborah argued.

'I'm her brother. Besides, it's because of me she's that way. I owe her.'

Deborah hung up the phone. Of course Steve wouldn't have taken off for Wheeling without letting her know. Wheeling was 160 miles away. She thought of calling Steve's parents, but that was useless. They spent every Christmas in Hawaii. Besides, Steve hadn't visited them for ten years.

She tried Pete Griffin. Pete's son Adam answered the phone. Rock music blared in the background and Adam told her his father had made a quick run to a discount store to buy a lighted reindeer for the front yard. 'The guy acts like I'm eight,' Adam grumbled, although humor edged his voice. 'We've already got about a thousand lights strung over every hedge and tree in the yard. I expect the fire marshal to stop by any minute.'

'You'd better be more appreciative or you'll find a lump of coal in your stocking,' Deborah warned.

'A lump of coal?' Adam asked in confusion.

'Never mind. Just an old custom.'

'Why are old customs always so *weird*?'

Deborah smiled. Adam Griffin enjoyed adopting the pose of a rather shallow teenager to hide his remarkable sensitivity and astounding intelligence. He'd confided to her one time he planned on becoming a biophysicist. 'Don't tell Dad, though,' he'd said. 'It's too much fun to make him think I'm going into some different daredevil career every week.' And as intelligent as Pete was himself, he always seemed to believe Adam.

'Have you seen Steve today, Adam? I can't locate him,' Deborah said.

'No, and I've been home all day, but I'll ask Dad when he comes in, although he's been in and out since morning. Is something wrong?'

'I don't think so. It's just odd that he'd vanish like this . . . oh, never mind. I'm probably getting all worked up for nothing. Just ask Pete to call me when he comes in.'

'I sure will.'

'Oh, and please make a big deal over the reindeer your dad buys. This kind of thing means a lot to him.'

Adam laughed. 'I know. And don't worry. I'll tell him it's the coolest thing I've ever seen, no matter how corny it looks.'

Well, no luck at Pete's. The uneasy feeling she'd had all day was becoming overpowering. In desperation, she called Evan again. 'I still can't find Steve,' she said. 'It's a quarter to nine.'

'He's not at the office.'

'I know. I already tried there. Evan, do you have any idea where he might have gone?'

'No, but I'll make some calls. You sit tight.'

Sit tight. Deborah had always wondered what that phrase meant. Sit tightened with anxiety?

She flipped through the address book for the number of Joe Pierce. After all, it had been Joe who'd called last night and thrown Steve into such a state of agitation. She should have called him earlier, she thought as she dialed. The busy signal. She slammed down the phone. *Now* what?

She went into the living room again. 'You're gettin' sparkles all *over*,' Brian ranted as Kim took the decorated cotton from the box.

'I am *not*. Besides, they just fall off.'

'We're not ready for the cotton! Mommy, tell her the cotton doesn't go around the train until the train's set up!'

'I *know* that,' Kim said furiously. 'I'm just taking the wrinkles out, but I won't *touch* your stupid cotton any more!'

41

'Kids, knock it off,' Deborah said, rubbing a hand across her forehead. Pain throbbed behind her eyes.

'Where's Daddy?' Brian demanded again.

'I don't *know*.'

His face suddenly turned red the way it always did when he wanted to cry but wouldn't let himself. He waved a piece of model railroad track in the air. 'How're we s'posed to put the train together?'

'We'll manage,' Deborah said, going to him and taking the track from his hand. Even Kim looked contrite as she put the cotton back in the box and scrambled down on the floor beside her brother. Scarlett, too, rushed to his side, instantly sympathetic. She lay down, put her head on Brian's knee, and looked up at him with such love and sorrow that all three of them burst into laughter.

'Now look what you've done,' Deborah said. 'Scarlett's going to cry, too.'

'Dogs don't cry,' Brian said, wiping at a tear that had slipped from one eye.

Kim nodded her head. 'Yeah, they do. Inside, where we can't see it.'

Deborah ran her hands over each child's head of shining hair. 'Why don't we forget the train for now? It's way past bedtime.' The children threw her hostile looks, and she didn't have the energy to argue with them. 'Tell you what, I'll fix some hot chocolate with cinnamon sticks and marshmallows. By the time we're done, Daddy will be home.'

Twenty minutes later, when both children sported foamy chocolate mustaches, Steve had not appeared. 'I'm gettin' sleepy,' Kim finally admitted.

Thank you, God, Deborah thought with relief. If she could just get the children into bed and have some quiet time to think . . .

At that moment, the doorbell rang. Scarlett went into a frenzy of barking, and for an instant elation flooded Deborah. Steve! Then her happiness faded. Steve always used the door leading from the garage into the kitchen. He wouldn't come to the front door and ring the bell.

She flipped on the porch light and looked out through one of the paned windows high in the door. Evan and Barbara. And someone else behind them, someone who stood just out of range of the light.

While Brian held Scarlett's collar to keep her from dashing out, Deborah opened the door. Evan smiled tightly. 'Steve not home yet?'

'No. Please come in. Oh, Joe, I didn't see you at first.'

Joe Pierce, with his sandy-brown hair and lean face, stepped in saying something she didn't hear in a soft voice. All she could think of was Steve.

'What's happened?' she blurted, aware that the children were gathered behind her, suddenly silent while the television rattled on in the background.

'We just thought we'd stop by,' Evan said in a tightly controlled voice.

Deborah glanced at the children. 'Kids, would you show Joe and Barbara your train-set?'

'They've seen it,' Brian said.

Joe moved past Evan. '*I* haven't. Come on, Brian. I want to see if it's like the one I had when I was a kid.'

Brian looked doubtful. 'You want us to go away so Evan can tell Mommy something bad's happened to Daddy.'

'If something bad has happened to your daddy, we don't know anything about it. We just came for a visit,' Joe said. 'Come on, kids. You too, Scarlett.' Deborah was surprised he remembered the dog's name. He'd only been in their home a couple of times. 'Let me see the train.'

Barbara smiled encouragingly with pale lips. 'Please, children. Your daddy wouldn't like it if you were rude to guests.'

Reluctantly the children led the two adults into the living room with Scarlett trailing suspiciously behind. Deborah took Evan to the kitchen, then said in a strangled voice, 'What *is* it?'

Evan clasped his hands together. A crease appeared between his bright blue eyes. He looked tired and deeply concerned. 'Deborah, you know about Artie Lieber, don't you?'

'Artie Lieber?' she repeated vacantly. 'The man who assaulted Steve's sister? What about him?'

'He got parole two months ago.'

'So soon? It's only been fifteen years.'

'He played the game, Deborah. Got counseling, maintained the model prisoner role. Anyway, everything was going okay until last week.'

Deborah continued to look at him imploringly. 'I didn't know Lieber was out on parole, but please don't make me drag every word out of you, Evan. What is going on? Where's Steve?'

'We don't know. After you called the second time, I phoned Joe and we've been looking ever since. Then Barbara said we'd better get over here to you and leave the searching to the police.'

Deborah froze. 'The police?'

'Yes.'

'I don't understand.'

Evan's tanned face seemed to tighten. He glanced away uncomfortably, then looked back at her. 'Listen, Deborah, it was Steve's testimony that put Lieber away.'

'Yes, I know that much.'

'Maybe you didn't know Lieber always claimed Steve was lying – that *Steve* was the one who attacked Emily.'

'That's ridiculous,' Deborah burst out, appalled at the accusation but equally shocked that Steve had never told her of it. 'Steve wouldn't hurt anybody, especially his own *sister*!'

'I know that as well as you do. But Lieber stuck to his story for all those years. And Deborah, he was spotted in Charleston yesterday. That's what Joe called about last night. He wanted to warn Steve that Lieber was here in town – just half a mile from your house, as a matter of fact.'

'Oh, God.' Deborah closed her eyes. 'There's more, though, isn't there? Go ahead – tell me,' she said dully.

'Just that Lieber once told a cellmate that when he got out he was going to make Steve pay for putting him away. And now Steve is missing.'

5

Steve's not missing – he's just misplaced, Deborah almost said, then started giggling. Evan threw her a disconcerted glance. 'I'm sorry,' she said, gasping. 'I'm just . . . I'm just . . .' The room darkened and she sagged. Evan caught her before she hit the floor. 'Good lord, I've never fainted in my life,' she mumbled.

He sat her on the bench of the refectory table and went to the cabinet where they stored the liquor. She saw him pour dark liquid into a glass. 'Chivas Regal, twelve years old,' she could hear Steve saying to Pete. Oh, lord.

'Drink this,' Evan ordered.

'I hate whiskey.'

'Drink!'

Deborah drained the glass, then almost choked as fire burned down her throat and into her chest. Barbara rushed into the kitchen. 'Deborah, are you all right?'

'She will be,' Evan said.

'I'll bet Steve walks through that door in the next ten minutes,' Barbara told her.

Deborah looked at her through a haze of tears. 'No, he won't. I knew it when we came back from shopping. Deep down I knew it.'

'You did not,' Evan said as if he were speaking to a child. 'You're just scared. Anything could have happened. Steve might be stuck someplace with a flat tire.'

'He knows how to change a tire, Evan.'

'Well, some kind of car trouble.'

'You don't believe that or you wouldn't have told me about Artie Lieber.'

'Maybe I jumped the gun. I should have kept my mouth shut about Lieber.'

'Lieber?' Deborah looked up to see Pete Griffin standing in the door, his face red from the cold, his thinning hair mussed. 'Sorry to burst in on you like this, but Adam said you were worried about Steve, and every time I've called your phone's been busy, so I decided I'd come and check on things for myself. I thought I was going to have to present identification to that guy who opened the front door. Now what the hell's going on and what's this about Lieber?'

'Artie Lieber is in town. I'm afraid he's gotten to Steve.'

Pete's face sagged. 'How? When?'

'This afternoon. And I don't know how.'

'Deborah, it could easily be something else,' Evan said. 'You mentioned that he had an appointment this afternoon. But you don't know who it was with, do you?'

'No. I'm not even sure there *was* an appointment. He didn't sound like he was telling the truth. I think maybe he was just trying to get me off his back about going to the mall Christmas shopping.'

'You two didn't have a fight, did you?'

'No. We've had about five fights since we've been married. Over stupid stuff. And today we had words because he was acting so mysterious about this so-called appointment.'

Evan's expression stiffened. 'So you two had a bad argument today?'

'No. We were irritated with each other, that's all. We've never had a *real* argument. Just a few infrequent spats.'

Her eyes filled with fresh tears. Barbara took her shoulders in her firm hands with their short nails. 'We shouldn't have come here and scared you like this over nothing.'

'I think I needed to know that Lieber is in town and maybe got to Steve,' Deborah said raggedly. 'Oh God, now I understand. We had a prowler last night. Someone hiding in the evergreens. Steve acted like a wild man, running out there barefoot. Now I know why. I also know what he was saying as he circled the trees – Lieber. He thought Artie Lieber was out there. And he must have been. He just waited until he got Steve alone. And then he—'

'Look, Deborah, the police are already in on this,' Evan said crisply. 'Normally a person isn't officially declared missing for twenty-four hours, but Steve's an assistant prosecuting attorney and under the circumstances . . . well, they aren't going to let it slide until tomorrow afternoon.'

'I'm glad. But I think it's too late.'

'Stop saying that,' Pete ordered. 'It's probably nothing. Maybe Steve went to a movie.'

'Oh, Pete, you know he *never* goes to movies. He says he can't stand the sound of people chomping on popcorn and slurping soft drinks while the film is showing.' Deborah held her glass out to Evan. 'Another shot, please.' Evan hesitated, then poured. She sipped this one more slowly and spoke, almost to herself. 'He was a very serious, reserved man, and sometimes he could be inconsiderate without meaning to be, but he was never cruel. *Never*. We've been married seven years. He's never disappeared like this. If he's going to be *very* late, he calls.'

'Always?' Evan asked.

'Well, there have been a couple of times . . .'

'And this could be one of them.'

Deborah shook her head. 'The only times he hasn't called is when he's caught up in work, but he's not working today. Mrs Dillman said he left at 2.30.'

'Mrs Dillman?' Barbara repeated. 'That crazy old lady next door?'

'Sometimes she's accurate.'

'And most of the time she isn't. Deborah, he could have left right before you got home from the mall. In that case, he would have only been gone . . .'

'About three hours,' Deborah said. 'But if he *did* leave at 2.30, he's been gone over seven hours. He might even have left shortly *after* we did, which would mean he's been gone eight hours. What about the hospitals?'

'We've checked,' Evan said. 'No one matching his description has been brought in.'

Joe came into the kitchen. He was taller and slimmer than Evan although not nearly so classically handsome. His face was weathered, his tanned forehead slashed by a thin two-inch-long scar above the right eyebrow, his smile less easy and dazzling than Evan's. He was originally from Texas and he'd always reminded Deborah of an old-fashioned cowboy, tough and sinewy, used to riding the range enduring storms, droughts and Indian attacks. He belonged in a Louis L'Amour novel. Like Evan, he was wearing jeans. Unlike Evan, he wore a scuffed leather jacket instead of a well-tailored suede one, with a tee-shirt underneath and cowboy boots. He had a slight beard stubble, and Deborah noticed the lines shooting from the corners of his gray eyes, as if he'd been looking at the sun too long.

47

'Joe, did Steve say anything to you last night that might explain all this?' Deborah asked.

'No. Nothing. I just told him Lieber had been spotted in Charleston.'

Deborah rubbed a hand over her forehead. 'I don't understand. If he thought Lieber was here and dangerous, why didn't he tell me?'

'He said he didn't want to worry you.'

'*Worry* me?' Deborah repeated loudly. 'The children and I were *out* today and he wouldn't even go with us. How worried could he have been?'

'Plenty,' Joe said firmly. 'But Evan told me you'd gone to the mall this afternoon. Steve probably thought you'd be safe there with all those people. And he'd already asked me to get in touch with a friend of mine at a local PI agency. They were going to provide around-the-clock protection for the three of you starting tomorrow morning. He was more scared for you and the kids than for himself. Lieber already damned near killed his sister. He didn't want him going after his wife and children.'

'So you knew all about this, too?'

'Yeah.'

'And you?' Deborah asked Pete.

'I knew Lieber had gotten parole, but not that he was in town or that Steve was worried about anything. He seemed fine at the party.'

'I can't believe Steve didn't tell *you* about Lieber,' Evan said to Deborah.

Joe threw Evan a sidelong look. 'You know what he said.' His slow, husky voice was so different from the loud, commanding tones of Steve and Evan, who were used to delivering dramatic closing arguments in court. 'He didn't want to scare her. And that's exactly what you're doing.'

'Better to scare her than keep her in the dark.' Evan brushed his hair back from his forehead. 'God, here we are arguing when Steve's missing and Deborah's a basket case. Sorry, Deborah. Lawyers are naturally argumentative.'

'I'm not a lawyer,' Joe said.

Evan's jaw tightened in irritation, but he ignored Joe. 'Deborah, we're going to need some information from you.'

'Like what?'

'Steve's license plate and driver's license numbers, his credit card numbers, that sort of thing. And we also need to know if any of his things are missing.'

'His things?' Deborah echoed.

'Yes. Like clothes.'

'Why would his clothes be missing?'

Evan looked uncomfortable. 'It's just procedure. The police will want to know.'

'They want to know if there are any indications that he ran off voluntarily,' Joe said.

Deborah was stunned. 'Voluntarily? Of course he didn't go voluntarily. Why would he?'

She suddenly had a vision of Steve and Alfred Dillman in Las Vegas with their gambling and liquor and 'tarts'. She smiled for a moment before her eyes filled again. If only that ridiculous scenario were true. It was so much better to think of him there than missing, perhaps at the mercy of Artie Lieber.

'All the numbers are written on a paper in Steve's desk,' she said shakily. 'You know how meticulous he was. Barbara, if you'll get that paper – I think it's in the top right-hand drawer – I'll go upstairs and check for missing clothes.'

The house had old-fashioned, narrow closets. When Deborah opened Steve's, she almost cried. Meticulous. Yes, that was Steve, even when it came to his clothes. Everything was in order – shirts all together, pants neatly folded over hangers, suit jackets hung with precision, shoes polished and standing in an even line. The gray wool suit she'd picked up from the cleaners on Friday was still swathed in plastic, as if it was to remain forever pristine.

'Stop it,' she said aloud. 'He'll wear it again. Just concentrate on what you're doing.'

She closed her eyes, trying to picture what Steve had been wearing that morning. Jeans, a navy-blue crew-neck sweater, and Nike running shoes. Of course, none of those articles was in the closet. Everything else was.

She went to the dresser drawer. There lay his underwear, wrinkle-free and almost regimentally ordered. He hadn't quite broken those childhood habits of obsessive neatness instilled by his mother. Lined up were seven pairs of undershirts, seven pairs of jockey shorts, eleven pairs of dark socks and three pairs of white crew socks. Only the underclothes and socks he'd worn yesterday and today were missing.

She glanced at the dresser top. His watch was gone, but his wedding ring lay forlornly next to a bottle of aftershave he never used. At first she was startled, then she remembered he'd developed a rash beneath the ring a few days ago. He hadn't worn it since. Still, its presence seemed to say something significant, as if it signaled the end of the marriage.

She came back downstairs to find Pete, Evan and Barbara in the kitchen. Joe and Adam were with the children in the living room. 'Nothing is gone except what he had on today.'

'How about a coat?' Evan asked.

Deborah motioned toward the coat tree beside the kitchen door. 'His blue down jacket is gone.'

'Nothing else?'

'Not that I can find.'

'Was there much cash in the house?'

'A couple of hundred dollars, maybe.'

'Where did he keep it?'

'In his desk drawer.'

'I went through every drawer of his desk,' Barbara said reluctantly. 'I didn't find any money.'

Pete frowned. 'He could have used the money for Christmas.'

Evan didn't answer as he looked at a sheet of paper with typed numbers. 'I'm going to the police with this.'

'Thank you,' Deborah murmured, feeling as if she were speaking from under water. Everything seemed muffled and unreal.

'I'm spending the night,' Barbara said.

'Oh, Barbara, you don't have to do that,' Deborah answered automatically.

'I want to. Besides, you and the kids don't need to be alone.'

'They sure don't.' Joe had appeared at the door again. He's like a wraith, Deborah thought. He's suddenly just there without warning. 'I'm staying, too.'

Barbara, Deborah, and Pete looked at him in surprise, and he went on in his slow, husky, measured voice, 'You women don't need to be alone with two little kids and Lieber on the loose, so don't give me any women's lib crap. I'm staying. Steve would want me to.'

Evan threw him a sharp glance. 'I'm perfectly capable of staying with them.'

'Or I could stay,' Pete offered.

Deborah smiled at Pete. 'Thanks, but I know you don't like to leave Adam alone at night.'

'He's not a little boy, Deborah. I think he can make it through one night alone.'

Joe interrupted. 'Don't worry about it, Mr . . .'

'Griffin,' Pete supplied. 'Pete.'

'Don't worry about it, Pete. I said *I'll* stay,' Joe repeated firmly. 'You look after your boy and Evan can go to the police.'

Evan's jaw flexed again. Deborah knew Evan didn't like Joe. 'Evan thinks Joe should walk around in a suit looking like an FBI man,' Steve had once told her, but there was something vague about his voice.

'I thought Evan never judged on appearances,' Deborah had challenged.

'Well, maybe it's more than that. Evan doesn't trust Joe.'

'Why?'

'He thinks Joe's dangerous.'

'But you've said Joe is such a great investigator.'

'He is, but you know how it is with some people. Evan and Joe are like oil and water.'

That old conversation faded away as Evan said testily to Joe, 'I'm not going to waste time bickering with you. Barbara and you can *both* stay. I'll call after I talk to the police.'

I hardly know Joe, Evan doesn't trust him, and he's going to stay in my home tonight, Deborah thought. But Steve liked Joe. At this point, that was enough.

Moments later the front door slammed. Although Pete and Evan had left together, Deborah knew who'd done the slamming. Barbara looked up at Joe, annoyance deepening the lines around her mouth. 'I wish you wouldn't do that.'

'Do what? Try to look after the four of you while Evan and Steve are gone?'

'You know what I mean.'

Joe leaned easily against the door frame. 'You mean, why don't I let Evan call all the shots?' he drawled. 'Well, Barbara, I don't want to rile you, but just because your boyfriend comes from a rich family and has a law degree and I don't doesn't mean he's in charge of every situation. I've noticed you giving him a few orders now and then yourself.' Barbara flushed and Joe softened his words with a self-deprecating grin. 'Besides, I'm the ex-cop, the one who knows martial arts and carries a gun. I'm the tough guy here, so let me play my role without giving me grief, okay?'

Deborah suddenly knew why Evan distrusted him. There was something reckless, almost uncivilized in Joe's gray eyes in spite of his grin. She got the feeling that beneath his quiet exterior there was something dangerous, something you wouldn't want to cross, something almost looking for trouble. She quailed again at the thought of him spending the night in her home. What did she know about him? Very little except the fact that he was a good investigator. But Barbara was smiling back at him, her body relaxing. 'Okay, Joe, you're right. I'm glad you're here.'

'Me, too,' Brian said, standing behind Barbara and Joe. 'Mommy, he set up the train. Come look.'

The last thing on Deborah's mind was the train, but she pulled herself up and went into the living room. The train chugged merrily through mounds of cotton, whizzing past miniature villages and a mirror made to look like a snow-surrounded lake. 'Isn't it neat!' Brian exclaimed.

'Neat,' Deborah repeated, her voice thick. This was the first year someone besides Steve had set up the train and it looked better than ever. The thought made her feel guilty, and she rushed over, switching it off. 'Bedtime.'

Kim was already huddled into a corner of the couch, sleeping soundly, one of her shoes lying on the floor. Even Scarlett had given up. She lay collapsed on the floor beside the couch, although she managed to open her eyes and look at them briefly before stretching to what seemed twice her normal length and lapsing back into a doze. Brian was still on his feet, but barely. His hair stood on end and his eyelids sagged.

Joe started to scoop the limp Kim off the couch, then looked at Deborah. 'Okay if I carry her up?'

Deborah tensed at the sight of this unfamiliar man touching her little girl, but he held Kimberly gently and the little girl slept on. 'Yes, please,' she said. 'I don't think I could manage her alone tonight.'

The children still slept together in the room across from her and Steve's. That situation would change this coming summer, when they remodeled the small room at the end of the hall above the kitchen for Brian. According to the former owners, the room had not been renovated since 1930. Mrs Dillman had told her in confidential tones over the fence one summer afternoon that the room was haunted. 'A young man *killed* himself in there,' she'd said darkly. 'Took arsenic because of some girl who'd left him. He was Catholic and couldn't have a proper Christian burial, so his spirit haunts the place. Sometimes you can still hear him moaning in pain from the poison.' Steve had actually laughed out loud at the story when Deborah told him later. 'No wonder we got such a good deal. The damned place is haunted. When does the moaning and chain-rattling start?' Deborah had never confirmed whether the tale of suicide was true or merely another figment of Mrs Dillman's increasingly wild imagination. All she knew was that the room was little, dark, and uninsulated, obviously abandoned for years. They now used it as a storeroom, rarely entering it and keeping the door closed.

After she'd undressed a drowsy Kimberly and deposited her in the bottom bunk, she left Brian to get himself ready for bed. Scarlett always slept in the children's room, and she was passed out on her plaid doggie cushion when Deborah closed the bedroom door and went downstairs to Barbara and Joe.

'Any word from Evan?' she asked.

The two sat quietly in front of the beautiful Christmas tree whose twinkling lights cast multi-colored reflections over their solemn faces.

'He called about ten minutes ago,' Barbara said. 'The police want a recent picture of Steve. They also asked about a passport.'

'A passport?'

'They still can't discount the theory that Steve took off,' Joe said. 'If he headed out of the country, he would need his passport.'

'This is *incredible*! He didn't leave the country,' Deborah said hotly. 'I can't believe they think he'd run off from his family.'

'Men do it all the time,' Joe answered calmly. 'Women, too, for that matter, although not as often.'

'Well, Steve didn't. Besides, he didn't have a passport. He's never been out of the country.'

'What about a picture?'

'Steve wasn't fond of having his picture taken. I'll look through the album tomorrow morning, though, and see what I can find.' She suddenly felt tired enough to drop on the floor. But there were two guests to take care of. 'I'm afraid there's only one guest room,' she said.

'So who gets it?' Joe asked Barbara, humor edging his voice. 'Do we flip a coin?'

Barbara gave him a playful slap on the hand. 'You said no women's lib crap tonight, so *I* get it. You sleep on the couch.'

'There are extra blankets and pillows upstairs,' Deborah said.

Barbara stood. 'I know where everything is. I'll get Mr Macho here fixed up on the couch. You get into bed before you collapse.'

Deborah smiled meekly. 'Thanks, Barb. I don't know what I'd do without you.'

'You don't have to find out.'

Upstairs in her room, Deborah slipped tiredly out of her slacks and turtleneck sweater and into the first nightgown her hand fell upon in her drawer – a long, flowered flannel thing Steve had given her for her birthday. With her long braid, she thought she looked like someone from *Little House on the Prairie* when she wore it, but it was warm and soft and she was freezing. She was too worn out to remove her make-up, a sin the editors of beauty magazines would never forgive, but right now she wasn't concerned with clogged pores or the inevitable mascara rings beneath her eyes which would appear in the morning.

She wandered to the bedroom window, looking out on the back yard. The twins' swing-set, Scarlett's rarely used dog house, the small metal garden shed – everything looked bleached out in the small area of cold winter moonlight showing through a hole in the cloud cover. Hard to believe that just last summer the yard was alive with cherry-rose nasturtiums, yellow marigolds, vari-colored moss roses, and lilies of the valley which grew in the shade of an apple tree. On Sundays the children had laughed and played on the swing-set while she lay in the sun, sipping lemonade and reading a mystery novel, and Steve, with his amazing gift for gardening, tended the flowers.

Deborah finally climbed into bed and pulled the comforter up to her chin. Exhausted as she was, she was certain she couldn't sleep. She lay quietly for a while, begging deep sleep to obliterate this terrible evening, when at last she fell into a fitful doze.

She dreamed she sat in a rocking chair placed before a large window shrouded with dusty lace curtains. Evening was falling, the temperature dropping. She didn't rock – she held perfectly still, listening to an old house snap and groan around her, settling in the chill air of approaching night. Finally the images faded and she was aware only of sounds – scraping and creaking. The snapping and groaning of wood. She mumbled 'no' a couple of times in half-conscious annoyance, wishing the sounds would go away so she could sleep.

Then she jerked awake. At first she held rigidly still, frightened but not knowing why until she heard a faint creak of boards again. She wasn't asleep this time. She was wide awake and the sound was coming from the room next to hers – the storage room over the kitchen.

Steve? she thought instantly. Was it possible that Steve had been in the storage room all along? Had he gone in there to find Christmas ornaments and gotten hurt somehow? Had he been lying in the room, unconscious, for hours? But that unlikely scenario didn't explain his missing car.

Mrs Dillman's story about the room being haunted flashed through her mind. 'Don't be absurd,' she mumbled. Even in childhood she hadn't believed ghost stories, and in the six years of their occupancy of the house, she'd never noticed anything unusual about the room. But then she'd never heard boards creaking in there, either. Artie Lieber? No. The room was on the second floor and Joe was downstairs. No one could have gotten past him.

She thought of going to get Joe, but she didn't want to seem like a hysterical woman. Besides, she had the odd feeling that she didn't want to run downstairs and leave the children up here. Alone.

She slid out of bed and flew to her door, not bothering with slippers and robe the way people always did in movies, no matter how dire the circumstances. She opened her door and ran across the hall to the children's room. Peeking in, she saw that both were sleeping peacefully, although Brian was curled on the plaid dog cushion with Scarlett, a blanket thrown over both of then. He really is frightened about his daddy, she thought with a pang, seeing his little arms wrapped around the dog who sat alert, her ears perked. So she had heard something, too.

Deborah motioned to the dog who deftly extricated herself from Brian's grasp and trotted to her. 'Be really quiet,' she murmured. 'We have to check on something without scaring anyone.'

Scarlett looked at her with uncanny intelligence, as if she understood every word. Deborah closed the children's door and she and the dog went down the hall to the guest room. She opened the door a crack and was relieved to see Barbara lying on her back, mouth slightly open, breathing regularly. All present and accounted for, Deborah thought, before she heard another sound, this one obviously a footstep, coming from the storage room. Scarlett stiffened, the hair along her spine rising.

Someone was in there.

Still reluctant to leave the others upstairs by themselves, Deborah went to the railing and called to Joe, but there was no reply. Damn. He was probably sleeping as deeply as Barbara. If she yelled loudly enough to wake him, she would wake everyone else and make the situation worse. All she needed was two little kids milling around in the hall, frightened out of their wits. Besides, maybe it was nothing. Maybe Scarlett was simply picking up on her own tension.

Reluctantly, Deborah stepped into her room, picked up a heavy trophy

Steve had won in a college debate tournament and now used as a doorstop, and walked down the hall. She pressed her ear to the storage-room door. Nothing. Of course not. It was just the house settling, making noises she'd never noticed before but which tonight, in her high-strung state, sounded odd, frightening. She should just go to bed and ignore them. Instead, she twisted the knob and slowly opened the door.

Immediately she was aware of a light – the beam from a flashlight – before she caught a blur of movement and the glint of something that looked dangerously like a gun pointed directly at her. Scarlett burst into a volley of barks and charged into the room. A tiny scream escaped Deborah before a male voice said, 'Jesus, you two scared the hell out of me! Scarlett, let go of my pants.'

Joe. Deborah's heart gave one giant thud, and she realized that for a moment it had stopped. She finally knew what people meant when they said their heart skipped a beat. She felt tears of physical shock and fear pressing behind her eyes. 'What are you doing in here?' she croaked, clutching the trophy.

Thankfully, Scarlett had immediately stopped barking. As if suddenly aware he was still holding the gun on her, Joe lowered the automatic he favored, holding it slightly behind his right leg where she couldn't see it. 'I couldn't sleep so I went into the kitchen to get something to drink when I thought I heard noises up here.'

Deborah flipped on the light – a naked, dusty bulb hanging from the ceiling – then cast her eyes around the small room piled with boxes and luggage. 'I heard noise, too, but it must have been you because Barbara and the kids are asleep.'

'*Were* asleep,' Barbara said behind her. 'What's going on?'

'It's the ghost of that boy who couldn't get a Christian burial because he did a sin!' Kim wailed.

So Mrs Dillman had told them her story of the boy who committed suicide. Damn. 'There's *no* ghost,' Deborah said, assuming a false calm.

'How do you know?'

'It's too cold for ghosts,' Joe said. 'Your mother just thought she heard something.'

'*What*?' Kim asked fearfully.

'Nothing bad – just a loose shutter.' The lame explanation was the first thing that came into Deborah's mind, but it might work on a couple of five-year-olds. 'I'm sorry I woke everyone up.'

'I'll get them back to bed,' Barbara murmured, with a look at Deborah that said, 'Afterward, I want to know what *really* happened.' For now she smiled brightly. 'Come on, kids. Fun's over.'

'I don't believe in ghosts, but I'm still not goin' back to bed without Scarlett,' Brian announced.

When children and dog had been shuffled back down the hall by Barbara, Deborah turned to Joe. 'It must have been you I heard in here when I was in bed. What are you looking for?'

'I'm looking for whoever was walking around up here earlier.'

'But you were awake.' Deborah heard her voice becoming more high-pitched. 'No one could have gotten up here without you seeing them.'

'There's more than one way into this room.' Joe turned off the flashlight and pointed with it to a small window on the back side of the house. It was open.

'You mean you think someone came in through the *window*?' Joe nodded.

'No,' Deborah said, starting to shiver. 'We're on the second floor. Maybe Steve came into the room this afternoon. He could have opened the window.'

'In an uninsulated room when it was thirty-five degrees outside? Besides, there's a ladder leaning against the house beneath the window.'

'A ladder?' Deborah repeated numbly.

'Yeah. Take a look if you don't believe me.'

Deborah did believe him, but she went to the window anyway, oblivious of the feel of the cold, dusty floor against her bare feet. She looked out at the tall wooden ladder whose top was only inches below the window. 'We have one just like it.'

'That *is* your ladder, Deborah. I know because I borrowed it last summer and I noticed the top step has a big nick in it.'

'Steve dropped it against the chain-link fence,' Deborah said distractedly. 'What's it doing here?'

'Providing a way into the house,' Joe said grimly. 'What I want to know is *who* got in and why they were hiding in this room next to yours.'

6

ONE

Deborah didn't sleep the rest of the night, turning restlessly in bed, filled with fear and despair. She knew Joe stayed awake, also. About every half an hour she heard him pacing through the house, checking rooms and windows like a sentinel. At six in the morning she came downstairs and fixed coffee. Barbara arose soon afterward, and by seven she and Deborah and Joe were on the second pot of coffee while Brian and Kim watched cartoons and ate microwave oatmeal after asking over and over, 'Where's Daddy?'

'Do you two want toast?' Deborah asked Barbara and Joe, although her own stomach was clenched so tight she knew she couldn't eat a bite.

'Deborah, you look ready to drop,' Barbara said, coming to help her. 'I'm not much of a cook, but I can at least work a toaster. You sit down.'

Barbara appeared more familiar today, her lips now bearing her usual muted copper-toned lipstick instead of the hideous bright pink she'd worn to the party, her short dark hair combed neatly into place. Deborah, however, sported puffy eyelids and hair carelessly pulled back with a rubber band. Steve liked her hair back, but suddenly she found it unbearable and tore out the rubber band, letting it fall black, straight, and shining halfway to her waist. Joe looked at her with a mixture of curiosity and surprise in his gray eyes, and she realized he'd never seen it down before. She gazed back at him defiantly. 'I know I look awful,' she snapped.

'You don't look awful, you just look so different,' he answered easily. 'I didn't know how long your hair was.'

Embarrassed by her flare of defensiveness, Deborah murmured, 'It *has* gotten pretty long. I guess I'm due for a cut.'

Joe shook his head. 'When I was growing up, our housekeeper on the ranch, Ramona, sometimes let her hair hang free. It was just as black and just as long as yours. I always liked it.'

'I didn't know you lived on a ranch,' Deborah said, suddenly self-conscious at the oblique compliment.

'Yeah. Three hundred acres down near the Mexican border. We raised horses and cotton.'

'Do you miss it?'

'Sometimes.' No, all the time, Deborah thought, judging by the tone of Joe's voice. But he quickly got up to pour another cup of coffee and the subject was dropped.

At eight o'clock Evan arrived, looking as if he hadn't slept all night. His eyes were slightly sunken, his skin not as golden-brown as usual. He dropped his coat on a kitchen chair, took a cup of coffee from Barbara, and looked at Deborah gravely. 'Kids upstairs?' he asked.

'Yes. They're getting ready for kindergarten. Joe said he'd take them this morning.'

'Then they can't hear us.'

Deborah's spine stiffened. 'No. What's happened?'

'The state police found Steve's car about five o'clock this morning. It was parked near Yeager Airport.' He hesitated. 'There's blood inside.'

Barbara gasped and Deborah's heart began a slow, steady thudding. Her vision darkened, then cleared. 'Blood?'

Evan nodded. 'Not a lot. Just a streak on the back seat.'

'Oh, God.'

'Take it easy. Be calm and think. Do you know Steve's blood type?'

'B positive. I know because I lost a lot of blood when the twins were born. Steve wanted to be my donor – he always had this fear of AIDS being transmitted by transfusions in spite of all the screening they do these days – but we had different blood types. I'm AB positive. That's the rarest type. We weren't compatible.'

Deborah ran out of words and breath at the same time. Suddenly air flooded painfully back into her lungs and she gulped, then knocked over her coffee. Barbara was beside her, wiping up coffee with a paper towel and crooning softly to her, as if she were a child. 'Deb, it's okay. Just take it easy, honey. This doesn't mean anything.'

'Doesn't mean anything?' Deborah cried, ignoring her reddening hand and the hot coffee dripping down on to her white terry-cloth robe. 'My husband has been missing for almost twenty-four hours, his car turns up abandoned with blood on the seat, and it doesn't *mean* anything?'

Joe's face had taken on a stony look, the gray eyes more narrow than usual although his voice sounded steady and off-hand as opposed to Evan's, who was barely able to mask his intensity. 'How close to the airport was the car?' he asked Evan.

'Half a mile.'

'Was there any damage to it?'

'Not a scratch.'

'And they're checking flights?'

'Sure. Nothing so far.'

'Checking *flights*!' Deborah exclaimed. 'What do they think? My husband left the car a half-mile from the airport, smeared blood on the back seat, then took a *flight*?'

Evan looked distressed. 'Deborah, checking departing flights is—'

'Standard procedure. I know. But none of his clothes except what he was wearing is missing.'

'But the money is gone from his desk—'

'Two hundred dollars. Where is he going on that? Rio? Paris? Rome? Besides, *why* would he go away?'

'Deborah, please calm down,' Evan said.

'Why should I calm down?' Deborah's voice rose. 'Isn't what happened to Steve obvious? Artie Lieber got him. He may have killed him!'

'Somebody killed Daddy!'

Everyone looked, appalled, at Brian and Kimberly standing in the doorway, dressed for kindergarten, their mouths open, their eyes wide. 'Oh, gosh, no, kids,' Barbara said quickly. 'No one killed your daddy. Your mommy is just upset.'

'Who's Artie Liter?' Brian demanded.

'No one important.'

'He's a mean person and he killed our daddy!' Kim cried. 'You're just not telling us.'

Deborah was too horrified by what she'd said and the looks on the children's faces to move. Evan, however, bent and wrapped his arms around them. 'No one killed your daddy.'

'How do you know?' Brian asked fearfully.

'I just know. I've got instincts about these things, and believe me, I'm right about this.'

'That's true,' Barbara added. 'Your daddy is one of Evan's best friends. Best friends *know* things about each other. We don't know where your daddy is right now, but he'll turn up and have an exciting story to tell all of us about where he's been.'

Kim's thumb immediately plunged into her mouth, the way it had until last year when the habit was finally broken. She asked around it, 'Will Daddy be here for Christmas?'

Barbara was still in command. Her voice rang with certainty. 'Honey, don't suck your thumb like a baby. There's no reason to be scared. I'm sure your daddy will be back for Christmas. Now, are you two ready for school?'

The children were pale and Deborah noticed that Brian's shirt was buttoned unevenly while Kim wore her skirt backward. They still needed help dressing, which she usually gave, but this morning she'd been too upset to supervise them. She had actually wanted them to skip kindergarten this morning, feeling they shouldn't be out of her sight under the circumstances, but Barbara had reminded her that keeping them home would only frighten them more. 'Let them follow their normal routine,' she'd said. 'They only stay half a day anyway and when Joe takes them this morning, he can tell the principal what's going on, have everyone keep a special eye on them. I'll take the day off from work and pick them up at noon.'

Deborah had reluctantly agreed, and she now felt the routine *would* have been the best thing for them if only they hadn't overheard her blurting out the possibility of Steve's being killed. She could have kicked herself, but the damage was done. She smiled with what she hoped was a semblance of normalcy. 'There's nothing to worry about. You two just have a good day and think about all the fun we're going to have at Christmas.'

'You're not lyin', are you?' Brian asked suspiciously.

She had never lied to the children. How could she expect them to be truthful when she filled their heads with falsehoods? But this situation was different. It would be cruel to inflict the same kind of fear as she was feeling on to two small children. 'I'm not lying. Everything will be all right. I want you to put this right out of your heads. Isn't your school Christmas party today?'

'Yeah,' Kim said, slowly removing her thumb from her mouth.

61

'Then you two have to be in a party spirit. I left the gifts for you to exchange with the other kids on a table by the door and Barbara will straighten up your clothes before you go out.' Taking her cue, Barbara immediately began turning Kim's skirt around before she moved on to Brian's shirt. 'When you get back, we'll know a lot more about where Daddy is and when he's coming home,' Deborah said with false cheer. They immediately detected the insincerity of her tone and looked at her with large, doubting eyes, although they said no more.

The morning was blustery, wind whipping bare tree-limbs around and catching at the children's hair when Joe took them out to his Jeep. They were unnaturally subdued, and Deborah's heart ached for them, but there was no way she could comfort them now.

After Joe had driven away with them, Deborah told Evan about the intruder in the spare room the night before.

'What time?' Evan asked.

'Around one o'clock. I heard boards creaking.'

'Did the dog bark?'

Deborah shook her head. 'No, but she heard something. She was awake. She *would* have barked if the creaking of the boards hadn't been so faint. If I'd been sound asleep, I'd never have heard them myself.'

'But Joe heard them, and he was downstairs,' Evan said, frowning into the coffee Barbara had poured for him.

'Joe was in the kitchen,' Deborah explained. 'The room was right above him.'

'Ummm.' Evan took a sip of coffee. 'Was it your ladder propped against the side of the house?'

'Yes. It was the one we store in the gardening shed.'

'Was the shed locked?'

'No. This is such a quiet neighborhood, Evan. We've never had anything stolen. We've never had trouble of any sort until the night before last, when that man was hiding in the evergreens. But he didn't steal anything. At least, I don't think he did. We didn't check the shed. But I find it hard to believe he made off with any gardening equipment.'

'And nothing was missing from the storage room last night?'

'Not that I could tell. The light was bad and I don't go in there often, so something could be gone and I wouldn't immediately miss it, but I don't think so.'

'But you think you heard creaking for at least ten minutes and Joe claims he heard it longer.' Evan looked up from his coffee, his eyes suspicious. '*Why* would someone go to all the trouble of climbing a ladder into the house, then do nothing but lurk in that room?'

Deborah ran her hands through her hair. 'I don't *know*. It doesn't make sense.'

'No, it doesn't,' Evan said emphatically. 'I'll let the police know. They'll want to check for evidence, if Joe didn't contaminate the scene too much last night.'

'Joe is a trained investigator,' Barbara interrupted in a chastizing tone. 'Certainly he was careful. And he already called the police.'

'Well, pardon me,' Evan said frostily.

Barbara blushed, clearly realizing she'd come on too strong again, and Deborah added hurriedly, 'They told us not to touch anything and they'd be here this morning. Of course, they didn't know about Steve's car then.' Her voice broke. Barbara's forehead creased in distress, as if she were frantically trying to think of the right thing to say. Deborah took a deep breath, forcing herself to pull her spiraling fear back to earth. 'I should go upstairs and get dressed before the police get here. If they come before I get back downstairs—'

'I'll take care of everything,' Barbara said.

'As usual.' Evan flashed her a resentful look.

Trouble in paradise, Deborah thought vaguely as she left the kitchen. But at the moment, she couldn't be concerned with Evan and Barbara's conflicts. She had her own much more serious situation to handle.

She hurriedly pulled on a pair of jeans and a heavy sweater, forgetting about make-up or pulling her hair back into its neat French braid. When she got downstairs again, Barbara was already talking to uniformed state troopers. Because Steve's car had been found outside the city limits, this was their investigation now, not that of the city police. 'The ladder is still propped against the house, just as it was left,' she was saying. 'We haven't even let the dog out there to mess things up.'

'We'll take a look outside first,' the man said, smiling falsely beyond Barbara at Deborah. 'And you are?'

'I'm Mrs Robinson,' Deborah said, realizing she'd let Barbara take over completely and the troopers had mistaken her for the lady of the house. 'It's my husband who's missing.'

'I see. Well, you two stay inside. Cold out today, isn't it?'

Deborah knew he was trying to minimize the situation just as she had with the children, but his empty comment grated on her. As if she'd even noticed the weather, Barbara said, yes indeed, it was cold, and shut the door behind them.

'Thank God you're here,' Deborah sighed. 'I'm no good in situations like this.'

Barbara smiled compassionately. 'How many people ever get in situations like this? Besides, it's not my husband who's missing or my house that's been invaded. Quit criticizing yourself. You're doing fine, everything considered.'

Dear Barbara, Deborah thought. She'd been a loyal, if sometimes bossy, friend for years. Her domineering personality had often gotten on Deborah's nerves, just as it was apparently working on Evan's, but now she was grateful for it. Barbara could manage anything. Deborah had never had much faith in her own ability to handle serious matters.

'Where's Evan?' she asked.

'At the office. Joe's taking the day off, too, and we couldn't all be gone. Besides, Evan had a court appearance at ten. Someone has to prosecute the bad guys out there.'

'I wish someone were out there to prosecute Artie Lieber,' Deborah said dismally.

Barbara walked over and put her hands on Deborah's shoulders, looking up at her. 'Don't make assumptions. We don't know that Lieber had anything to do with Steve's disappearance.'

'What else could it be?'

'A hundred things. Steve could come walking in that door any minute.'

'You keep saying that, but he won't. You know it and I know it.'

Barbara's short-lashed dark eyes slid away from her.

She believes the same thing I do, Deborah thought. And she's not being much more convincing with her reassurances than I was with the kids. 'I think I'll make another pot of coffee,' Barbara said suddenly. 'That blend you have is scrumptious. What is it?'

'Gevalia,' Deborah answered absently. 'It's Swedish. I order it.'

'I think I'll order some, too. Evan seemed to like it. It would be good in the mornings. Of course, he doesn't spend the night with me too often. Claims my mattress is bad. I don't stay with him too often, either.' She looked troubled and Deborah feared Barbara was about to confide intimate details of her relationship with Evan, which Deborah was *definitely* not in the mood to hear this morning, but she was spared as Barbara went on about the coffee. 'I could order some delivered to his house. I think he'd like that.'

Barbara poured coffee grounds into the filter and flipped on the automatic coffee maker. They talked desultorily, both screamingly aware of the troopers searching the back yard. Barbara seemed jittery, and five minutes later she leaped up from her chair and announced with desperate gaiety, 'The coffee's ready!'

And strong enough to snap already frayed nerves, Deborah thought, but she took the mug Barbara offered and smiled as the bitter concoction slid down her throat. Barbara took a sip and said thoughtfully, 'Maybe I should have added a little more water.'

'It's fine.'

'Lots of body, right?' Barbara said drily. 'You don't even need a backbone with this stuff in you.'

Deborah was laughing softly as the troopers came back into the house. There were two of them. The young, homely one introduced himself as Muller. The older, handsome one with immobile features and a tall, spare frame was named Cook. 'We'll be going upstairs now, ma'am,' Muller said as Scarlett danced around his legs, begging for attention. He bent and petted the dog. 'He's real cute. Not any particular breed, is he?'

'It's a she,' Deborah said. 'Her mother was a beagle-terrier mix and her father a German Shepherd.'

'That's quite a blend,' the young man laughed.

'I like purebred dogs myself,' Cook announced loudly as if everyone was interested. 'And I don't like them inside the house.'

'How fascinating,' Barbara snapped. 'Come on – I'll take you up to the storage room.'

The older man gave Deborah a stern look. 'You'll have to keep this dog out of the way. Got to keep the scene as clean as possible.'

'I'll shut her in the garage.'

Scarlett looked at her reproachfully as she spread an old throw-rug on the cold garage floor and motioned for the dog to lie down on it. 'What a sourpuss that Cook is,' she muttered. Tail between her legs, Scarlett crept over to the rug, interpreting Deborah's actions as punishment. 'I'll get you out of there in a jiffy,' she said, rubbing the dog's ears in reassurance. Scarlett relaxed and lapsed into what Steve often called her 'stupid look', her expression growing increasingly vacant. 'I swear you can see her IQ drop by the second,' Steve would laugh. Deborah couldn't help smiling as the dog flopped on her side in complete abandonment. 'You're a good girl, Scarlett. Just don't get into any trouble for the next few minutes.'

Joe arrived a moment later. 'Kids delivered, principal notified,' he said shortly. 'He also said they could stay for the party, but he'd rather they not finish out the week. Too much responsibility for the school to accept.'

'I guess I can't blame him,' Deborah said.

'Cops upstairs?'

'Yes.'

'Know who it is?'

'Cook and Muller,' Barbara said.

'Muller's okay. Sort of a friend of mine. Cook's a pain.' Without another word Joe left her and Deborah heard his boots beating on the stairs. She sat in front of her abominable coffee, her mind revolving helplessly. Steve, where *are* you? she thought. 'God, I'll give ten years of my life if you'll just return him to us safe and sound,' she murmured. But her mother had told her long ago you shouldn't try to make deals with God. 'Everything that happens in this world is God's will,' she would say as she sat over sewing or pasting recipes into an album, as if they were family pictures. 'What will be, will be. God's got a divine plan and we can't change it.'

'But if there's a divine plan and we can't change it, why do we bother to pray?' Deborah had asked.

Her mother would look at her, disturbed. 'What on earth do you mean, child? We pray to thank God.'

'Not most of the time,' a twelve-year-old Deborah had argued. 'Mostly we ask for things to turn out a certain way. Just last Sunday in church we prayed for old Mr McCallister to be healed of his black lung.'

'You don't understand.'

'No, I don't. Explain it.'

'I can't. It's too complicated. But don't let your daddy hear you talkin' like that.'

'What's wrong with asking questions?'

'Just keep your questions to yourself, Deborah. Daddy doesn't like questions.'

Especially from me, Deborah had thought, the child who had lived while her two older brothers had died as babies. He'd resented Deborah, as if it were her fault each of the two boys had been born too premature to live, while she'd been a healthy eight pounds. She'd always been aware of that resentment, even when she was too young to analyse its cause.

So Deborah *had* kept her questions to herself, but she'd never stopped wondering at the contradiction. Even now, as she sat at the kitchen table, she felt that, on the one hand, she should be praying for her missing husband, but on the other, that prayers were useless.

Thoughts of her parents triggered thoughts of Steve's. They should be apprised of the situation, but she didn't know where to reach them in Hawaii. Besides, would they even care? Of course they would care. He was their only son. They must have some shred of feeling for him. But if she could phone them, she couldn't tell them without bringing up Artie Lieber's name, and she wasn't sure she wanted to do that. But what if Lieber were still a danger to Emily? Was it possible that he could get into the nursing home? Should the staff be alerted?

Her thoughts were interrupted by the policemen coming back down the stairs, Barbara and Joe trailing behind. 'Do you always leave the window to that storage room unlocked?' Muller asked Deborah.

'No, of course not. Not on purpose, anyway. Why?'

'Because there's no sign of forced entry.'

'So the window was unlocked. I guess it's possible. We hardly ever went in there. I suppose one of us could have unlocked and opened it in the summer, then forgot to lock it. It's just that my husband was so careful about those kinds of things.'

'But you said the door to the tool shed was left unlocked,' Joe pointed out.

'The tool shed, yes. But locks on the house – no, Steve was very careful about that. After what happened to Emily . . .'

'Who's Emily?' Cook asked.

'My husband's sister,' Deborah said. 'She was raped and beaten when she was a teenager. Her attacker got parole a couple of months ago and was spotted in Charleston two days ago. I thought Evan Kincaid had already gone over this with you people.'

Cook's handsome face flushed. 'He talked to the city cops, not us. Nobody mentioned the sister's name to us, and we're not mind-readers.'

Joe held up his hands in a placating manner. 'Okay. No big deal. Mrs Robinson isn't an expert on jurisdictional matters.'

But I know that much, Deborah thought unhappily. I'm too flustered to think straight. 'Did you get any fingerprints?' she asked.

'We'll have to wait for the evidence team,' Cook said. 'They'll have quite a job ahead of them since I heard you had that big blowout here Saturday night.'

'I'd hardly call our Christmas party a *blowout*,' Deborah bristled. 'Besides, we didn't entertain guests in the storeroom.'

'Whatever,' Cook said, unfazed by her sarcasm. 'Someone should be here within the hour. They'll have to get yours, too, Mrs Robinson. Unfortunately, Mr Pierce here said your husband's prints aren't on file.'

'But Lieber's are,' Joe said. 'If he was the one in the room last night and careless enough to leave prints, we'll get him.'

'I just don't understand why Artie Lieber would break into the house,' Deborah said. 'Steve had been missing for hours. What would be the point of Lieber breaking in here if he already had Steve?'

'We don't know that this guy, this Lieber creep, has anything to do with your husband's disappearance,' Muller said.

Cook cast a cold gaze at Deborah. 'Or maybe he isn't satisfied with just Mr Robinson.'

Deborah went rigid. 'You mean he could come after the children and me?'

Cook shrugged, looking disdainful and self-important. 'Why not? Lieber probably has a big hate thing going about the guy who put him away, and meanwhile got himself a successful law career, a young wife and a couple of kids while *he* was rotting away in prison.'

'Oh, lord,' Deborah murmured, feeling weak. 'Then we're all in danger. *Real* danger.'

Joe gave her a long, level look. 'You could all be in danger *if* Lieber really is out for blood, *if* he's really done something to Steve. We have absolutely no proof of any of this.'

'No, Lieber just happened to turn up in Charleston this week and Steve just happened to vanish last night,' Deborah said grimly. 'That's enough proof for me.'

Thirty minutes later the troopers left. Deborah had been fingerprinted, had found a fairly recent photograph of Steve, and had presented the troopers with one of Steve's sweaters and his hairbrush – the sweater to give bloodhounds his scent, the brush for hair so they could get a DNA sample to match with the blood left in the car.

Before going out the door, Cook said, 'You hear anything, you let us know.' He flung an accusatory look at Deborah, as if he thought she was going to object for some nefarious reason.

Muller lingered behind, muttering a soft apology for his partner's abrasive manner. 'He's got troubles at home, ma'am. Don't hold it against him.'

'I won't,' Deborah said, although she thought if she ever saw Cook again it would be too soon. Barbara let Scarlett back into the house. The dog spent the next five minutes shivering violently. 'For heaven's sake, you'd think you'd been in the Yukon for the last hour,' she laughed.

'Kim picked the perfect name for her,' Deborah said. 'She definitely has Scarlett O'Hara's gift for the dramatic.'

Shortly afterward, the doorbell rang. 'I'll get it,' Barbara offered.

Deborah shook her head. 'I haven't completely fallen apart. I can still answer my own door.'

On the front porch stood a man of medium height with very short light brown hair and deep crow's-feet around unflinching light blue eyes. 'Mrs Deborah Robinson?' he asked. She nodded. 'I'm Charles Wylie, FBI.'

'FBI?' she repeated in confusion. He showed her identification. 'You're here about my husband?'

'Yes. May I come in?'

Joe and Barbara were sitting in the living room. 'This is Mr Wylie with the FBI,' Deborah said. Barbara's expression was as confused as her own, but a quick, wary look passed over Joe's face. 'He's here about Steve. Mr Wylie, this is Barbara Levine and Joe Pierce. They both work in the Prosecutor's office with my husband.'

Wylie nodded to them, then turned to Deborah. 'I'd like to speak with you alone for a few minutes.'

'There's nothing about my husband's disappearance that Barbara and Joe don't know,' Deborah said.

'Nevertheless, I need to ask you some questions. I'd rather do it alone.'

'Do you have evidence that Steve was taken across the state line?' Barbara asked, not at all daunted by the agent's unsmiling demeanor. Deborah wondered briefly if practicing a stone-face was part of the FBI training.

'I just found out a couple of hours ago about Mr Robinson's disappearance,' Wylie answered. 'I have no evidence as of yet.'

'How did you find out my husband was missing?' Deborah asked.

'The West Virginia state police put a notice about your husband's car on the teletype system and we saw it.'

'But I still don't understand why you're here.'

'As I said, I have some questions for you, Mrs Robinson.'

'All right,' Deborah said. 'Barbara, Joe, since Mr Wylie wants to talk with me alone, would you mind waiting in the kitchen?'

Joe and Barbara rose simultaneously. Barbara still looked puzzled and more than a little suspicious, but Joe's face had that odd, closed look that meant he knew something. He and Evan *both* knew something they weren't telling her, something that Evan had apparently not even told Barbara.

Deborah motioned to the couch. Agent Wylie sat down and took a small notebook out while surreptitiously surveying the room. Deborah felt absurdly guilty and wondered why. Was it because of the cold penetration of Wylie's gaze? Or was it merely because she'd never come into contact with the FBI before?

'I understand your husband disappeared yesterday afternoon,' Wylie began.

'Yes. The children and I had gone Christmas shopping around one. The lady next door says Steve left about 2.30, but she's not always reliable.' Wylie's eyebrows lifted. 'She's ninety-two. Sometimes she gets mixed up or invents stories, but not all the time.'

'I see. Did she say if your husband left alone?'

'Yes, she said he was alone.'

'And none of his things are missing?'

'Nothing but the clothes he was wearing. And his jacket. And his car, of course.' She did not mention the money gone from Steve's desk.

'The car was found near the airport early this morning.'

'Yes,' Deborah said unsteadily. 'I was told there was blood on the back seat.'

Wylie nodded, writing in his notebook. He showed no shock, no compassion, and Deborah suddenly felt angry with his cold-blooded efficiency. And what was he here for, anyway?

He looked up suddenly. 'Your husband visited his sister at the nursing home in Wheeling about once every two months, right?'

'His sister?' Deborah repeated, startled. 'Yes, he did. But what has that got to do with anything?'

'He left on Saturdays and spent the night in Wheeling.'

'Yes. It's a long drive and he liked to see her twice – on Saturday afternoon and Sunday morning.'

'Did you often accompany him?'

'No. I only went once, right after we were married. That was seven years ago.'

'Why didn't you go back?'

'Steve didn't want me to. He said it was depressing – Emily doesn't move or speak. At least, she doesn't say much, although last night a nurse told me she *does* speak sometimes. Anyway, there were the children. I always stayed home with them.'

'Did your husband usually call you from Wheeling on Saturday night?'

'No. Well, he did a few times, but mostly when I was pregnant.'

'He hasn't called you from Wheeling on a Saturday night for over five years? That's how old your twins are, aren't they? Five?'

Why did Agent Wylie know so much about their family and their routines? 'Yes, my children are five. They'll be six in April. And he *has* called since their birth.'

'But not often.'

'Well, not every time he's gone to see Emily.'

'Have you ever called him at his motel on those Saturday nights when he's in Wheeling?'

'Maybe three or four times. Usually he's quite depressed after he's seen his sister – he's not in the mood for chit-chat. Besides, he doesn't always stay in the same place. Mr Wylie, will you *please* tell me why you're asking all this?'

Wylie ignored her, going on with passionless determination. 'Did your husband go to visit his parents in Wheeling during these trips?'

'No. He's estranged from his parents. He hasn't seen them for years.'

'No chance meetings at the nursing home?'

'Not that I was aware of. The Robinsons know he visits his sister the second Saturday and Sunday of every other month, and they stay away.'

'What is the reason for this estrangement?'

Deborah hesitated. She resented Wylie's presumptuous manner. What business was it of his why Steve was estranged from his parents? But she responded to the authority in his voice. 'Emily, Steve's sister, was attacked by a man named Artie Lieber. He'd been the Robinsons' handyman, but he had a bad reputation and they'd fired him when he showed too much interest in Emily.' She realized how stiff she sounded, but she couldn't seem to speak naturally to this cold-eyed man. 'One weekend they went away and Steve was supposed to be looking out for Emily, only he left the house for a couple of hours. That's when Lieber got to her. She was raped, strangled and beaten.'

'What were the extent of her injuries?'

'Lieber hit her in the head with a pipe and she suffered brain damage. At least, I think she did.' Wylie looked at her enquiringly. 'What I mean is, Steve told me doctors say there was some brain damage, but it wasn't irreparable. They claim her problem is mostly psychological, not physical. It's still the result of the attack, though. But you know all this, don't you?'

'I'd like to hear it from you.'

Growing angrier and more frustrated by the minute, Deborah glared at him. 'Well, you've heard it from me. Now I'd like to hear something from you, such as why you're here.'

'I can't go into that right now.'

Deborah's jaw sagged. 'You want me to answer all these questions, but I'm not to know why?'

'I'd appreciate your cooperation.'

'I will cooperate in any way possible to find my husband, but I don't see how these particular questions are going to help locate Steve. You must already know about Lieber and how he vowed to get even with Steve for giving testimony that put him in jail.'

'Lieber knows going after your husband would land him back in jail. Why would he risk that?'

'I don't know. He's crazy, but I don't see how this concerns the FBI.'

'If that's what happened, and unless, as Ms Levine suggested, Lieber took your husband into another state, it doesn't.'

'*If* that's what happened? What else could have happened?'

'A lot of other things.'

'Things that concern the FBI?'

'Yes.'

'Like what?' Deborah demanded. 'Why is the Bureau looking for my husband?'

'I can't go into that right now.' Wylie frowned, looking at a plant placed on the wide mantel. 'Is that oleander?'

'What?'

'Is that plant an oleander?'

Deborah gazed at him, bewildered. 'Yes, it is.'

'Who has the green fingers?'

'My husband.'

'Is he particularly fond of oleanders?'

'Yes, I suppose. They aren't easy to grow in this area. He was proud that he could do it.'

'I see.'

'I don't. What on earth does that have to do with—'

'You've been a great help,' Agent Wylie said abruptly, standing. 'I may need to talk with you again.'

Deborah's tolerance, which had already reached strained levels, suddenly snapped. 'I will not answer any more of *your* questions until you answer some of *mine*.'

'Thank you for your cooperation, Mrs Robinson,' Wylie said calmly, his gaze flat. 'I'll see myself out.'

TWO

Stunned by Wylie's visit, Deborah walked into the kitchen where Barbara and Joe were sitting at the kitchen table. Barbara looked at her expectantly. 'Well? What did *he* want?'

'I don't know,' Deborah said quietly. 'But Joe does.'

Her eyes met Joe's. He glanced down for a moment, tapping his tanned fingers on the table. 'Joe, you know something we don't?' Barbara asked in a surprised voice.

Joe took a deep breath, and Deborah was afraid he was composing himself to tell a lie. Instead, he looked at her, regret showing in his usually steely eyes. 'Deborah, you'd better sit down.'

'I think I'd rather stand.'

'My mother always said that when someone had bad news to give her,' Joe said absently. 'Okay. Steve didn't want you to know. But he told Evan and me because he was scared to death. He wanted our help.'

Deborah swallowed. 'What did he tell you?'

Joe folded his hands, and for the first time Deborah noticed the turquoise ring he wore. It looked American Indian in design and the silver caught the weak winter light coming in through the window behind the table. 'You've heard of The Dark Alley Strangler.'

Deborah blinked. 'The Dark Alley Strangler?'

'The serial murderer?' Barbara asked.

'Yeah. In the past three years he's murdered eight women in Ohio and Pennsylvania. Last Saturday night he attacked a woman named Sally Yates in Wheeling.'

Barbara had gone completely still, but Deborah continued to look at Joe, baffled. 'I read about Sally Yates. The last I heard she was in a coma but not expected to live. But I still don't get it. What does all this have to do with Steve?'

'All the women were murdered within a hundred-mile radius of Wheeling. They were beaten, raped, and strangled, always on weekends when Steve had gone to Wheeling to visit Emily.'

Deborah gaped, then started laughing. 'Are you telling me that the FBI thinks *Steve* is this Dark Alley Strangler? That's the most ludicrous thing I've ever heard! My God, it sounds like something Mrs Dillman might come up with.'

Joe's eyes dropped. 'An FBI agent came to see Steve Friday morning, Deborah. It seems on Thursday a witness came forward. This person was in a bar named Kelly's, where Sally Yates had been earlier the previous Saturday evening when she was attacked. The witness didn't see the actual attack, but he or she, whatever, saw a man coming out of the alley shortly after Yates was raped and beaten. The man had also been in the bar earlier and now he seemed to be in a real hurry, although he was talking to himself and snickering. The witness didn't know about Yates yet but thought it was all pretty strange – a guy coming out of the alley acting weird – so out of curiosity watched him. He got into a white car. The witness couldn't identify the make but got a partial reading of the West Virginia license plate – *8E-7*.' He raised his eyes. 'Steve drives a white Cavalier and his license plate number is *8E-7591*.'

7

ONE

Deborah stared at Joe, aghast. Her mouth had suddenly gone dry, her hands cold. Finally she muttered in a feeble voice, 'You can't be serious.'

'Wasn't an FBI agent just here?' Joe asked softly.

'But he could have come for some other reason. Maybe he thought Steve's disappearance involved interstate crime or—'

Joe was shaking his head. 'No, Deborah, that's not what the Feds think.'

Deborah sank on to the bench across the table from him. The shock made her feel dull-witted. 'I can't believe this.'

'Neither can I,' Barbara echoed faintly.

'Why didn't Steve tell me?' Deborah asked.

'He was thunderstruck. And scared.'

'But he told you and Evan.'

'He thought we could help. Deborah, the evidence against him is circumstantial, but in spite of what we hear in the movies, circumstantial evidence can convict a person.'

Barbara leaned forward, her voice strong and sure again. She was no longer the puzzled friend – she was an attorney. 'Did this person who claims to have seen a man come out of the alley get a good look at him?'

'Apparently good enough to identify him as a man who'd been in Kelly's earlier,' Joe said.

'Why did the witness wait so long to come forward?' Deborah asked.

Joe looked at her. 'This kind of thing happens all the time. For one reason or another someone doesn't go to the police with what they know.

Maybe they have something to hide, or maybe they just don't want to get involved. Then conscience gets the better of them.'

'And you don't know the witness's name?'

'The police aren't careless enough to release that information and jeopardize another life. Anyway, this person said the guy was about six feet tall, with dark brown hair, slender. Looked to be in his late thirties, good shape. Had a mustache. He wasn't a regular at the bar.'

'What about eye color?' Barbara asked.

'He had on tinted glasses.'

'Steve doesn't wear glasses,' Deborah said. 'He also doesn't have a mustache or dark hair.'

'The FBI believes he could have been in disguise – a fake mustache, spectacle frames with non-prescription tinted glass. Maybe he even used a wig or temporary dye to give him the dark hair.'

'And they're absolutely sure the man who attacked the Yates woman is The Dark Alley Strangler?'

'Yes. He pulls a woman who has just come out of a bar into an alley. He beats, strangles, and rapes her, although there's never any semen for DNA testing.'

'What about hair samples?'

'None.'

Barbara looked perplexed. 'Okay, if he wears a condom, there might not be any semen, but how can there be a rape without hair samples?'

'I think the theory is that he's using an object for the rape.'

'You mean he's not actually . . .'

'Right,' Joe said abruptly. 'How better to be absolutely sure you don't leave semen or hair? They've never managed to get a blood sample, either. Apparently this guy knocks the women senseless almost immediately so they don't have much time to struggle. All they've picked up are some fiber samples. This killer is careful. And strong. Another part of his ritual is that he takes his victim's jewelry, often ripping earrings right out of the ear-lobes.'

Deborah cringed, but Barbara was frowning. 'The car,' she began. 'Couldn't the witness be mistaken about the license plate?'

'Maybe, but you have to admit, it would be quite a coincidence if the mistake just happened to match Steve's license plate number. And don't forget, the car was white, the same color as Steve's.'

Deborah looked at him in disbelief and reproach. 'You sound like you think Steve really is this Dark Alley person. Surely you can't believe Steve would *murder* someone!'

'We're not talking about what I believe,' Joe said calmly. 'We're talking about what the FBI believes based on some pretty damning evidence. It doesn't help that these women were raped, strangled and beaten, the same as Steve's sister.'

'Oh, God,' Deborah gasped. 'But it was Lieber who attacked Emily.'

'According to Steve. He was the only witness.'

Deborah put her head in her hands, her long hair falling over her face. 'This is too awful.'

'That's why Steve didn't want to tell you.'

Barbara looked angry. 'Why do men always have to play the big heroes? He couldn't have thought he could keep it from her for ever.'

'Believe it or not, I think he did. That's why he turned to Evan and me – he wanted us to help clear him before Deborah ever knew. But now, since his disappearance . . .'

'His disappearance,' Deborah said slowly. 'The FBI doesn't believe Artie Lieber did anything to him, do they? They think he faked a disappearance because he felt the net closing in on him.'

Joe looked at her gravely. 'Wouldn't you think the same thing if you were an outsider? This makes him look more guilty than ever. They've even set up surveillance on the house.'

'If they're watching the house, why didn't they see where Steve went yesterday?'

'Surveillance probably wasn't supposed to start until this morning. At least, that's what Steve guessed. Looks like he was right.'

'Oh, hell,' Barbara muttered. 'That's just great. Steve tells you and Evan he's expecting surveillance to begin on Monday, and he disappears on Sunday. It *does* look bad.'

Joe was still gazing steadily at Deborah. 'They think you know more than you're saying. They think he might call or even come back here.'

Deborah's voice turned fierce. 'If he supposedly went to all this trouble to stage a disappearance, I don't believe he'd come back the next day. But he didn't stage a disappearance. I know it. My God, if he were suspected of being this Strangler person, why would Steve have told you and Evan? Why would he have asked for your help?'

'We were there when Wylie came to the office and questioned Steve. It was obvious from Steve's reaction to the visit Wylie hadn't been there on any routine kind of business. They would say he thought he couldn't hide it from us, and they'd be right.'

'But he could hide his fear from me,' Deborah said desolately. 'He was always hiding things from me. Sometimes I felt like I didn't know him at all.' She saw Barbara and Joe exchange a look and her voice tensed. 'I don't mean he could have been a cold-blooded serial killer and I wouldn't have known it. I just mean that he kept small things from me, the confidences that husbands and wives usually share. At least, I think they do.'

Joe looked at her intensely. 'Deborah, don't say to the FBI you felt you didn't really know your husband. They'll jump on that and ignore the subtleties that explain exactly what you meant.'

'I . . . of course I won't,' Deborah said, feeling foolish and blundering. What if she had blurted out such a statement to Agent Wylie? The thought frightened her and immediately she began a mental replay of her conversation with the man. Had she said anything wrong? Anything that might hurt Steve? She couldn't remember. The whole conversation with the FBI agent seemed like a dream. In fact, the last two days seemed like a dream. Or a nightmare. Steve should be at work and she should be diligently typing her current project, the sleep-inducing manuscript on an obscure, mediocre poet by a local author. Instead, Steve was missing, a man who had threatened to get even with him was on the loose in Charleston, and the FBI was convinced Steve was a serial killer. The situation was almost too absurd for her to accept, but it was all true and she couldn't handle it alone, she knew that. She looked at Joe.

'Were you going to help Steve?'

'Yes.'

'Then neither you nor Evan believed – even for a second – that Steve could be a killer?'

'No.'

She nodded. 'In that case, I need for both of you to help me now. I don't know what to do. I don't know how to help Steve. God, I don't even know if he's still alive.' Tears welled up in her eyes. 'I don't know *anything*!'

Barbara put her hand with its graceless onyx ring – the only jewelry she ever wore – on Deborah's shoulder. 'Everything's going to be all right. Somehow, everything is going to be all right and your life with Steve will be just the same as it's always been.'

But Deborah knew that no matter what the explanation for Steve's disappearance was, things would never be the same again.

TWO

Sharp December wind nipped at Kimberly's fingers as she stood in the schoolyard at morning recess. She'd lost her new blue gloves. She'd already lost the red pair, and Mommy had told her the blue ones would be the last for that year. She didn't really think Mommy meant it, but neither did she want to say she'd left another pair at school where some kid had taken them. Mommy would go on and on about something she called 'respon'bil'ty' and tell her money didn't grow on trees, which she already knew. Did Mommy really think she was so dumb she didn't know they made money at 'The Bank' and gave it to people who went to the machine outside and typed in the secret code? Kim shook her head. Mommy just didn't know how smart she was, even if she kept losing her gloves.

Kim plunged her cold hands into her coat pockets. Wind pulled at her long blonde hair, which reminded her she'd left her fuzzy wool scarf inside. She didn't want to go back for it. She glanced over at some of her friends jumping rope. They'd asked her to play, but she didn't want to. She felt too sad about Daddy. Mommy thought someone had *killed* him. She said she didn't mean it, but she did, Kim could tell. But Mommy *had* to be wrong. Daddy wouldn't let someone kill him, especially right before Christmas. Still, Mommy had been crying, and Mommy never cried.

Her own eyes filling with tears, Kim looked around the playground until she spotted Brian. He was hanging upside down on the Jungle Jim. Mommy didn't allow him to climb on the Jungle Jim because he usually got hurt. Rubbing her tears away, Kim marched toward him. 'Get down,' she ordered. 'Get lost,' Brian responded.

'You're not s'posed to be on the Jungle Jim,' Kim continued in her most grown-up voice. 'Mommy said you'd fall and crack your head open.'

Climbing like monkeys, three other little boys snickered. Brian glowered at his sister. 'If you don't leave me alone, I'll tell Mommy you lost your new gloves.'

Kim considered this possibility and decided getting tattled on wasn't worth preserving Brian's head. Besides, if he cracked it open, the doctor could fix it like he did last Christmas when Brian fell down the attic stairs.

She made a face at him and wandered toward the big tree where their teacher, Miss Hart, said robins would make nests in the spring. Last spring Daddy had carried her and Brian, separately, up a big ladder and let them peer in at a robin's nest in a tree in the back yard. Inside were four tiny blue eggs. Kim had been delighted, especially when the eggs hatched. For a while, Scarlett had only been allowed out on her leash until the baby birds learned to be good fliers in case one of them nose-dived and couldn't make it back up into the air before Scarlett reached him.

Thinking about the baby birds and Daddy made her want to cry again. She turned to the gate in the schoolyard fence and froze. A man stood there, motioning for her to come to him. He wore a blue coat like Daddy's, but he had the hood pulled up and Kim couldn't see his face clearly. She squinted like Mommy did sometimes. Was it Daddy? From so far away, she couldn't be sure.

She slowly walked toward the figure. He was tall like Daddy. His hair was about the same color as Daddy's. But he had on dark glasses. She couldn't see his eyes.

'Kimberly, come here.'

His voice seemed soft and kind, but the wind carried it away and she couldn't be sure it was Daddy's. The wind was also stinging her eyes, making them water. He beckoned to her again. Kim hesitated, thinking. If he was Daddy, and she found him, everybody would be *so* happy. But if he *was* Daddy, why didn't he just go home? Her thumb shot to her mouth again. She was mixed up. He looked an awful lot like Daddy, but Daddy wouldn't come to school and stand outside the gate with a hood pulled so tight she couldn't even see most of his face. Unless . . .

Her thumb drifted from her mouth as she remembered a television show she'd seen once about a man who forgot who he was. Mommy said the man had . . . what was it? *Am*-something. It didn't matter. He'd gotten hit on the head and he didn't remember his name or where he lived. Maybe Daddy got hurt and didn't remember where he lived, either.

'Kimberly, please come to me,' the man called again. 'Come on, honey. I want to give you an early Christmas present.'

Kim smiled. 'Daddy!' She burst into a run toward the gate where the man stooped, arms outstretched.

She was only inches away from him when suddenly Miss Hart screamed, 'Kim! No!'

Startled, the child slowed. The man shot to a standing position, his head jerking toward the teacher.

'Kim, don't go near him,' Miss Hart shouted, her young face white, her eyes wide.

Kimberly stopped, confused. Miss Hart acted scared, and so did the man, yet his arms thrust out to grab her. An abrupt, instinctive fear flashed through Kim as the man's fingertips touched her coat. She stumbled backward. 'Come *here*,' he hissed, no longer sounding nice at all. Kim whimpered, tripping over a clump of tough, dried crab-grass. She went sprawling to the ground and the man rushed foward. He was almost on her when Miss Hart swept down, jerking Kim into her arms. 'Get *away* from her,' she shrieked. 'Help! Someone help me!'

The man turned and bolted down the street. He ran so fast his hood fell backward, but his face was turned away from them. Kim burst into tears as a crowd of excited young children gathered around her.

THREE

After the state troopers left Deborah's house, Joe was quick to follow. 'Got a couple of errands to run,' he said brusquely, 'but I'll be back in time to pick the kids up from school.'

'I wonder what that's all about?' Barbara asked.

Deborah shrugged. 'I don't know, but we're really disrupting his life. Maybe he needed to pick up some things at home.'

Twenty minutes later the phone rang and Deborah rushed to answer it. 'Mrs Robinson?'

The female voice was vaguely familiar but quavery. She didn't sound like a reporter or a policewoman.

'Yes, this is Mrs Robinson,' Deborah said guardedly.

'This is Lois Hart, Kim and Brian's teacher.'

Panic rushed through Deborah. 'What is it?' she asked loudly. 'Are the children all right?'

'There was an incident today at recess—'

'Oh, God, is one of them hurt?'

'No, they're fine. Kim is just a little upset. You see, there was this man . . . I looked away at two little boys fighting and I didn't realize at first . . . I only looked away for a couple of minutes . . . and then—'

'You're scaring the life out of her. Let me talk to her.' Deborah recognized the booming, impatient voice of Howard Morton, the principal. Her heart hammered during the moment of silence before he began speaking with false cheer. 'Mrs Robinson, the man who brought the children to school today, Pierce I believe he said his name was, apprised me of your unfortunate situation. You have my condolences. He asked that we keep a close eye on Kimberly and Brian, and it's fortunate that he did. I informed Miss Hart. At recess, a man came to the gate of the schoolyard and tried to lure Kimberly away.'

'*What?*' Deborah shrilled.

'I assure you, everything is all right. Miss Hart saw what was happening and reached Kimberly just in time.'

'Just in time?' Deborah repeated dumbly.

'Just before the man got his hands on Kimberly and spirited her away.'

Who but the pompous Howard Morton would say 'spirited her away'? Deborah wondered in spite of her fear. 'Is Kim hurt?' she asked tremulously.

'No, no, not at all, Mrs Robinson. She's just a bit shaken, but under the circumstances we feel it would be best for both her and Brian to go home today.'

'I'll be there in ten minutes.'

'That would be fine. And I'd like for you to know we've called the police. Miss Hart will be giving them a complete description of the man.'

'Did she recognize him?'

'No, but Kimberly said at first she thought he was her father. Now she's not certain. Miss Hart has never met your husband, so she can't say.'

Slowly, Deborah hung up the phone. A man had tried to abduct her daughter, a man the little girl had thought was Steve. Could it have been? Or was someone else out to harm her children?

* * *

82

FOUR

Artie Lieber leaned on bed pillows he'd propped against the headboard and stared intently at the grainy color picture on the portable television across from him. It was 12.20 and the noon news was ending. Weather maps flashed in front of him. Warmer weather was predicted for tomorrow with a high of thirty-seven degrees, the weatherman announced gleefully. Hot damn, Artie thought sourly. Might as well be in Miami Beach. Let's have a party over this great weather.

The news anchors were back on, interviewing the star of some new series. The star declared the series location, the staff, and the scripts were in turn terrific, wonderful, and fantastic. It was an honor to work on the show. Why don't they ever say they're starring in a piece of crap for the money? 'Because then they'd lose the show and wouldn't be making the big bucks any more,' Artie answered himself. Now the anchors were making 'happy talk', seemingly delighted with each other's inane chatter. Finally they promised another scintillating news cast at six o'clock before they relinquished the stage to a soap opera. Artie tilted his head back and looked at the ceiling, ignoring the beautiful, perfectly made-up and coiffed blonde who drooped around her sumptuous house in supposed mental turmoil.

Nothing had appeared on the news about Steve Robinson. Artie's square jaw tightened. He couldn't even think of the man's name without a wave of revulsion shaking his slender frame which he'd kept strong by at least two hours of excrcise a day while he was in prison. Robinson hadn't been home all night and the police were at his house this morning. Still, it was too early for him to be considered officially a missing person. That's why there hadn't been anything about him on the news.

Artie breathed heavily, thinking about what he'd seen at the house that morning. People besides the police were there, too. He'd spotted a woman with short dark hair. She wasn't much of a looker. There'd also been two men. Robinson's wife must have called in help.

Artie had also seen the two little kids. Brian and Kimberly. He knew their names as if they were his own children. They'd acted upset as one of the men put them in a Jeep Cherokee and drove off with them. Artie's own little girl, Pearl, used to look like that sometimes. In fact, she'd looked like Kimberly the last time he saw her before he went to prison, when his ex-wife – whom he now always referred to as The Slut – had brought Pearl to the courtroom to see him convicted. He'd never forget the confusion and fright in Pearl's big brown eyes when they'd dragged him, shouting curses, from the courtroom. Pearl was twenty-two now, but he hadn't seen her since that day. The Slut had taken her away to Florida. He'd learned Pearl was married and had a kid of her own – a boy. Jeez, he was a grandfather! He'd contacted her when he got out of prison, but she always hung up on him after telling him she didn't even acknowledge him as her father.

He'd been crushed at first, then decided Pearl just needed time. He wasn't one to give up so easily. Maybe with patience he could repair the damage her mother had done, turning the kid against him, filling her head with all kinds of garbage. And when he'd fixed everything with Pearl and got to know his grandson, he'd get even with The Slut.

But now his concern was Steve Robinson. What the hell was going on at his house, anyway? They knew he was missing – that was a given. But he wanted to know every little detail. What did they think had happened to him? They'd found his car. Did they assume he'd been murdered? Did they know that he, Artie, was in Charleston? Was he a suspect in Robinson's disappearance? Had anyone talked to his parole officer and found out he'd missed his meeting that morning? Hell, what he wouldn't give to have the house bugged. Then he could keep more accurate tabs on the whole situation. He wanted to know how much *they* knew about him. He had to know, for his own safety. He hadn't meant to stay in Charleston for so long, hadn't meant to miss even one parole meeting. He sure as hell hadn't meant to be spotted on Saturday when he got that traffic ticket. Why hadn't he just gone home then? Why had he let his obsession get the better of him, overriding his instinct that this wasn't the time to get Steve Robinson? Now he couldn't leave. The police would pick him up before he got anywhere near Wheeling.

His mind skittered around like a mouse trapped in a room with a cat. He suddenly thought of Robinson's young wife, Deborah. He'd caught a glimpse of her when she'd gone out on the porch to bid the kids goodbye. Now *she* was a looker, not like the older one with short hair. The bastard. Robinson had robbed him of his little girl and sent him to prison for fifteen godforsaken years while he'd made a big career for himself and married some young, sexy broad. Like he couldn't have done better with his own good looks which even prison hadn't been able to obliterate.

Suddenly furious, Artie jumped up from the bed and flipped off the TV. He'd had a rough morning and a narrow escape. Still, he had to resume his surveillance, providing the cops weren't still crawling around. The jerks would bury him under the prison if they caught him anywhere near the Robinson house. He'd been a fool to come, but now he couldn't leave. He also couldn't make himself sit here in this dismal motel room all afternoon. He felt like he was tingling all over. He couldn't hold still for more than a few minutes at a time. A tic he'd developed last year began to wiggle around his right eye. His nerves and emotions were on fire.

He opened the bottle of vodka sitting on the scarred bedside table and poured some into the glass he'd been drinking from for the past hour. One more shot to calm him down, and then he'd make another pass by the Robinson house. In a coat with the collar turned up and that stupid hat and the sunglasses he'd bought yesterday, they'd never recognize him driving the white heap he'd 'borrowed' a couple of hours ago when he found it in the unlocked garage of an empty house near the Robinson kids' school. At least, Artie hoped they wouldn't recognize him. He also hoped the car hadn't yet been reported missing. Driving it around was risky, but it was a chance he had to take. He couldn't stand not knowing what was going on at Robinson's house. Damn, he just couldn't stand it.

8

ONE

Barbara had gone home to pack a bag – she insisted on staying with Deborah until 'we find out something', she'd said tactfully. The children were in the back yard playing ball with Joe and Scarlett. Deborah slumped at the kitchen table feeling abandoned and self-pitying beneath her fear. *Why* hadn't Steve told her about this serial killer business? Why hadn't he told her about Artie Lieber? He'd felt free to confide in Evan and Joe, but not her, his own wife, and no matter how many times they told her it was because Steve didn't want to worry her, she felt hurt and excluded. She reprimanded herself for being immature and selfish when Steve might well be dead, but that didn't help, either. Nothing changed how she felt about her husband's secrecy. She deeply resented it. To her it did not seem like mere protection of her peace of mind – it felt like one more way in which Steve had kept her at a distance throughout their entire marriage.

She sighed, ran her hands through her hair for what seemed the hundredth time, longed for a cigarette, and checked the spaghetti boiling on the stove. Beside it bubbled a pan of canned spaghetti sauce. She didn't like to take short cuts with the cooking, but the children loved simple, 'fun' meals. Without Steve's presence, they would probably have a contest to see who could suck in the longest piece of spaghetti and make the most noise while doing it. Tonight she didn't care how messy they were as long as their minds were diverted from their missing father and the incident at the school. Kimberly had talked about it incessantly for an hour after she got home, one minute saying the man who'd tried to grab her was Daddy, the next

86

saying he was like Daddy but he wasn't like Daddy, either. Then she went upstairs to play with her dolls and had said no more about the man.

Deborah wandered over to the dining-room window that looked out on the back yard. The children laughed as Joe tossed the ball. Kimberly repeatedly caught it while Brian missed, even when Joe threw it directly to him. Deborah could see the frustration growing on his little face. Maybe he needed glasses. She'd been wondering about the acuity of his eyesight for a few months. She'd take him for an exam soon. She wasn't sure how he'd react if he *did* need glasses. After all, he was only five. She had been ten when she'd started wearing them – a horrible peacock-blue pair her mother had selected – and cringed through the teasing she'd taken at school, the sudden label of 'four-eyes' and the disdain of a 'boyfriend' who said he didn't like a girl who couldn't see good and had to wear dumb-looking specs. But Brian was a resilient little boy. He would probably ignore any barbs thrown his way. Both children possessed a confidence she'd never had as a child, a confidence she still didn't command.

She moved away from the window to the wall lined with shelves of plants Steve grew inside. She loved the rich African violets that blossomed under his touch. Five pots of them rested on the top shelf, and she wondered if they needed watering or something. Steve would be so disappointed if he came home to find she'd allowed them to die. If he came home . . .

Deborah shuddered. She looked at the two pots of oleander sitting near the violets, high out of the children's reach. Why had Agent Wylie been so curious about oleander? Maybe he, too, was an amateur horticulturist, but Deborah didn't think so.

Her gaze drifted down to the hardy heartleaf philodendron, the English ivy, the jade plants, and, of course, a huge poinsettia. Steve's parents always sent one at Christmas. They never visited and rarely called, but a poinsettia arrived without fail a week before Christmas every year, sent by a florist who had a standing order from them. Deborah had noticed this was the one plant Steve never cared for scrupulously. By March the poinsettia was usually dead.

Looking at the plant reminded her that his parents still didn't know about Steve. Earlier in the day she'd had an inspiration and called the nursing home. She thought they would certainly have left the address of their hotel in case anything happened to Emily, and she'd been right. She had called the hotel, but no one answered in their room. She'd been told at the desk they'd gone off for a boat trip around the Hawaiian islands. They wouldn't be back for two or three days. She told herself she should leave word about Steve being missing. Their friends would probably hear it on the news and break it to them when they got back. Intellectually she knew that was a cruel way for them to find out, but emotionally she couldn't work up much pity for them. They'd unfairly shut him out years ago. Now it was their turn to hurt, if they still felt enough for him to care.

Joe and the children burst through the kitchen door smelling of the chilly outdoors. 'When's supper?' Brian asked, shrugging out of his coat.

'Five minutes. Everyone go wash their hands.'

'C'mon, Joe,' Brian said. 'We wash hands upstairs.'

Joe made a wry face at Deborah, who smiled back. He was really being so good with the children, much better than she was. She would never have guessed that he could be so patient. She knew he'd never been married, and had no children of his own. Maybe he had nieces and nephews, though, because he certainly had a way with kids. He was now trooping dutifully upstairs behind Brian and Kim as Scarlett skittered ahead of them. It was a miracle that neither child had questioned her about Steve again. 'Is Daddy home yet?' had already been asked at least twenty times since they'd come home from kindergarten at noon. It would probably be asked twenty more times before they went to sleep.

When they came back downstairs, Deborah set steaming plates of spaghetti in front of everyone and took a loaf of Italian bread from the oven. As she'd anticipated, the children had a contest and Joe joined in, slurping spaghetti until even Deborah was amused. After winning the contest, Kim announced, 'I love s'qetti. And I like your hair that way, Mommy. You look like Rapunzel.'

Deborah smiled. 'I don't think my hair is quite long enough to hang out a tower window to reach the ground. And I sure wouldn't want someone climbing up it. Ouch!'

Kim giggled. 'It wouldn't be an ouch if a prince climbed it.' Sadness swept over her face. 'Or Daddy.'

'Your daddy doesn't have to climb her hair to get in,' Joe said quickly. 'He's got his own door key.'

Fear swept over Kim's features. 'What if that was Daddy at school today and he has a key and comes in and takes me?'

'That wasn't your daddy,' Joe said. 'He wouldn't scare you like that. The man was just someone who *looked* like him.'

'Are you sure?'

'Yes, I'm sure. But you must never go near anyone like that again.'

'I won't,' Kim said fervently.

'And don't worry. Your daddy will be home soon.'

'I hope.'

Brian laid down his fork. 'He's been gone an awful long time.'

'Not really,' Deborah said. 'It just seems long to us because we miss him. But he'll be back.'

Brian's face abruptly assumed a mournful and hauntingly mature look. 'I don't think so. I don't think Daddy's coming back at all.'

TWO

Pete Griffin passed his son's opened bedroom door and peered in. The handsome boy, with his longish black hair, slender face, and azure eyes, sat on the bed holding a gold frame, his expression wistful. Pete felt the familiar sinking sensation in his heart. After three years the boy hadn't forgotten his mother, Hope, who gazed out at him with laughing azure eyes exactly like his own and a perfect, dimpled smile. 'We haven't heard from her for a long time,' Pete said.

Adam jumped, looked guilty, then flashed his father a charming grin, offset by the wounded look that in unguarded moments sometimes crept into the gay eyes. 'She kind of looks like Deborah Robinson, don't you think?'

Pete looked at the picture critically. 'Well, she was only about twenty-three when this was taken. She was more vivacious than Deborah and I think she was much prettier, but the coloring is very similar. I see a slight resemblance. Maybe that's why you've always liked Deborah so much.'

'I guess. I never thought about it.'

Pete doubted this. He'd often wondered if the boy had a secret crush on Deborah. He wasn't bothered by the possibility – Deborah was thirteen years older than Adam and certainly not one to encourage a young boy. But his son's overly nonchalant dismissal of Deborah struck him as touching. Adam was embarrassed by his crush.

Adam studied the picture. 'She doesn't look like the kind of person who'd abandon her family, does she?'

'She had a different way of seeing things than most people do,' Pete said easily, sitting down on the bed beside his son. 'She was very gentle – she loved flowers, poetry, animals—' He paused and smiled. 'And Judy Collins. Have you ever heard of her?'

'Sure. The singer. I found some old albums downstairs and played them. I especially liked that song "Suzanne".'

Pete threw him a surprised glance. 'That was your mother's favorite, too. I never dreamed you'd like that kind of music.'

Adam shrugged and said with joking egotism, 'Hey, what can I say, Dad? I'm a versatile guy.'

'Apparently so. The Renaissance man. Anyway, Hope was a very good woman in her way. She wanted to do great things in the world. You know, leave a mark. And she had these passionate devotions to things – the environment, whales, baby seals—'

'And now it's wolves.' Pete and Adam smiled at each other. 'Do you think I could go up to Montana to see her?'

Alarm flashed across Pete's face. His tongue nervously touched his lips. 'I don't think this time of year would be so good.'

'I don't mean now. This summer.'

Pete's eyes searched the room, as if looking for inspiration. He twisted his hands, as he always did when he was uncomfortable. He still wore his wedding ring.

'Dad, what is it?'

'Well, actually, I'm not sure she's in Montana any more.'

Adam stared at him. 'What do you mean? She sends me birthday cards and Christmas cards. She never says anything except "Love, Mom", but she *does* remember. And I write to her every few months.'

Pete's eyes dropped. 'I knew this moment would come. I thought I'd be able to handle it better, but diplomacy has never been my strong point. All I can do is be blunt. Your letters have been returned with "Address Unknown" stamped on them for years. I always managed to intercept them.'

Adam gaped. 'But the cards '

'I had a friend of hers in Montana send them to you for the last couple of years. You were so young and I didn't want you to be hurt.' Pete's eyes begged for understanding and forgiveness. 'Son, I'm so sorry.'

Adam's hands tightened on the picture frame as he gazed down at the smiling face of his mother. Then he looked back at his father. 'I feel like a dope, but I understand what you did, Dad. You were trying to protect me. But what if she's *dead*?'

'Unless she destroyed her identification, I would have found out. Her parents would have let me know so I would take care of funeral expenses. I don't believe she's dead. I think I'd *feel* it, if she were, if that makes any sense.'

'You loved her a lot, didn't you?'

'I adored her. I don't think she ever felt the same way about me. I believe she was looking for stability at the time. There had been a lot of trouble in her family. A sister the parents had kicked out of the family for marrying outside the Catholic Church, a father who was chronically ill.'

'When did she leave Montana?'

'Nearly two years ago. It was my fault, really. I'd written to say I wanted to bring you to visit her. There would be no pressure to come home, I promised – I just wanted her to see what a fine young son she had.' Pete laughed ruefully. 'All I accomplished was to scare her away.'

'She never wants to see us again,' Adam said flatly. His eyes had taken on a sheen of unshed tears. 'I just don't understand. I remember her as so much fun. Everyone thought I had the coolest mom in the world – she was so pretty and laughed a lot and she *never* nagged, not like everyone else's moms who were always bitching about something stupid. And she seemed to really *love* me.' His expression hardened. 'But I guess she didn't.'

Pete's face contorted slightly, then he said in a broken voice, 'I can't have you believing she didn't love you, and I guess you're old enough to hear the truth now. If you want to, that is.'

Adam paused, dread showing in his eyes, then nodded.

Pete looked away. 'It's so sordid and clichéd, it's embarrassing – but all right. For a couple of months she'd been acting secretive. Then there had been phone calls when someone hung up if I answered the phone. Never if she answered. One day I came home at noon to pick up some papers I'd forgotten and I could tell something was wrong. She was in bed, very flustered, and, well . . . without going into details, it was obvious she'd been in bed with a man.'

Adam's eyes widened. '*Who?*'

'I don't know. She would never tell me, although she confessed to the affair. I was devastated, but after a lot of talking and crying, your mother and I decided to try to work things out. After all, the man – whom she claimed to love madly and who'd told her the same thing – didn't want to see her any more when he found out I knew about the affair. Her illusions about him were destroyed. He didn't really give a damn about her. Under the circumstances, why not stay with good old Pete?'

Bitterness crept into his voice, but he quickly controlled it. 'Sorry about that. I decided a long time ago not to turn into some hostile loud-mouth, always talking about his faithless wife. Besides, there was so much more to Hope's behavior than an indiscretion. I just wasn't the right man for her. I was too staid, too unimaginative for her.'

Adam said nothing. 'Then she found out she was pregnant,' Pete went on tonelessly. 'It couldn't have been my baby. We hadn't been . . . intimate for weeks. I was too stupid to even consider her lack of interest in . . . romance was because she was in love with someone else and didn't want me touching her. The problem was she didn't believe in abortion and neither did I.'

'So you made her leave.'

'God, no! I'm not saying I was gracious about the whole thing. I ranted, raved, pouted, generally acted like a stereotype of the wronged husband, but I couldn't throw her out, pregnant, unskilled, with a family who would never understand her predicament, to whom she would eventually have confessed the truth. Her mother would have badgered it out of her, then thrown her out. Your *very* Christian maternal grandparents aren't the most forgiving people in the world, not like my grandmother. Besides, I still loved Hope and she was your mother. You needed her. Things seemed to be going as well as could be expected for about a month, although she was unusually quiet.' Pete looked troubled. 'Well, quiet is an understatement. She just sat and stared. I talked about getting her psychological counseling, which threw her into a tailspin. Then suddenly she left. Once again I came home from work to get a major surprise – she'd moved out.'

'I remember that day,' Adam said softly. 'You told me she went to see Grandma and Grandpa LeBlanc in Quebec, but I didn't believe you. I called Grandma and she didn't know what I was talking about. I'd noticed how strange everything had been for weeks – she'd even started sleeping in the guest room – and I got it into my head you'd made Mom leave. I rode all over town on my bike like a crazy person looking for her.'

Misery shone in Pete's eyes. 'You got back here at ten that night and collapsed in the front yard, too exhausted to even cry. I had to carry you in. It took weeks for you to finally believe I hadn't driven her away. You wouldn't even look at me.'

'I was really a jerk.'

'You were a hurt kid who didn't know what was going on. I understood. I tried to find her for you, Adam, for both of us, but gave up after about six months. The private investigator's bills were extraordinary. Finally, about a year after she left, I got a card from her. She was in Montana. She said the baby, a girl, had been stillborn, which she guessed was God's will. That sounded so unlike her. She wasn't just a fallen-away Catholic who claimed to have doubts – she was truly an atheist. I decided she'd had some kind of breakdown. I never heard from her again.'

'And you haven't tried to see her since then?'

'No, Adam, I haven't. Two years ago she ran at the very thought of seeing us. If staying away from her husband and son means so much to her, I say it's best to leave her alone.' Pete drew a deep breath. 'Listen, son, I've given up hope. I know she's no longer the woman I married. She's been gone so long, expressed so little interest in her own child that . . . well, I hope you understand, but I'm finally going to start seeing other women. If I can ever locate her, I'll divorce her.'

The breath went out of Adam. He stared at the wall for a moment, his face hardening into the planes of manhood. He'll never again look like a fifteen-year-old boy, Pete thought.

'I'm glad you're going to divorce her,' Adam said at last, stonily, his voice rougher and deeper than Pete had ever heard it. Adam opened his nightstand drawer and slid the picture frame in, face down. The beautiful smile of his mother disappeared. 'I suppose it's time we both put old memories behind us.'

THREE

Barbara threw clothes into a battered suitcase while Evan sat on the bed, watching her. 'Are you sure you want to stay with Deborah through all of this?' he asked.

Barbara looked at him in surprise. 'Of course I do. She's my best friend. Why wouldn't I?'

'Because it's dangerous at that house.'

'You mean because of Lieber?'

Evan nodded, his blond hair burnished by the harsh overhead light. 'He's gotten rid of Steve, but I don't think he'll stop there.'

Barbara dropped a white nylon half-slip into the bag. 'Why are you so sure he'll go after Deborah and the kids?'

'I've read his record. Before the rape of Emily Robinson his wife got a restraining order one time after he slapped her around for being late from work. Broke her nose and two fingers. He has a history of violence.'

'That's all the more reason why Deborah and the children shouldn't be left alone.'

'And what are you going to do if Lieber shows up? Shoot him? You've never shot a gun in your life. Beat the hell out of him, all one hundred and twelve pounds of you? Deborah needs a man there.'

'Joe's staying.'

'Joe!' Evan scoffed, standing up and walking to Barbara's messy dresser. He began fiddling with the ragged brown teddy bear named Boo Bear she'd been given as a child by her grandmother, the woman who had encouraged her to be whatever she wanted to be, even if it wasn't a housewife. Boo Bear always sat propped against Barbara's mirror as a reminder of the old lady who had given her so much love when her mother was always too busy or too tired. 'I trust Joe about as much as I would Lieber,' Evan said.

Barbara glared at him. 'My God, Evan, that's a terrible thing to say!'

'I don't care. Do you know why he quit the Houston police department? He was sleeping with a prostitute who ended up with her throat slashed.'

'She wasn't a prostitute, she was a call-girl.'

'Oh, excuse me. That makes a big difference.'

'And he wasn't just sleeping with her. He was in love with her.'

'So he claimed. He also claimed he had nothing to do with her unfortunate and very gory murder even though she'd told people she was afraid of him.'

'She was doing a lot of cocaine and saying all kinds of things. Besides, he had an alibi. Ever heard of one of those?'

'It was shaky, very shaky.'

'The Houston police department believed him.'

'They were protecting one of their own.'

'Oh, Evan.' Barbara walked over to him, wrapping her arms around his waist, leaning her head against his back. 'Evan, what are you so upset about? What do you think is going to happen? Do you think Joe's going to kill Deborah or me?'

'I think it's possible, and I cannot for the life of me understand why the two of you would spend one night around him. God, the guy gives me the creeps.'

Barbara frowned. 'I don't think he gives anyone else the creeps. Besides, what do you want Deborah to do?'

'Let *me* stay, what else? Do you think Steve would want that guy sleeping in his house, sleeping near his *children*?'

'Joe and Steve were friends. Besides, you have to work.'

'So do you.'

'But Joe's taken the vacation time he passed up last year. He can be there all day when we aren't.'

Evan dropped the teddy bear's ragged paw and turned to face her. 'That's something else that bothers me. Barb, have you ever known Joe Pierce go out on a limb for anyone?'

'What do you mean?'

'I mean he's a loner. He doesn't get involved. Now here he is, Deborah's knight in shining armor. Why?'

Barbara lifted her shoulders. '*Why?* Because he likes Steve. Because he wants to protect Deborah and the children.'

'Because he wants to protect Deborah, or because he wants to protect himself?'

Barbara's eyebrows drew together. 'Protect himself? What do you mean?'

Evan took a deep breath. 'Barbara, we know there's a serial killer on the loose, don't we?'

'Yes.'

'And we also know that killer isn't Steve.'

'Of course it isn't. And stop talking to me like I'm twelve.'

'However,' Evan went on, ignoring her, 'someone has done a really good job of setting up Steve. Now, who better than someone who works with Steve, someone who knows his schedule, to set him up for these crimes?'

Barbara stared at him in disbelief. 'You're not saying that *Joe* is this Dark Alley Strangler! That's absolutely crazy. Besides, you're Steve's friend, too. You also work at the Prosecutor's office.'

'And I've been Steve's friend for a long time. Joe's a different story. I

95

mean, what do we know about him except that he quit the Houston police department because of his involvement with a woman who was violently murdered, that he's worked closely with Steve since *two* months before these murders began, that he's showing a hell of a lot of uncharacteristic concern over Deborah and the children, *and* that he knows an awful lot about the Strangler?' He looked deep into her eyes, his own serious and darkened to slate-blue with concern. 'You're a logical woman. Think about it, Barb. Think about it hard and then tell me if you think my suspicions are so crazy.'

9

Joe offered to help clean up after dinner, but Deborah refused. 'I'd rather you took the kids into the living room and watched TV with them. Anything but the evening news. It's unlikely at this point, but there might be something on about Steve.'

'They watch the news?' Joe asked incredulously.

'They change channels constantly.'

Joe nodded. 'Don't worry. I'll keep a firm grip on the remote control.'

Fifteen minutes later, as she was drying the last pot used to make their simple dinner, Joe appeared in the kitchen. 'Pete Griffin and his son are in the living room.'

Deborah looked down at her baggy sweater and thought about her hair carelessly pulled behind her ears. She'd never looked as sloppy in her life as she had the last few days. Suddenly she felt as totally out of control emotionally as she was physically. 'I'll put on a fresh pot of coffee,' she said. 'Pete likes herbal tea and artificial sweetener. I'm out of both. And I don't have any Coke for Adam. Or is it Pepsi he likes?' She realized she was babbling and stopped abruptly, her cheeks pinkening.

Joe smiled. 'Don't worry. The kids are showing them the train-set under the tree and I can find my way around a kitchen well enough to manage coffee and a soft drink. Go talk to your guests.'

Deborah finally emerged from the kitchen to find Kim pointing out individual ornaments to Adam and explaining solemnly, 'This is a reindeer, and this is a church, and this is a rocking horse . . .'

Adam listened intently, as if he could never have figured out all of this high art on his own. Brian looked at Deborah and rolled his eyes. She smothered a grin. In some ways he seemed so much older and more sophisticated than his sister.

'That's a really great tree,' Adam said when Kim finally ran down like a wind-up toy. 'But I've got something to make it even better.' From his coat pocket he withdrew a beautiful blown glass ornament with a golden-winged angel inside. 'Oh, how pretty!' Kim gasped.

Adam hung the ornament in the center of the tree. While Kim continued her wide-eyed, delighted compliments, Deborah stared at it. She recognized it. Her gaze shot to Pete, whose eyes bore an almost hypnotic glaze as the delicate angel glowed in the tree lights. The bulb, so exquisite, so obviously expensive, had belonged to Hope Griffin. Deborah had a sense of the world whirling. Something disturbing was happening between Pete and Adam concerning Hope. Good lord, had they heard from her after all this time? Was she dead? Hope and Steve, both missing yet haunting everyone's thoughts, she mused. Why was it so easy to take people for granted when they were present, and impossible to forget them when they were gone?

Joe emerged from the kitchen, clumsily carrying her most battered serving tray on which a coffee pot, Coke can, and cups balanced with what seemed sheer force of will. Deborah rushed to him, taking the tray and quickly depositing it on the coffee table. 'I think we're missing a few things here, but there's plenty to drink. I also have harder stuff, if anyone would care for it.'

In great seriousness, Adam announced, 'I'll have Scotch. Make it a double. No ice.'

'Go home and go to bed,' Pete said. 'You're a disgrace.'

They grinned at each other and Deborah felt her stomach muscles loosening. She still didn't know why Adam had brought over Hope's most prized Christmas ornament, supposedly made in France over a hundred years ago, but apparently everything was fine between Pete and Adam.

As Deborah served coffee and tea, Barbara and Evan arrived. 'We didn't call first because we knew there'd be a trace on the phone,' Evan said. 'No sense throwing everyone into a tizzy for nothing.'

Barbara looked at her solemnly. 'Have any . . . significant calls come in?'

She was asking if there had been calls from kidnappers or from Steve, but she was watching her words in front of Kim and Brian. Deborah shook her head. She hadn't expected either, so she wasn't disappointed. Ever since they'd located Steve's car, she'd merely waited one endless hour after another for word that his body finally had been found.

Sensing that the subject of Steve would come up again in one form or another throughout the evening, Deborah made a great show of looking at the clock. 'Kids, why don't I set up the VCR in my bedroom and let you watch that tape of *Aladdin* Daddy bought for you? You just have time to see it before bedtime.'

'We have to leave the comp'ny?' Kim asked.

'Well, you can't watch it in here. You couldn't hear a thing with all of us talking.'

Brian looked torn for a moment, but Deborah knew how much he wanted to see the videotaped movie that had been a pre-Christmas gift. 'Can we have Cokes up in your room?' he asked.

'Hot chocolate, if you're careful not to spill it.'

The children looked at each other with that wordless, expressionless means of communication that baffled Deborah. 'Okay,' Brian said.

'I'll set up the VCR,' Adam said, already unplugging it from the living-room television set.

Deborah stood. 'While you're doing that, I'll make the hot chocolate.'

Fifteen minutes later the children and Scarlett were sitting on the floor of Deborah's bedroom as the movie started. She closed the bedroom door and went downstairs. 'Everyone is settled,' she said as all eyes fixed on her when she returned. 'Steve had promised them we'd all watch the movie tonight.'

She heard the quiver in her voice and swallowed. Barbara looked sympathetic. The men looked uncomfortable. 'I'm sorry,' she said. 'I can't keep my mind off Steve.'

'It's all right,' Pete said. 'I don't think any of us can keep our minds off him. But I'm just as concerned about you and the children, especially after that trouble at the school today.'

Deborah looked at him quizzically. 'How did you know about that?'

'Have you forgotten that the great Howard Morton, Principal, lives next door to me? I got a full report, although I think it was slightly skewed. According to Morton, he saved the day.'

Deborah shook her head. 'The children's teacher, Miss Hart, saved the day.'

'That's what I figured. But who in the world could the man have been? Surely it wasn't Steve.'

'Kimberly isn't certain. He had on a hood and dark glasses.'

'Well, why on earth would Steve be trying to lure his daughter away from the playground?'

'I can't think of any reason.'

'Then it wasn't Steve,' Pete said briskly. 'Steve would never do something so irrational or so frightening to a little girl.'

'Certainly he wouldn't,' Barbara chimed in.

Deborah smiled tiredly as she sat down on the couch. 'I can't imagine him doing such a thing, either, no matter what the circumstances. I'm just so thrown by all this FBI stuff on top of Steve's disappearance. Thank goodness the serial killer business hasn't made it to the television news.'

'The FBI is very good at keeping things quiet,' Evan said. 'They wouldn't let information like that out.'

'What's this about the FBI?' Pete asked.

Deborah's eyes flashed to Evan. She'd forgotten that Pete and Adam knew nothing about the FBI's suspicion that Steve was a deranged killer colorfully known as The Dark Alley Strangler. She racked her brains for an excuse for the remark, then decided that lying to Pete was ridiculous. He was Steve's oldest friend. As succinctly and unemotionally as she could, with occasional interjections from Evan and Joe, she told Pete the story. His initial reaction was the same as hers had been – he laughed. Then, when he realized no one was exaggerating, he looked incredulous.

'I can't believe it,' he exclaimed. 'How could anyone think something so absurd?'

'Steve Robinson, prosecuting attorney by day, Dark Alley Strangler by night,' Adam said.

Pete cast him a stern look. 'Adam!'

'He's right,' Deborah said. 'It's crazy.'

'Then why are they persisting in this investigation?' Pete asked.

'There's so much evidence,' Evan put in. 'If I didn't know Steve, I'd be convinced they were right. Look at the facts – the dates of the attacks coincide with Steve's visits to Emily, the murders were all so close to Wheeling, then there's the witness who got the color of the car and partial license plate number of the man coming out the alley after the Yates woman was attacked, which matched Steve's car. It would strain anyone's credulity to believe it was all a coincidence.'

'Then *you* believe Steve is guilty of all this?' Pete asked.

'No. But he's in a hell of a lot of trouble.'

'*If* he's alive,' Deborah said. 'I can't believe that no matter how much trouble he's in he'd voluntarily vanish like this. If nothing else, he adored the children. He wouldn't desert them.'

Adam murmured, 'Maybe he wanted to save them from seeing their father charged with murder.'

'Adam!' Pete snapped again.

Deborah took a deep breath. 'He didn't say Steve *was* a murderer, only that he'd be charged with murder. And it's true. Steve *wouldn't* want that. Still, he was always so strong about facing tough situations. A lot of people in his position would have shied away from visiting Emily more than once or twice a year, if at all. Instead, he visited her every two months.'

'How ironic that those visits are part of what caused the FBI to suspect him,' Joe said. 'Hell, they even think he might have tried to kill Emily himself.'

'What?' Pete gasped.

Deborah nodded. 'I forgot to mention that earlier.'

Pete looked disturbed. 'Well, there was talk at the time of Emily's attack, mostly because Lieber kept insisting it was Steve who'd hurt her.'

'I didn't know that,' Deborah said, amazed.

Pete looked at her earnestly. 'Well, good lord, Deborah, that was years ago, and no one really believed it.'

'I don't know about that,' Evan said. 'You see, all the recent victims were raped, strangled and beaten just like Emily. The FBI is making a connection.'

'But unlike Emily, the Strangler's victims are all married,' Joe said.

A strange expression passed over Pete's face. His eyes dropped. 'What is it?' Deborah asked tensely.

'It's . . . well, you see, Emily *was* married.'

Shock rockected through Deborah. 'What?'

'Didn't Steve ever tell you?' Deborah shook her head, unable to speak. 'Oh, God, I certainly didn't mean to tell secrets,' Pete stammered. 'She was only sixteen. It wasn't legal. But a ceremony had been performed. I guess she lied about her age. Apparently she planned to keep the whole thing a secret, but that weekend, the weekend of her attack, Steve overheard her giggling on the phone with the guy – her *husband* – about it. *That's* why Steve left her alone that day. He went off in a blind rage to get the man who'd *married* his little sister.'

'I always thought it was unbelievable that the most responsible man I've ever known would just casually leave his sister when he knew she was in possible danger from someone like Lieber,' Barbara said.

Pete nodded. 'He told me he was so horrified and so furious, he wasn't thinking clearly for a couple of hours.'

'But he said he was at his girlfriend's,' Deborah said numbly. 'Why didn't he tell the truth?'

'Because the Robinsons wanted the marriage kept a secret. Aside from it being illegal and Emily being so young, the man involved was unsavory.' Catching Deborah's eyes, Pete added hastily, 'That's one thing Steve never told me – the identity of the husband. I just know he was older than Emily.'

'It would be a matter of public record,' Evan said.

'*If* you knew where the ceremony took place. I never knew that, either.'

'But didn't Steve's girlfriend corroborate his alibi? Didn't she say he was with her at the time of Emily's attack?' Barbara asked.

'Yes, she did,' Pete said reluctantly. 'And according to Steve, he did stop at her house to see if she knew anything about the whole marriage mess. But he didn't go directly home. He tried one more place where the husband might be. The guy wasn't there and no one saw Steve. But Lieber was screaming that it was Steve who raped and beat Emily. Steve didn't have an alibi and he was the only witness against Lieber. The tables could have been turned so easily, making him the rapist, so his girlfriend lied for him.'

'Lied for him,' Deborah murmured. 'Steve – my Steve – encouraged a teenaged girl to lie for him?'

'He didn't encourage her – she just did and he let it ride. After all, Deborah, you have to remember that Steve was only an eighteen-year-old kid himself, not the man you married. He was scared *and* innocent. Besides, his parents said that if he hadn't protected his sister from physical danger, the least he could do was protect her reputation. He was laboring under so much fear and guilt, I don't think he knew *what* he was doing. Don't fault him for letting someone help him out of a terrible situation he didn't make.'

But that doesn't change the facts, Deborah thought dismally. The facts are that Steve allowed someone to lie for him. And worst of all, he truly didn't have an alibi for the time when Emily was nearly murdered.

10

After the videotaped movie ended, Deborah put the children to bed amid loud protests that neither one was sleepy. 'You'll get sleepy when you lie down,' she said.

'I won't,' Brian insisted.

Deborah sighed. 'I don't want to argue with you two. Now it's bedtime and that's that.'

'But it's almost Christmas,' Kim argued in a last-ditch attempt to make her mother see reason.

'All the more reason for you two to be well rested. Now, into bed and not another word.'

'Okay, but leave the door open,' Kim said. 'I won't go to sleep if the door's shut.'

Knowing the little girl was still frightened after her encounter with the man at school, Deborah agreed, even though she thought the voices from downstairs might keep them awake. She kissed both of them goodnight, and stood down the hall for a few moments, listening to them both grousing. 'I'm not *sleepy*,' Brian repeated. 'We shouldn't have to go to bed if we're not sleepy.' 'And it's almost Christmas,' Kim repeated querulously.

Back downstairs, Deborah tried to keep her equilibrium, tried to keep the conversation flowing, but she couldn't. All she could think about was the maelstrom of lies and omissions that encircled the Emily Robinson case, lies and omissions her husband had sanctioned. Her sense of not really knowing Steve deepened dramatically.

Pete, obviously aware of her distress and feeling great discomfort at having upset her, made awkward excuses and left with Adam shortly afterward. Deborah sat with Joe, Barbara, and Evan, trying to sort out the new information Pete had given her. 'Why didn't Steve ever tell me?' she asked aloud. 'Why didn't he tell me why he left Emily alone that day?'

'Because then he'd have to tell you his girlfriend lied to the police for him,' Barbara said flatly. 'He clearly didn't want you to know about that.'

'But like Pete said, he was scared,' Evan added. 'He might have been young, but he wasn't stupid. He *knew* how bad things could get for him.'

'Who would have believed he attacked his own sister?' Deborah asked. 'What possible reason could anyone have for believing something so monstrous?'

'Maybe there was a reason, maybe there wasn't,' Joe said softly. 'Maybe he was just doing what Pete said – trying to keep the fact of Emily's marriage out of the whole mess.'

Deborah slowly shook her head. 'Emily was married to someone. Who could it have been? Why did the family consider him so "unsavory", as Pete said?'

' "Unsavory" is a fairly vague word,' Joe commented. 'It could mean a hundred things. Probably he came from a family the Robinsons didn't approve of. Or maybe he'd been in trouble. Once again, we just don't know, and since Pete doesn't know the guy's identity, he can't tell us.'

'I wonder where the husband is now?' Deborah mused. 'I wonder if he ever goes to see Emily?'

'I doubt if the Robinsons would permit that,' Barbara said. 'You'll never find out who he is by discovering who visits Emily in the nursing home.'

'I still wonder who he is. How did he feel when this happened to Emily and he couldn't come forward?'

Evan raised an eyebrow. 'Who says he couldn't come forward? The Robinsons couldn't have stopped him.'

'No, they couldn't have,' Deborah said thoughtfully. 'Maybe he just wanted to stay clear of the whole mess. Not a very romantic picture.'

Around nine o'clock, Evan declared he had a ton of work to do and had to go home. Barbara walked him to the door and kissed him goodnight. Before he left, he called, 'If you have *any* trouble, phone me. I can be here in ten minutes.'

'We will,' Deborah promised. 'But with Barbara and Joe here, I'm sure we'll be fine.'

Joe grimaced and he muttered out of Evan's earshot, 'Evan doesn't think anyone will be fine without him around.'

'Why are you two so hard on each other?' Deborah asked softly.

'I can't stand him and he hates me.'

'Never one to mince words, are you?'

Joe shrugged. 'Why try to hide the obvious?'

Half an hour later, Deborah cocked her head, listening. Kim had started coughing, the loose, rattling cough she developed every winter. Several trips to the doctor had convinced her that at this stage cough syrup was all the child required. Deborah went to the medicine cabinet and found that she had only one dose of cough syrup. That would do for a few hours, but sometimes the child had violent coughing fits in the night which required a second dose. 'Oh, great,' she muttered. 'What a terrific evening.' She went downstairs and told Joe and Barbara the problem.

'I'll go get some more medicine,' Barbara said, rising from the couch. 'The drug store is open until ten.'

'No you don't,' Joe countered. 'This isn't the time for a woman to be wandering around by herself at night.'

Barbara looked sarcastic. 'Joe, believe it or not, women don't just *wander* around. We're capable of reaching a destination and then returning home without getting lost.'

'Oh, hell, Barbara, will you stop pouncing on every word I say?' Joe fired back in irritation. 'That's not what I meant. I just don't think it's wise for either you or Deborah to be out. Besides, it's cold. Tell me what kind of cough syrup you need, Deborah, and I'll get it.'

When he'd left, Deborah turned to Barbara. 'Why do you become such a flaming feminist around him?'

Barbara sighed. 'I don't know. I just always expect him to call me "little lady" or something. I don't think he likes strong women.'

'I think you're wrong. But there comes a time when you have to stop flexing your independence and exercise a little caution. Artie Lieber could be out there, you know. I, for one, would rather have Joe tangle with him than you.'

Barbara laughed. 'You're right. As Evan has pointed out, I don't cut an imposing figure when it comes to self-defense. Okay, I'm officially off the soap box during the duration of this crisis.'

'Wonderful. I appreciate it.'

Deborah went upstairs to check on Kim again. 'Can I come downstairs?' she asked.

'No, I want you to stay in bed and keep warm.'

'I'm *not* sleepy,' she fussed.

'Then lie quietly and rest.'

Kim coughed again and gave her the stubborn, sulky look she so often wore when she wasn't feeling well, as if she thought Deborah was responsible for her discomfort. Deborah moved toward the door. 'Don't shut it!' Kim commanded.

'I *won't*. I told you that earlier. Now settle down.'

'Everything okay up there?' Barbara asked when Deborah returned to the living room.

'Kim is mad at the world. I hope Joe comes soon with the cough syrup.'

'It seems to me he should have been back by now.'

'Maybe the store was crowded.'

'At this time of night?'

'It's almost Christmas,' Deborah said, thinking she sounded like Kim. 'Lots of people stop in at night for decorations and gifts. The drug store is like a little department store.'

A wail of terror ripped down the stairs. Deborah and Barbara stiffened, their eyes flying wide in frightened astonishment. Then Deborah bolted through the living room and up the stairs, barely feeling the steps beneath her feet.

She reached the children's room and stood for a moment in the doorway, looking at Kimberly. The little girl lay face down on the floor, howling. Brian sat on the top bunk, staring at his sister in baffled horror, Scarlett pawed at Kimberly, the hair along her back standing up in the dog's instinctive response to encroaching danger.

Deborah rushed forward, pushing Scarlett aside, and gathered up her quaking child. 'Kimmy, what *is* it?'

The little girl babbled through her tears. Light glared overhead and Deborah sensed Barbara behind her. 'Honey, I can't understand a word you're saying,' Deborah said. 'You're safe. Barbara and I are here. You're all right, Kim. Now tell Mommy what's wrong.'

Kim pulled back and looked at Deborah as if she didn't know her. Her green eyes had a blind, dazed look, exactly like her Aunt Emily's. Cold fear touched Deborah's heart. 'Kim, it's *Mommy*,' she said firmly. 'Look at me. It's Mommy and you're safe.'

Gradually Kimberly's rigidity melted, and her gaze became more familiar. 'Mommy?'

'Yes, Kim, of course it's Mommy. Don't be afraid.'

Kimberly suddenly flung her arms around her mother and buried her face in Deborah's neck. Deborah held her close, rocking back and forth.

She glanced up at Brian, who still sat tightly on his bed, clutching his blanket. 'What happened?'

'I don't know,' Brian said defensively. 'I was almost asleep. I didn't do anything to her.'

'I know you didn't, Brian.' Deborah uncoiled Kimberly's arms from around her neck and held the child a few inches away from her. 'Kim, I want you to tell me what frightened you.'

Kim sniffled, then said in a tiny, trembling voice, 'I got up to look out the window and I saw . . .'

'You saw what?'

'A *thing*,' Kim breathed. 'A thing with big shiny eyes. Silver eyes. And it was lookin' at *me*. It was gonna come and *get* me, Mommy!'

11

ONE

Mrs Dillman turned the bar of soap over and over in her hands, working up a lather, then began scrubbing her face. She followed with splashes of cold water, and finally blotted with a faded towel. She'd read in one of those women's magazines that you shouldn't use soap on your face – too drying. Nonsense. She'd used soap for ninety years and it hadn't hurt her. She leaned closer to the mirror, peering at the pale, crêpey skin that had once been so soft Alfred had said it was like rose petals. Well, maybe soap hadn't done her complexion any good, but it was too late to fix it now.

She walked into her bedroom and began fumbling with the buttons on her sweater. She hung it on a hook on the back of the door and slipped off the cotton dress that had been much too thin for a cold day. Next came a cotton slip whose lace edging was beginning to fray.

Clad only in bra and pants, she sank to her knees beside her bed and clasped her hands. 'Now I lay me down to sleep,' she began, then frowned. 'Oh, how silly. That's a children's prayer. What I meant to say, God, was thank you for another day. Bless my children, even if they don't come to see me. Also bless Alfred and let him know I love him.' She paused. 'But he *cannot* come home. Make sure he knows that. I will not allow him to come crawling back, and I'm sure You don't blame me.' She fell silent, frowning more ferociously than before. 'Oh, yes, now I remember. Bless that poor woman next door and those little children. I know he's run out on them. I never saw him all day, but I did see the police. Such a shame. They don't deserve this. Men! Honestly! I don't know why You can't make them behave better.' She shook her head in sorrow. 'Oh well, thank you and good night.'

She groaned as she stood up. Then she looked down at her underwear. 'Mercy! I was praying nearly naked. Where is my nightgown? Where is my *mind*?' She looked up at the ceiling. 'Dear God, a postscript. *Please* improve my memory. This forgetfulness is humiliating.'

She headed for the chest of drawers. As she passed by the window, whose curtains she'd forgotten to draw, her still relatively sharp eyes caught a flash. Her head whipped to the right and she saw him, limned by the light, staring at her. Her heart slammed against her fragile ribs. The man from next door, the missing man, was watching as she moved around her bedroom only half dressed. As she stood transfixed, color flooding her sunken cheeks, he tossed back his head and laughed.

TWO

'A dream,' Barbara said as they sat together on the couch, Kim's head cradled on Deborah's lap.

'Was not,' Kim said. 'I wasn't even asleep.'

'She's not prone to nightmares,' Deborah agreed.

'But after today . . .' Barbara let the words hang in the air, obviously referring to the incident at school.

'I *wasn't* sleepin',' Kim argued.

Barbara persisted. 'Maybe it was an animal whose eyes caught the light.'

'Nope,' Kim said stubbornly. 'No animal. A *thing*.'

Deborah shook her head at Barbara, indicating that the questioning should stop. She didn't believe Kim had been dreaming. It *was* possible that a cat had climbed a tree and that its eyes reflected eerily in the light, but she wasn't sure about that, either, although Kim maintained the eyes were 'up in the air'.

Kim began to cough again. 'Where on earth is Joe with the medicine?' Barbara asked.

'I don't know,' Deborah answered tiredly. 'I wonder if I should take her to the emergency room.'

'I'm not goin' outside,' Kim announced.

Deborah sighed. A trip to the emergency room probably would be foolish. The cough was a familiar ailment, and dragging Kim out in the cold might only make it worse, so the three of them remained silently on the couch, looking through the sheer curtains at the lights glowing merrily on the shrubbery along the front walk.

'Good heavens, here comes Mrs Dillman,' Barbara said suddenly. A moment later furious pounding sounded at the front door. Barbara rose. 'I'll get it.'

Seconds later, the woman stood in the living room. Deborah gaped at her, startled by her condition. Her long white hair fell in a thin veil over her shoulders and her eyes were wild. She wore cracked pink leather bedroom slippers beneath a winter coat flapping open over a flowered nightgown.

'Mrs Dillman, come and sit down,' Deborah said. 'Is something wrong?'

'I will *not* sit down,' Mrs Dillman announced, her faded blue eyes bulging. 'I'm here about your husband.'

'What about Steve?' Deborah asked, puzzled.

'Your husband was watching me as I got ready for bed. I was in my *undergarments*! Oh, dear lord, I never in all my life . . .' She patted her chest, breathing raggedly.

'Mrs Dillman, I wish you'd sit down and let us get you something warm to drink,' Deborah said, noticing the woman's bare white legs covered with gooseflesh. 'My husband isn't here.'

'I know he's not here! He's outside, peeping and spying.'

Kim sat up. 'Daddy's here?'

'Hush, honey,' Deborah said, wishing the child wasn't in the room but still trying to make sense of what the woman was saying. 'Mrs Dillman, I don't understand. When did this happen?'

'I told you, I was getting ready for bed, saying my prayers. It was no more than ten minutes ago.'

'I thought your bedroom was on the second floor,' Deborah said.

'It *is*. That devil! And the glowing eyes couldn't fool me.'

'Glowing eyes?' Deborah repeated.

'That's what it looked like at first. Nearly scared the life out of me.'

'Mrs Dillman, I know you've been complaining about a peeping Tom, but why did you suddenly decide this man was Steve? It's dark.'

'He had a light behind him, of course,' Mrs Dillman said witheringly, as if Deborah were being particularly dense. 'You know about the light.'

'What light?'

'Oh, for pity's sake, you're protecting him, aren't you? Well, I won't put up with it. You tell him that! I have a shotgun and I will use it!'

Deborah took a deep breath. 'Mrs Dillman, my husband has been missing since Sunday—'

'That's because he's going around spying on unsuspecting females. Filthy, perverted man! I think you should seek a divorce immediately. I will tell a judge all about him and you should have no trouble regaining your freedom.'

Deborah briefly closed her eyes. She did not need this woman's hysterics on top of everything else this evening. 'Mrs Dillman, maybe you saw a reflection in your window,' she said tiredly. 'I assure you my husband wasn't watching you undress.'

'You're just like I was about my Alfred,' Mrs Dillman said woefully. 'I always wanted to believe the best about him. But when he ran off to Europe with that opera singer, I had to face the truth.'

Poor Alfred Dillman, Deborah thought. First he'd been accused of going out for bread and ending up in Las Vegas, and now he was in Europe with an opera singer. In reality, Deborah suspected, the most exciting thing the kindly old minister had ever done was play a rigorous round of golf.

'Mrs Dillman, can you tell me anything else about this man?' she asked, almost certain the woman was suffering from delusions, but still feeling she should follow up on any sighting of Steve on the slim chance it might be valid. 'Was he standing on your lawn?'

'He wasn't on the ground,' Mrs Dillman said in exasperation. 'He couldn't look directly into my bedroom from the ground.'

'He wasn't on the ground? Where was he?'

'Oh, you're impossible. Just impossible!' the old lady burst out, then whirled around and headed for home.

'Mrs Dillman, wait,' Deborah called. 'I'll walk you home.'

'I can find my own way, thank you very much!'

As the woman hurried down the walk, Deborah looked at Barbara, who had returned to the living room. 'Apparently Steve has learned to hover in the air like a vampire,' Deborah said drily, although her hands shook slightly.

'He's also developed a desire to watch ninety-year-old women undress,' Barbara said.

'She saw the *thing*,' Kim said ominously, her small body shaking. 'I told you it wasn't on the ground.'

Deborah bit her lower lip, feeling the back of her neck tingle. What was the likelihood of a five-year-old girl and a ninety-two-year-old woman living in separate houses both seeing something in the night? Something with glowing eyes far above the ground?

Twenty minutes later, Joe arrived. 'I had a damned flat tire,' he muttered before Deborah or Barbara could ask any questions. 'It's thirty-two degrees out there and I had a flat tire. Then they were out of the cough syrup you wanted at your drug store so I had to go downtown.'

'I'm sorry you had so much trouble,' Deborah said meekly. Joe seemed flustered and angry. 'I just wish you'd called to let us know about the flat. We were worried.'

'Sorry. It never occurred to me. I've lived alone too long, I guess.' He handed Deborah the bottle. 'If you tell me I got the wrong kind I'm going to cuss a blue streak.'

'Save your breath. It's the right kind. And just in time,' Deborah said as Kim burst into another coughing fit. 'I'll give her a second dose right now.'

As she led Kim to the kitchen, she heard Barbara ask with studied carelessness, 'Did you change the tire yourself, Joe?'

'Yeah. No one even stopped to help. Why?'

'Oh, nothing. It's just that you look so clean. I thought tire-changing was a messy business.'

What's gotten into her? Deborah wondered. And from the tone of Joe's snappish reply, she knew he wondered the same thing.

12

ONE

The next morning Deborah was awakened by the sound of Scarlett frantically barking in the back yard. She opened eyes that felt grainy from lack of sleep and peered at the bedside clock: 6.10. Usually Scarlett didn't go out until the children awakened around seven. Something was wrong.

Deborah shot out of bed, grabbing a robe on her way out of the bedroom. Joe was not on the couch when she reached the living room. She ran into the kitchen where the back door stood open. Dim light was just beginning to dissipate the black of night. She stepped out on the porch and spotted Scarlett in Mrs Dillman's yard running back and forth beside what in the semi-darkness looked like a pile of rags. Then she saw Joe hurdling the fence and landing beside the rags. He bent and touched them gently, then looked up at Deborah. 'It's Mrs Dillman,' he shouted. 'Call the paramedics.'

'Is she dead?' Deborah gasped.

'No, but she's not far from it. Hurry.'

The next few minutes passed in a blur for Deborah. She made the call, surprised at how calm she sounded, grabbed a blanket off the couch where Joe had slept, then went out into the back yard, where Joe was still kneeling beside the woman. 'What on earth happened?'

'You're barefooted,' Joe said, spreading the blanket over Mrs Dillman.

'I always walk around out here barefooted these days,' Deborah responded absently. 'I asked what happened.'

'I don't know. Scarlett came downstairs and woke me up. She kept running toward the kitchen, then coming back. I thought she needed to go

113

out in a hurry, so I opened the door. I came back into the kitchen and put on a pot of coffee, thinking she'd bark when she wanted in. Well, she barked all right. I looked out and she was digging like mad, trying to get into this yard. By the time I got out here, she'd made it. She was licking Mrs Dillman's face and still barking. I didn't want to fool with that clip you have on your gate, so I jumped the fence. That's when you came out.'

'What's wrong with her?'

'A nice-sized lump and cut on the top of her head. And I don't know how long she's been lying out here in the cold.'

'My God. I knew one day she was going to have a bad fall.'

Joe looked up at her. 'Deborah, she didn't get this lump by falling on the ground. I'm not a pathologist, but I'd say it was made by something like a club – maybe a baseball bat. The woman was attacked.'

'Attacked?' Deborah repeated dumbly.

'I think so.'

Later Deborah barely remembered running back inside for Joe's jacket. She was shivering with cold and couldn't stop thinking of the thin, limp body of Mrs Dillman lying on the freezing ground wearing only a flannel robe and the same cracked leather house slippers Deborah had seen when the woman had come to the door the night before claiming Steve was watching her.

What had happened? Deborah wondered as she hurried back into the house and ran upstairs, where she pulled on jeans, a sweater and a pair of loafers. Mrs Dillman had been terribly upset and convinced she was being watched. Had she gone outside to investigate and . . . and what? Joe couldn't be certain she'd been struck. Maybe she *had* merely fallen. But what if Joe was right? What if there really was a watcher and he'd struck her on the head?

Struck her on the head. The words jangled through Deborah's mind. Struck on the head like Emily? Struck on the head like all the Strangler's victims? But all of them had also been strangled and raped. She hadn't seen Mrs Dillman's neck. Had she been strangled but lived? Had she been raped? Many people believed rape was an act of lust, but Deborah knew it was actually a violent act of dominance. Mrs Dillman's advanced age could not protect her from such savagery.

As she started down the hall, Barbara's door opened. She looked at Deborah with bleary eyes. 'What's going on?'

'Mrs Dillman has been hurt. She's lying in her back yard. Joe is with her and the paramedics are on the way.'

'My God! What happened?'

'We don't know. Joe thinks she was hit on the head.'

Barbara's eyes widened. 'Who would do such a thing? Oh, Deborah, you don't think she was right about someone watching her, do you?'

'Something was out there. Both Kim and Mrs Dillman saw it.'

'*It?* You think it was an *it?*'

'I don't know what I think any more,' Deborah said in exasperation. 'I have to get back outside.'

'I'll get dressed,' Barbara said. 'How can I help?'

'Make sure the children don't come outside if they wake up,' Deborah replied as she ran downstairs, now grateful for the carpet that muffled her footsteps. She fervently hoped the children would sleep through this emergency. They'd already been through too much.

Five minutes later the paramedics arrived. Along with his jacket, Deborah had handed Joe Scarlett's leash and he brought her back to her own yard. Deborah shut her, whining and straining against the leash, inside the house. Back outside, she watched as the paramedics took Mrs Dillman's vital signs, then checked her for broken bones or other injuries aside from the one on her head. Deborah barely breathed until she learned there were none. The woman hadn't been strangled. 'But she's in shock,' the female paramedic said. 'We need to get her to the ambulance to elevate her feet and try to raise this blood pressure.' She looked at Joe and Deborah. 'Can one of you come to the hospital?'

'I will,' Deborah said. 'Her son left a key to her house with me a few months ago. I'll get her insurance information and be right along.'

'I'll take you,' Joe said.

'You can't. Barbara has to go to work and someone needs to stay with the kids.'

Joe frowned. 'I don't like you going off by yourself.'

'It's daytime, Joe. And I'm heading straight for the hospital.'

'I'm going into her house with you. It's a slim chance, but someone could be in there. And I don't think you'll need that key. I don't think she came out here in her nightgown and locked the door behind her.'

Joe was right. The back door stood open. 'Well, we know she didn't lock herself out,' Deborah said. 'She must have heard or seen something and come outside.'

They entered the kitchen where the overhead light still burned and went into the living room. Although the room was neat, the furniture was old and worn and gave off a faint musty odor. 'Circa 1955?' Joe asked, pointing to a bulky armchair with lace antimacassars pinned to the arms.

'Probably older than that.'

'The place looks awfully run-down. It's in bad need of paint. Is she short of money?'

'I'm sure she's not well off, but she's not struggling, either. She's just not up to arranging for home repairs. Steve used to help her some, but during this last year she's told him that it was her husband Alfred's job to take care of these things and sent him home. Steve talked to one of her sons who lives in Huntington about the necessity of either hiring someone to stay with her or placing her in a nursing home, but the son did nothing except leave a key to the house with us. That was three months ago. No one has been back to check on her since then.'

'That's a damned shame,' Joe said. 'Do you have the son's phone number so you can let him know what's happened?'

'No, but I'm sure it's listed in Mrs Dillman's address book on the table by the phone. His name is Fred Dillman. Would you look it up while I search for her purse? Her insurance card is probably in her wallet. At least, I hope it is.'

Deborah had been in the Dillman house only a few times, but she was always amazed that in spite of the woman's increasing loss of memory and fantasies concerning people, she was extremely organized about her paperwork. She paid bills promptly and sent out a myriad of birthday cards, which according to Fred Dillman always arrived on the correct date.

'I have the card,' she called, relieved she'd found it so quickly.

'And I have the phone number.'

'Great. Would you mind calling Fred from my house so you can keep an eye on the kids while Barbara gets ready for work? I want to leave for the hospital immediately.'

'Okay. That will save Mrs Dillman the cost of a long-distance call.'

Twenty minutes later Deborah was filling out hospital forms to the best of her ability, forced to leave many blank spaces because she didn't know Mrs Dillman well. A family member would have to complete the forms later. While she waited for some word on the woman's condition, she called Joe. He told her he'd reached Fred Dillman, who said he would be there by afternoon. 'Afternoon?' Deborah repeated. 'He only lives an hour away.'

'Sorry. That's the best I could do. He sounded flustered and I heard a woman griping in the background.'

'I hope Steve and I get better treatment when we're old.'

Joe was silent, and Deborah experienced a strange sinking sensation. He doesn't believe old age is something Steve will have to worry about, she thought sadly.

She was downing her third cup of bitter coffee from the coffee machine when a doctor appeared. 'Mrs Dillman is suffering from shock and hypothermia,' he told her. 'And that was quite a blow on the head. She has a concussion and is still unconscious.'

'Will she be all right?'

'Frankly, I'm not sure at this point. The CT scan didn't show any intracranial bleeding, which is encouraging. She also seems to be in unusually good physical health for a woman her age. But she's been through a lot for a ninety-two-year-old woman. Do you know what happened?'

'No. We found her lying in her back yard.' She hesitated. 'Someone suggested that she'd been struck with a club of some kind rather than just hitting her head in a fall.'

'The blow *is* on the top of her head. Injuries to the head caused during a fall are usually found on the sides, front, or back of the head. We also found wood splinters in the cut.'

'She wasn't near anything wooden,' Deborah said slowly. 'Could she have stood up, banged her head on something, then gone into her yard?'

The doctor shook his head. 'I don't think so. The head injury is severe and probably resulted in immediate unconsciousness.'

So Joe had been right, Deborah thought with a chill. Someone had assaulted the frail, elderly lady and left her to freeze to death.

TWO

Deborah returned home to find the children and Joe laboring over a jigsaw puzzle with large pieces. Kim was still coughing, although not as often as she had the night before. Brian looked at her. 'Is Mrs Dillman dead?' he asked.

117

'They saw the ambulance leaving,' Joe said.

'No, honey, she isn't dead. She just got a bump on the head, and then she got chilled from lying outside.'

Kim looked excited. 'Joe said Scarlett found her.'

'That's right.'

'Mrs Dillman likes Scarlett,' Brian informed Joe. 'She doesn't like Pierre Vincent.'

'Who's Pierre Vincent?' he asked.

'That's the Vincents' poodle,' Deborah told him.

Brian looked at Joe. 'She says he's a little varmint. Mommy says that's like a rat.'

'He dug up her flowers three years ago and she's never forgiven him,' Deborah said.

'Scarlett made a hole under the fence,' Kim noted worriedly. 'Maybe she won't like her any more.'

Deborah touched Kim's hair. 'I think she will, sweetheart. She'll know Scarlett was only trying to help.'

Seeming satisfied with the answer, the children went back to the puzzle, which they soon finished. Afterward they wanted go outside, but Deborah insisted Kim stay in because of her cough. They decided instead to go to the basement where Kim's play kitchen and Brian's 'woodshop' were set up in the big room with the washer and dryer.

Joe questioned her more closely about Mrs Dillman. 'The doctor agrees with you that she was struck on the head,' Deborah told him. 'There were splinters in the cut. But we didn't find a club or anything like it in the yard.'

'Whoever hit her wasn't stupid enough to leave his weapon.'

'Every time I think of someone deliberately bashing that woman in the head . . . ' Deborah closed her eyes. 'Why? Why would someone attack her?'

'Maybe she had a prowler like you did the night of your party. Maybe she looked out and saw someone in her back yard.'

'So she went out to confront them? That's absurd. She's ninety-two.'

'Deborah, she isn't always rational. She thought Steve was lurking around spying on her, but that didn't stop her from storming over here in her nightgown.'

'You're right. But I'm sure she saw something. So did Kim, although they both claim it was hovering above the ground.'

'I know. Barbara had a bee in her bonnet about that detail this morning. She said she had an idea about what Mrs Dillman meant and she was going to check it out.'

'She didn't tell you what her idea was?'

'No. I guess we'll find out this evening.'

THREE

Barbara pulled into the parking lot of Capitol Realty. Inside, a young receptionist threw her a radiant smile. 'House-hunting today?'

'In a way.' The girl's smile faltered slightly at Barbara's vague reply. 'Is Roberta Mitchell free?'

'I'll check. May I have your name?'

'Barbara Levine.'

'Fine.' She buzzed Roberta's office, and after a few moments of hushed conversation announced that Roberta was on another phone line but would be able to see Barbara in ten minutes. 'Why don't you have a seat while you're waiting, Ms Levine?' she invited with the same brilliant smile.

Barbara walked into a small waiting area decorated in shades of taupe and light blue. On one wall hung a large bulletin board bearing photographs of houses that were current listings. Barbara studied it and didn't find what she was looking for. She sat down and began wiggling her foot nervously. She had a lot of work to do today. Hopefully this wouldn't take much time.

In less than ten minutes the receptionist looked at her brightly. 'Ms Mitchell said she's ready to see you now. Back down the hall, third office on the right.'

Barbara tapped on the door before entering. Roberta sat behind a beautifully crafted walnut desk. An attractive black woman who looked much younger than her fifty years, she smiled broadly at Barbara and stood up. 'Barbara Levine! I haven't seen you for over a year. Are you finally going to move out of that spartan apartment and into a decent house?'

'I'm afraid not. At least not now.'

'People like you make my business tough.'

119

'From the looks of things, I'd say you're doing very well.'

'I've had bad years, but I've always managed to stay afloat. Now, what can I do for you?'

'I need some information.'

'All right. Would you like some coffee first?'

'I'd love some.'

As Roberta walked to an automatic coffee maker, Barbara admired her forest-green wool suit, brightened with a topaz silk scarf flung with expert carelessness around her neck. I could never wear a scarf like that with such aplomb, Barbara thought. The best I can manage is a pair of button earrings. 'Cream? Sugar?' Roberta asked.

'Cream.'

Roberta fixed the coffee and handed it to her in a gold-rimmed china cup. No styrofoam here, Barbara thought.

Roberta sat down on the edge of her desk. 'Okay, what do you need to know?'

'There's a house on Woodbine Court that used to be one of your listings. It's lovely – two-story, bay windows—'

'The O'Donnell house,' Roberta said promptly.

'Yes. I know the house was listed with you for almost three years, but your sign disappeared and the house isn't being shown any more. What's the story?'

'Is this official business?'

'No, but it's important to me and to a very close friend of mine who lives across the street from the house to find out something about it. I get the feeling something strange is going on over there.'

Roberta studied her. 'I know you well enough to be sure you're not enquiring out of idle curiosity. And frankly, that house has troubled me lately, too.'

'The house?'

'Well, not the house. The inhabitant. Or rather, the supposed inhabitant.'

Barbara set her cup and saucer on the desk. 'You know how to get someone's attention.'

Roberta smiled. 'I already had your attention.'

'So tell me what's going on.'

Roberta retreated behind her desk and sat down. 'I was handling that house. About four months ago a man approached me wanting to rent it for six months. I told him it was for sale, not rent. He asked me to present his offer to the owners anyway. To my surprise, they accepted. Of course, the house had been on the market for quite a while, and I know the O'Donnells need the money, but one of the man's stipulations was that the house not be shown during his occupancy. I advised against the deal, but the O'Donnells insisted. So the house was rented in September.'

'Roberta, there's no sign of anyone living in that house.'

'I *know*. That's what troubles me. Who would rent a house like that and not live in it? It didn't go cheaply, I can tell you that.'

Barbara leaned forward. 'What was the man's name.'

Roberta hesitated. 'Edward J. King.'

'Do you know what he does for a living?'

'He said he was self-employed. I was dubious. I wanted to do a credit check on him, but when he paid the whole six months rent in *advance*, the O'Donnells were overjoyed and stopped me. They said he might end up buying the house and they didn't want him offended by a credit check.'

'How could he be offended? Isn't a credit check just good business practise?'

'Yes, but the O'Donnells aren't very savvy about business procedures. Actually, they remind me of two thirteen-year-olds.'

'How did Edward King pay?'

'With a check drawn on an account in a Charleston bank.' Roberta cocked her head. 'Barbara, what's going on in that house? Is he using the place to deal drugs?'

'If so, he's got a scanty clientele. My friend has never seen *anyone* around that house.'

'Then what is it?'

'An elderly lady who lives across the street and my friend's five-year-old daughter both saw something last night. From what they described, I think they saw someone on the second floor of that house.'

'If it's Mr King, he has every right to be there.'

'My friend's husband has been missing for a couple of days. Her little girl saw only what she says was a *thing* with big silver eyes. The old lady says she saw my friend's husband looking at her and he had glowing eyes.'

'Are you trying to tell me a ghost story?'

'No. I think they saw light reflecting off binoculars.'

Roberta leaned back in her chair. 'Do you think it was the missing husband? Or did I simply rent the house to some pervert who's using it as an observatory?'

121

'I have no idea, but I want to know about this Mr King. Tell me about him.'

Roberta looked disquieted. 'I had a bad feeling about him. It wasn't anything he said or did, it was just this sense that there was something *wrong* about him. Have you ever had that feeling about someone?'

'Many times. What did he look like?'

'I remember him because I felt so uneasy around him for no apparent reason.' Roberta closed her eyes, concentrating. 'He was tall, around six feet, and slender. He was dressed well but not expensively. He had dark brown hair, and a mustache. He wore glasses with dark-tinted lenses. I'd guess him to be in his late thirties or early forties. Nothing unusual.'

Barbara fumbled in her purse for a Polaroid photograph of her, Evan, Deborah, and Steve taken the previous summer. She held it out to Roberta. 'Do you see Edward King here?'

Roberta held the picture under a desk lamp in her already bright office. She bit her lip. 'I can't be sure, but with dark glasses, darker hair, and a mustache, it very well could be.'

13

ONE

Artie Lieber sat on the side of his bed, drawing a deep breath, holding it until he counted to ten, then releasing it. Long ago a doctor had told him this would help the hyperventilation he experienced in times of stress. He was feeling stress now. A *lot* of stress.

He'd been unable to stop himself from driving past the Robinson house again that morning, but the cops watching the place in an unmarked car parked in a driveway had spotted him. He knew they were cops. He could *smell* cops. The one on the passenger's side had sat up and peered closely at his car. He'd panicked, certain they were going to pull out and pursue him. It had been all he could do not to push his foot down on the accelerator and drive like hell. He'd controlled himself, though, maintaining fifteen miles an hour until he emerged from the cul-de-sac, but he couldn't control his eyes, which flashed continually to the rearview mirror. The cops hadn't followed, but in spite of the cold weather Artie was sweating profusely and huffing like a steam engine by the time he reached his shoddy hotel.

Well, that's it, he thought, taking his fifth deep breath. That was the third time he'd cruised slowly past the Robinson house since Steve's disappearance and they'd gotten suspicious. They were probably running a check on the car right now. They'd sure gotten a good look at the license plate. Of course, he'd switched it with another car's, but they'd figure the whole thing out soon enough. He'd left the old white Buick Regal in a parking lot four blocks away and knew he'd have to steal another car that night. That would be relatively easy. He couldn't believe the number of people who carelessly left the keys in their cars. But what if the cops had gotten a good look at him? He poured a shot of vodka and downed it. Well, what if they *had* seen him clearly? He'd grown a beard during the last month and he was wearing that stupid cap that came down over his ears. He'd never liked covering up his thick dark hair with hats of any kind, but this one had served a purpose in helping disguise him.

Still, today's encounter had been way too close, he thought, pouring another shot of vodka. He would have to curb the nearly irresistible impulse that drew him to the Robinson house. He'd been spying for a week, but it was time to stop. The cops were already looking for him – they had to be, now that Robinson was missing. He hadn't reported to his probation officer on Monday as scheduled, and he'd been spotted in Charleston. So he should go to the police, not let them find him. 'I'll explain everything,' he told his reflection in the wavery mirror. 'I'm a good liar – they'll believe me.' But as he stared into his own burning eyes, he knew he was kidding himself. He couldn't go to the police with some lame story about why he'd been in Charleston. And he couldn't leave. Not yet.

TWO

The children were still playing in the basement when the doorbell rang. Deborah answered it and found Agent Wylie standing on the porch. She stiffened as his cool blue eyes bored into hers. 'Mrs Robinson, I need to talk with you. May I come in?'

Wordlessly, Deborah stood back and motioned the FBI agent inside. As they entered the living room, Joe looked up from a magazine. 'Wylie? What's up?'

'I'd like to speak with Mrs Robinson alone.'

'Mr Wylie, can't Joe stay?' Deborah asked, her nerves beginning to quiver. This could only mean bad news.

'I'd rather he left.'

'All right, Wylie,' Joe said, tossing down the magazine, his eyes rebellious. 'Have it your way, but she'll tell me everything you've said as soon as you leave.'

'That's up to her,' Wylie responded tonelessly.

He stood, intractable and unsmiling. Joe shrugged and left the room. Deborah sat down on the couch. 'What's wrong, Mr Wylie? Have you found Steve?'

Wylie sat on a chair across from her. 'No, but we've learned something important. We've searched your bank accounts.'

'Our bank accounts?'

He nodded, withdrew a small notebook from his pocket and flipped it open. He glanced at it, then said, 'You have one thousand and thirty-three dollars and forty-five cents in your checking account. Does that sound accurate?'

'I don't know our balance to the dollar, but yes, it sounds about right. How is that important?'

'It isn't.' He paused. 'But this is. Your savings account reads "Steven J. Robinson *or* Deborah A. Robinson". The *or* instead of an *and* means you don't need both signatures to make a withdrawal.'

'I know that,' Deborah said, fighting for patience. 'What's your point?'

'My point is that as of closing time on Friday the account balance was seven thousand and twenty-three dollars and fifty-one cents.' He looked at her. 'On Saturday your husband withdrew six thousand dollars.'

Deborah stared at him. 'Six *thousand*?'

'That's right.'

'It *can't* be right.'

'I'm afraid it is. Didn't you know anything about the withdrawal?'

'No,' she said faintly.

'So it wasn't for home repair or anything of that nature?'

'No. We were going to remodel the storeroom this summer, but we didn't have any other jobs planned, especially at this time of year.' Deborah let the significance of Wylie's announcement sink in, but asked anyway, 'What can this mean?'

'It appears your husband withdrew the money because he needed a lot of cash in a hurry.'

'And you think it was to escape.'

'That's what it looks like.'

Deborah twisted her wedding ring, not glancing at Wylie although she felt him watching her closely. 'I don't care what it looks like. That's not why he withdrew the money.'

'Then why? He didn't vanish until Sunday. Why didn't he tell you about the withdrawal? Or did he routinely keep financial matters to himself?'

'Sometimes.' Wylie's eyes were fastened on her, and she remembered Joe telling her not to reveal any doubts she had about Steve in front of the FBI. 'What I mean is, he didn't account to me for every dollar he spent. But any sizable expenditure we discussed. I don't know why he didn't tell me about withdrawing the money. All I know is that he must have had a good reason, and it *wasn't* to help him run away. My husband wouldn't do such a thing.'

'You're sure about that.'

'Absolutely.'

Wylie closed his notebook. 'Well, at least you know you have six thousand dollars less to live on than you thought.'

Deborah couldn't tell if he was being flippant or if this was another ploy to gauge her reaction. 'We'll manage,' she said shortly. 'We'll manage until Steve gets home.'

After Agent Wylie left, Deborah stood in the front hall, shaken and worried. She'd adamantly told the FBI agent that her husband would not empty a bank account and run. But until last night, she would never have believed he would allow a teenaged girl to lie in order to provide him with an alibi. Now she wondered if she could be sure of anything her husband of seven years would or would not do.

THREE

'I have a secret,' Kim announced as Deborah buttoned her pajama top.

'Are you going to tell me what it is?' Deborah asked.

'Nope.'

Brian looked sulky. 'She won't even tell me.'

'Can you give me a hint, honey?' Deborah persisted absently as she poured cough syrup into a teaspoon.

'I hate that stuff,' Kim said. 'Brian doesn't have to take it.'

'Brian doesn't have a cough.' Kim swallowed the dose of syrup and grimaced ferociously.

'Oh, come on, Kimberly. It isn't that bad.'

'Is too.'

'Make her tell the secret,' Brian said.

'If Kim has a secret, we'll just let her keep it.'

Kimberly looked disappointed. 'I might tell tomorrow.'

Deborah winked at Brian. 'Suit yourself,' she said nonchalantly.

'It's a good secret,' Kim insisted as she got into bed and Deborah pulled the blanket up to her chin. 'A *real* good secret.'

'I'm sure it is, honey.' She kissed Kim on the forehead and watched Brian climb the ladder to the top bunk. He'd decided two months ago he was too old for kisses, so humoring him, Deborah merely ruffled his hair. 'I'm going to leave the door open again tonight so I can hear Kim if she starts coughing. Now you get a good night's sleep.' She looked at Scarlett settling on to her dog bed. 'All three of you.'

When she came downstairs, she found Joe opening the door for Evan and Barbara. 'I saw you pulling up,' he said.

Barbara shrugged out of her coat. 'We meant to get here sooner, but we went out to eat and the service was incredibly slow. Evan wanted to leave the restaurant.'

Deborah noticed that Evan looked tired and irritable, a crease fixed between his eyebrows. She wondered how much of his bad humor was caused by Barbara spending so much time away from him.

'Any news today?' he asked as Deborah ushered everyone into the living room.

She and Joe exchanged a look. 'Yes, there was. Agent Wylie from the FBI was here. It seems that on Saturday morning Steve withdrew six thousand dollars from our bank account. He nearly wiped it out.'

'Oh my God,' Barbara breathed. 'That's terrible! It looks like he took the money so he could run.'

'That's what Wylie said. And I'm not sure he believes I knew nothing about it. Maybe it would have been better for Steve if I'd lied and said I did know about it – that he spent the money on something.'

'No, you shouldn't have lied,' Evan said vehemently. 'Wylie would want to know what it was spent on, and then you'd trip on another lie and make things look even worse. But that doesn't mean Steve *didn't* withdraw the money for something besides an escape.'

'Such as?' Joe asked.

'Such as an extravagant Christmas present.'

'On the Sunday before he vanished he said he couldn't go to the mall with us because he had to attend to a surprise for Christmas,' Deborah told him. 'But I didn't believe him then and I still don't. It was an excuse. And I can guarantee you, Evan, he didn't spend almost our entire savings account on a Christmas gift. What else is there?'

'Maybe he decided to pay off his car.'

'At a time when he's got more trouble coming at him than he can handle, including a possible lawyer's fee if he's arrested and indicted, he decides to pay off his *car*?' Joe asked incredulously. 'I don't think so.'

Evan shot him a scalding look, but acquiesced to Joe's logic with a curt nod. 'Deborah, can you think of *anything* else he might have used the money for?'

'No. Absolutely nothing.'

'Damn,' Evan muttered. 'This *is* bad. Really bad.'

After a moment of silence, Barbara said slowly, 'As much as I hate to suggest it, maybe he did run. Maybe the enormity of all this just got to him and he bolted.'

'A couple of days ago I would have told you that was impossible,' Deborah said. 'Now I don't know.'

Someone knocked lightly on the front door. Deborah answered. Pete Griffin stood in the front porch with grocery bags in both arms. 'I didn't ring the bell because I thought the children might be asleep. But I saw how you were scrambling around for refreshments last night and I realized in all the turmoil of the last few days you probably hadn't gotten a chance to go to the grocery store, so I brought you some supplies.'

'Oh, Pete, that was so sweet of you!' Deborah exclaimed.

'There's more in the car. Maybe Joe could help me.'

'I'm on my way,' Joe said, pulling on his jacket.

Fifteen minutes later, after Deborah had put away five bags of groceries, smiling when she saw that Pete had included herbal tea and artificial sweetner, she joined the others in the living room. Barbara was telling Pete about Mrs Dillman.

'Good lord, who would do such a thing to an elderly lady?' Pete exclaimed. 'When I think of someone hurting my grandmother that way, I feel sick. Is she conscious yet?'

'Not as of two hours ago,' Deborah said. 'She may never regain consciousness, Pete. The doctor didn't seem to hold out much hope for her.'

Pete frowned. 'So she won't be able to say who attacked her.'

'Well, even if she *does* regain consciousness, she may not be able to tell us much. Her mind isn't very clear. Last night she was convinced Steve was spying on her and he wasn't standing on the ground.'

'She may not have been wrong, at least about someone spying but not standing on the ground,' Barbara said excitedly. 'I couldn't get what she and Kimberly both claimed to have seen out of my mind. And then it came to me. The person watching them *wasn't* on the ground. They saw him from a second-story window.'

'We thought of that, but no window in this house looks into Mrs Dillman's bedroom,' Deborah said.

'Not *this* house. The O'Donnell house. It's two stories, directly across the street from Mrs Dillman's, and you said Mrs Dillman's bedroom is at the front of the house, just like Kim and Brian's is at the front of yours. An upstairs window in the O'Donnell house would have a direct view into Mrs Dillman's bedroom. The view would be at more of a slant into Kim and Brian's bedroom. Binoculars could have reflected the glow of a street light, which made the lenses look like two big silver eyes.'

'But that house is vacant,' Deborah argued.

'Wrong. I did some checking today. You mentioned to me that the real estate sign had vanished from the lawn some time ago. I know the woman who owns the real estate firm that was handling the house and I went to see her today. She said the owners were desperate and decided to rent the house. The sign was taken down four months ago because the house was leased for six months to a man named Edward King.'

Deborah looked at her in astonishment. 'But no one ever moved in. Who rents a big, beautiful house like that and leaves it empty? Where is this man?'

Barbara shrugged. 'My friend, Roberta, has no idea. But six months' rent was paid in advance by a check drawn on a Charleston back account.'

'You're joking,' Pete said. 'Could she tell you anything about this guy?'

'Only that he said he was self-employed.' Barbara hesitated. 'She also remembered that he was probably in his late thirties or early forties, tall, slim and dark-haired.'

Deborah swallowed. 'Just like Steve.'

14

At 9.30 Pete left, followed shortly afterward by Barbara and Evan. Barbara wanted to stay, but Deborah took her aside. 'Evan is strung tight as a piano string.'

'Of course he is,' Barbara had said. 'He's worried to death about Steve and now there's all this stuff about the bank account and Mrs Dillman.'

'I know all that. But I also think he misses you. Spend the night with him – make him forget about all this for a while.' Barbara started to protest. 'Don't argue. We're fine. The police or the FBI or maybe both are outside and Joe's inside with us.'

'Yes – Joe . . .' Barbara looked worried.

'What is it?'

'Just something Evan said about Joe.'

'What did he say?'

'Nothing definite. Just that he doesn't trust Joe. You know – all that stuff in Houston.'

'Steve told me about it. Joe was cleared of all wrongdoing. What's the problem?'

'I don't know.' Barbara had looked as if she regretted saying anything. 'I suppose they just don't like each other. Forget what I said.'

Exasperated, Deborah felt like saying it wasn't fair of Barbara to bring up doubts about the man staying in her house, then tell her to drop the matter. She bit back the words, however, as Evan came up holding Barbara's coat.

'We can both stay,' he told Deborah, his blue eyes solemn. 'Say the word and you have two more watchdogs.'

For an instant Deborah considered saying yes. Barbara's words had shaken her, but only slightly. She wasn't going to let Evan and Joe's personal differences sway her growing confidence in Joe. If she started doubting everyone, she'd completely lose control in this dangerous situation, and she could *not* lose control – she had the children to protect.

Still, she remembered her father telling her many years ago that she had bad instincts about others. 'You don't have the sense God gave a goose when it comes to people,' he'd shouted angrily when her best friend, Mary Lynn, had been arrested for shoplifting. 'I knew she was bad soon as I looked at her. But not you. Always thinkin' the best of folks. One of these days, girl, you'll learn.' She had trusted Steve, only to come to doubt that she'd known her husband at all. Now she was trusting Joe. Was that just as big a mistake?

TWO

Evan stood at the window of Barbara's third-floor apartment staring out at the cold December night. 'We should put up a Christmas tree,' he said.

'Have you forgotten?' Barbara came up behind him and wrapped her arms around his waist. 'I don't celebrate Christmas.'

'Would having a Christmas tree condemn you to hell?'

'I'm Jewish – we don't believe in hell.'

'Then where do you believe someone like The Dark Alley Strangler goes when he dies?'

Barbara forced him to turn around and frowned up at him. 'What's brought on this mood? We've been seeing each other for nearly a year and never discussed religion.'

'It's our first Christmas together, and under the circumstances . . .'

'Under *what* circumstances?'

'This thing with Steve.'

'What does Steve have to do with a Christmas tree?'

'I don't know. Nothing.'

131

Barbara put her hands on his shoulders and looked into his eyes. 'Yes, it's something. Just tell me.'

'I suppose because everything is so screwed up, I need to maintain a few of the traditions.'

'Do you think Steve is dead?'

'No. I'm afraid he's guilty.'

'Evan! How can you say that?'

'How can I say it? Look at the evidence. There's more every day.'

'Coincidence.'

'Sure. One coincidence after another. I don't buy it.'

'Before, you were suspicious of Joe. Now you're suspicious of *Steve*?' She took her hands away from his shoulders. 'Evan, I know you don't like Joe, and I admit, you got me thinking about his sudden overwhelming concern for Deborah. But I can't believe you've known Steve for so long and you're talking like this. How can you possibly believe Steve Robinson is capable of not one but multiple brutal murders?'

'He's not beyond reproach, Barbara. Look at the events surrounding his sister's attack.'

'He was a kid.'

'He *wasn't* a kid. He was eighteen.'

'And how mature were you at eighteen?'

'Apparently more so than Steve.'

'I wonder about that. He was scared, Evan. And he was under terrible pressure from his parents.'

Evan jerked his hand impatiently, almost as if he were brushing her aside like a fly, and walked to the brown vinyl-upholstered couch. The cushions squeaked when he sat down. 'When are you going to get some decent furniture?' he asked irritably.

'The apartment is furnished, Evan.'

'Then why don't you find an apartment that isn't furnished and fix it up? Make it look warm, not like an office decorated from a department-store bargain basement.'

Barbara's lips tightened. 'You know I couldn't care less how the apartment looks as long as it's clean. Why do you want me to move? Because you'd like to move in with me?'

Evan looked startled. 'No.'

'I didn't think so.'

'Barb, our living together or getting married just isn't possible right now.'

'Why not?' Barbara was aware of the sharp tone her voice had acquired, but she couldn't help it. Nevertheless, she could see Evan bristling. 'We need to plan for something like that. We've never even discussed it.'

'A church wedding takes time.'

'Evan, I'm not getting married in a church.'

'Oh, for God's sake,' he exploded. 'What is this religious kick you're suddenly on?'

'The religious kick *I'm* on? What about you? I've never known you go to church. You're worried about your parents. You know they wouldn't approve of a civil ceremony, but it would be *our* wedding.'

'They're older, Barb. These things mean a lot to them.'

'They mean a lot to my family, too.'

'And then we'd have to discuss the issue of children. I mean, if we were going to have a child, it would have to be soon. You don't have much more time.'

'Thank you very much for reminding me,' Barbara said acidly.

Evan rolled his blue eyes. 'I didn't mean that as an insult. If your age bothered me, I wouldn't have started seeing you in the first place. But facts are facts.'

'Yes, they are. And the fact is that you aren't interested in marrying me.'

'We have things to work out. It would be a bad move for us *now*.'

Barbara placed her hands on her hips. 'And when *wouldn't* it be a bad move?'

Evan stared at her. 'You look like the stiff-necked schoolmarm glaring over me. Has the young whippersnapper overstepped himself again? Do you feel you need to jerk him back in line, force him to listen to an older, wiser voice?'

Color flooded Barbara's cheeks. 'How dare you talk to me that way?'

Evan stood. 'Listen to yourself. You sound like my parent, not my lover.'

'I don't.'

'You *do*.' Evan reached for his coat on the arm of the couch. 'I think it's time for me to leave.'

'*Leave*? Evan, you were going to spend the night.'

'Well, you've hardly set the mood for romance. I'll take a raincheck.'

'A *raincheck*! Do you have to sound so cavalier?'

'I could sound a lot worse than cavalier.'

Barbara's anger faded and she took an entreating step toward him. 'Evan, I left Deborah alone so we could spend some time together.'

'She's not alone. She has the rough and ready Joe Pierce with her.'

'Evan, *please*,' Barbara begged as she followed him to the door. 'Don't leave like this.'

'Better to leave like this than to stay and make things worse.'

Barbara clutched his arm. 'Evan—'

'Don't *pull* at me,' he snapped, jerking his arm away. 'I'll see you tomorrow. Goodnight.'

Barbara closed the door behind him, then leaned against it, tears filling her eyes. What had happened? What had she done to ruin the evening? Or had Evan merely *wanted* an excuse to leave?

THREE

Evan stalked from Barbara's apartment building and out to his red Toyota Camry. He sat in the car for a moment, his hand tight on the steering wheel. He half expected to see Barbara barreling out of the door and tearing after him. If she looked down from her living-room window and saw him, she would. Quickly he started the car and headed out of the lot.

He tuned the radio to the classical station. Barbara hated classical music, which was just one of their differences. She also had no interest in art films, gourmet food, or horses. When he'd taken her to his parents' graceful twenty-room home with its surrounding fifteen acres in Fairfax, Virginia, she'd been lost. She had nothing to talk about with his fragile, artistic mother or his genteel and very social sister. And when she'd been thrown into the midst of his old social set, with the young, affluent married couples and the unmarried women who despite their various careers all wore the patina of old money and privilege, Barbara seemed like a wild and hardy dandelion amid a bunch of delicate tea-roses.

He'd felt ashamed of himself for thinking so, ashamed of caring that his friends, for all their good manners, had been openly astonished at his choice of a girlfriend. And his parents, though they hadn't said a word, were unable to hide their own disapproval.

Or had they really tried to hide it? he asked himself. His parents were masters at conveying negative emotions without saying a word. For instance, they'd never said they were appalled that he'd become a prosecuting attorney instead of going into the law firm his great-grandfather had started, but they'd let him know it all the same. And if he was going to disappoint them with his career, he was at least expected to marry someone 'suitable', someone reared with money, someone who had traveled in Europe, gone to all the right schools, someone who knew how to leave work at the office and become the charming, lilting-voiced hostess at home. Especially someone young enough to have several children to carry on the Kincaid name. After all, Evan was the only male child. The line would end with him if he didn't have a son.

'Good God,' he said aloud. 'It sounds like we're some royal family.' But ridiculous as it sounded, he'd been brought up knowing what was expected of him, just as his father had been. And his father had done what he was supposed to do. He was the rebel in the family, but he wasn't sure he was as comfortable with rebellion as he thought he'd be.

With a curse, he turned off the radio. What he needed was an evening in a bright, sleazy bar, where the cigarette smoke, the liquor, and the noise would temporarily ease the painful conflict in his mind.

FOUR

I'm gonna get *murdered*, Toni Lee Morris thought as she emerged from the bar. She stood on the sidewalk a moment, pulled a lock of her long dark hair under her nose and sniffed. Ugh! She reeked of cigarette smoke. Clothes she could shed. She could even hop in the shower before climbing in bed with Daryl, but she couldn't explain washing her hair at midnight. And he'd notice, she thought glumly. As soon as she got back to the trailer court and crept into their bed, Daryl would awaken from what seemed a death-like sleep and be all over her. After all, it *was* only his third night back from hauling chemicals out of Nitro to God knew where. And he was leaving again tomorrow morning. Yeah, he'd notice, and she couldn't pass off the smell as the lingering smoke of a couple of cigarettes she'd had while babysitting for her sister Brenda's kids.

Then there was the problem of money. Brenda always paid her for babysitting. She'd promised to lie if Daryl called ('Yeah, Daryl, I got back early but I'm beat and I asked Toni to pick up a pizza for me. I'll have her call as soon as she gets back'), then give Toni Lee a warning call at the bar. But the problem was that Toni Lee had no money to show for her evening of 'babysitting'. Maybe Daryl would ask to see it. Yeah, sure, Toni Lee thought. In the morning he'd ask for a five for cigarettes, and after the drinks she'd bought tonight, she only had a couple of dollars. She'd have to make something up. How about saying Brenda was short and would pay her later? It wasn't bad. It wasn't good, either.

Shit. Marrying Daryl right out of high school was her biggest mistake. She was pretty. Better than pretty. Everyone said so. She could have had anybody. Maybe even some rich playboy. Maybe some day she would have ended up on *Lifestyles of the Rich and Famous.* Instead, she'd married Daryl Morris because she thought she was pregnant. She wasn't, but now she was trapped. He'd never let her go. He was crazy about her. Besides, she'd never held a job. What would she do for a living?

She'd parked her car in an alley just in case Daryl got suspicious and came looking for her. Which was really dumb, she thought as she turned into the wide, badly lit alley. *I should have just come out tomorrow night* after Daryl left. But she'd met that cute salesman in the bar last Monday night and he'd said he was usually around on Mondays. But not *this* Monday, as it turned out. She'd taken a big risk for nothing. She hadn't even seen anyone interesting. Well, there was that one guy sitting at the bar, but he'd seemed kind of shy. He'd left after the woman with bushy, bleached-blonde hair attached herself to him. He'd waited until she went to the restroom and then he'd taken off. No wonder, Toni Lee thought. *That* one looked like she'd been around the block a few times. A few *hundred* times.

Smiling at her own witty observation, she fished in her purse for the car keys. There they were on her pink pom-pom key chain. Other women laughed at that key chain, but she laughed right back when she immediately found her keys while they rooted interminably through their purses for some silly little key ring that might be tasteful, but certainly not practical.

Aside from an empty delivery truck pulled up beside the bar, Toni Lee's blue Ford Escort was the only vehicle in the alley. Her high heels echoed hollowly on the concrete. Her feet were killing her, but she'd stood all evening because she was wearing her short black skirt and the high black heels that made her dynamite legs look even better. Of course, once she got in the car she'd remove the skirt and heels in favor of jeans and her white leather Keds, because if Daryl happened to be awake when she got in, he'd never believe she'd been babysitting in a mini-skirt and heels. So maybe it was better the alley was so deserted, even if it was a little creepy. At least she'd have some privacy to change clothes.

She had just inserted her key in the car doorlock when a man stepped out of the shadows around the delivery truck. Toni Lee froze. He walked toward her, casually, non-threateningly. 'Hi,' he said in a friendly voice. 'Kind of a dangerous place to park, isn't it?'

'Not if you carry a gun like I do,' Toni Lee responded, hating the quiver in her voice.

'Are you a policewoman or PI?'

'Huh?' Toni mumbled, fumbling in her purse as if she were going for a gun.

'You need a license to carry a gun.'

'Oh, yeah. I'm a policewoman. A detective.'

The man smiled. It was an open, guileless smile. 'I don't think so. I think you're just scared. But you don't have to be. I saw you in the bar.' Toni squinted in the bad light, then recognized him. 'I was trying to work up the courage to talk to you when I was accosted by that blonde.' He shook his head, laughing. 'Who was she supposed to be? Dolly Parton or Madonna?'

Toni Lee relaxed slightly. 'The lights in her house must be real soft if she thinks she looks like either one of them.'

'Maybe she dresses by candlelight.'

'Yeah, that'd be best. Say, how come you're hiding here in the alley?'

'I'm not *hiding*. It's such a nice, clear night I just thought I'd have a cigarette. And to be perfectly honest, I kept a watch on the bar door. I thought if Miss Bleached Blonde left before you, I'd come back in and strike up a conversation. I never dreamed I'd be so lucky as to have you come to me.'

Toni Lee's blush of pleasure was hidden in the dusky light. 'I see. So why'd you wanna talk to me?'

'Have you ever looked in a mirror? Besides, you didn't look like you belonged in a place like that. Oh, it's an okay bar for most people, but not you. You looked like a rose among thorns.'

Toni Lee was entranced. 'A rose among thorns?'

'Yes. You're too good for that place. I can see you somewhere like the TriBeCa Grill.'

'What's that?'

'A Manhattan restaurant owned by Robert De Niro.'

'I *love* Robert De Niro,' Toni said, although at the moment she couldn't think of one movie he'd starred in. But she knew he was classy. 'Have you been to his place?'

'A couple of times.'

'Do you *know* him?'

'We've said hello, but he's pretty distant. Just shy, I guess.'

'It must be great to meet a movie star.' Gee, this guy's okay-looking, Toni Lee mused. He was quite a few years older than she – maybe ten – and it was hard to tell much about his body because he had on a lined raincoat, but he had nice brown hair and his smile was good. Kinda boyish, yet sexy. He reminded her of someone. If she could see his eyes, she'd know who, but they were hidden by horn-rimmed glasses with tinted lenses that remained slightly dark even in the shadows of the alley. 'Are you from New York?'

'No, but I travel a lot.'

'Are you a salesman?'

He laughed. 'No, thank God. I'm not aggressive enough to be a salesman. I'm an MD – a pediatrician, really – but my parents died last year and left me some money, so I decided to take a little time off and just enjoy life. It's nice not to see sick kids every day.'

A *doctor*, Toni Lee's mind screamed. A doctor who was independently wealthy and good-looking. Actually, now that she knew he had his own money, she decided he was *great*-looking, unstylish glasses or not. Was he married? She stole a look at his ring finger, but he was wearing gloves. He saw her glance, though, and said, 'I'm divorced. Two years now. How about you?'

She thought about saying she was divorced also, but instead opted for, 'Soon to be divorced. We're separated.'

'I see. I'm sorry.'

'I'm not. It was a big mistake from the beginning.' She wanted to go someplace and talk to him for hours, but there was Daryl to think of. Daryl, the husband from whom she was *not* separated. She dropped back into reality with a thud.

'Well, I really have to get home now.'

'You must be freezing.'

'Yeah, it's pretty chilly out tonight, but I'd love it if we could get together again.'

He smiled. 'That would be great. Do you have a favorite place around here?'

'Ummm, well, there's a restaurant I like. It's called The Fifth Quarter,' she said hesitantly. Meeting him at a restaurant was risky, but none of Daryl's friends frequented The Fifth Quarter. 'It's across the street from the Town Center Mall—'

'I know where it is,' he said. 'Excellent choice. What night?'

'How about tomorrow?'

'Tomorrow it is. Around eight o'clock?'

Toni Lee usually ate off a television tray at 5.30 while she watched *Geraldo*. She'd be starving by eight, but she promptly said, 'That's perfect.' She could always have a snack while she bathed and got dressed up. But not a big snack. She didn't want her stomach to bulge in the tight green dress she'd already decided to wear.

'Wonderful,' he said enthusiastically. 'I'll see you tomorrow.'

'Yes, tomorrow.' She wished she could think of something clever to say, but she wasn't a clever person. She'd have to let a dazzling smile do.

As Toni Lee reinserted her key in the lock, she realized she didn't know the guy's name. 'By the way,' she said, turning, 'I'm Toni Lee. And you're—'

A cord slipped around her neck and jerked her so hard she was pulled off her high-heeled feet. One pitiful squeak escaped her before the cord cut into her throat. She kicked and made futile grabs at the horrible thing choking her. It dug so deeply into her throat, though, that even her long nails couldn't slip under it. She reached farther back, trying to rake the man's face, but he dodged her groping fingers. Her hands fell, dragging down the length of his coat sleeves. Then something slammed against her temple. White light flashed behind her eyes. Her hand flew to her face, but not before another blow hit her cheekbone. She heard the bone snap.

While she reeled from the blows, he captured her clawing hands and tied them behind her back, binding them unbearably tight. Then he dragged her away from the car. She emitted grating, strangling sounds as she struggled to breathe. But she couldn't get any air.

The alley grew fuzzier. For a moment she thought she was in the trailer court where she lived. She mouthed the name 'Daryl', but Daryl wasn't there. Big, uncouth, territorial Daryl who'd never even slapped her wasn't there to beat the crap out of someone trying to hurt his woman. He'll be so mad at me, Toni Lee thought. He'll know what I was doing. In spite of the intense physical pain, she felt wrenchingly sad, tears spilling from her eyes as she suddenly longed for the man she'd thought she couldn't stand. What a time to realize she cared for the jerk. Daryl, help me, she cried silently. Oh, Daryl, please, *please* help me.

The man pulled her, still kicking feebly, behind the delivery truck and administered one final, shattering blow to her jaw. Inwardly she screamed in agony as he pried open her broken jaw and stuffed something in her mouth, something that felt like twigs and leaves. Then he hiked up her skirt and began tearing at her pantyhose. I'm sorry, Daryl, she thought dully before her mind began to close against the unbearable pain and the atrocity that would follow. Daryl, I'm so very, very sorry.

FIVE

Deborah lowered her paperback copy of Michael Caine's autobiography and looked at the clock: 1.20. She sighed and laid the book aside. She was so tired the words were running together, but she wasn't sleepy even though she'd been awake since early morning when Scarlett found Mrs Dillman. She kept seeing the woman's delicate body lying on the frosty grass. She also kept thinking about the savings account Steve had nearly emptied the day before he disappeared. Her tranquil life had been turned upside down Sunday night, and her brain felt overloaded with the deluge of strange and frightening events of the past few days. She wasn't sure how much more she could take.

Restlessly she tossed aside the blankets and pulled on her robe. Maybe hot milk would help. Hot milk with a generous shot of bourbon. This experience is going to turn me into an alcoholic, she thought. Just one more thing Dad can attribute to my ill-advised marriage. If I'd married Billy Ray Soames, like he wanted, probably alcohol would never have crossed my lips.

The door of the guest room stood open. Deborah hoped Barbara was enjoying her night with Evan. He'd seemed so tense. As much as he wanted to help, Deborah was afraid he resented all the time Barbara was spending here. And it had to be taking its toll on Barbara, too. After all, she was working her usual ten-hour days, and this house hardly provided a relaxing evening atmosphere.

She glanced into the children's room. Both were sleeping soundly. Scarlett opened sleepy eyes but didn't seem inclined to follow her.

Tiptoeing downstairs, Deborah pulled her robe tighter around her. A week ago she wouldn't have dreamed she'd be walking around Joe Pierce in her night clothes. Now such modesty seemed silly.

Joe had refused to sleep in the guest room in Barbara's absence. 'I need to be downstairs,' he'd said. 'If anyone is prowling around here, I'll hear them.' But as Deborah passed the living room, she saw that the couch was vacant. In fact, it didn't look as if it had been slept upon at all. She went into the kitchen, expecting to find him at the table drinking coffee. The room was empty. Alarm shot through her. Had Joe heard something and gone out to check on it?

Her hands began to tremble. She took a deep breath and went to the back door. It was securely locked, as was the door into the garage. She looked out the kitchen window but saw nothing. Then she rushed to the front door. It was locked and dead-bolted. Pulling the draperies aside, she peered into the front yard. Empty, as was the street, although she knew a surveillance car lurked somewhere near. That knowledge didn't make her feel any safer, though.

Where was Joe? Well, she couldn't go outside to investigate, but she couldn't calmly return to bed, either. She went back in the kitchen and poured milk into a mug, then set it into the microwave oven. Milk wouldn't help, but preparing it gave her something to do.

The microwave bell sounded at the same time as the phone rang. She picked up the kitchen extension, expecting to hear Joe's familiar, husky voice. Instead a rough, dramatically distorted male voice said, 'Deborah?'

She hesitated. 'Yes?'

'I love the way you look tonight.'

She held the phone for a startled instant, then slammed down the receiver. A burning jolt of panic raced through her. Her eyes darted to the window over the sink. The blind was drawn. No one could see through it. Still, she felt eyes full of malignant amusement roving over her.

She wrapped her arms around herself, feeling small and vulnerable. What should she do? Run outside to the surveillance car? The thought of dashing out into the night terrified her. Someone out there was watching her.

'Or maybe not,' she said aloud, just to break the silence of the kitchen. 'He didn't say anything specific about how I look. Maybe he couldn't see me at all.' So calling the police would be useless. They would probably chalk it up as a harmless crank call. And although she knew the phone was tapped, the connection had lasted less than thirty seconds. That wasn't long enough for a trace. She'd been a fool not to hang on longer.

Deborah took the mug of milk from the microwave. It was lukewarm now, but she didn't bother reheating it. Instead she found a bottle of bourbon in the cabinet and poured some into the milk. Then she sat down at the table, still shaking, her eyes drifting irresistibly to the phone. As if on cue, it rang again.

Deborah sat, frozen with uncertainty. Should she let it ring? Should she answer and try to get him to hang on for a few minutes? She closed her eyes. It rang again. And again.

She stood and rushed to it, nearly yelling, 'Hello?'

'You seem tense,' the voice said. 'Worried about being alone in the house with your children?'

'Who is this?' Deborah said inanely. How often had she complained about characters in movies asking such a stupid question? But it was instinctive.

'Just call me an admirer.'

The line went dead.

Her hands trembling, Deborah cowered at the table, waiting for another call. Ten minutes passed. She'd finished the milk without even tasting it. Now she was thinking about fixing a second drink, only she found she was too frightened even to stand up. This is what they call paralyzing fear, she thought.

The back doorknob jiggled. Deborah sucked in her breath, then went motionless, rooted to her chair. Her gaze fastened on the knob. A grating sound. Then the door swung open.

Joe stepped in. Trapped air flooded from her lungs. 'Where on earth have you been?' she croaked.

'Outside.'

'I *know* that,' she snapped, her fear turning to fury at Joe for frightening her so badly. '*Where* outside?'

Joe closed the door behind him and relocked it. 'I thought I saw a light in the O'Donnell house. I went over to investigate.'

'And?'

'And nothing. By the time I got over there, the light was gone. If there ever was one. I'm not sure now. Maybe it was just a reflection.'

'I had two calls when you were gone. A man said, "I love the way you look tonight." '

Joe frowned and she noticed his eyes traveling over her, taking in her disheveled hair and bulky terry cloth robe. 'What the hell did he mean by that?'

In spite of her earlier terror, Deborah couldn't help a wry smile. 'Obviously you don't share his opinion.'

'I'm sorry. I didn't mean—'

'It's okay. Believe it or not, I have some lovely negligées. Now just doesn't seem the time to wear them, but I don't *always* look like this.' She stopped and ran a hand over her forehead. 'What am I babbling about? Anyway, the first call came around fifteen minutes ago. I slammed down the receiver, which I shouldn't have done.'

Joe sat down across from her, still wearing his leather jacket. 'Did you recognize the voice?'

'No. It was deep, gravelly, disguised. The second time he said I sounded tense and that I must be worried about being alone in the house with my children. He called himself my admirer.' She paused. 'Joe, do you think he could actually see into the house?'

'No,' Joe said thoughtfully. 'But he knew you were alone and chose then to scare the wits out of you. He may not have been able to see inside, but I'd bet my life he *was* watching the house.'

'From where?'

'He had to be near a phone to call before I got back, and you now have the only occupied house in the cul-de-sac. He could have been in any one of them. Or he could have been calling from a mobile phone. In other words, he could have been anywhere around here. He might still be. These days traces are instantaneous. I'll try to find out where the call came from.'

And he did. It originated from a pay-phone in the parking lot of a self-serve gas station a block away. No one at the station remembered seeing who made the call.

Just as I expected, Deborah thought bleakly. In spite of all the police technology, no one seemed able to help. She was basically on her own in this nightmare.

Later, after Deborah had gone back to bed and lay under an extra blanket, trying to ease the chills racing over her body, she wondered why Joe had used the back instead of the front door, and where he had gotten a key.

15

The next morning Deborah woke up early and came downstairs to find Joe already sipping from a mug of coffee. 'Do you ever sleep?' she asked. 'No matter what time I get up, you're awake.'

'I had to get up at five every morning when I was growing up on the ranch,' he said.

'To milk the cows?'

Joe smiled. 'It's a horse and cotton ranch, Deborah.'

'That's right. You told me. I really was listening – I'm just absent-minded these days.' She poured coffee and sat down. 'Did you raise thoroughbreds?'

'Quarter horses. Have you ever ridden one?'

'I've never been on a horse in my life. I can't even bear to watch the Kentucky Derby because I'm afraid one of the horses will fall and injure one of those slender legs and they'll have to shoot it.'

'They don't always shoot them now.'

'I'm glad. Shooting those beautiful creatures always seemed like a sacrilege.'

Joe grinned. 'My mother would like you. You're kindred spirits.'

'Really? Tell me about her.' Talk to me about anything except my missing husband, Deborah thought desperately.

Joe leaned back in his chair. 'My mother's name is Amanda and she's originally from Massachusetts. After my dad died when I was nine, everyone thought she'd sell the ranch. You see, I have a younger brother, Bob, and two younger sisters. People figured with that brood, and very little experience in handling a ranch, Mom would just give up and head back to Massachusetts. But she held on. Things were tough at first. We had to sell off a few hundred acres – we're down to about three hundred right now – but the ranch is going strong.'

'Living in Texas must have been quite a change for her after Massachusetts.'

'That's an understatement. She came from one of those Boston Brahmin families – all very correct, very genteel. Right out of Henry James.' Deborah stifled a look of surprise that Joe was familiar with Henry James. He'd most likely be quite insulted that she thought he'd only read Zane Gray. 'Her parents thought she should come home and spend her life pouring tea and having literary parties. Instead she took on rough-and-tumble life on a ranch, so they refused to help her out financially.'

'Good heavens, she sounds like a daunting woman.'

Pride shone on his face. 'She is, but not on the surface. People are always surprised by her because she looks so delicate, she's soft-spoken, and she's still every inch the lady. But I remember one time when my brother Bob was ten and he went riding off by himself to do some exploring. He was bitten by a rattlesnake and even though we'd been taught how to handle snake bites, he panicked and just rode like hell for home. It was over a mile. We had company that day. Everyone was sitting on the veranda and Bob came tearing up on his horse, yelled, "Ma, I think I'm dying," and fell to the ground. The other ladies started screaming. Even the men were blundering around like a bunch of frightened cattle. But my mother very calmly sent our housekeeper in to call for the doctor, then grabbed a knife, made a neat little incision in his leg, and began sucking out the venom.'

'And Bob was all right?'

'He sure was. He still lives on the ranch with his wife and their little girl.'

'Your mother *does* sound amazing. I'm afraid I would have been screaming and blundering with the rest of the guests.'

Joe looked at her speculatively. 'No, I don't think so. You have a lot more grit than you think, Deborah Robinson.'

'I didn't show a lot of grit last night.'

'Those calls would have shaken up anyone. I'm sorry I wasn't here.'

She ran her fingers around the rim of her coffee mug. 'Joe, where did you get a key to the back door?'

146

'Oh the hook *beside* the door,' he said casually. 'Did you forget one was hanging there?'

'Yes, actually I did,' she said, embarrassed.

'And you were suspicious.'

'A little. I'm sorry.'

'Don't be. You had every reason to wonder why I was coming and going with my own key.'

'You're trying to make me feel better.'

'Evan Kincaid would be the first to tell you I *never* try to make people feel better. I just say what I think, and I think you're handling all this pretty well.'

'Well, thank you for the compliment,' Deborah said, feeling silly and girlish and angry with herself. The guy wasn't flirting with her. He was just being nice. Still, her mind darted for a new conversational topic. 'There's something I've always wanted to ask you. How did you get the scar on your forehead?'

He touched the narrow scar above his eyebrow. 'Bob wasn't the only one who took a spill off a horse. I got this when I was ten. I fell on the only rock within a mile radius. Afterward I was sort of proud of it. I thought it made me look tough.'

'Why didn't you stay on the ranch with your family?'

Joe tossed her a self-deprecating smile. 'Before my grandfather bought the ranch, he was a Texas Ranger. I was brought up on tales of his exploits. Do you know the Rangers' motto?' Deborah shook her head. ' "One riot, one Ranger." I took that to heart. I was going to be that ranger standing alone, guarding good against evil.' He emitted a short, bitter laugh. 'Instead I got involved with a call-girl and left the police force in disgrace.'

Deborah studied him for a moment. 'Joe, would you mind telling me about that woman in Houston?'

'Didn't Steve tell you?'

'Just the bare outline. He said you were cleared of any wrongdoing.'

He began slowly, not looking at her. 'When I was in high school, I was crazy about a girl named Lisa. We dated for two years. Then during our senior year, her parents split up, and her mother took her east. We wrote for a while, then her letters stopped coming. I was stunned when I ran into her in Houston ten years later. We started seeing each other again. She told me she was an investment counselor.'

'And you believed her.'

147

'I had no reason not to. She'd always been smart, and she was obviously successful. She had beautiful clothes, a nice apartment.' He smiled wryly. 'Then, after a few weeks, I noticed she never talked about her work. When I asked questions, she hedged. And there was never any sign of her business dealings in the house – no papers, no computer, not even a briefcase. And she seemed inclined to mood swings, sometimes hyperactivity. I wondered if she was taking drugs.'

'So you got suspicious.'

Joe nodded. 'It didn't take long to find out what her business *really* was. I should have walked away, but I loved her. I tried to talk her into changing her life. I even offered to help send her to college. That brought a huge laugh. Then I did more digging and found out that one of her clients was a high-powered drug dealer we'd been after for months. I wasn't working that particular case, but I suddenly realized how often she'd asked me to talk about police business. She was pumping me for information. There was no excuse at that point for my not staying completely away from her. Instead I decided to play savior. I put pressure on her to get away from this dealer – he was dangerous as hell. She got really hostile then. Looking back, I think she knew she was in over her head. She was *expected* to produce information or else. For some reason she started telling people she was afraid of me. Maybe she was afraid that I was using her like she was using me or that I'd already found out too much. Anyway, I finally made myself leave her. I hadn't seen her for about two weeks when she was found with her throat slashed.'

His voice was cool and emotionless, but Deborah saw a slight tremor in his hand. 'Did they find who did it?' she asked.

'After dragging me over the coals, which I guess I deserved, they arrested some poor jerk who was obsessed with her and had been following her around. But I know in my bones he didn't do it – the dealer did because she was doing too much cocaine and talking too much.'

'But he wasn't arrested.'

'Hell, no. He'd covered his tracks too well. So Lisa's murderer is still free and I left the force under a cloud, as they say. End of tragic, stupid story.'

'Stupid?'

'The way she lived her life was stupid. And the way I lost my career was stupid. But I guess that's life.'

'I'm sorry.'

'Yeah, me too.'

Uncomfortable silence hung in the air. 'Have you brought in the newspaper?' she asked quickly to hide her emotions.

'No. I'll get it right now.'

Joe rose from the table and went to the front door while Deborah poured a cup of coffee. When she sat down again, Joe entered the kitchen slowly, his face pale, his eyes full of dread. 'Oh my God,' Deborah exclaimed. 'They've found Steve.'

'No. If they had, they'd notify you before they put it in the newspaper.'

'Then what *is* it?'

'The Strangler killed again last night, this time right here in Charleston.'

TWO

Deborah stared at Joe, although she felt as if her eyes weren't quite focusing. 'Read the article to me.'

As Joe read, particulars jumped out at Deborah. The victim was Toni Lee Morris. She was a twenty-two-year-old housewife. She'd been attacked in the alley beside a local bar – raped, beaten, and strangled. She hadn't fared as well as Sally Yates. She was dead when she was found around 1 a.m. by a wino who stumbled over her body. Her earrings had been ripped from her ear-lobes. The medical examiner placed the time of death at between eleven and twelve. Patrons of the bar said she was a regular and had left around 11.30. She was survived by her husband, Daryl, and a sister, Brenda Johnson.

Joe looked up at her. 'The Strangler has changed his pattern. He's always waited a few months between killings, and he always struck on a Saturday night.'

'But this time he hit less than two weeks from the last attack and he did it on a week night. Why the change?'

'Sometimes that happens with serial killers. They start out slowly, cautiously. Then they get more confident. They don't do all the preparation they did in the beginning. And they pick up speed.'

'Pick up speed?'

'They kill more frequently.'

'Why? Because they want to be caught?'

Joe smiled sadly. 'Maybe some killers want to be caught, Deborah, but this guy is a psychopath and a psychopath doesn't have a conscience. However, he can lose control.'

Steve, wildly murdering young women as he spun out of control? Ripping out their earrings, smashing their faces, raping and strangling them?

Deborah's stomach lurched. She took a deep breath and steadied herself. 'It's Lieber,' she said fiercely. 'Artie Lieber is in Charleston and *he* murdered that woman last night. Not Steve. Not *Steve!*'

THREE

She'd read the article about Toni Lee Morris twice more during the morning, and each time fear tingled through her at the thought of The Dark Alley Strangler killing right here in Charleston. Finally Joe took the paper from her. 'Enough, Deborah. Going over and over the details isn't going to change anything, and you get whiter every time you read this piece. I'm almost sorry I brought it to your attention.'

'And you think I wouldn't have noticed it otherwise? Besides, I had to know. I have to know as much as possible. After all, as far as the FBI is concerned, I'm right in the middle of this whole thing. I believe Agent Wylie actually thinks I'm protecting my serial-killer husband.'

Joe had said nothing, and she knew there was nothing for him to say. It wasn't just Agent Wylie who believed Steve was The Dark Alley Strangler. She was beginning to think Joe thought so, too.

Later, as she rinsed the last plate from lunch and set it in the drainer, the phone rang and she picked up the receiver with a damp hand.

'Is this Deborah?' a woman asked.

The sharp-edged, somewhat imperious voice was unfamiliar and Deborah feared it was yet another reporter. 'This is Deborah Robinson,' she said cautiously.

'This is Lorna Robinson, Steven's mother.'

Deborah had always wondered how she would react if one of Steve's parents called out of the blue. Now she knew. She was speechless. 'Are you still there?' the woman demanded.

'Yes. Hello, Mrs Robinson.'

'Hello. My husband and I are in Hawaii. We heard from friends last night that Steven has been missing for days. Why didn't you let us know?'

'I tried to,' Deborah said, annoyed that Mrs Robinson had rebuked her before even asking if there was news of Steve. 'You were traveling around the islands.'

'You could have left word.'

'Mrs Robinson, I didn't want you to come back to your hotel and find this out from a message and I wasn't sure you'd return my call. Besides,' she couldn't help adding, 'I didn't think you would be so worried.'

'That wasn't a very kind thing to say.'

On the phone two minutes and we're already sparring, Deborah thought. It was time to pull the reins on this conversation. 'This is a very rough time, Mrs Robinson. We still have no idea what's happened to Steve, but we're fearing the worst, especially with Artie Lieber hanging around.'

'Lieber! Good lord, I didn't know *he* was involved!'

'As I said, he's around. Or he was at the time of Steve's disappearance.'

'I see. Then the police haven't located him *or* Steven?'

'No.'

Anxiety crept into the unpleasant voice. 'You don't think Lieber will try to harm Emily, do you?'

The woman's concern for her daughter was natural, yet Deborah felt even angrier. She sounded more alarmed about Emily, who was safe, than Steve, who had been missing for days. 'I've alerted the nursing home about the situation. They've promised to take extra precautions to safeguard Emily, and I would have heard if anything were wrong.'

'That's a relief. Nevertheless, my husband and I will be coming home as soon as possible. Unfortunately, he picked up some kind of bug. He'll probably be too sick to fly for a couple of days.' She sounded disgusted and accusatory. Deborah pitied the man who had to spend the next two days trapped in a hotel room with her.

'Couldn't you come ahead by yourself?' she asked.

'I'm not good at traveling alone,' Mrs Robinson said stiffly. 'Besides, my husband needs me.'

And your son is missing, perhaps dead, but you're not coming home

151

because you've found out your daughter is safe and that's what really counts, Deborah thought bitterly.

'You will let me know if Steven is found, won't you?'

'Of course,' Deborah said, wondering how Mrs Robinson could sound as if Steve might have just gone out for the day, wanting to know when he returned.

'And Deborah, I hope you won't talk to the press. This family has already suffered so much because of negative publicity.'

Deborah now knew what people meant when they said they were so angry they saw red. She felt a rush of fury so intense it almost blinded her. Of all the shallow, stupid things to be worried about at a time like this. 'I will talk to reporters if I feel it will help locate Steve.'

Mrs Robinson sighed. 'Well, I can't stop you, although I'm asking you as Steven's mother.' Deborah rolled her eyes at the woman's softened voice which begged for pity. Deborah didn't answer and finally Mrs Robinson went on. 'If I don't hear from you in the next few days, I'll get in touch when I return to Wheeling. Then we'll decide what to do.'

We'll decide what to do? Deborah thought. What on earth was there to decide? Whether or not to keep searching for Steve?

Mrs Robinson uttered a curt goodbye, and as Deborah hung up, she noted that the woman hadn't even inquired about her grandchildren.

FOUR

Linda Amato, RN, looked at her watch and sighed in exhausted relief. Forty-five minutes and she could go home. Of course, when she arrived there would still be at least two loads of laundry to do if the kids were to have anything clean to wear tomorrow, and no doubt there would be a sink full of dirty dishes. She could let the dishes go until tomorrow, but by then the food remains would be petrified. No, better to wash them and be done with it. Considering all she had to do, she'd be lucky to get to bed by midnight. These double shifts were killing her, but she'd have to endure them until her ex-husband came through with the overdue child support.

Since old Mr Havers in 201 had mercifully quieted down after being given a Valium, and Mrs Weston had worn herself out demanding to be helped with unnecessary trips to the bathroom every fifteen minutes, the halls in ICU had become quiet. Funny, Linda thought. On a bad night the constant noise nearly drove everyone crazy, but when the clamor suddenly died, the silence turned eerie.

She quietly opened the door to Sally Yates's room and moved toward the motionless form on the bed. Every time she looked at Sally she felt like crying. When Sally was hired by the hospital six months ago, Linda thought she was one of the most beautiful girls she'd ever seen. Now Sally's jaw was wired shut, the left side of her face was horribly bruised and still disfigured by stitches where her jaw bone had ripped through the delicate skin, part of her hair had been shaved where that lunatic had bashed her skull, causing a massive hematoma, and her arms were discolored from countless assaults with needles delivering painkillers and drawing blood. An IV tube hung beside the bed, and Sally was catheterized. Miraculously, the swelling from the rope they'd found around her neck had gone down and she'd been taken off the respirator. The doctors said there hadn't been a real attempt to murder by strangulation. That seemed to be for show. Apparently, the blows to the head had been meant to kill her and very nearly had.

They knew now it was The Dark Alley Strangler who had attacked Sally. It was the most horrifying thing that had ever entered Linda's disappointing but mundane world, and brought out a ferocity in her she'd never known she possessed. For the first time in her life, she felt like she could kill someone and not experience a twinge of remorse over her act. Well, at least the bastard had worn a condom while raping Sally, so the risk of AIDS was reduced, even though she could have come into contact with infected blood through any of her many lacerations.

Sally's mother claimed that her baby girl Amy cried constantly for her mama, but she wouldn't have been allowed to see her even if she were older than eight months. Sally was no sight for a child, no matter how young. But Amy was in good hands. Sally's mother might be critical and tart-tongued, but she adored her daughter and granddaughter. Although she was too stoic to cry when she saw Sally, the anguish in her eyes revealed the depth of her feeling. Sally's husband was another matter. Jack Yates had stomped into the hospital room the day after Sally's attack, looked at her with his blunt, stupid face and expressionless eyes, and muttered, 'Is she gonna live?'

'We hope so,' young Dr Healy said. Linda thought the world of Dr Healy. He was handsome, brilliant, and never yelled at the nurses, which was a rare trait among doctors. Jack Yates continued to stare at his savagely beaten, comatose young wife, not going near her, and Dr Healy added gently, 'I must tell you, Mr Yates, even though we're doing all we can, it doesn't look good right now.'

Yates turned his cold eyes on him. 'You reap what you sow,' he pronounced in a voice of sanctimonious doom. 'She's a tramp, hangin' out in a bar like that. If she lives, I'm gonna divorce her. And I'll tell you another thing – I'm not payin' you or this hospital one dime. Let her ma take care of her bills. If she'd raised her better, Sally wouldn't be here.'

As he stalked out, Dr Healy looked after him with fire in his usually mild blue eyes and said loudly, 'Son of a bitch.' Yates stiffened but otherwise didn't acknowledge the doctor's words. He also never visited Sally again.

Linda shook her head angrily at the memory and bent over Sally, grasping her right wrist to take the girl's pulse. In the ghostly quiet of the room, she nearly yelped when Sally hissed, 'Linda?'

'Good heavens, Sally!' Linda gasped. She peered at the young woman. 'Sally, are you coming out of it?' She leaned closer to her face. 'Honey, can you open your eyes?'

At first there was nothing. Sally lay utterly still, and Linda was beginning to think she'd imagined Sally's voice, but she wasn't going to give up easily. She grasped Sally's limp, cold hand and said soothingly, 'Honey, you're alive. You're in the hospital. Everyone loves you and is praying for you.' Everyone except your cretin of a husband, she thought. 'Sally, please say something.'

Finally Sally's right eye opened slightly. The other was still swollen shut. 'Amy?'

Linda beamed and looked upward. 'Oh, God, thank you for this miracle!' She gazed at Sally. 'Amy's with your mother. She's fine, although she misses you terribly. Don't worry, Jack's not going anywhere near her,' she added, knowing that Sally always worried about the child when she was in Jack's care. 'Listen, Sally, everything is going to be *fine*. You're *alive*, thank the Lord.'

Sally drew a labored breath. 'How long?'

'How long have you been in a coma? Oh, a few days,' Linda said airily. If she told Sally it had been eleven days, the girl would be badly frightened.

Usually patients who were comatose for longer than three days stayed that way.

Sally drew a labored breath. 'Finger?'

'Finger?' Linda repeated blankly, then remembered that Sally's ring finger had been nearly severed. 'You have your finger. They reattached it. You probably won't have full use of it, but what's the difference? It'll still look just fine. A little scar, that's all,' she said gaily.

'Catch him?'

Linda sobered. She wanted so badly to say, 'Yes, they caught the monster who did this to you,' but that would be a blatant lie, not a little evasion. Linda drew the line at lies. 'No, honey, they didn't get him.' Fear leaped in Sally's beautiful, opened eye. 'But they *will*. The police are going wild over this, and I heard there's a witness.' Sally continued to look at her fearfully, and Linda added, 'I'm going to leave you for a few minutes and get a doctor. Healy's on duty tonight. You would not *believe* how that man has hovered over you. I always knew he was sweet on you. My gosh, he's going to be *thrilled*!'

Sally's hand abruptly tightened on hers. 'No! No doctor.'

'No *doctor*! Why, honey, what in the world are you talking about? You *must* see a doctor.'

Sally's grip increased. '*No!*' she croaked and hissed at the same time around the wires holding her jaw in place. Now she looked terrified. 'Didn't get him.'

'No, they didn't get the man who attacked you, but now that you're awake, you can identify him. You *can* identify him, can't you?'

'Not sure.' She touched a dry tongue to dry lips. Linda poured water from a pitcher into a plastic cup, held it near Sally's face and guided the straw to her lips. Sally took a couple of swallows and started coughing. Linda withdrew the cup. 'Well, you could give it a try. Identifying the man, I mean.'

'*No!*' Linda drew back at the force of Sally's voice.

'I don't understand. Why not?'

'Maybe can't. But if he sinks I can . . .'

'If he thinks you can, what?'

Sally's battered face managed an expression of complete frustration. 'He's still *out* dere. Come after me.'

'Oh,' Linda said slowly. 'But you're safe here.'

'No! Not from him!'

155

'Sweetie, he's not superhuman. There are people all over this place.'

'Lithen.'

Linda looked at her in complete confusion. 'Listen to what? I don't hear a thing.'

'Where all de people?'

Comprehension dawned on Linda's narrow, lined face. Hadn't she been aware of the unnerving silence earlier? Wasn't it true that sometimes at night the halls *did* seem deserted? Of course, they never were for long. But sometimes nurses were in patients' rooms or absorbed with paperwork in the nurses' station. It was possible, just barely possible, that someone could sneak into a patient's room.

'What do you want me to do, Sally?' Linda asked helplessly.

'Don't tell. Pretend I still in coma.'

'Oh, Sally, how can I pretend you're still in a coma? You need a doctor's attention!'

'No! If doctor knows, other people find out. End up on news. He's still out dere. *He'll* know. Linda, *pleath*.'

Linda closed her eyes, ignoring Sally's hand clenched on hers. It wasn't right not to tell Dr Healy. Not right at all. But she loved Sally like a younger sister and she'd been through so much. And she was so upset.

'Okay,' she said at last. 'I don't feel good about this, but I won't tell for now.'

'Promith?'

'Promise,' Linda said reluctantly.

A tear trickled down Sally's purple and mauve cheek. The air seemed to go out of her. She was exhausted. 'Sank you.'

'You're welcome, honey.' Linda bent down and gave Sally a light kiss on the forehead. But as she left the room, she was deeply troubled. She knew she was a woman of little imagination. That's why she *always* went by the book. No variation of routine, no reliance on her own judgment. She didn't trust herself. And now look what she was doing – hiding the fact that a critically injured patient had awakened from a coma. No, it wasn't right. It would backfire, she knew it. She could lose her job over it. Worse still, Sally might suffer because of it. Linda's fingers twisted nervously. Maybe she should ignore her promise to Sally. After all, the woman probably wasn't thinking clearly at all. Sally had just awakened from an eleven-day coma after a brutal rape and beating. She probably didn't even fully realize what she was saying. She was jeopardizing her health, her *life*, because of some paranoid fear.

A voice somewhere deep in Linda's mind spoke up, a voice she usually tried to ignore because it *always* brought up disturbing possibilities and complications. Normally she could shut it out, but not this time. This time it kept saying, 'Maybe Sally *isn't* reacting to some paranoid fear. Maybe if you tell, *you'll* be the one jeopardizing Sally's health, her very *life*.' And a chill rippled across Linda's neck when she remembered Sally's tortured, terrified words – 'He's still out there.'

16

ONE

Although the children still asked every few hours if she'd heard from Daddy, Deborah noticed that the hope had faded from their eyes. Her deepest pain came from their hurt acceptance of the fact that Steve wasn't coming home. She wanted to tell them to cheer up — Daddy would probably be home for Christmas, but that would be cruel. If Steve didn't turn up – and she had an increasing certainty that he wouldn't – they would be crushed. As for herself, she suffered a perpetual coldness deep inside her. No matter how many sweaters she layered on, no matter how high she turned up the heating, the chill remained.

She was adjusting the thermostat for the third time since she'd awakened when someone rang the doorbell. She stiffened and hesitated. Joe had gone home for a couple of hours to pick up his messages and get fresh clothes. It was a wild, blustery day, and she'd already been startled a couple of times by the spiny, naked limbs of a forsythia slapping against the living-room window. The children, who had quarreled most of the morning, were now playing quietly in the basement and the house felt uncomfortably silent.

The doorbell rang again, and she chided herself for being so frightened. It was 11 a.m. Artie Lieber was not going to come to the front door and ring the bell in broad daylight with surveillance posted on the house.

She opened the door. Fred Dillman, Mrs Dillman's son, stood windblown and shivering on the front porch. 'Mrs Robinson? I hope I'm not stopping by at a bad time. I would have called first but I've been at the hospital—'

158

'Come in,' Deborah said. 'I've been so worried about your mother. How is she?'

'Just the same,' Fred told her. He was a burly man, at least six feet two with thick brown hair heavily laced with silver. Last year Mrs Dillman had told her Fred was a test pilot. In reality, he was an optometrist. 'I don't think Mom's going to pull out of this.'

Fred looked genuinely sad, and Deborah wondered why he had neglected his mother if he cared so much. As if reading her mind, he said, 'If only Mom had gone to live with my sister in Florida, this wouldn't have happened.'

'She could have come to live with you,' Deborah couldn't resist saying.

He flushed with embarrassment. 'My wife wouldn't allow it. She and Mom have never gotten along. You know how it can be with in-laws.' Oh, *did* she. 'Besides, you can't *make* someone like Mom live where she doesn't want to. She'd just run off.'

'Maybe so.'

'She's managed fairly well on her own, with a lot of help from you and your husband. I appreciate your kindness. I couldn't come often – I'm so busy. She also got it into her head that I was trying to poison her. Can you imagine anything so fantastic?'

'I had no idea. She never said anything about *that* particular fantasy to me, but I've heard others.'

Fred grinned. 'No doubt concerning the wild shenanigans of my poor father.'

'He does seem to have led quite a life these last few years.' Deborah suddenly realized they were still standing in the entrance hall. She invited Fred in, but he declined. 'I really came to ask another favor. I've been staying in a motel, but I think I'll move into the house today since I'll probably be here for a few more days. And even though Mom's unconscious, I can't stand seeing her in that thin hospital gown. I'd like to take a robe, slippers, some toiletries – whatever women need when they're in the hospital. I wondered if you'd mind going to the house with me and gathering up some things. I'm sure you'd know more about what I should take than I do.'

Although Fred seemed personable, Deborah felt like telling him taking a brush and lipstick to his unconscious mother was doing far too little much too late, but now didn't seem like the time to dole out unwanted moral judgments. She hesitated, then said, 'Would you mind if I brought my children along? We've had some trouble — '

'I know all about it,' Fred's cheeks pinked again. He had an unsettling way of becoming embarrassed easily, but Deborah told herself how easy it was for people to feel nonplussed in this situation. 'It's been all over the news,' he added hastily. 'I'm very sorry. I suppose you haven't had any word about him?'

'Nothing good,' Deborah said cautiously. She had difficulty remembering that the general public did not know that the FBI suspected Steve of being a serial killer. The news broadcasts had mentioned only the details of his disappearance. Reminding herself of this, she relaxed slightly. 'I'm still hoping my husband is all right, but he vanished without a trace.'

'What a terrible situation. You don't think what happened to your husband had anything to do with the attack on Mom, do you?'

She hesitated again, then decided to be open with him. 'I don't know if there's a connection, but there is something you should know. The night your mother was attacked, she came over here claiming my husband had been watching her get ready for bed. She said he wasn't standing on the ground, and there was a light behind him.'

'That's ridiculous,' Fred said.

'That's what my friend Barbara and I thought at first. But after we found your mother, Barbara was troubled by the idea that maybe someone *had* been spying on her from the house across the street. It's been vacant for years, or so we thought, but Barbara discovered it had been rented several months ago to a man we've never seen.'

Fred looked incredulous. 'You mean you think the man who lives there was watching Mom and then *attacked* her?'

'We can't know for sure, but it would be possible to look into your mother's bedroom window from an upstairs room in that house, and the person who rented it is a mystery.'

'Do the police know about this?'

'Yes.'

'Did they search it?'

'Yes, but they found nothing.' She omitted to tell him that they were only able to obtain a search warrant because they were convinced that *Steve* might be the mysterious renter.

'Can anyone look in the house?'

'No. It's private property, whether it's empty or not. But a private investigator, a friend of the family who's been staying with me and the children, sneaked over one night and looked in the windows. He didn't see anyone.'

'Well, how much could he see at night? Why didn't he go during the day?'

'As I said, this house is under surveillance. The police watch every move we make, and I don't think they'd let Joe get away with an illegal search. What little he could do had to be done at night with him being careful not to be seen.'

'And whoever attacked Mom had to do the same thing. He came out at night. But why on earth would anyone want to hurt *her*? She's harmless.'

'Maybe she isn't so harmless,' Deborah said. 'She's very observant, although she's not always able to give you an accurate description of what she's seen. Still, I believe there's something strange going on in that house, and your mother might have witnessed something she wasn't supposed to see.' She shrugged and smiled sheepishly. 'I know that sounds like I've watched too many Alfred Hitchcock movies, but I think it's a real possibility.'

Fred frowned. 'It doesn't sound so far-fetched to me. Maybe it's a good thing I'll be staying in the house. Maybe I can see something interesting from her bedroom window.'

Ten minutes later, after the children had been bundled up against the bitter wind, Fred opened the door to his mother's house. A slightly damp mustiness wafted over them. Kim wrinkled her nose and opened her mouth to speak, but Deborah nudged her. 'I turned the thermostat down the other day,' she told Fred. 'Your mother worries about the heating bills and since the house is empty . . . '

Fred nodded. 'That's fine. The odor is coming from the furniture. I don't know why my parents didn't buy some new things through the years. It's not as if these pieces are valuable antiques – they're a collection of junk.'

The children went to a table laden with pictures. 'We know who everybody is,' Brian said. 'Uncle Robert, Grandma Daisy—'

'You look at the pictures and I'll go upstairs with Mr Dillman,' Deborah said. 'Be back in just a few minutes.'

Fred followed her upstairs, although he did nothing but stand around while Deborah rummaged through the closet and dresser drawers. She found a pretty navy robe with a ruffled white collar which looked as if it had never been worn, pitifully ragged underwear with loose elastic, a decent

161

pair of white house slippers, a tube of dryish red lipstick, and a new bottle of Emeraude cologne which Fred said he'd sent his mother for her birthday. Last of all, she placed Mrs Dillman's well-worn Bible on top of the clothes in a suitcase she'd brought from home. 'I guess that about does it,' she said.

Fred took the suitcase and started downstairs. Deborah lingered in the bedroom, wandering over to a cedar chest beneath the window. Although the rest of the furniture was worn, this piece seemed to have been lovingly polished. She couldn't resist raising the lid. It was obviously handmade and inside an inscription had been burned into the wood: 'To Virginia from Mother and Father, 1922.' Virginia. It was impossible for Deborah to think of her as anything except 'Mrs Dillman'.

She lowered the lid and looked through the sheer curtains. The wind had picked up a paper bag and sent it skittering down the street like tumbleweed on the prairie. Across the street a stray cat wandered across the lawn of the O'Donnell house. It stopped and looked up. Deborah followed its gaze and went rigid when for just a moment she caught the flash of a pale face in an upstairs window looking back at her.

She bolted down the stairs and out the front door. She caught a brief glimpse of Fred gaping at her while the children rocketed along in her wake like playful puppies. Out on the walk, Deborah looked all around the cul-de-sac for a car or van that could be the surveillance vehicle and saw none. She knew it had to be around, concealed so as not to scream its presence. That didn't help her, though. The street was empty, and so was the upstairs window in the O'Donnell house.

TWO

Ever since she awakened from the coma, Sally had tried not to sleep, especially at night, especially after Linda told Dr Healy that she had regained consciousness. She accepted with bleak resignation that Linda could not keep such a serious secret. Linda thought she was doing what was best to preserve her life. Sally knew she'd inadvertently done what would most likely cause her death.

She didn't have a watch or a clock in the room, but the television had been turned off, and that was always done at 11 p.m. She'd drifted to sleep during the nine o'clock movie, at least an hour ago. Maybe *hours* ago. She had no way of knowing how much time had passed.

Her eyes darted around the room. At least it was small and spare and she could see fairly well by the light coming in through her open door. No hulking shapes that didn't belong. No odd noises. Just the usual chatter from the nurses' station and an occasional shout from the man down the hall who thought he was back in the Philippines during World War II. Normal. Everything was normal.

A yawn formed and, unable to escape her wired jaw, flared her nostrils until they hurt and filled her eyes with tears. She was amazed that after being in a coma so long she was so terribly sleepy. She knew it was because of her severe injuries. Also, she'd managed to stay awake after she'd talked to Linda last night. Twenty-four hours she'd spent wide awake. And how sickeningly dismayed she'd been when a beaming Dr Healy strode in that afternoon with Linda skulking along behind him. Tears had run down Sally's face at the sight of them, and for the first few minutes she couldn't make herself speak to Linda. But she'd never really had any hope that Linda would keep her consciousness quiet. If only she'd awakened when she was alone, then *no one* would know.

Her eyelids felt leaden. I *can't* go to sleep again! she thought fiercely. If only I could have a cup of strong black coffee. But this isn't a hotel. They won't give me coffee at this hour. Maybe I could ask for speed, she mused. That would set them talking at the nurses' station.

Even as she inwardly smiled, her eyes were closing. She struggled, but the dark waves of sleep overpowered her.

She was back in the alley, bending over the man with a bloody handkerchief pressed to his forehead. He pulled it away, stood to put his arm around her shoulders, and she saw there was no cut on his head – only a red stain, probably a drop of food coloring. His hand went to his pocket and in a flash a rope tightened around her neck. His fist slammed into her face and, as she reeled, he pulled her off her feet and dragged her—

Her eyes snapped open. Her heart beat against her ribs in strong, painful strokes. How long had she been asleep? And why was her door now *closed*?

She caught a whiff of scent – not cologne, just the scent of another warm human being. A whimper escaped through her wired jaw. Frantically she reached for the buzzer to summon a nurse, but a hand closed around hers. 'Now you don't want to do that, do you, Sally?'

She drew in breath for a scream, but another hand closed over her mouth, brutally gripping her broken jaw. 'You look so delicate but you're a hard one to kill,' the husky whisper went on with terrifying gentleness. 'Some of the others were easy, some not. But none of them was like you. Tell me, where do you get your strength, Sally? That interests me. Why are you so damned *strong*?'

Fear raged through her. She kicked under the sheet and blanket, kicked with all her strength. He chuckled. 'Feisty to the end, eh? Going to go down fighting like the street trash you are? Well, even though it makes this thing more difficult for me, I admire you. But only for your strength. *Not* for your morals. Women like you don't know what morals are.'

The pain grew in Sally's jaw and the hand pressed upward, blocking her nose. She made noisy attempts to get her breath and whimpered again behind the hand. 'Word that you regained consciousness traveled through the hospital like wildfire, and I've made it my business to have contacts in this town, thank goodness. Otherwise, there could have been a disaster. Oh, I know you've refused to talk to the police so far,' the awful, caressing voice went on. 'I know they've been here, but you won't speak. But they'll wear you down. At least, they'd wear you down if you were still alive. But unfortunately for you, your luck has run out.'

He forced her head back. She looked up at the face, but couldn't focus on the features. All she really saw was the gleaming switch-blade knife in front of her eyes. 'Not my usual style, but under the circumstances—'

Sally kicked violently and tried to scream, her voice rasping in her throat. Then the door flew back, light flooded the room, and a nurse exclaimed, 'What in the world—'

Sally saw a white-jacketed figure hurl itself across the room. The nurse flung out her hands, grabbing at the man's shoulders. His arm shot forward and buried the switch-blade in the nurse's abdomen. With a soft moan, she crumpled. He darted from the room. Sally expected a great commotion in the hall, but there was nothing except the ordinary sounds. Stunned and gasping, Sally stared at the fallen nurse a moment, her mind numb until she saw blood seeping across the floor from beneath the woman's body. Then Sally pressed the buzzer, over and over, until help finally arrived.

17

Christmas Eve arrived with a flurry of snowflakes that sent the children into whoops of delight. 'White Christmas, white Christmas!' Kimberly chanted. 'Daddy said it'd be a white Christmas!'

Deborah had already placed the gifts from her and Steve under the tree, her throat tightening when she saw the tags that read 'From Mommy and Daddy'. The black and white wool sweater she'd bought for Steve remained unwrapped, hidden away in her own sweater drawer. She had no idea what Steve had gotten for her, if anything. Maybe he had planned on buying something right before Christmas, and then it had been too late.

Determined to make the evening a festive occasion in spite of Steve's absence, she'd invited Pete and Adam as well as Barbara and Evan to join the family. The family, she thought, now seemed to consist of her, the children, and Joe. A week ago that possibility would have seemed ludicrous.

She pushed the thought out of her mind and buttoned the red satin blouse she'd bought two weeks ago along with the white dress she'd worn to the party. Before going downstairs, she checked to make sure her black wool pants were free of lint and dog hairs, and fastened a thin gold chain around her neck. Gazing at herself in the mirror, she saw the faint shadows under her eyes which concealer didn't hide, and cheekbones that stood out more sharply than usual. She'd lost four pounds since Saturday night. Defiantly, she pulled a pair of dangling gold earrings with red rhinestones from her jewelry box and clipped them on, pleased with the flashy gaiety they conveyed. She owed it to the children to forget about Steve for a few hours and make their favorite night of the year a happy one.

When she went downstairs, she took a deep breath and smiled. The house smelled of evergreen, cherry pie, and the gingerbread house she'd labored over all afternoon, painstakingly decorating it with white icing

165

and jelly beans. She lighted several fat candles she'd placed around the living room, then went into the kitchen to assemble a refreshment tray and check if there was enough ice. Had it been less than a week since Steve had complained that they'd run out of ice, she'd gone out to the freezer in the garage to retrieve a bag, and come back in to find Steve, white and shaky-handed, talking curtly on the phone? She closed her eyes. 'Not tonight,' she whispered. 'Don't think about that tonight.'

Ten minutes after everyone arrived, Deborah realized with a mixture of dismay and irritation that Evan and Barbara were furious with each other. Barbara was overly merry, almost giddy. Evan's forced smiles came out as grimaces. They never touched, never met each other's eyes. Wonderful, Deborah thought glumly. Apparently the tension she'd sensed when she'd sent Barbara home the other night had only escalated. Everyone in the room except the children noticed. Joe watched expressionlessly, Pete threw them wary looks, and Adam openly gazed at them with a gleeful glint in his eyes, as if he thought this dull gathering might turn out to be interesting after all.

The evening limped along with the adults struggling to make pleasant talk while Barbara kept interrupting with stridently bright comments followed by high-pitched laughter, usually cut short by an acerbic burst from Evan. After the first half-hour, Joe caught Deborah's eye and winked. She had to force herself not to laugh, although she was increasingly annoyed with the bickering lovers.

The children played, blissfully unaware of the stress in the air. They ran the train under the tree, pointed out their red stockings which Deborah had hung on the mantel, and anxiously asked everyone if they thought the fireplace was big enough for Santa's landing. 'He's *real* fat, you know,' Kim solemnly told Pete, who assured her with equal gravity that Santa was very flexible and could get into anyone's fireplace, or even use the front door.

She and Steve always allowed the children to open one present each on Christmas Eve. Kim selected a long one wrapped in red with a gold bow and squealed happily when she withdrew a beautiful golden-haired bride doll nearly as tall as herself. 'Her name is Angie Sue Robinson,' she announced promptly. 'She's marrying a rich man with a lot of mansions and an airplane.' Brian selected a slightly smaller package but seemed equally happy with his 'Strobe Robot.' 'My grandmother always got me licorice,' Pete said. 'I hate licorice.'

Deborah laughed. 'Where *is* your grandmother this year?'

'Her closest friend Ida fell and broke a hip. Grandma is convinced Ida will never be able to walk again unless she is there to oversee her medical treatment. I suggested Adam and I spent Christmas with her, but Adam had some plans for Christmas Day. We'll go up next weekend.'

Adam didn't look too happy at the prospect. Deborah knew he loved his grandmother, but at fifteen, weekends had too much potential to be spent sitting around a grandmother's house.

Kim scrambled under the tree until she found a wrapped gift for Scarlett. The children laughed as the dog eagerly tore off the wrapping paper and triumphantly withdrew a giant beef-basted chew bone. '*That* should keep her busy for a while,' Adam commented as the dog retreated to the corner and began furious, noisy gnawing.

'Now you, Mommy,' Brian said.

'Don't you want me to wait until tomorrow?'

'Nope. We have presents for tonight *and* tomorrow.'

They brought her two clumsily wrapped presents, each bearing approximately half a roll of Scotch tape. From Brian she received a Coke can decorated with Christmas stickers and bearing holes in the top.

'A pen holder,' he told her.

'It's beautiful!' Deborah exclaimed.

'We had to make stuff 'cause Daddy was gonna take us to buy your gifts,' Brian went on sadly.

'I like this much better than a gift from the store,' Deborah assured him.

Kim had wrapped red felt around a piece of foam rubber and fastened it with paste. 'Pin cushion,' she said simply.

Deborah enthused over the gifts as did everyone else. The children seemed happier than they had for days, and later, when Deborah put them to bed, Brian even allowed her to kiss him.

Before everyone else left, Deborah handed out gifts amid pleased protestations. 'Don't worry, the gifts are by no means extravagant. Just little remembrances. Besides, you all seem to think I didn't see you slipping gifts under *my* tree.'

'We all brought fruit cake,' Evan said, his first pleasant remark of the evening.

'That's great,' Deborah laughed. 'Unlike a lot of people, I *love* fruit cake.'

Pete and Adam were the first to leave, Pete reminding her again to call if she needed anything. A few minutes later, Barbara asked half-heartedly if Deborah wanted her to stay. 'It isn't necessary,' Deborah said, longing for a moment alone with Barbara to ask what was wrong between her and Evan. 'Joe's doing a great job of looking after us.'

Barbara looked relieved, and Deborah knew she was deeply troubled. Otherwise, she would never have left her alone another night. They didn't have the intensely close friendship a lot of women had with each other, but they had great loyalty.

Five minutes later Evan and Barbara were back. 'Car won't start,' Evan said tightly. 'We'll have to call a cab.'

After three phone calls, however, he announced they couldn't get a cab for at least an hour. 'I'll take you home,' Joe said. 'That is if Deborah doesn't mind being alone for half an hour.'

Deborah took one look at Barbara and Evan's stiff, angry faces and knew that within an hour it would be all-out war. 'I'll survive. It's not even very late.'

Silently the three of them trooped out to Joe's car. Deborah locked the door behind them and set to work cleaning up the paper, ribbons, and wads of tape left on the floor, then washing the dishes left by her guests. Finally she fixed a snifter of brandy and sat down in front of the fire, wondering if things would ever get back to normal in this house. Even her attempt at a pleasant Christmas Eve had failed because of Barbara and Evan. Normally she would have been concerned, but tonight she was only annoyed that they'd dragged their troubles into her home. As if she didn't have enough to worry about . . .

The phone beside her armchair rang. Steve's mother home from Hawaii? she wondered. Or worse, maybe the police with bad news. She picked up the receiver. 'Hello?'

There was a long sigh, then the familiar husky, disguised voice said, 'Merry Christmas, Deborah.'

Her hands turned icy, but this time she didn't slam down the receiver. 'Who is this?' she quavered.

'You know who it is. Did you have fun tonight? You certainly had enough men around you '

'Men?'

'Well, I wouldn't call one of them a man. But you know those raging teenage hormones. He'd probably be happy to bed you.'

Although she was alone, Deborah's cheeks turned crimson. The hand holding the receiver involuntarily jerked toward the cradle, but she forced herself to stop the motion. She swallowed. 'You must mean Adam.'

'I must.' He paused. 'I have to go now. Enjoy your Christmas.'

He hung up and Deborah sat motionless, holding the receiver and barely breathing. Finally she, too, hung up. Rigid with fear, she stared at the Regulator clock ticking calmly above the couch until Joe finally returned.

'Where the *hell* have you been for the past hour?' she demanded.

Joe's eyes widened. 'Barbara and Golden Boy aren't cohabiting tonight. I had to take them to their respective apartments. God, they're mad at each other.' He looked at her closely. 'What happened?'

'I got another call. He wished me a merry Christmas.'

'Is that all he said?'

'No. He also said I should have enjoyed the evening because I had so many men around me, and that even the teenager would probably be happy to *bed* me.'

'Holy shit.' Joe dropped his jacket on to the couch and sat down, leaning forward with his hands hanging down between his knees. 'It probably came from a pay-phone, but not the same one that was used last night. That one is being watched.'

'But the police can't watch every phone in the city. That means I could keep getting these calls.'

'Did you recognize his voice?'

'No, but it was so distorted. All I could tell was that it belonged to a man.'

'What about speech patterns?'

'I've never heard Steve talk about "bedding" someone, but then I've never known anyone but a character in books or movies use the expression, either. Nothing else stood out.'

Joe watched her quietly for a moment. Then he said, 'I'm getting you another brandy and myself a whiskey and water. Be right back.'

While he was out in the kitchen, Deborah went to the hall closet and took out a heavy sweater. Her hands were trembling and she felt as if a block of ice had lodged in her stomach.

Joe returned quickly with the drinks. She took a sip of brandy and leaned her head against the back of the chair. 'Dear God, is this ever going to end?'

'It's only been a few days, although it seems like a lifetime.'

'He was watching us again, probably from the O'Donnell house.'

'Maybe, but he didn't call from there. That would be too easy to trace. Besides, the police are keeping a closer eye on that place since you saw someone in the window. I don't think someone could come and go as easily as they used to.'

'What about the man who rented it? Who *is* he? *Where* is he?'

'The police don't know yet. Or if they do, they're not saying anything.' The doorbell rang. 'Oh great,' Joe snarled. '*Now* what?'

'Joe, who would be stopping by now? It's ten o'clock.'

Joe looked at her. 'Wait a minute.' He left the room, then came back holding his gun. 'You stay behind me. I'll answer the door.'

Deborah's palms suddenly grew wet. How absurd it seemed to have an armed man answering her door. Still, she couldn't have answered it herself, not after that phone call.

She hovered in the hall while Joe yelled, 'Who's there?' through the closed, windowless door.

'Delivery,' a young male voice yelled back.

'Who sent you?'

'Dale Sampson of Dale Sampson Deliveries,' a young male voice answered. 'I'm Dale.'

'I've heard of him,' Joe whispered to Deborah.

'What are you delivering?' he called through the door.

'I don't know, man. It's something in Christmas paper. Weighs three or four pounds. And it's *cold* out here.'

'Leave it on the porch,' Joe ordered.

'Hey, I'd love to, but I got a policy. Somebody's gotta sign for it.'

'Who is the package addressed to?'

'Oh, jeez,' Dale Sampson said in disgust. 'Wait a minute. There's a tag. I can barely see it. Ever think about putting a stronger bulb in this porch light? Deborah Robinson. That's what the tag says.'

Joe looked at Deborah. 'Want to take a chance?'

'He sounds far too young to be Artie Lieber.'

Joe nodded and unlocked the door, holding the gun behind him. A thin young man of about nineteen stood shivering on the front porch. He thrust a medium-sized package at Joe. 'If this is a bomb or something, I wish you'd hurry up and take it.'

'I don't hear any ticking,' Joe said calmly. 'Sorry to give you such a rough time, but this is an unusual hour to be delivering Christmas presents.'

'You're tellin' me. But that's why I got the job. The big companies in

170

town don't deliver to private homes at this hour. Not cost effective, they say.' He grinned. 'That's why young entrepreneurs like me get the extra work.'

Joe set the package down on the hall table and took the clipboard Dale held out to him. 'Who asked for this special delivery?'

'I don't know. I go to college and my girlfriend takes calls when I'm in class. This evening she told me this package had to be delivered at ten o'clock on the dot. I thought maybe ten had some symbolic meaning. A lot of people go in for that, you know. Symbolism, I mean.'

'I know what you mean. Do you know who sent the package?'

'She said it was some guy.'

'Any idea about a name?'

Dale rolled his eyes. 'Maybe she took it down. If they pay cash, though, sometimes she doesn't. She forgets.' Dale shrugged. 'Sloppy, I know, but she works for free.'

'Didn't she say anything about the sender?' Deborah asked. 'It's very important.'

Dale sighed. 'Okay. Let me think.' This took a few moments of foot-tapping as he stared to the right. 'Okay, I do remember her saying something about him. His name was . . . Travis. Let's see . . . yeah, Travis McGee. Name seemed familiar to me – that's how come I remembered.' Joe's eyes flashed at Deborah. Clearly he, too, recognized the name of John D. MacDonald's famous private detective. 'Come to think of it, you look kind of familiar,' Dale said to Joe. 'Do I know you?'

'You've made deliveries to the Prosecutor's office where I work,' Joe answered, handing him back the clipboard.

'Hey, that's it! You don't look like a lawyer, though.'

'I'm not. Listen, Dale, could your girlfriend give us any more information about this Travis McGee?'

'Does this involve a big case?' Dale asked excitedly.

'Maybe. I can't be sure until I get a description of the man who sent the package.'

'Well, my girlfriend notices guys' looks. That bothers me, but maybe she could help you.'

'But she didn't tell *you* what the man looked like?'

'No, but if it's so important, you could call her later. Her name's Marcy. I got my own listing in the Yellow Pages. Dale Sampson Deliveries. Got a little corner store. My dad financed it. I live upstairs. Marcy lives with me and she'd be glad to tell you anything she knows.'

He smiled ingratiatingly but made no move for the door. Joe reached into his pocket and withdrew a five dollar bill 'Thanks for going to all the trouble of delivering this so late, Dale. And I will call your girlfriend later. You won't mind, will you?'

'Shoot, no. You're way too old for her.'

In spite of the situation, Deborah smothered a smile at the boy's innocently egregious remark, but Joe didn't seem insulted. 'Yeah, I'm probably old enough to be her father. Thanks, son. Better get back in your car out of this cold.'

When Dale had gone, Joe turned to Deborah. 'This is no ordinary Christmas gift. Do you have some rubber gloves?'

'Gloves?'

'I don't know how many people have handled this package, but I'd bet it's no more than Dale, Marcy, me, and the sender. It looks perfect – no frayed corners, bow not mashed. I might be able to get some physical evidence from it.'

'I see. I have gloves in the kitchen.'

Joe stood in the hall while she went into the kitchen, picked up her rubber gloves from the cabinet under the sink, and rinsed them off. Then she remembered she'd bought a new set just a couple of weeks ago. She rummaged through the cabinet and found them, still in their plastic wrapper. She carried them into the hall. 'Brand new.'

'Great. I think they're too small for me. You put them on and open the package.'

'You're just afraid this really *is* a bomb,' Deborah said, trying for lightness while her hands shook.

'I'll stand outside while you open it.'

'Very funny. You stay where you are. I refuse to be blown up by myself.'

Once she'd stuffed her cold hands inside the gloves, she picked up the box from the hall table. It was wrapped in silver paper decorated with green and red wreaths. The bow was red, large, and had obviously been bought at the store, not tied by hand.

'Open it very carefully, touching as little as possible.'

'I always open packages that way. My mother was a fanatic about saving Christmas paper. I was never allowed to just tear into a gift.'

She ran a hand under one of the flaps on the end and gently loosened the tape. Peering inside, she saw a brown cardboard box. She slipped her hand into the tunnel of loosened paper and managed to slip out the box without tearing the wrapping.

'Good job,' Joe said quietly. He peered at the box, which read, 'Kitcheneer. Combination Meat Grinder and Food Chopper'.

'This can't be a meat grinder.' Deborah's voice quavered. The words conjured up a terrible image.

'I don't think it's a meat grinder,' Joe said reassuringly. 'Open the top.'

Being as careful as she had been before, Deborah slowly peeled back the tape that held the lid closed. When she opened the box, she saw styrofoam chips. She looked at Joe. 'It must be something fragile. Do I just dig through this packing?'

'Yeah. Go ahead.'

Deborah plunged her hands through the chips until her fingers came into contact with something hard. She pulled it up and gazed at a box made of cherry wood with ornate carvings around the sides. A small gold clasp held the lid. Slowly, she turned the clasp and lifted the lid. Musical notes tinkled through the hall.

'It's a music box.'

'And a pretty nice one,' Joe said. 'What's it playing?'

Deborah frowned. 'I know it. It's an old song.'

'I know it, too, but I can't quite get it.'

'Something about a glow . . . oh hell, why can't I remember?'

'Close your eyes and concentrate a minute.'

Deborah did as Joe directed. They both stood very still, eyes closed, Deborah holding the beautiful music box in her yellow-gloved hands. They listened for at least thirty seconds and Deborah was on the verge of saying, 'I can't remember,' when abruptly a scene popped into her head. Fred Astaire. Fred Astaire singing to Ginger Rogers, whose hair was full of shampoo. ' "The Way You Look Tonight!" ' she said triumphantly.

'That's it!' Joe beamed. 'How does it go?'

'I can't remember all the words. Snatches. "Someday, when I'm low . . . a glow." Oh, wait a minute. I think I'm getting it.' She closed her eyes again and the words floated out of her mouth, words that seemed to come from nowhere. ' "Someday, when I'm awfully low/When . . . the world is . . . cold/I will feel a glow . . . just thinking of you/And the way you look tonight." '

'Great!' Joe congratulated her.

Deborah smiled for a moment, then grew serious. 'Joe, the man who called me the other night said, "I love the way you look tonight." What does it mean? Why would someone anonymously send me a music box that plays this song?'

Joe was peering into the cardboard box. 'It may not be an anonymous gift. There's an envelope inside.'

Deborah set down the music box and looked in the box. In the bottom lay a red envelope. She picked it up. It was not sealed although a card was tucked inside. She pulled out the card, on whose glossy cover was a beautiful Christmas tree. Inside, the card simply read, 'Season's Greetings'. There was no signature, but a note on cheap white paper dropped to the table. Deborah picked it up. Joe looked over her shoulder so she didn't have to read the typewritten words that turned her cold all over:

My dear wife,
To keep you company all year long,
A box to play your favorite song.

18

'Is "The Way You Look Tonight" your favorite song?' Joe asked quietly.

'No. My favorite song is "Greensleeves".'

'Did Steve know that?'

Deborah felt as if she could hardly get her breath. 'I'm not sure. I may have mentioned it, but I don't know that he'd remember.'

'Was "The Way You Look Tonight" Steve's favorite song?'

'I don't think he had a favorite song. He never paid much attention to music.' She paused. 'At least, not that I know of. But then I don't seem to know much about my own husband.'

'Do you like the Travis McGee series?'

'Very much.'

'Did Steve know *that*?'

'I don't know,' she said miserably. 'When he read, it was mostly history. He never asked what I was reading.'

'Well, Artie Lieber certainly couldn't know you liked MacDonald's work.'

'No . . .'

Joe looked at her sharply. 'What is it?'

'Only that I have several boxes full of books in the storeroom upstairs. The whole Travis McGee series is in those boxes. Whoever was in that room could have looked through the books. Oh Joe, I'm scared.'

'You're supposed to be. And the damned thing is, I don't think we're going to find out much about this package. The note is typewritten and I'd bet my last dollar whoever sent it wore gloves when he handled it.'

'But the sender *couldn't* be Steve.' Her words emerged almost as a wail and she swallowed, regaining control. 'I mean, *why*? Why would Steve, or Artie Lieber for that matter, send me a music box and a note that doesn't make any sense?'

Joe looked reflectively at the box. 'I think the note does make sense,' he said slowly, 'I think this song has some significance, not for you but for the person who sent it.'

'Such as?'

'Could be anything. Something so obscure we'd never understand it.'

'Then what would be the point of sending it to me if I'd never understand it?'

Joe's right hand tightened into a fist, then relaxed. She'd begun to recognize this as a sign that he was thinking deeply. 'You're right. Why send you something you couldn't understand? The message has to be more obvious.' His forehead wrinkled. ' "The Way You Look *Tonight*." '

Deborah glanced down at her red blouse and black slacks. 'I'm semi-dressed-up tonight, but I wasn't the other night when he called. I was in an old robe.'

'Now wait. Let's try this. "The Way You *Look* Tonight." ' Deborah stared at him questioningly. 'Maybe the emphasis isn't on transitory appearance depending on what you're wearing, but on your physical appearance. Your build, your features. *That* could be the significance.'

'What about appearance? I don't understand.'

Joe's eyes went from wondering to consternation. 'Oh, hell, I'm afraid I do.' He rushed into the living room again and came back with a notebook. 'After the FBI visited Steve a few days ago, I made a list of The Dark Alley Strangler's victims and their descriptions.'

'What for?'

'Like everyone else, I've followed the killer's activities, but not in detail. When Steve told me the FBI suspected him and he asked for my help, I decided to study The Dark Alley Strangler as if I were a homicide detective working the case.'

'How did you get your information?'

'I still have contacts,' Joe said abstractedly. 'Now, I want you to hear the list so you'll understand where I'm headed with this line of reasoning, okay?' Deborah nodded. 'Here goes. Victim number one was killed in August 1991. Mandy Lambert of Waynesburg, Pennsylvania. Age twenty-two. Bank teller. Five foot eight, one hundred and thirty-two pounds, long dark brown hair, blue eyes. Victim number two was murdered in February 1992. Jane Kawalski of Bellaire, Ohio. Housewife. She was twenty-nine, five foot seven, one hundred and thirty pounds, long black hair, brown eyes. Next came a grocery-store manager, Margaret Snyder, in June 1992.

Margaret lived in Washington, Pennsylvania. She was twenty-three, five foot nine, one hundred and thirty-six pounds, and had long dark brown hair and green eyes. October 1992, our guy killed Patricia Latta, twenty-four, of Cambridge, Ohio. She was a waitress with long, dyed black hair and gray eyes. She was five foot seven, one hundred and twenty-eight pounds. In August 1993, the victim was Karen Macy of Zanesville, Ohio. She was a student at Ohio State University home on summer break. She was twenty, five foot seven, one hundrend and twenty-five pounds, with long dark brown hair and brown eyes. October 1993, Leona Chesbro of Bethel Park, Pennsylvania, was murdered. She was an aerobics instructor, five foot ten, twenty-nine years old, one hundred and thirty pounds, with long brown hair and blue eyes. Victim seven was Sally Yates, twenty-one, of Wheeling. She was a nurse. Height five foot seven, weight one hundred and twenty-five pounds, and she had long black hair and green eyes. Sally's still alive, although she's in a coma and not expected to live. Last victim was Toni Lee Morris, housewife, five foot eight, one hundred and thirty pounds, long dark brown hair and blue eyes.' He looked at Deborah. 'So what do they all have in common?'

'Long hair.'

'Long *dark* hair, above average height, slenderness.'

Deborah's eyes instinctively flew to the mirror over the hall table. 'I have long dark hair.'

'Height and weight?'

'I'm five foot eight. My weight fluctuates between one hundred and twenty-five and one hundred and thirty.'

'And you're in your twenties.'

'I'm twenty-eight.' Deborah swallowed. 'So you're saying the killer picks his victims on the basis of their looks and age?'

Joe looked at her steadily. 'Also the fact that they're married. And Deborah, you fit the profile perfectly.'

19

ONE

Deborah stood staring at Joe for what seemed an age. Sound roared in her ears and she experienced a feeling of unreality. Finally she managed to say in a rough voice that didn't sound like her own, 'Joe, this has to be a coincidence.'

'That's what you said about the woman who spotted Steve's license plate.'

'You're saying you think Steve *is* this killer and I'm a potential victim?'

Joe looked at her gravely. 'I *do* believe you're a potential victim.'

'But what about Steve?'

'That part gives me a lot of trouble.'

Deborah hesitated. 'Why?'

He put a comforting hand on her arm and smiled. 'Come sit beside me on the couch and I'll tell you.'

He led the way and Deborah followed, almost blindly. At this moment she wanted someone to take control, to tell her everything was going to be all right.

She didn't so much as sit on the couch as collapse on it. Joe sat nearly a foot away.

'I'm not basing my point of view on my personal feelings about Steve,' he started slowly. 'Impressions can be wrong. I'm looking at the facts. I don't know exactly what's going on. I do think you're being targeted, and that scares the hell out of me. But targeted by Steve, the man you've lived with for seven years? It doesn't make sense. If he was this person, the

Strangler, why would he wait until now to come after you? What's changed about you? Nothing. Besides, he has to know you're under surveillance. You're not wandering around by yourself, hanging out in bars. Besides, the FBI theory is that he staged his own death because the net was closing in on him, so why would he surface again *here*, in Charleston, only days after this elaborate disappearance, to terrorize his own wife? That's not the best way to make it look like he's dead at the hands of some ex-con.'

Deborah thought. 'No, it wouldn't be the wisest thing for a *rational* man to do, but the Strangler isn't rational.'

'Isn't he? Maybe his reasoning isn't the same as ours, but he has a very strong sense of reason all his *own*. These people always do. And he's wily as hell. Now does this stunt with the music box seem like the act of a frighteningly calculating man, a man cautious and smart enough to elude the police for all these years?'

'Then you think it's a prank?'

'Maybe. But that doesn't feel right, either. I think whoever sent you that music box is dangerous and has an agenda all his own, one that would seem crazy to us but makes perfect sense to him.'

'This is getting too convoluted for me,' Deborah said stubbornly. 'I don't understand all this FBI behavioral scientist bull.'

'Oh yes you do, or you wouldn't have even known I was talking "FBI behavioral scientist bull" as you put it.'

'I watch television.'

Joe grinned. 'Deborah, come off it. Don't hide behind ignorance because you're scared. We're talking about the workings of a man with sick but incredibly convoluted logic.'

Deborah's eyes dropped. 'The mind of the Strangler,' she said hollowly. She raised her eyes. 'Which may be the mind of my own husband.'

TWO

Deborah slept uneasily that night. Twice she tiptoed in to check on the children, and once she realized she had been standing at her bedroom window peering through the mini-blinds for twenty minutes. The night was cold and clear. A stiff breeze had risen earlier in the evening and the evergreen branches moved restlessly against a star-strewn sky. Deborah thought of the birds that had probably taken refuge from the cold in their thick, feathery limbs. 'These trees are better than birdhouses,' Steve had told the children last summer when he was cutting them in a way necessary to prevent malformation after they'd been trimmed into the conical Christmas-tree shape. 'The birds stay warm and safe in these branches, even if it snows.' Would a man who showed such concern for plants and animals – even birds – beat, rape, and strangle all those young women? It seemed hard to believe – no, impossible to believe. The FBI had totally missed the mark on this one. Her husband was missing and probably dead. But had he been a killer in life? Absolutely not.

Still, she couldn't stop thinking about the Strangler's victims. Emily flashed into Deborah's mind, Emily with her long dark brown hair and slender frame. Was she tall? Deborah had only seen her seated. But she *was* married.

She also thought of all the things Steve had left unsaid. Why hadn't he told *her* Emily was secretly married and he'd heedlessly gone in search of the husband when Emily was attacked? Was it because he knew Deborah had never heard the rumors about him being Emily's attacker and he therefore wasn't on the defensive? And what about the music box? The note had read, 'My dear wife'. True, anyone could have written that salutation. But what about the description Dale Sampson's girlfriend Marcy had given of the sender? Around six feet tall, early thirties, slender, brown-haired, and wearing dark-tinted glasses. That could be Steve. It could also be a thousand other men in the city.

However, there was the raid on the savings account. What was the explanation for Steve withdrawing six thousand dollars the day before he disappeared? Was it for an elaborate Christmas gift? No. Steve leaned toward the practical, not the extravagant. He would never have spent such a sum on a gift, especially at the cost of wiping out their savings account.

Nervous and unbearably frustrated from the unending turmoil of her thoughts, Deborah's craving for a cigarette returned. I'm too weak to resist right now, she thought, going to her bedside table where two aged Salems rested in a crumpled pack. She lit one, inhaled deeply, and felt her stomach lurch. The cigarette tasted like burned rags. She tried two more puffs and when her mouth began watering dangerously, she stubbed out the cigarette. Everyone told her that after a long hiatus from smoking, the first cigarette tasted awful, but she thought they'd been exaggerating. They weren't.

Her eyes filled with tears. Damn it, on top of everything else was she to be denied the simple comfort of a cigarette? She went into the bathroom and looked at her reddened eyes, knowing she was acting as childishly and petulantly as Kim and Brian did sometimes. 'Pull yourself together,' she said sternly into the mirror. 'Everything is out of control, but you can't let yourself go, too. You have to stay strong for the children.'

She sniffled into a tissue, guiltily took a sip of Pepto Bismol directly from the bottle (how many times had she told the children what a nasty habit *that* was?), then brushed her teeth vigorously.

She walked back into the bedroom, her mouth tasting pleasantly like peppermint. The house seemed so quiet. Earlier she'd heard the television downstairs, but Joe must have turned it off and gone to sleep on the couch. Otherwise she would have gone down for some company. Unhappily, she climbed back into bed and pulled up the comforter. In spite of the warmth, she shivered. What had her mother always said when a person inexplicably shivered? She announced in a sepulchral voice that someone was walking on your grave. 'Well, that's ridiculous,' Deborah said aloud. 'No one can be walking on my grave if I'm not in it.' She shivered again. 'If I'm not in it *yet* . . .'

THREE

A figure stood in the shadows, beckoning. Deborah strained to see through the dark. She took a step forward. Something jabbed her on the shoulder. She tried to brush it away, but the jabbing continued. She moaned, then slowly became aware of someone saying, 'Mommy?'

She opened her eyes. Brian stood beside the bed, steadily tapping her on the shoulder. 'Mommy, get *up*.'

'What's wrong?' Deborah cried, immediately alert.

'Kim and Scarlett are gone.'

She jerked up from the pillow. 'Gone? What do you mean, gone?'

Brian looked bewildered and a little frightened. 'They're gone, Mommy, and it's still dark out.'

Deborah glanced at the clock: 3.30. She flung back the covers, her heart pounding. 'Kim must be downstairs,' she said, struggling to sound calm in spite of her fear.

'Nope. I already looked.'

'You looked *everywhere*?'

'Yeah. She's not here.'

'Where's Joe?'

'Sleepin' on the couch.'

Deborah grabbed her robe. 'Did you wake him?'

'Nope.'

No, he wouldn't, Deborah thought. Brian was still a young child, and in times of trouble he would instinctively run for a parent. 'Did you check the storeroom?'

Brian shook his head. 'Kim wouldn't go in there. She's scared of the dead boy's ghost.'

Deborah rushed down the hall and flung open the door of the dusty storeroom. Cold air hit her in the face. She flipped the switch and the naked bulb sprang to life. Her eyes shot around the room. 'Kimberly, are you in here?' Silence. Nothing except boxes and big footprints made by the policemen and Joe. There was no sign of a little blonde-haired girl. Still, Deborah circled the room, looking in every corner and behind every box.

'Mommy, I told you she wouldn't come in here,' Brian persisted.

'Yes, all right,' Deborah said distractedly. She turned off the light and, without closing the door, hurried to the guest room. It, too, was empty.

Downstairs she shook Joe awake. He looked at her groggily and mumbled, 'Go 'way.'

'Joe, wake *up*,' Deborah said breathlessly. 'Kim is missing.'

'And Scarlett,' Brian added.

Comprehension slowly dawned in Joe's eyes. He threw off his blanket. He was wearing a tee-shirt and gray sweat pants. Deborah had never seen him in anything except jeans. 'Kim's gone? She can't be. She has to be in the house somewhere.'

'Kim? Scarlett?' Brian yelled. He puckered his lips and made a futile attempt to whistle. 'Here, Scarlett! Here, girl!'

The three of them were still for a moment, but there was no response. 'Where could she be?' Joe asked.

Deborah's mouth worked but nothing came out. All she could think about was the man who'd tried to lure Kim away from the school.

'Damn it, I'm usually a light sleeper,' Joe fumed, breaking the silence. 'I guess I've lost too much sleep lately and it caught up with me. I can't believe Kim went out the front door and I didn't hear her, though.'

'I already checked it,' Deborah said. 'The dead-bolt is secured. You can't secure the dead-bolt from the outside without a key, and Kim doesn't have a key.'

Joe was pulling his boots on to bare feet. 'Deborah, you search all the downstairs rooms. I'll look in the back yard.'

The house was not large. 'All the downstairs rooms' consisted of the living room, dining room, Steve's study, and the kitchen. They were empty. Frantic, Deborah ran to thc back door. 'Any luck?' she called to Joe, who was circling the evergreens with a flashlight.

'Not a trace,' he called back.

'Damn,' Deborah muttered. She started out the door to join him when a terrible thought hit her. For a moment her muscles locked in a paralysis of fear. 'Oh, God, no,' she whispered.

'What is it, Mommy?' Brian asked.

She didn't answer. She pushed past him, flying to the door leading to the garage. Once again she'd forgotten to put on slippers, and the cold concrete floor sent chills up her legs.

'Please, *please* God, let me be wrong,' she muttered desperately, reaching the big freezer in which she'd found Brian's toy fire truck the night before Steve disappeared, the freezer for which she'd forgotten to buy a padlock. 'Please don't let her be here.'

With trembling hands and closed eyes, she pulled on the handle and slowly lifted the lid. She took a deep breath and opened her eyes.

Her scream tore through the frigid quiet of the garage.

20

Deborah wasn't sure how much time passed before she realized she was in Joe's arms. 'What is it?' he demanded. 'Deborah, what *is* it?'

Her body shook violently and she couldn't see clearly. She couldn't speak, either. She pointed mutely at the freezer whose lid had fallen from her hands, slamming shut.

Joe paused, then turned her loose. He lifted the freezer lid while Deborah shook and whimpered. She was dimly aware of Brian standing stiff with fear in the doorway, staring at them. Joe peered into the freezer. He drew in his breath sharply. Then he reached inside.

'Oh, God,' Deborah moaned. 'My little girl.'

'It's all right,' Joe said softly. 'It's only a doll.'

Deborah's ears roared and she thought she hadn't heard him correctly. 'What?' she croaked. 'What did you say?'

'It's Kim's bride doll.' He held it out to her. 'Her doll.'

Deborah looked at the big doll with its fall of golden hair so like Kimberly's. The hair was stiff and the doll's beautiful face was clouded by a shroud of frost. It was wrapped in Kim's pink afghan, the bridal gown barely showing.

As Deborah stared at the doll, her vision darkened and for a moment she thought she was going to faint. Then the light returned along with her breath. She promptly burst into tears.

Joe closed the freezer, laid the doll on the lid, then folded Deborah in his arms again. 'For a second I thought it was Kim, too. That afghan makes it look bigger. But it isn't Kim.'

'I've never been so horrified in my whole life,' Deborah sobbed. 'If it *had* been her . . .'

'It *wasn't*. But you've got to get hold of yourself. We still have to find her.'

'I'm right here.'

Deborah and Joe both whirled to face the little girl who was holding tightly to Scarlett's leash. The dog's tail wagged vigorously, as if she were delighted with the crowd in the garage. A young man wearing a suit stood beside Kimberly. 'Found her running down the street,' he said. 'Deakins, FBI.'

'Boy, are *you* in trouble,' Brian told Kim in an awed voice. 'I bet you go to jail.'

Deborah's terrible fear and relief were immediately converted into anger. 'What on *earth* were you doing?' she shouted at Kim.

The child quailed. 'Nothin'.'

'Nothing? You were outside because of *nothing*?'

Kim's face crumpled and tears flowed. 'I thought I heard Santa,' she cried.

'Santa!' Deborah exploded. 'With everything that's been going on, you went out looking for *Santa*?'

Joe put a hand on her arm. 'Take it easy, Deborah. She's just a little girl. You're scaring the hell out of her.'

'She scared the hell out of *me*,' Deborah flared. Then she looked at the shivering child who just a few minutes ago she'd thought was dead. Her anger vanished. She rushed to Kim and clutched her in her arms. 'Oh, Kimmy, I'm sorry I yelled. We were all so worried about you.' Kim sniffled pitifully. 'Honey, why did you go out searching for Santa?'

'I heard the bells on the reindeer.'

'Bells?'

'Yeah.' Kim wiped the back of her hand across her wet face. 'I thought Santa and Rudolph were in the back yard.'

'But Joe looked for you in the back yard.'

'I was a little scared so I took Scarlett with me. I put her on the leash, just in case she was gonna chase the reindeer, but she started growlin' and pulled away from me. The gate was open and she ran down the street. I had to get her.'

'And you were wearing just your robe and bunny slippers,' Deborah scolded gently. 'Your cold will get worse for sure.'

'What was Scarlett growlin' at?' Brian asked. 'The reindeer?'

'We didn't see any reindeer,' Kim told him in disappointment. 'I never saw anybody.'

Agent Deakins shrugged. 'My partner and I didn't see anything, either. We did hear bells a few minutes before the little girl came tearing down the street. We thought someone in the neighborhood must be ringing them. Then we remembered that the only people on the street are you folks and Mr Dillman next door. Didn't seem likely any of you would be ringing bells, though.'

'Could the sound have been coming from another street?' Joe asked.

'This isn't a housing development,' Deakins said. 'The next street is nearly a quarter of a mile away. The sound was too loud to have come that far.'

Kim gazed beyond Deborah to her bride doll lying on the lid of the freezer. 'Angie Sue!' she cried. 'What happened to her?'

'Kim, did you put the doll in the freezer?' Deborah asked.

Kim looked affronted. 'The freezer? No! I'd never do that to Angie Sue!' She turned furiously on Brian. 'You put her in there!'

'Why would I do that?' Brian stormed back at her. 'I never touch your dumb old dolls. Besides, I'd get into trouble.'

'Well, someone put the doll in the freezer,' Deborah said in a small, tight voice.

Joe looked at her bleakly. 'And it just happened to be on a night when somebody thought you might be looking for Kim.'

TWO

Deborah didn't think she could possibly go back to sleep, but she was dozing when someone began tapping on her shoulder again. 'Mommy,' Kim stage-whispered.

Deborah jerked upright, her nerves tingling. 'What's wrong?'

Kim recoiled, startled. 'It's *Christmas*. Santa's been here.'

Deborah fell backward. 'Oh, is that all?'

'Is that *all*,' Kim repeated, appalled.

'It's fifteen minutes till seven o'clock,' Brian said.

Kim nodded vehemently, apparently for once not bothered by her brother's time announcements. 'Yeah. Fifteen minutes till seven o'clock. *A*.m.'

'Oh, heavens. You two wouldn't by any chance still be sleepy, would you?' Deborah asked, feeling too exhausted by the night's events to step out of bed. 'We could open presents a little later.'

'*No*,' the children said in firm unison.

Oh, to have the resiliency of a child, Deborah thought. They acted as if last night had been as peaceful as any other. They didn't even look tired.

'Okay,' Deborah groaned. 'Someone hand me my robe. I'm too sleepy to find it.'

To her relief Joe was already up and had made coffee. They sat, just as she and Steve did every Christmas morning, drinking coffee and watching the children tear into presents with abandon.

Kimberly squealed over her AM/FM headphone radio and Brian smiled in satisfaction when he saw his toy night-laser gun. They immediately began writing on their doodle pads. Then both looked up and said, 'Now you two give presents.'

'We didn't get anything for each other,' Deborah said.

'Well, actually, I picked up a little something for you the night I went to the drug store for Kim's medicine,' Joe said. He thrust a package at Deborah. Embarrassed, she opened it to find a piece of Napier jewelry, a chain with a rhinestone heart. Joe must have realized it seemed slightly romantic because he said quickly, 'I saw the necklace and it reminded me of what a warm heart you have, just like my mother. I got her one, too.'

The same gift he'd given his mother. No one could misconstrue that message. Deborah smiled. 'It's lovely. Thank you so much. But I don't have anything for you. I haven't been able to go shopping—'

He held up his hand. 'I didn't expect anything. Besides, you've fed me for days. That's a fine gift, if you ask me.'

'We've got real gifts for you,' Kim piped. Once again they produced mangled-looking packages which Joe opened with great ceremony. Kim gave him a Bic pen which Deborah knew came from Steve's desk. Brian produced Volume Seventeen of the West Virginia Code. Deborah could see a smile dancing around Joe's mouth as he held Steve's law book. 'I can read the book and take notes with the pen. Thanks, kids.'

Vastly pleased with themselves, the children brought out two more gifts for Deborah. Brian's was a photograph of him and Scarlett glued to red construction paper. 'One of my favorite pictures,' she said. 'Thank you so much, honey.'

'It's not as good as mine,' Kim said, handing her a soft, oddly shaped package wrapped in green paper. 'What could *this* be?' Deborah asked enthusiastically.

'It's my secret,' Kim beamed.

'The one you've been talking about?'

'Yeah. You're gonna really, *really* like it!'

Deborah tore through the familiar mass of Scotch tape and pulled back the paper to reveal a plastic sandwich bag filled with jewelry. She unsealed the top and dumped the pieces on to her lap. Wedding bands and earrings. Puzzled, Deborah picked up a wedding band and read aloud the inscription: 'Sally and Jack'.

Stunned, she dropped the band and picked up a filigree earring. 'Good God,' Joe muttered as the sunlight fell on traces of red and a tiny bit of something that looked like shriveled mushroom clinging to the wire hook.

Deborah stood, ran to the bathroom, and vomited.

THREE

Ten minutes later she returned to the living room to find Joe holding Kim on his lap as she cried. She looked fearfully at Deborah and said, 'I'm sorry, Mommy. I thought you'd like it.'

'The jewelry is beautiful, honey,' Deborah managed shakily. 'Where did you find it?'

'In the hidey-hole.'

The 'hidey-hole', as Kim had christened it, was a three-foot-by-three-foot hole that led to the part of the house without basement beneath it. Steve had covered it with a small, latched wooden door and warned the children away from it with warnings of 'big, horrible bugs' that lived in the dirt inside, but apparently Kim's curiosity outweighed her fear.

'When did you find it?' Joe persisted.

'A couple a days ago.' Kim wiped her tear-streaked face. 'Did I do something wrong?'

'You looked in the hidey-hole,' Brian informed her censoriously. 'We're not s'posed to do that.'

'It's all right,' Deborah said. 'Did you see . . . Daddy put this stuff in the hole?'

'Nope.' Kim looked at her wide-eyed. 'It's *pirate's* treasure from the olden days.'

Deborah and Joe exchanged glances. 'Think pirates left it?' Deborah asked him lightly, aware of the children's worried faces. This must not touch them, she thought. Someday Kim would know what a ghastly 'treasure' she'd found, but for now Deborah had to put the best possible face on the matter.

'I'm not sure if pirates were in this area,' Joe said solemnly. 'We're pretty far away from the ocean, but this is a *very* old house. Somebody could have hidden it *years* ago.'

'How many years ago?' Brian asked.

'Ummm . . . fifty.'

The answer seemed to satisfy both children. Even Kim's eyes dried and she quickly scrambled back to the floor to retrieve her headphones.

'You kids play with your toys and I'm going to make some more coffee for Joe and me. Do you two want toast or cereal?'

'Pancakes,' Brian said distractedly. 'But not now.'

With distaste she could barely mask, Deborah clutched the plastic bag and went into the kitchen. Joe followed, took the bag from her, and sat down at the kitchen table while she vigorously washed her hands. 'There's blood and flesh on those earrings,' she said shakily. 'How long do you think the jewelry has been there?'

'Considering the wedding ring you picked up, since after the attack on Sally Yates. That was two weeks ago.'

'There's nothing from the last murder?'

'I don't know what was taken from the Morris woman. Besides, didn't Kim start talking about having a secret before then?'

Deborah's forehead wrinkled. 'I think so. Yes.' She took a deep breath. 'I guess this just about seals it, doesn't it? Steve put that jewelry in the hole in the basement.'

Joe's eyes slewed away from hers, and she realized that at last his own faith in Steve was wavering. 'It looks that way.'

'And yet . . .'

'And yet?' he repeated alertly.

'Remember when we were talking about the possibility of the Strangler wanting to be caught and you said he didn't?'

'Sure.'

'Suppose Steve is this psychopathic killer. He wouldn't want to get caught. So why hide this jewelry in the basement where the kids play?'

'He told them never to open that door and look in the hole.'

'Unless children have changed a lot since my day, that's a sure-fire way to make sure they look in it.'

Joe looked at her thoughtfully. 'You're right. Steve would have known that eventually one of them would investigate.' He paused and glanced away. 'And if he *did* go away to create a new identity, he wouldn't want to drag this stuff with him. Someone might find it. But with him being gone from this house, it wouldn't matter if the jewelry was found here or not, would it?'

FOUR

Deborah spent the rest of the day trying to make light conversation, trying to act like she was enjoying the turkey dinner she'd fixed complete with chestnut dressing, two vegetables, and cranberry salad. 'I'm going to weigh three hundred pounds when I leave here,' Joe said, leaning back in his chair after dinner. 'I don't know how Steve managed to keep his weight down.'

'We don't always eat this way,' Deborah said. She sighed. 'I usually fix a plate for Mrs Dillman. I guess I could take something over to Fred.'

Finally it was decided that Joe would deliver the plate, which he reported was accepted gratefully. 'He was on the phone with his wife when I got there. I don't think the conversation was going too well.'

'Speaking of unhappy couples, I wonder how Barbara and Evan are doing?' Deborah mused as she scrubbed the roasting pan with a steel-wool pad.

'She'll be calling later to give you a full report.'

'Not on a tapped phone. Maybe she'll come by.' Deborah stopped scrubbing and looked at Joe. 'I've been so concerned about taking Barbara away from Evan, I haven't even considered your love-life. I hope my problems aren't causing trouble for you.'

Joe grinned. 'Are you asking if I have a jealous girlfriend? No. There are a couple of women I see occasionally, but that's it. I haven't been serious about anyone since Lisa back in Houston.'

'I'm sorry, Joe.'

'It was years ago. I'm over it.'

'Are you happy?' she asked impulsively.

Joe considered the question. 'I'm not happy and I'm not unhappy.'

'Sounds boring.'

'Sometimes. Any more dishes, Mrs Robinson?'

'Not for about an hour. The children will be ready for a snack then.'

Joe laid down the dishtowel and looked at her. 'Do you know how proud Steve was of you and the children?'

Deborah stared. 'Proud. Of *me*? I don't think so.'

'He was. He didn't talk about you very much, but when he did, he got a certain look in his eyes.'

'And now you think he might be trying to kill me.'

'I guess that is a hard one to swallow. And I only said the Strangler *might* be Steve. But Deborah, whoever the Strangler is, he's very complicated.'

'So is Steve,' Deborah said. 'He's smart. Dedicated.' She paused. 'And troubled.'

Joe nodded. 'I know. That's the part that worries me. I always thought the trouble was caused by what happened to Emily. Now I'm not so sure. I can't forget Pete saying some people thought *Steve* attacked Emily. Would they think that just because Lieber said so? Or had people noticed something unusual about his relationship with his sister?'

'I guess that's something we'll never know.' Deborah looked out the kitchen window at the patches of white that remained from last night's brief snowfall. 'We *can* know if we go to Wheeling and talk to some people.'

'You want to go to Wheeling?'

'Yes, I think I do.'

'Deborah, the Emily business happened a *long* time ago.'

'But people remember that kind of thing. There has to be someone with more answers than Pete has.'

'And what if you find out more about Emily's assault? What does that have to do with now?'

'You know the FBI thinks Steve might have attacked Emily. They believe the pattern was set then. I think that has a great deal to do with what's happening now.'

'Maybe you're right,' Joe said. 'But maybe you'd just be opening up a whole can of worms and regret it later.'

'At this point I'd rather know something awful for certain than know nothing and tear myself apart with doubts and questions. I want to go to Wheeling,' Deborah said determinedly. 'I want to go tomorrow.'

FIVE

As Deborah predicted, Barbara did want to talk with her, but not over the phone. She arrived at seven o'clock looking haggard and thin, her eyes red-rimmed from crying. Joe tactfully disappeared to the basement to play with the children while Barbara accepted a drink and sat on the edge of the couch, too nervous to relax against the back cushions. 'I'm the worst friend in the world,' she began dramatically. 'With all you're going through, I haven't been here for you. And now I'm here to talk about my own problems.'

'You were here when I needed you most,' Deborah said mildly. 'You *do* have a job and your own life with Evan.'

Barbara's dark eyes filled with tears. '*What* life with Evan? I hardly see him any more. Deborah, he's been so strange lately. He makes excuses to get away from me. The evening you sent me home to spend a romantic night with him, he picked a fight about my not wanting to put up a Christmas tree of all things! Oh, God, I don't know what to do.'

'You can calm down for starters.' Barbara took a sip of her Scotch and soda and looked expectantly at Deborah, as if awaiting more advice. 'I don't know Evan very well. I've been around him for years, but we always stuck to small-talk, so I can't give you any insight about how his mind works. All I know is that everything seemed fine the night of the Christmas party. Maybe he's just upset about Steve.'

'He *is*,' Barbara said. 'He even . . . well, never mind.'

'He even what?' Deborah demanded, hating it when people started to tell her something obviously important then broke off.

'Well . . . he's begun to think maybe Steve *is* the Strangler.'

'Oh, really?'

'Deb, please don't look like that. You've wondered yourself. I've seen the doubt in your eyes.'

How could she deny it after her reaction to the jewelry this morning? She wasn't going to tell Barbara about the wedding bands and earrings, though. She didn't want to endure a hundred questions. She also didn't want to think about it any more that day.

'I suppose we've all considered the possibility that Steve is the Strangler,' she said neutrally.

Barbara took another sip of her drink. 'At first Evan thought it had to be someone Steve worked with because that person would know Steve's routine, be able to set him up.' She said this last in a rush and Deborah blinked at her. That particular possibility hadn't occurred to her. She'd focused only on Steve and Artie Lieber. 'Frankly, I've begun to wonder . . .'

'You've wondered what?'

'If he was right. If Steve isn't the killer, then it *could* be someone he works with. And Evan has been acting so bizarre.'

'You think *Evan* might be a serial killer?'

'It crossed my mind,' Barbara said abjectly. 'Of course, Joe's been acting a little odd, too.'

Deborah looked at her in astonishment. 'Joe? What odd thing has he done?'

'He's become your watchdog.'

Aware that Barbara's voice, its normal volume raised through tension, was probably floating down to the basement through the furnace ducts, Deborah cut her off. 'Barb, Steve was . . . *is* Joe's friend. Joe is protecting his friend's wife and children.'

'That's what I told Evan, but he wasn't convinced. At least, he acted like he wasn't.' She looked away, biting on a thumbnail, then burst out, 'Evan picked the fight about the Christmas tree the night that Morris woman was murdered. What if he was just trying to get away from me so he could . . . so he could . . .'

'Rape and strangle a young woman outside a bar? You can't really believe that.'

Barbara's gaze dropped. 'Deborah, do you know that Evan and I have *never* been together on a night when one of those women was murdered? I keep a diary and I went through it last night That's how I know for sure. And the O'Donnell house was rented to someone named Edward King. Evan Kincaid. E. K.'

Deborah gaped at her. 'Barbara, do you know how flimsy all this sounds? It's as if you *want* to believe Evan is guilty. Is that preferable to thinking maybe he just doesn't want this relationship any longer?'

Barbara's eyes opened wide as if she'd been slapped. 'That was a *vile* thing to say.'

'And what you're implying about Evan isn't? Barb, you're my dearest friend, but you're going off the deep end because Evan has been edgy and distant for a few days.'

Barbara gave her a long, hard look. 'You're mad because I haven't been staying with you, so you're trying to hurt me.'

'That's absurd.'

Barbara set down her drink and stood. 'I can see I came to the wrong person with my problem.'

'Oh, Barb, get off your high horse. I'm your friend and I'm not trying to hurt you, but you're letting your imagination run away with you. I have to tell you what I think.'

'Thank you for your learned opinion,' Barbara said stiffly. 'I'll be going now.'

'Barbara, *please* don't act this way—'

Her words were cut off by the slamming of the front door.

Deborah leaned forward and put her head in her hands. She was still sitting that way when Joe walked into the room. 'You have more important things to think about than Barbara's tantrum.'

'You heard,' Deborah said, lifting her head.

'Every word, including those about my own suspicious actions.'

'I'm sorry.'

'Don't be. And Barbara shouldn't be either.' Deborah lifted her eyebrows in surprise. 'You were a little hard on her, Deborah.'

'But you heard the accusations she was throwing around. They were dangerous.'

'Deborah, we don't know who The Dark Alley Strangler is,' Joe said gravely. 'Is it dangerous or is it *smart* to consider all the possibilities?'

'But she thought that you, or even *Evan*, could be guilty.'

'And just how well do any of you really know me? As for Evan, well, I thought she made some pretty good points. *He's* the one who brought up the angle of Steve's being set up by someone he worked with. I figure he was trying to throw suspicion on me, maybe because he really suspects me, but maybe he did it to deflect suspicion from himself. And it's quite a coincidence that he and Barbara have never spent the night together when a murder has taken place. Remember, all except the last one happened on a Saturday night. Isn't that when people usually go out on a date or spend the night together? And what about this "E. K." business? Don't ask me why, but people have a tendency to pick assumed names with the same initials as their real names. Also, those checks to the realty company come from a Charleston bank. As you said when you first heard about Edward King, why would someone rent a house and leave it vacant, especially someone who probably lives in this city?'

'Stop,' Deborah said, rubbing her temples. 'I feel like I'm floundering around in quicksand. I can't think about the possibilities because there are too many and they're too frightening. For now all I can concentrate on is Steve and Emily and Artie Lieber.'

'Then you still want to go to Wheeling tomorrow?'

'More than ever.'

'And you still want me to take you?'

'Yes,' she said firmly, although later in bed she kept hearing him say, 'And just how well do any of you really know me?'

21

ONE

'How well do any of you really know me?'

Deborah shut her eyes. I will not think about what he said, she told herself. Joe is not a killer and neither is Evan. 'But you're not so sure about your own husband, are you?' her mental voice intoned derisively.

She glanced at the clock: 6.30. If they left by eight, they could be in Wheeling well before noon. That would give them plenty of time to do what she wanted and get back around nine o'clock.

The night before, she had called Pete to ask if he would look after the children for her. She had refused to say why because of the phone tap, although she knew she and Joe would probably be followed. At least she didn't have to provide an itinerary, though. If the FBI wanted to follow, they'd just have to keep up with her and Joe.

The children were unaccountably cranky. 'Where are you goin'?' Kim kept asking. 'How come we can't go?'

'It's a long trip,' Deborah told her. 'You wouldn't have any fun.'

'But Pete doesn't have any toys at his house,' Brian said.

'We'll take toys. Now quit grousing and get your clothes on. And I expect you to behave today.'

She left them griping in their room while she packed up some of the toys they'd received for Christmas. Pete had also agreed to keep Scarlett. Deborah didn't like leaving her alone all day, and she knew the dog would help entertain the children. Along with the children's toys she collected Scarlett's food and water bowls and her yarn tug-of-war toy. The huge beef-basted chew toy would stay at home because it sometimes left stains, and Pete had expensive rugs.

By 7.30 they were pulling up in front of Pete's large white colonial home less than a mile from Deborah's. She'd always admired the house, especially because Pete had tried to maintain the colonial feel with carefully selected antiques. Joe waited in the car while Deborah took the children and Scarlett, straining at her leash, up to the door. Pete greeted them and ushered them into the living room, where sunlight poured in through a Palladian window, making the furnishings of saffron and cream even brighter.

'Pete, this is so nice of you,' Deborah said, removing the children's coats.

'It's no problem whatsoever. I do wish you'd tell me what's going on, though.' She hesitated, and Pete abruptly said, 'Children, why don't you set Scarlett's dishes in the kitchen, wherever you think she'd like. I'll be right in to fill her water bowl.'

The kids looked at each other. 'They don't want us to hear,' Brian said owlishly, and they marched off with the dog trailing behind.

'They don't miss much, do they?' Pete said, smiling. 'I remember Adam at that age. Hope and I resorted to spelling. We kept it up for a year before we realized he could spell remarkably well.'

'I don't think Kim and Brian can, but I don't have the patience for spelling today,' Deborah said. 'Joe is taking me to Wheeling.'

Pete's eyes flickered. 'Wheeling? Whatever for? To see Emily?'

'Among other things. I have this feeling, Pete, that somehow what's going on now is connected to what happened to Emily all those years ago.'

'How could that possibly be?'

'I'm not sure,' she evaded, then saw the knowledge in his eyes. He knew she was wondering if Steve had indeed attacked his sister.

'Deborah, I don't think this is a good idea,' he said sternly. 'Lieber is still on the loose. Besides, what I think you're hoping to find the truth about happened a *long* time ago. The trail is cold, as they say on those police shows.'

'Maybe not. Maybe there's something everyone else missed.'

'And you're going to find it in one day?'

'I hope so.'

Pete sighed. 'Deborah, I can't help saying I'm a bit worried about you going off with Joe. He seems nice enough, but—'

'What do we really know about him?' she finished automatically. 'I

197

trust him. He's been a tremendous help. And so have you.' Impulsively, she flung her arms around Pete and hugged him, her eyes filling with tears. He stiffened in surprise, then relaxed and patted her back.

'Deborah, you're really not in shape for this trip.'

She pulled away, wiping her face. 'I'm okay. Besides, I *have* to go. If I don't find out anything, then I don't. But at least I'll know I tried.'

Pete lifted his hands in resignation. 'I suppose I can't stop you.'

'But you can help me in one more way. What was the name of Steve's girlfriend, the one who provided him with an alibi for the time of Emily's attack?'

Pete's eyes flickered, then he frowned. 'Deborah, I can't remember. He hadn't been seeing her for long and I think she moved away after high school. Let's see. Jane? Joyce? Something like that, but neither of those sound exactly right, and the last name is completely gone.'

'Oh well, I guess it's not that important.'

'I'm sorry. But there is one stop I'd like you to make if you have time, and that's at my grandmother's house. I missed not seeing her over Christmas and I want to make sure she isn't overdoing the Florence Nightingale act with her friend Ida.'

'Of course, Pete. I'm sure we can work in a short visit.'

'Wonderful. I'll jot down the address.'

Before she left, Adam came downstairs, his hair as rumpled as his tee-shirt and jeans. 'Where are the kids?' he asked abruptly.

'The kitchen,' Deborah told him.

'And you brought the dog?'

'Yes.'

He smiled. 'Great. I've got a big day planned for them.'

'Maybe Deborah doesn't want them to run around all day,' Pete said. 'Kimberly did have that cough.'

'She's okay now, isn't she?' Adam asked.

'She's much better. Just don't let her overdo it.'

'I'll take good care of both of them,' Adam said, looking into her eyes.

Deborah was touched. How many fifteen-year-old boys would so happily assume responsibility for two little children?

'Don't you worry about a thing,' Pete said, handing her an index card bearing his grandmother's address. 'Adam and I will watch over the children. And Deborah – even though I don't have much faith in this mission of yours, good luck.'

TWO

Deborah and Joe hardly spoke until they drove out of Charleston and headed north. Deborah kept searching her mind for topics of conversation and coming up blank. She knew her mouth was pressed into a grim line, but she couldn't relax. Finally Joe said, 'It's too quiet in here,' and pushed a CD into the player. A moment later guitar sounds followed by those of a haunting flute filled the car before The Marshall Tucker Band broke into 'Can't You See'. Deborah hadn't heard the song for years and after a few seconds realized her foot was bobbing along to the rhythm. She caught Joe's eyes on the moving foot. Then, suddenly, he burst out with 'Can't you see what that woman's been doin' to me?' in a strong singing voice. She smiled and a moment later began singing with him. They followed with 'Heard It in a Love Song', then 'Searchin' for a Rainbow', both exaggerating western twangs until, laughing, Deborah said, 'Sorry, Joe, that's the end of my Marshall Tucker repertoire.'

'Well, I learned something about you,' Joe said, turning down the volume. 'You're a closet rock star.'

She blushed but nodded. 'I remember one night when I was fourteen I stayed overnight with my friend Mary Lynn. She had hundreds of cassettes, and while her parents were out to dinner we put on a concert in her bedroom. I've never been so mortified in my life as I was when her parents opened the door and I was standing on Mary Lynn's bed belting out "Stayin' Alive" into a hairbrush.'

Joe threw back his head and laughed. 'My brothers and I started a band. We got two gigs – a family barbecue and my sister's sixteenth birthday party. After the party I heard one of my sister's friends, a girl I had a huge crush on, say, "If they think they're good, they've been out in the sun too long. Jack knows about five notes, Joe sounds like a dying cow, and Bob looks like he's having some kind of seizure." '

'That must have hurt,' Deborah giggled.

'We were devastated. No world tours. No adoring groupies. No *Rolling Stone* covers. Then we thought about what a pain all that rehearsing was and abandoned our musical futures.'

'So you became a policeman and I became a secretary.'

'And the music world lost two of its brightest lights.'

They continued chatting lightly about their childhoods for the next two hours, and Deborah felt the tightness leave the muscles of her back. Then the sun disappeared and Deborah's tension returned as a slate-blue sky pressed down on them. By the time they entered the Wheeling city limits, her hands were trembling. 'Have you ever been here?' she asked Joe.

'No.'

'I only came once with Steve to see Emily. I've never even been to the historic district.'

'What's there?'

'Shops and restaurants built during the Victorian era. Oglebay Park is here, too. November through early February they have a light festival with around five hundred thousand lights in the shapes of things like snowmen and wreaths. Steve said we'd bring the children up this year right before Christmas—'

Her throat contracted and she stifled a sob that startled her as much as it did Joe. He reached over and patted her hand. 'Take it easy, Deborah.'

She swallowed hard. 'I'm sorry.'

'Want to go home?'

'No. I can't. I don't understand my own certainty that I'm going to find something out here. Maybe it has to do with the fact that Steve only brought me here once even though I asked repeatedly to come. He didn't want me here. *Why?* Because he didn't want to drag his new life into his old one? Or because he was afraid I'd find out something?'

'Deborah, I'm not trying to talk you out of spending the day here. You just looked a little shaky for a minute.'

'I'm all right.'

'Good. Where's our first stop?'

'The nursing home to see Emily.'

THREE

Artie Lieber was on the move. Christmas Eve he removed a blue Toyota from a driveway and exchanged the license plate with that of a station wagon he found parked by a curb three blocks away. He made himself endure Christmas Day in his motel room, sitting through one saccharine Christmas special after another. He could remember watching such shows with his little Pearl so long ago. He wondered if she watched them with her kid.

At last evening came and he made a pass by the Robinson house, feeling relatively safe in his new car. He'd seen that short-haired woman he'd spotted the day after Steve Robinson's disappearance storming out of the door. She'd paused by her car and stared at the big two-story brick place across the street. With a start he knew what she was looking for. Well, she wouldn't see it. No face in the window now, baby, he thought with satisfaction. But she had a determined expression he didn't like. She wasn't one to leave things alone. She was the type who'd go snooping, and that wouldn't be too smart of her.

Now it was the morning of 26 December. He'd always found Christmas depressing and he was glad it was over. He ran a razor over his chin, noting that except for that damned tic around his eye he was still a good-looking guy. And he was *whole*. They hadn't broken him in prison. Not by a long shot. He was a man of action and he was mad at himself for wasting so much time waiting, spying, playing games. Now it was time to get going again. Now it was time to get things done.

FOUR

The smells of medicine and illness assailed Deborah as she and Joe approached the nursing-home reception desk. A harried-looking nurse with short, gray-laced blonde hair and a peevish expression glanced up. 'Yes?'

'We're here to see Emily Robinson.'

The nurse's dark eyes grew wary. 'Miss Robinson isn't allowed visitors at the request of her family.'

'I made that request,' Deborah said. 'I'm her sister-in-law.'

The nurse's eyebrows shot up. 'You're Steve's wife?'

'That's right. You know my husband?'

'Yes. I'm Jean Bartram. Didn't he ever mention me?'

'No, I'm sorry, he didn't.' Jean looked even more peevish. Deborah

201

had an absurd impulse to apologize for Steve, but controlled herself. 'Could we see Emily?'

Jean's eyes narrowed. 'If you want to visit Emily, I have to see some identification. Ever since all this news broke about your husband disappearing, reporters have been pestering the life out of us, trying to get a picture of Emily, passing themselves off as family members. And I've never seen you before.'

Deborah was outraged that reporters had been attempting to get to Emily. What did they expect? A statement from her concerning the possible whereabouts of her brother?

She fought to keep her expression composed, in spite of her churning emotions. 'Steve and I have two young children,' she said, rummaging in her purse for her billfold. She withdrew her driver's license and handed it to Jean. 'I don't visit Emily with Steve because I have to stay home with the kids.'

Jean looked at the picture on the license and handed it back to her. 'I understand. It's not like you can really visit with her anyway.'

'But I was told she does say something now and then.'

'Oh, yes. She could talk if she wanted to, but she won't.'

'I think the problem is a bit more complicated than mere obstinance,' Deborah couldn't help retorting.

'Are you a doctor?' Jean flared.

'No.'

Jean shrugged, then looked at Joe. 'Who's he?'

'Joe Pierce. He is a very good friend of the family and working with the police in their search for my husband.'

Jean looked at him dubiously. He met her gaze with his own, and Jean's eyes dropped. Deborah put her license back in her purse as Jean came around the desk, clearly, if not graciously, intending to take them to Emily's room. 'Sometimes she says several words together,' Jean said. 'At least, I think they're several words. You can't really understand her when she does that. Other times she says one word very clearly.'

'Is it the same word?'

'Yes. Usually it's "Steve".'

'Not Mom or Dad?'

Deep creases formed between Jean's eyebrows. 'No, I don't believe I've ever heard her mention them, although they come to see her most weekends.'

'Does she say anything else?'

'Christmas.'

Deborah and Joe both looked at her. 'Christmas?'

Jean raised her shoulders. 'Your husband said she loved Christmas. She says it just as plain as day. He always brought her gifts.'

Deborah felt stricken. Christmas was yesterday and there had been no present from Steve, nor had she brought one. It had never occurred to her that Emily was aware of the holiday.

'Here we are,' Jean said, stopping beside a heavy wooden door. 'She has a private room. Those are hard to come by around here. Ready to go in?'

'Yes,' Deborah murmured, although she didn't feel ready at all. She'd visited Emily years before, when she and Steve were first married, but he'd controlled the visit then, talking to his sister as if she understood every word he said and keeping up a steady stream of chatter that had taken the awkwardness from the encounter. Now Deborah was in charge, and she didn't know what to do.

Jean swung open the door. Emily was sitting in a chair facing a large color television. A soap opera was playing. Emily's eyes were fixed on the show, but it was impossible to tell whether or not she comprehended anything. As they drew nearer, Deborah spotted a trace of gray in her long, brown hair, which had grown dull since her last visit. Her skin also looked paler and dryer than when Deborah had seen her last. She was wrapped in a kimono-style robe made of silk and bearing a delicate pattern in lilac and yellow. Someone had tied back her hair with a lilac ribbon, and her feet were encased in white leather house slippers.

Joe paused in the doorway, but Deborah walked directly up to her. 'Hello, Emily,' she said softly, kneeling beside her chair. 'You probably don't remember me, but I'm Steve's wife, Deborah.'

Emily's face remained immobile. Up close, Deborah could see that her long-lashed green eyes were just as beautiful as ever, but her lips were chapped and tiny lines surrounded them. Still, even in this unadorned condition, she bordered on beautiful. Marring the picture, though, was a jagged scar on her forehead where she'd been hit by the pipe, and a narrow ligature mark around her neck where her assailant had drawn a wire tight, cutting the fragile skin.

'I've brought a friend with me to visit you,' Deborah went on brightly, trying to mimic the way Steve had talked to her long ago. 'This is Joe Pierce. He works with Steve.'

Joe slowly stepped forward. Deborah sensed his reluctance and was surprised. She had thought nothing fazed Joe, but apparently the sight of this lovely, eerily motionless woman daunted him 'Hello, Emily,' he said in a bright, unnatural voice.

Jean lingered at the door. Deborah wished she would go, but didn't want to ask her. Besides, maybe there was a reason why she stayed. Maybe she didn't quite trust these two strangers around Emily. Or maybe Emily was prone to unexpected outbursts of some kind. Deborah decided to ignore the woman, and sat down on the bed beside Emily's chair while Joe stood, uncomfortably tapping his fingers on the television top.

'You're wearing cologne,' she said. 'It's very nice.'

'It's *Charlie*,' Jean piped up. 'Ever since she came in here she's worn it. She gets really riled up if we don't put it on her every day. Her mother said she always wore it before . . . well, you know.'

'I've always liked the fragrance,' Deborah said.

'It's okay. I like *Giorgio* myself, but I can't afford it.'

How fascinating, Deborah thought. She turned her attention back to Emily. 'I suppose Steve has told you about your niece and nephew,' she continued, thinking she sounded like a fool, chattering gaily away to someone as unresponsive as a statue. 'Their names are Kimberly and Brian. They're very bright, but full of mischief. I have a picture here , , . ' She fumbled for her billfold again, then drew out the most recent picture of the children, smiling broadly and unnaturally for the camera. She held the picture in front of Emily, who blinked and said nothing.

'We also have a dog,' Deborah went on. 'Her name is Scarlett. Kim named her after Scarlett O'Hara. Steve told me *Gone with the Wind* used to be your favorite book. I have a picture of her, too.' She displayed a photo of Scarlett, her eyes turned alien red by the camera's flash, clenching a rawhide chew bone in her mouth. What on earth am I doing, rattling on like an idiot and showing Emily a photograph of the family dog? Deborah thought. She started to put the picture away, feeling foolish, when suddenly Emily said, 'Sex?'

Deborah jumped at the sound of the voice, rusty from disuse, issuing from the immobile face. 'Sex?' she repeated, glancing at Jean, who looked stupefied, then grinned. 'What are you talking about, Emily?'

The right corner of Emily's mouth lifted slightly. 'Sex,' she said softly, affectionately.

'Was Sex your dog?' Deborah asked desperately.

Joe looked at Deborah with humorous disbelief. 'A dog named "Sex"?'

Emily gazed at the picture. 'Sex. Christmas.'

Deborah glanced at Jean, who spread her hands in bafflement. 'This is a new one on me. I never heard her say "sex" before.'

Deborah turned back to Emily. 'Was Sex a dog you got for Christmas?'

'Christmas.' Very slowly, Emily raised her hand toward the photo. 'Sex.'

Deborah handed her the picture of Scarlett. Emily's hand closed loosely around it and dropped back to her lap. 'Sex,' she said again, this time with a note of sadness.

Deborah felt like crying. What was Emily trying to say? Whatever it was, it had something to do with a dog, but certainly 'Sex' hadn't been its name. They would probably never know. For now she must be satisfied with giving Emily the photo. That would have to be her Christmas present.

She looked at Joe, who seemed to realize suddenly that she expected him to do more than shift back and forth like a restless elephant. He came over and knelt opposite Deborah beside Emily's chair. 'Hi, Emily, I'm Joe,' he said stiffly. 'Deborah wanted to visit you at Christmas, so I brought her.'

'Christmas.'

Deborah looked at Jean again, who commented, 'She's a regular chatterbox today. I haven't heard her say this much for ages.'

You don't have to talk like she's not in the room, Deborah thought in irritation. Obviously Emily understood quite a bit of what was going on around her.

Joe smiled at Emily. 'Do you remember the last time you saw Steve?'

The corner of Emily's mouth that had lifted earlier fell back into place. 'Ed.'

'Ed?' Deborah repeated.

'He's an orderly here,' Jean said. 'Always makes a big fuss over her. She's confused.'

Joe tried again. 'No, Emily, not Ed, your brother Steve. He came to see you.' His eyes shot to a plant in a pot swathed in red foil sitting on the chest of drawers. It was oleander. 'Did Steve bring you the plant?'

'Steve. Christmas.'

Deborah looked at Jean, who nodded. 'He brought that the last time he was here. Gave us all kinds of instructions about how to take care of it, like we don't have enough to do around here without running a plant nursery.'

Deborah's feeling towards Jean had turned from annoyance to dislike. Her petulant voice grated on her nerves.

'Did Steve bring you the plant for Christmas?' Deborah asked.

Abruptly, Emily turned her head, lifted her hand and ran it down the length of Deborah's hair, which she hadn't pulled back in the braid. 'Sally!'

'Sally?'

'Sally Yates,' Jean said, and Deborah felt as if a jolt of electricity had passed through her.

'She knows Sally Yates?'

'Yeah. Sally used to work here. Not for long, though. Found out she could make more money somewhere else. Quit a few months ago. The old geezers here were devastated. She was kind of pretty and had a body like some fashion model. Probably spent all her free time doing exercise. She flirted like crazy with the old guys, acting like they were Kevin Costner, or Richard Gere, or Favio.'

'Fabio,' Deborah corrected absently. Jean scowled. Obviously the woman couldn't stand Sally Yates, but Deborah wasn't concerned with Jean's personal feelings. She was still reeling from the news that Sally had actually worked in the nursing home. 'Did Mrs Yates spend much time with Emily?' she asked.

'Sure. Another one of her special pets. Brushed Emily's hair. Did her nails. Put make-up on her.'

'Did my husband know Sally?'

'I guess so. I don't keep up with everyone's social lives.' Jean seemed to become aware of her catty tone. 'I feel real sorry for her, nearly being killed and all. And then it happened again.'

'What do you mean, it happened again?' Joe asked sharply.

'She regained consciousness and someone got in her hospital room night before last and tried to slit her throat. Sally wasn't hurt – a nurse surprised him. He stabbed *her* in the abdomen. She's going to live, but she's so scared she can't remember what he looks like. Or else she's lying. Sally won't say anything, either. Not that I blame them. I wouldn't want some homicidal maniac out there thinking *I* could identify him.'

Deborah had begun to tremble inside. She wanted to ask a dozen questions, but not in front of Emily. Jean might think the patient had the awareness of a stone, but Deborah knew better.

She turned back to Emily and forced another bright smile. 'Emily, did you enjoy Christmas? Did you enjoy seeing Steve last week?'

Emily abruptly dropped the strand of hair she'd been caressing. She stared again at the television, but Deborah was aware of her hands tightening almost imperceptibly. 'Emily, are you listening to me?' she asked, leaning closer to her. 'I asked if you enjoyed seeing your brother—'

Suddenly Emily gasped, her eyes widened, and she screeched, 'Steve, no! Hurt! Steve, hurt!'

Deborah nearly fell backwards in shock and Joe jumped to his feet. Jean ran to Emily. 'You'd better leave,' she ordered, while trying to restrain Emily's flailing hands.

'But what's wrong?' Deborah asked in horror.

'I don't know. You upset her,' Jean said accusingly. 'I've only seen her like this a couple of times, years ago.' Emily's hand caught Jean sharply on the cheek, and the woman cursed. 'Great. Now we'll have to give her Thorazine and that causes her to have periods of apnea. Hold *still*, dammit! I'll probably have to sit with her the rest of the whole damned day.' Another nurse passing by the door stopped. 'Get Dr Hatten,' Jean snapped, then looked at Deborah. 'Please get out. Now!'

Deborah and Joe rushed from the room, but even in the hall Deborah could hear Emily keening, 'No! Steve, hurt! No!'

22

They sat in the Jeep in the parking lot of the nursing home for ten minutes while Deborah drew deep breaths, trying to calm down. Emily's terror at the mention of Steve's name had sent her reeling. Was it true that *Steve* had been her attacker? Could he possibly have done something so awful to his own sister? And was she only the first of several victims?

'You're white as a sheet, Deborah,' Joe said. 'Had enough for today?'

'Believe me, I'd like to head for home as soon as possible, but I can't. I still want to get into the Robinson house, providing they aren't back yet. But we can't do that until dark.'

'So what do we do in the meantime?'

'I would give anything to know the name of Steve's girlfriend at the time of Emily's attack. Maybe she could tell us something.'

'Pete didn't give you her name?'

'He said he didn't remember. However . . .'

Joe raised his eyebrows enquiringly. 'However?'

'I did promise him I'd stop in to see his grandmother Violet. Maybe I can get the name from her.'

Joe smiled. 'Very resourceful.'

'I'm learning a lot about myself lately.' She withdrew the address Pete had jotted down from her purse. 'Do you mind?'

'I'm a willing chauffeur today. Just tell me where we're headed.'

TWO

'We'll make this visit short, I promise,' Deborah told Joe fifteen minutes later as they climbed out of the Jeep in front of Violet Griffin's attractive brick home.

'I don't mind, but don't forget we have at least one more stop to make and the sky isn't looking good. The radio said snow by midnight, but I wonder if it's going to hold off that long.'

Deborah looked up and frowned. 'You're right. Maybe we should just forget this—'

The front door of the house swung open and a short, round woman with fluffy white hair stepped out. 'Why, hello!' she called in a high, fluting voice. 'Deborah. And you must be Joe. I talked to Petey today and he said you were coming to Wheeling.'

Deborah could never get used to hearing the woman call her slightly proper and dignified grandson Petey. But then he'd been reared by his grandmother since he was ten.

'I was hoping you'd stop by,' Mrs Griffin went on, motioning them into the house with staccato waves of her plump arm. 'Petey didn't say you would for sure, but I hoped. Deborah, you're even prettier than when I saw you last Christmas. A little thin and pale, but pretty as a picture.'

'Thank you, Mrs Griffin. I hope we're not bothering you. I know you're looking after your friend.'

'She's doing just fine. Sleeping like a baby in the guest room right now. And no more of this "Mrs Griffin" business,' she went on, pulling at the sleeves of Deborah's coat before she got it off and fluffing her long hair. 'I'm Violet or Vi. That goes for you, too, Joe.'

Deborah saw a faint smile hovering around Joe's mouth as Violet began tugging at his jacket. Deborah half expected the woman to fluff *his* hair when the jacket came off.

'Now you two come right inside and warm up. I baked a cake just in case you stopped by. It's vanilla with vanilla icing. Do you like vanilla? I thought that would be safest. It isn't everyone's favorite, but I've never met anyone who hates it. A piece for both of you?'

'Just a small piece,' Deborah said. 'We can't stay long.'

Violet's blue eyes sparkled behind her glasses. They were young eyes for a woman Deborah knew to be in her late seventies, but her complexion was florid from high blood pressure. 'I'll fix two big pieces and you just eat what you can. There's fresh coffee, too. You go into the living room and I'll be right there.'

'Do you need some help?' Deborah asked.

'No, no. Just relax. Sit by the fire. I just love a fire on a cold, dreary day like this, don't you?'

Without waiting for an answer she dashed into the kitchen. Joe shrugged, grinning, and they walked into the living room. A natural stone fireplace dominated one end. A fire crackled cheerfully inside. Early American furniture sat on a huge braided rug surrounded by shining oak floors. A console television set with a large screen flashed a game show although the sound had been turned down. Everything looked new, a sharp contrast to Mrs Dillman's pathetically worn decor.

Deborah wandered over to a wall where a grouping of photographs hung. A couple in 1940s wedding garb posed stiffly, their eyes wide above tremulous smiles. Violet and her new husband, Deborah guessed. Another picture showed a young man who looked remarkably like Mr Griffin. Judging from the clothing style, Deborah assumed it to be the Griffins' only son, Pete's father. Below it hung a photograph of a dark-haired woman holding a baby. The baby was obviously the focus of the photo, but the woman stood out with her large, smoky eyes and beautiful half-smile. Next was one of young Pete in a Boy Scout uniform, then one in a graduation cap and gown. Beside these hung the image of Adam as he'd looked a couple of years ago.

'Oh, I see you're admiring my collection,' Violet said, carrying in a tray. 'I'm a great believer in letting people see what a wonderful family I have, especially my boys.'

'Your son was a fine-looking man,' Deborah said, sitting down and accepting a piece of cake so large it threatened to overflow the sides of the plate.

'Yes, my Nelson was a handsome devil.' Her curiously unlined face grew troubled. 'But maybe that wasn't such a blessing. He always attracted the wrong kind of women. That wife of his . . . well, if it weren't for her, my son would be alive.'

Pete had told Deborah his parents died in a car wreck. She didn't know what Violet meant and she felt uncomfortable pursuing the subject, but the woman didn't need prompting. 'She was loose. Man-hungry. I thought she might change after Petey came along, but she didn't. Couldn't get enough men, and with Nelson being a salesman and on the road so much, she had the perfect opportunity to pursue all the men she wanted. His daddy and I told him to leave her, but he wouldn't. He stayed, but he drank. Then one night, one horrible night, he drank too much and went out in the car and . . .' Her lower lip trembled. 'At least he died instantly. That's what the doctors told me. He never felt a thing.'

Deborah was nonplussed by this outpouring, especially after the scene with Emily, but she felt it wouldn't be polite to switch the subject abruptly. 'Didn't his wife die in the wreck with him?'

Violet looked vague. 'What? Oh, yes. The neighbors said they had a terrible argument and Nelson left, probably coming to see me, and she ran out and jumped in the car as he was pulling away. Left Petey playing in the yard. Thank God she didn't drag him along. At least *he* was spared. And what a good boy he's always been. I think I would have lost my mind if it hadn't been for him.' She shook her head. 'Isn't it odd that he married someone just like his mother? Liked the men too well.'

Deborah stared. She'd never heard anything about Hope and other men, but then Pete's code of manners would not allow him to paint Adam's mother in a bad light to outsiders, even though she'd left him.

'Hope was a pretty girl,' Violet went on, 'but I never cared for her. She was strange. And deserting her family like she did! That was unforgivable. For years I was afraid Adam would be odd like her, but thank goodness he took after his daddy.' She paused and smiled. 'But listen to me run on. I never wanted to turn into one of those old ladies who ramble. Forgive me, Deborah. You're the concern now. Petey says you haven't heard a word from Steve.'

'No, I'm afraid we haven't.'

'You must be out of your head with worry.'

'It's a hard time.'

Violet shook her head again and made a clicking sound with her tongue. 'I remember Steve when he was young, before all that trouble with Emily. He and Petey were good friends.'

'I know,' Deborah said. 'What was Steve like in those days?'

'Smart. Wonderful in sports. Let me see . . . what was it the boys played?'

'Basketball.'

'Oh, yes. I used to go to the games, although I didn't understand them. But the other parents came. The Robinsons were always there. They were so proud of Steve.' She frowned and set down her cake plate. 'But they never seemed to *love* him like they did Emily. They thought the sun rose and set on that girl. Called her *angel*.' She smiled mirthlessly. 'She was no angel, I can tell you.'

Deborah felt Joe grow alert with interest beside her, but he wisely remained silent. It was Deborah who asked, 'What do you mean?'

'She was boy-crazy. And sneaky.' Her eyes widened. 'Oh my, she's your sister-in-law and so sick. I shouldn't have said those things. I just couldn't help being mad at the Robinsons for the way they treated Steve.'

'Violet, Pete told me Emily was secretly married, but he didn't know to whom. I don't suppose you heard any rumors . . .'

'Rumors? I've heard a hundred. But I don't know anything definite. I don't even know if she was really married, although Petey said Steve told him she was. In any case, it would have been illegal and the man went his merry way, which was best for everyone. The whole thing was such a tragedy. And now this. Poor Steve.'

Deborah sensed from the woman's demeanor that she knew nothing of the FBI's suspicion that Steve was a serial killer, and she was grateful to Pete for keeping that information to himself.

'I guess the boys did things besides go to school and play on the same basketball team,' Deborah said, keeping her tone casual. 'They probably double-dated.'

'Oh, yes.'

'I don't suppose you remember any of Steve's girlfriends.'

Violet looked at her waggishly. 'Now, honey, you're not looking for someone to be jealous over, are you?'

The idea was so ludicrous that Deborah almost laughed sarcastically, then reminded herself that Violet had no idea why she was asking such a question. 'It's just that I know so little about Steve when he was young. He never talked much about his years in Wheeling.'

'Well, he was quite popular, I remember that. More popular than Petey, I'm afraid, although Petey did have a girlfriend.' A look of distaste crossed her face and Deborah realized Violet hadn't liked the girlfriend. She hadn't liked his wife Hope, either. Was she jealous of any woman with whom Pete became involved? But she wasn't interested in Pete's past.

'Was there anyone special for Steve?' Deborah prodded. 'Anyone during his senior year of high school, maybe?'

Violet threw her a puzzled glance. 'This certainly seems to mean a lot to you.' Deborah couldn't again claim idle curiosity, but Violet was clearly a gossip who didn't need much excuse to spill her knowledge of people's private lives, so she simply smiled sweetly. 'Well, dear, it's hard to remember so far back,' Violet went on predictably. 'But yes, there were a couple of girls. Jennifer Stratton was one. His parents adored her – her daddy owns tons of land around here. They're quite affluent. But for some reason they broke up. Petey said the Robinsons were unhappy about *that*, let me tell you, Steve giving up a girl with rich parents. Then he started seeing someone they didn't like. Let me see now . . . what was her name? Oh yes, her name was the same as the girl on that television show. The one that lived in a bottle.'

'You mean *I Dream of Jeannie*?'

'Yes, that's it! Jeannie. Jeannie . . . Arnold. She moved away, became a nurse, and married some man named Burton or Bertram.'

'A nurse?' Deborah repeated. 'Jean Bartram who works at the nursing home?'

'The nursing home?' Violet frowned ferociously. 'Why, I think I did hear something about her moving back here a couple of years ago. But I don't know where she works. Does she have blonde hair?'

'Yes.'

'She would be in her early thirties, but I've heard she hasn't aged well. Did you meet her earlier today?'

'Yes. She took us to see Emily.'

'But she didn't say anything about dating Steve?'

'Not a word.'

'Well, maybe she thought you might not like it, dear.'

'Did you know Artie Lieber?' Joe asked abruptly.

Violet's eyes fluttered behind their glasses. 'Heavens, no! We couldn't afford anyone to do lawn work. My husband did everything, and later Petey. There wasn't much money in those days. My husband wasn't a go-getter like Petey. We didn't even live in this house. We had a tacky little thing hardly big enough to turn around in. It's because of Petey that I live so well now. He's a very generous man.'

She nearly glows when she talks about Pete, Deborah thought. She wondered what it was like to receive such unqualified love from a parental figure.

'Oh my!' Violet exclaimed, her gaze fastened on the window. 'Would you look at those snowflakes? Big as pennies.' She clicked her tongue again as if the weather were being particularly naughty.

'We really must be going,' Deborah said. 'We have another stop to make before we head home.'

'Oh? Where?' Violet asked.

We're going to break into my in-laws' house, Deborah felt like saying. How would Violet react to that nugget of information? 'I left something at the nursing home when we visited Emily,' she substituted.

'I see. How is the poor girl?'

'The same.'

'She doesn't talk, does she?'

'No,' Deborah said, unwilling to discuss Emily's disturbing outburst.

'Fifteen years of silence. I can't imagine it, me being such a talker and all. I suppose she doesn't know Steve is missing, Well, of course she doesn't. How silly of me. But his parents! They're off on that Hawaiian trip they take every year. Do they know?'

'Yes. I talked with Mrs Robinson on the phone. Steve's father is sick, but as soon as he's well enough to travel, they're coming home.'

'Well, that's something. I'll wager that Lorna Robinson didn't express a lot of concern, though.'

'You'd win the wager,' Deborah said.

'That woman! Puts on airs. She always tried to act like they were rich. They aren't. Very comfortable, yes, but not rich. Of course, their lifestyle went down a few notches when they had to start paying all of Emily's medical bills. I'll bet that bothers Lorna. She is *so* shallow. Why, if my Petey was in this situation, I'd be absolutely frantic.'

The woman was warming to her subject. She could probably tell Deborah volumes about Steve's early life, but not what she wanted to know, and the room suddenly felt hot. She was also growing nervous thinking about their planned trip to the Robinson home. It would be dark soon and she and Joe still had to plan how they were going to enter the Robinson house, which was undoubtedly under surveillance in case Steve returned there.

'Violet, thank you so much for the hospitality,' she said, forcing a smile, 'but we really must be going.'

'Oh, not so soon!' Violet cried.

At that moment a feeble voice called to her from the back of the house. The invalid Ida had come to their rescue. Violet helped them into their coats, patted them both as if they were little children, and stood on her porch waving goodbye with great sweeping gestures as they drove away.

THREE

They drove back to the nursing home to be told that Emily had been heavily medicated and Jean had left for the day. 'Sick headache,' another nurse told them. 'I wonder what brought that on,' Joe murmured to Deborah.

They asked for Jean's address. She lived in a narrow two-story shingled house not far from the hospital. Scrawny shrubs lined a cracked walk. A yellow cat watched them warily from a front window. Joe rang the bell and a moment later Jean swung open the door, looking pale and cross.

'Now what?' she snapped.

'Hello to you, too,' Deborah answered. 'Could we talk for a few minutes?'

'I'm sick.'

She was wrapped in a red plaid robe, and without lipstick she looked five years older than she had at the nursing home. 'Jean, please. We won't take up much of your time.'

The cat weaved around Jean's legs. She looked at it, then somewhere above their heads, and finally said, 'Oh, all right. But just for a few minutes.'

The house was small and crowded with too much cheap furniture and a plethora of knick-knacks sitting on every available space. Jean led them into a cramped living room and motioned toward a couch covered with a gaudy floral throw. 'Elegant, isn't it?' she said. 'My husband died four months ago, but thank God he left life insurance. I'm going to sell this place as soon as I can and move into something new and pretty.'

'I'm sorry about your husband,' Deborah said.

'He was sick for a long time. I think we were both relieved when he finally went.'

Deborah could think of no reply to this sentimental comment. She decided simply to launch into the subject without preamble. 'I've learned you dated Steve at the time of Emily's attack.'

Jean's hands gave a reflexive jerk and she looked away. 'I knew this was coming as soon as I saw you today.' Deborah remained silent. 'Okay, yeah, I dated Steve.'

'And you told the police he was with you at the time Emily was being raped and strangled.'

215

Jean's brown eyes blazed. 'It was a long time ago. It's hard to remember what I said.'

'Relax,' Joe said. 'We're not the police and we're not here to accuse you of anything. Steve's wife would just like a little information.'

'And what are you going to do with this information?' Jean asked Deborah.

'Nothing. My husband is missing and I'd like to know more about his early life.'

'Why? What's that got to do with him being missing?'

'It might have something to do with Artie Lieber. He was in Charleston at the time of Steve's disappearance.'

'Well, there you go,' Jean said. 'Artie hated Steve. He must have killed him.'

Deborah winced at Jean's bald pronouncement. 'We're not sure of that. Did you know Lieber?'

'I knew who he was. I saw him working at the Robinsons'. He threatened to kill Steve after the trial.'

'Do you think he would have followed through with that threat?' Joe asked.

'How should I know? Steve's gone, isn't he? I don't understand why you're trying to drag me in on all this.'

'Yes, you do know,' Deborah said firmly. 'You lied for Steve a long time ago and that lie could be important now.'

'Just supposing I did lie, how would that be important now?'

'There's more to Steve's disappearance than you've heard on the news,' Deborah said. 'I wish you'd just answer my questions.'

'What do you mean, there's more to Steve's disappearance?' Jean's face took on a mulish look. 'I'm not telling you a thing until I get some answers.'

The woman was becoming extremely agitated and Deborah knew she meant what she said. Although it caused her an almost physical pain to say Steve was suspected of being a serial killer, and she didn't like this woman, she could see that Jean wasn't giving information without getting some in return. 'The FBI think Steve might be The Dark Alley Strangler and that Emily was his first victim.'

She expected surprise. She did not expect the woman's face to turn crimson, then pale so dramatically that Deborah was certain she was going to faint. Jean drew a deep breath and whispered, 'Why do they think *Steve* is—' She broke off, her mouth going slack.

'It seems that all of the Strangler's victims were killed within a one-hundred-mile radius of Wheeling on nights when Steve was here visiting Emily,' Deborah said calmly. 'After Sally Yates was attacked, a witness saw a man fitting Steve's description get into a car the same color as Steve's with a license plate that read 8E-7. Steve's license number is 8E-7591.'

'My God,' Jean muttered. 'Sometimes over the years I wondered if Lieber was right about Steve, but I never suspected anything else.'

Jean had wondered if Steve had attacked Emily? Deborah felt as if she'd been punched in the stomach and suddenly she didn't want to hear any more. She wanted out of the room, out of the town—

'Tell us about Emily,' Joe said, not looking at Deborah.

Jean glanced away. Her foot jiggled. 'I'm not a drinker, but I need something. Just a minute.' She went into the other room and in a moment came back bearing a juice glass with clear liquid in the bottom. She didn't offer Joe and Deborah anything, merely took a gulp and stared at them, her lips chalky.

'Tell us about Emily,' Joe repeated.

'Okay, I'm going to. Just give me a minute.' She took a deep breath. 'You see, Steve adored her. It was kind of sickening, really.'

They waited for more, but Jean merely stared at them, as if dazed. 'We've been told that Emily was secretly married and Steve was out looking for the husband when she was attacked,' Joe persisted.

'Who told you all this stuff?' Jean's eyes narrowed. 'Oh, *I* know. That sanctimonious weasel Pete Griffin.'

'You don't like Pete?' Deborah managed.

'I can't stand him. Emily used to put up with him, but I don't know how.'

'What do you mean, Emily put up with him?'

'I *mean* she went out with him sometimes.'

Deborah was too surprised to say anything. It was Joe who asked, 'Was *he* her secret husband?'

'*Pete?* God, no.'

'Then who was?'

'I don't know.'

'If you don't know who the husband was, how do you know it wasn't Pete?'

Jean looked from face to face. 'I *know*. Look, I'm telling you the truth, although I don't really have to be talking to you at all.'

'We know,' Joe told her. 'And nothing you say is going beyond this room.'

'How do I know that?'

Deborah leaned forward. 'Steve is my husband and the father of my two children. Do you really think I want his name smeared? I'm only trying to find out for myself. I have two five-year-olds to protect, Jean. You have to realize how important that is.'

Jean smiled ruefully. 'I had a kid once. She died when she was two of meningitis. I would have given my own life to save hers.' For the first time she looked at Deborah with compassion. 'Yeah, I sympathize with you. And guess I'll help if I can. What do you want to know?'

'Everything about the day Emily was attacked.'

Jean took another sip of her drink. 'All right. Let me think. It was so long ago and I've tried to forget . . . Steve stopped by my place around one in the afternoon. He was crazed. He wanted to know if *I* knew anything about Emily's marriage. Well, you could have knocked me over with a feather. *Married! Emily?* I'd never been close to her. To me she was just Steve's spoiled, stuck-up little sister that I had to talk to when he took me over to his house, which wasn't often. And I guess I was jealous of her because he was so nuts about her. But I thought it was kind of funny that the kid had done something to throw those snotty parents of hers into a tailspin. I didn't have any idea who the husband was, but I did know she thought Pete was a bore. It couldn't have been him. That's all I could tell Steve. Then he took off like a bat out of hell and I didn't see him again that day. I heard that evening what had happened to Emily. They said it happened around two o'clock.'

'Why did you lie for Steve and provide him with an alibi for the time of Emily's attack?' Deborah asked.

'I didn't think he'd done anything to the precious Emily.' Her eyes dropped. 'And I thought we might get married. That couldn't happen if he somehow wound up in jail.'

Deborah looked at her searchingly. 'But you didn't get married.'

'No. After the mess was cleared up he just took off for the university and that's the last I saw of him until I went to work at the nursing home. I was long married then, and he acted like nothing had ever gone on between us. I guess he felt safe after such a long time. Actually, I thought he acted weird.'

218

'How did he act weird?' Joe asked.

'Well, like he really *didn't* remember that there'd been anything between us or that I'd lied to save his skin. And then there were times when Emily acted like she did today.'

'You said that had never happened before.'

'I lied. I'm good at it,' she said sarcastically. 'I really just wanted to get you two out of there.'

'But she's shown fear around Steve?'

'Yeah. Screaming about *Steve* and saying *it hurts*. It scared the hell out of me because, like I said, I'd already started wondering if maybe Lieber had been telling the truth all along. Steve knew what I was thinking. He gave me these creepy looks sometimes. I wished then I could tell the truth, but I couldn't without blowing the whistle on myself, and he damned well knew it.'

Bitterness edged her voice. Deborah realized that Jean still wasn't over the sting of Steve's rejection. Had Steve really acted 'weird' and given her 'creepy' looks? Had Emily often cried out in fear around him? Jean might be giving them a version of events colored by hurt and resentment. Or was she telling them a truth Deborah didn't want to hear?

23

ONE

After they left Jean's, Deborah called the Robinson home from a pay-phone. There was no answer, so she assumed they were not yet back from Hawaii.

Although she had never visited her in-laws, Steve had driven her past their house several years ago and she still remembered the general layout of the neighborhood, so she described it to Joe and they worked out a plan for entering the house.

Shortly after dark they stopped at a diner a couple of blocks from the Robinson home. They each ordered coffee and a grilled cheese sandwich. Deborah was too jittery to eat, but Joe wolfed down his sandwich as if he hadn't a care in the world. 'Aren't you nervous?' Deborah asked.

'I can't let myself be. I need to keep my head clear.'

'So what's the plan from here?' she asked, feeling ridiculously like a terrorist making earth-rocking plans in an inconspicuous meeting place.

Joe wiped his mouth and hands on his napkin. 'I know we're being watched, but no one followed us in here. In about two minutes I'm going back to the men's room. At the end of the corridor where the restrooms are, I saw a door. I'm sure it leads out the back. After I come out of the men's room, I'm going out that door. You're going to sit here for four minutes, then you're going to follow me. We'll walk to the Robinsons'.'

'There will be surveillance on the house.'

'The front, yes, but they probably don't have guards posted at every entrance. There's a back door, isn't there?'

'Yes. I've seen it in photographs taken in the Robinsons' back yard.'

'Okay, if we don't see anyone at the back, we'll go in that way. You did say there are a lot of trees and shrubs in that area, didn't you?'

'Yes, as I remember from the pictures. But those pictures are old.'

'Well, at least we can check it out. If nothing has changed and there's no surveillance on the back of the house, we're all set.'

Almost immediately Joe put enough money to cover the meal on the table, casually tossed down his napkin, and sauntered toward the restrooms. Deborah glanced at her watch. During the next four minutes she desultorily sipped her coffee, and even accepted a refill when the waitress came by. Then, with a casualness she hoped equalled Joe's, she went toward the restrooms. She glanced behind her to make sure no one was looking, then darted out the back door.

Outside snow was falling in a thick, wet veil whipped around by the wind. It was dark, and she almost cried out when Joe stepped up behind her and took her arm. 'Okay, Mrs Robinson, walk briskly but don't run.'

For twenty minutes they sneaked through back yards, dodging behind trees and shrubbery like cartoon characters. At one point Deborah bent double with nervous giggles. Joe gave her a stern look and she apologized. 'I just feel so *absurd*,' she gasped. 'Is this really necessary?'

'Do you want to get into that house?' Joe asked.

'Yes.'

'Well, if the FBI see you, you aren't going to get in. This is the only way.'

Forcing herself to keep her mind on the objective and not think about how silly she and Joe looked, she recovered only to be frightened half to death by a Doberman that came charging through a dog door and crashed against a chain-link fence. They were on the other side of the fence, but the dog was jumping so high Deborah was sure he was going to hurtle over the top and be on them. She backed away, but Joe stood his ground and spoke soothingly to the dog, who continued to show his formidable teeth for about a minute, then made whimpering sounds and allowed Joe to pat him on the head. The back door of the house opened and a man called, 'Jake? What's going on, boy?' Jake obediently ran back to his master. The man peered suspiciously into his dark back yard, unable to see Joe and Deborah crouched behind a shrub obscured by the blowing snow. 'What's wrong, fella? See a big, bad cat or something?'

He guffawed as if he'd said something amazingly clever, then took the dog inside. 'I think I've made friends with old Jake,' Joe murmured, 'but let's not push it. We'll circle around this yard and not try scaling the fence to go through it.'

'I had no intention of scaling a fence anyway,' Deborah hissed.

Finally they reached the Robinsons' long one-story home. Although the colors didn't show well in the darkness, Deborah knew it was painted a lovely dusky blue with snowy-white shutters.

'I hope they don't have a security system,' Joe muttered.

'I doubt it. This is a quiet neighborhood.'

'It was before we got here.'

'Let's just pray whoever is watching the place didn't see these two shapes skulking through everyone's back yard to get here.'

'You're the Robinsons' daughter-in-law. The neighbors can't get too upset about you being here.'

'It's not the neighbors I'm worried about,' Deborah said, shivering. 'It's Steve's parents. This is breaking and entering and they wouldn't say a word in my defense.'

'With any luck, they'll never know you've set foot in their precious house.'

'Oh, they'll know. I'm going to take a few things and I'll have to tell them. But that will be later.'

Joe took his laminated driver's license from his wallet.

'I thought you used credit cards for this kind of thing,' Deborah said.

'You can, but this is better. Credit cards are more brittle.'

'I'll remember that for my next B & E job.'

'Thank goodness this house isn't new.'

'Why?'

'Easier to get into.' Joe leaned against the door, inserted the license above the latch between the facing and the door, and pushed until half the license disappeared. Then he slid the laminated card down until it hit the strike bar, meanwhile pulling the door toward him. Deborah held her breath, then smiled when she heard a reassuring click. 'Voilà!' Joe exulted. 'Glad to see I haven't lost my touch. Ready?' he asked, his hand on the knob.

Was she? What if Steve were in there? What if he'd been hiding here ever since he disappeared from their home? Obviously the police thought he might come here or they wouldn't be watching the house. True, it would be hard for him to be living here with the house under surveillance, but it wasn't impossible. How awful it seemed to be afraid of going into a house because she thought her husband might be there. But that was the situation. She closed her eyes. You're not alone, she told herself, and you *have* to see what's in the Robinson home. 'Okay,' she said softly.

Joe opened the door and they stepped into the house. It smelled slightly musty, and Deborah immediately knew no one had entered it since the Robinsons left over two weeks ago. Joe flipped on the flashlight, keeping the beam below window level. Deborah blinked a couple of times before her eyes adjusted to the strange half-light. 'The kitchen,' she said needlessly, gazing at the narrow, scrupulously neat room with its white linoleum, cabinets, and appliances. The only touch of color was a small basket of silk ivy placed on the glass-topped kitchen table.

'Are you sure someone lives here?' Joe asked. 'It looks like a model home. Either that or an institution.'

'Steve told me his mother is obsessively neat. She can't stand to see a dirty ashtray or a crumpled towel.'

'And she's probably never eaten out of an open can over the sink.'

'Which you do.'

'Frequently.'

Deborah shook her head. 'Men!'

'A primitive but charming lot we are.'

'Yeah, there's nothing more charming than watching a man eat beans over the sink,' Deborah giggled. She was cold and frightened and she appreciated Joe's efforts to take her mind off the situation.

They moved out of the kitchen to the dining room. Another silk flower arrangement sat on the shining table which had six chairs arranged around it. In the corner stood a china cabinet bearing dishes with a narrow gold rim. 'Steve said they always ate dinner in the dining room,' Deborah said. 'His mother insisted on dinner being a rather formal affair and was livid if he was even ten minutes late.'

'Sounds like a fun meal,' Joe responded sourly. 'And so far you've only mentioned Steve's mother.'

Deborah stopped in surprise. 'Good heavens, I never thought of that. He didn't talk about his family very much, but when he did, he focused on his mother. I know hardly anything about his father except that he owns a chain of drug stores and plays a lot of golf.'

'What about Emily?'

'I don't know much about her, either. Just that she was pretty and popular—'

'And married. But who was her husband?'

'That's one of the things I hope to find out from this little illegal visit,' Deborah said. 'I don't know why, but I keep thinking it's important.'

'Well, I have to admit it seems pretty strange that no one seems to know who the guy is.'

'No one except Steve. And his parents, of course. But what is the deep, dark secret about his identity? Why did the family consider him so *unsavory*?'

Joe didn't answer. Instead, his eyes traveled to the living room where a lamp glowed against the closed draperies. 'I hope to God that lamp was turned on by a timer.'

'It was. The timer is there on the end table. Thank goodness. This means we don't have to be so careful about the flashlight in here.'

The lamp shed soft light over the highly polished hardwood floors Steve had hated. Imitation Queen Anne furniture sat on an oriental rug. A few knick-knacks were placed strategically on gleaming tables. There were no ashtrays, magazines, or books. An ornately framed mirror was hung over the sofa, coldly reflecting the room.

'Now this is what I call a warm, cosy place,' Joe said drily.

'I think there's a television room in the basement.'

'Let's hope so. Otherwise I'd feel like I was in a museum. Can you imagine two energetic kids growing up in this place?'

'Certainly not my two. Maybe Steve and Emily were more restrained. I know hardly anything about them when they were growing up. Steve always acted as if they just appeared full grown. But I think the answers to a lot of our questions lie in their past.'

'How are you going to learn those things? Photo albums? School yearbooks?'

'Exactly. Maybe we can find a few old letters or diaries.'

'I wouldn't count on that, particularly if they say anything revealing. I have a feeling Steve's mother would have destroyed anything like that.'

'It's worth a try. Here's a hall. The bedrooms must be this way.'

Even though there were no windows in the hall, Joe still kept the flashlight shaded with his left hand. Four rooms lined the hall, two on each side, with all doors closed. Deborah opened the first door on the right. The room was small, overpowered by a huge four poster bed smothered with a flounced bed-skirt, comforter, several small ruffled pillows, and a canopy. On a dresser to the left sat a mirror tray holding various perfume bottles. Another silk fern stood in front of the window. The table to the left of the bed bore a crystal-based lamp and a small alarm clock. The one to the right carried a matching lamp and the unheard of – a book. Deborah tiptoed over to look at it. *The Last of the Mohicans.* She smiled, remembering Steve saying that although his mother considered reading fiction a waste of time, his father had a deep interest in American literature. 'Dad wanted to be an English teacher,' he'd said, 'but his father forced him into the drug store business, which he hated. But what would the world be without five Robinson pharmacies?' So she did know a little more about his father than she thought.

'This is Steve's parents' room,' Deborah said, glancing into the small adjoining bathroom. 'I don't think we'll find anything interesting here.'

Joe had gone to the window that faced the street, and parted the curtains slightly. 'Quiet as a tomb out there.'

'No bright lights and Swat teams ordering us to surrender?'

'Not so far,' Joe smiled, 'but we don't want to push our luck. Let's make this quick.'

Without a word Deborah turned and left the room. The next door on the right was a large bathroom with a separate shower stall, double sinks in a vanity unit, soap shaped like rosebuds in a dish, and heavy embroidered towels lined regimentally on a rack. She quickly shut the door and turned to the left. The first room contained a twin-sized bed and a naked dresser. Nothing hung on the walls. Deborah was sure this was Steve's room, although there was no sign of his occupancy. It looked as if every trace of the Robinsons' son had been carefully swept from the room. Her throat tightened. Steve had vanished from this house just as completely as he'd vanished from her life.

'Let's try next door,' Joe said softly, as if reading her thoughts.

The next room was twice as large as Steve's and, unlike his, looked exactly as it must have twenty years ago when Emily occupied it. A white eyelet coverlet shrouded the double bed. A stuffed tiger resting against the pillows watched them with cloudy eyes, and a white Princess phone sat beneath a hand-painted china lamp. The dresser was lined with perfume bottles containing murky liquid, two jewelry cases, a collection of dried-out lipsticks in what once must have been corals and pinks, and a picture of Emily and two other girls wearing cheerleading outfits. On one wall was a large painting of a dark-haired girl wearing shorts riding a bike. Emily, probably at age fourteen or fifteen. There was no name in the corner of the portrait, only the scrawled initials P.G. 'Pete Griffin,' Deborah said aloud. 'He told me he used to dabble in art. And he was *good*.' On another wall was a poster of The Rolling Stones. A bookcase sat beneath the window. Deborah ran her eyes over the titles. Lots of Phyllis Whitney, Victoria Holt, and Mary Stewart. 'She liked romantic suspense and intrigue,' Deborah mumbled. 'I've read most of these myself.'

'Look for a diary, letters, whatever,' Joe said distractedly, handing her the flashlight. 'I'm going back to Mom and Dad's room to check the action out front.'

It didn't take Deborah long to hit paydirt. On the bottom bookshelf were three high-school yearbooks and a slender photo album. She didn't bother to look through them, but immediately began searching Emily's dresser drawers. One contained underwear, another stockings and socks, another sweaters. Everything remained as if Emily were coming home from the hospital any day. There were even fresh sachets in the drawers, but no letters or diaries. 'Of course not,' Deborah muttered, standing up. 'If she'd been dumb enough to hide things in her dresser drawers, her mother would have found them by now.'

She frantically searched her mind. Her room had been a shabby cubbyhole compared to this one, but where had *she* hidden things? She'd kept her diary in an old shoe box at the back of her closet. She rushed to Emily's closet. Clothes hung in a neat row, and shoes were stored in a clear plastic shoe case. Nowhere to hide something in the closet. She looked around the room, but reason told her it would be nearly impossible to hide anything as large as a diary unless it were under the mattress, and that too would have been found by now. What about something small? Where could that be stashed from prying eyes?

Her gaze fell on the bookcase again. Emily had obviously been an avid reader. Her mother was not. There would have been no threat of Mrs Robinson borrowing a book from her daughter, and Mr Robinson's taste seemed to run toward the classics. Quickly, Deborah began pulling books from the case, flipping hurriedly through the pages. A letter dropped out of the fifth book, *Kirkland Revels*, just as Joe reappeared.

'Deborah, I'm feeling prickly.'

'Prickly?'

'Nervous. Someone's coming. I can't see them but I can feel them. We should have gotten out of here five minutes ago.'

'Right.' Deborah checked to see that she'd gotten all the books aligned neatly on the shelf. Mrs Robinson might immediately miss the yearbooks and album, but it was a chance Deborah would have to take. There would be hell to pay for what she was doing anyway. 'I found a letter Emily must have hidden.'

Joe looked surprised. 'I really didn't think you'd find anything.'

'That's because you were never a teenage girl.'

'Full of secrets, are they?'

'Yes. Most of the secrets seem ridiculous ten years later, but they're deadly serious at the time.' She paused. 'Only in Emily's case, I think maybe they *were* deadly serious.'

'Maybe, but you'll have to find out later. We have to get out of here *now*.'

Deborah scrambled to her feet, clutching the yearbooks and album and stuffing the letter in her purse. 'Okay, I'm ready.'

They hurried back to the kitchen. Deborah's hand was on the doorknob when Joe hissed, 'Stop!' She froze as he doused the flashlight and put an arm around her waist, pulling her down to a stooping position. 'Wha—' she squeaked in shock before he glared her into silence. 'They're checking around the house,' he whispered in her ear. 'I *knew* they were coming.'

'They won't come in, will they?'

'Not unless they see something suspicious.'

'Our *footprints*.'

'The way that snow was falling, they're probably covered. Now hush.'

Deborah held her breath as light danced across the back windows. The silence was spun out for a moment, then the kitchen doorknob rattled. Deborah's eyes flashed to Joe's face. He didn't look at her, but his jaw tightened. How could we ever explain this? she wondered.

Her anxiety was reaching a peak when mercifully the doorknob stopped rattling. After what seemed like an hour, but couldn't have been more than a couple of minutes, the light disappeared. She and Joe both let out long sighs, and Deborah realized she was perspiring, even though it was only about sixty degrees in the house. 'I don't ever want to do something like this again,' she murmured.

'Let's hope you never have to.'

TWO

By the time they crept back to Joe's Jeep, their hair was wet, and Deborah's stockings and shoes were soaking. The windshield wipers worked furiously but seemed to do little to help. 'We can't go back to Charleston in this,' he said.

'We *have* to.'

'Deborah, would you look out there?'

She looked. He was right. The children were safe with Pete, and returning tonight wasn't worth the risk of having a wreck. 'Okay, we'll have to stay over.'

'Know of a good motel?'

'There's one Steve used to stay in,' she said. 'It's on the outskirts of town and I think the rates are pretty reasonable.'

The clerk had given them a sly look when they asked for two rooms. 'Will that be *adjoining* rooms?' he asked.

'No,' Joe told him firmly. 'Just two rooms, each with a double bed.'

He gave them adjoining rooms anyway. Joe rolled his eyes at Deborah when he saw the door between them. 'Oh, who cares?' she'd said, too wet and cold to be concerned about what anyone thought.

Joe had sat down on one of the beds, running his hand over the purple velour spread. 'How tasteful.'

'Gaudy, but serviceable.'

'I don't think we can expect room service.'

'I'm more concerned with the fact that we don't have toothbrushes, toothpaste – nothing.'

'That's easily remedied,' Joe said. 'You call Pete and tell him we're staying over, we'll go to a drug store and get what we need for tonight, and then have a good meal. I'm starving, in spite of that cake we had at Violet's and the sandwiches.'

'Me too,' Deborah admitted.

'Besides, you deserve it in honor of your first breaking and entering job.'

Deborah grinned. 'Don't remind me. That's one story I don't think I'll be telling the kids.'

'I saw a place down the road called The Blue Note. The sign said they serve dinners and have live music. Are you in the mood?'

Deborah started to say all she wanted was something from a fast-food place, then decided maybe a nice dinner with a couple of drinks and music might be just what she needed to relax. 'Sounds good to me.'

Joe went to his room and Deborah called Pete. 'We can't get back home,' she said. 'We're spending the night.'

'Oh,' Pete said flatly. 'I see.'

'It's *really* snowing here,' Deborah went on, for some reason feeling like a teenager making excuses to a parent.

'It's best that you stay, then.'

Did he sound disapproving? No, tired, she thought. He wasn't used to having two children and a dog around. 'I hope the kids aren't being too much of a bother.'

'They've behaved beautifully. They've already had dinner. I was going to fix steamed vegetables and chicken, but they wanted pizza.'

'They love pizza.'

'So I gathered from their appetites,' he laughed. 'Did you see my grandmother?'

'Yes. She was very sweet to us, and she's fine, Pete.'

'And who else did you see?'

'Just Emily. Oh, and Steve's old girlfriend, Jean Bartram.'

'Oh, *Jeannie*! That was her name. How did you ever come up with it?'

'Your grandmother.'

'How on earth did she remember that?'

'I don't know, Pete, but she did. Jean had lived away from here for a long time. She only came back a couple of years ago and she works at the nursing home where Emily is.'

'Well, of all the coincidences! Was she of any help?'

'Oh, she had a lot to say, but I don't want to go into it all right now. I don't know whether to believe her or not.' She paused. 'I don't really like her.'

'I never did either, and the feeling was mutual, as I recall.'

It *was* mutual, Deborah thought, but said nothing. 'Well, she didn't know who Emily's husband was. That was a disappointment.'

'I don't understand why you're so determined to find out his identity,' Pete said with faint amusement. 'Is this Nancy Drew syndrome?'

Deborah laughed. 'It must be. I just feel it's connected to what's going on with Steve. It's so maddening not to know. Oh well. I wanted to let you

229

know that Joe and I are going to have dinner at a place called The Blue Note if you need to call me before I get back to the room.'

'The Blue Note!'

'Yes. Do you know it?'

'That place has been around for ages.'

'Is the food good?'

'I've never been there. It's a jazz club. I hate jazz.'

'I didn't know that.'

'I have many fascinating secrets,' Pete said lightly.

'Anyway, I'll be there then straight back here.' She gave him the room and phone number. 'I'm really sorry to dump the kids off on you like this.'

'It's no problem, Deborah. We have plenty of room. You just have a nice dinner and a safe trip back tomorrow.'

'May I speak to the children for a minute?'

Pete hesitated. 'Deborah, would you mind not speaking to them? They've been very restless, but now they've settled down to watch a movie with Adam. I'd rather not get them excited again.'

So they *were* being a problem, Deborah thought. She wished she could do something, but getting home tonight was impossible.

'Oh well, I won't disturb them, then.' A wave of disappointment washed over her. She had never spent a night away from the children. Now she was forced to abandon them for a night because she'd been determined to come to Wheeling on what was probably a fool's errand. 'You will be very careful tonight, won't you?' she asked. 'Lieber is still out there somewhere.'

'I'll guard the children with my life,' Pete said lightly. 'See you tomorrow.'

THREE

After the phone call, Deborah held her long hair over a heat vent to dry it. Then they went to a drug store and collected toiletries and stopped at a budget shoe store where Deborah bought a flimsy, but dry, pair of loafers.

'Well, I certainly look spiffy,' she said ruefully, looking at the cheap shoes and feeling her hair falling in rough creases instead of its usual smooth waves.

'You look great and I'm mighty proud to be seen with you, ma'am,' Joe drawled.

'Yeah, sure,' Deborah returned drily. 'You're probably just glad you never have to be seen with me again in this town.'

'Not true. I'd sneak through back yards with you any time. You're just going to have to control that giggling if anyone's going to take you seriously as a partner in crime.'

'I'm so embarrassed about that. I'm thinking my husband might be a serial killer, I'm going to his parents' house to get evidence, and on the way I'm paralyzed with giggles.'

'Better laughter than tears, although you did look about fifteen.'

'Oh, be quiet and let's go eat,' Deborah laughed.

The Blue Note was only a short distance from the motel. As soon as Deborah stepped inside, she knew Pete was right – the place had been around for a long time. Still, it had been beautifully maintained and exuded a warm, relaxed ambience she loved. The knotty pine-panelled walls were decorated with hundreds of framed photographs of regular patrons and groups who'd once played at the club. In the center of the room sat large tables, most of which were occupied, and along the walls were deep and comfortable dark blue upholstered booths. Dim lights and candles set a somewhat sultry tone. One end of the club featured a dance floor, and above it loomed a dais bearing various musical instruments.

'Nice place,' Joe said as they sat down in one of the booths. He flipped open the menu. 'Reasonable prices, too.'

He chose a T-bone steak and Deborah selected shrimp. Both ordered drinks, and while she sipped her white wine she looked at the photographs on the wall to her left. 'That one looks like it was taken in the fifties,' she said. 'Look at those hairstyles!'

Joe peered at the one closest to him. 'This one was later. Late seventies or very early eighties, I'd say.'

'Then you'd be right.' They both looked up to see a heavy man around seventy wearing a black turtleneck sweater and a black jacket. His equally black hair was slicked back and he wore several rings. He looked like a singer in a bad lounge act, but his smile was wide and genuine. 'I'm Harry Gauge, owner of the place. Never seen you folks here before.'

'We've never been here before,' Deborah said. 'It's very nice.'

231

'I'm pretty proud of it and always happy to welcome new patrons. Now that picture you were lookin' at,' Harry went on, 'that *was* taken around 1980. See that black guy on the sax? That was Eddie Kaye. Biggest talent that ever hit this place.'

Deborah looked closer at the young man playing the saxophone. He looked to be in his early twenties and he was extremely handsome. He seemed to be playing directly at a table where two young men and two teenaged girls sat. The dark-haired girl was gazing at him almost rapturously.

'Weren't those people a little young to be in a place that serves liquor?' Deborah asked.

Harry grinned. 'Sometimes we bend the rules and hope we don't get caught. Of course, they can't have drinks – I draw the line there. But so far I've never had any trouble.'

'Whatever happened to the sax player?' Joe asked.

'That remains a mystery. Probably went to Hollywood or New York. Maybe New Orleans. He used to talk a lot about wanting to play in the French Quarter. Anyway, one day he just seemed to vanish off the face of the earth.'

There seems to be a lot of that going around, Deborah felt like saying. Joe flashed her a quick look. Her expression must have betrayed her distress because he jumped in immediately. 'How long have you been in business?'

'Forty years last month. Everybody said I was a fool to open this place. Said it would never go over.' He laughed without arrogance. 'Just goes to show that sometimes you've got to follow your instincts, not everyone's advice. Well, you folks enjoy your dinners. Music will be starting in about twenty minutes.'

Over dinner Deborah asked Joe what he had thought of Jean's story. He chewed a piece of steak for an unusually long time, then said reluctantly, 'The thing that bothered me the most was that she kept talking about how crazy Steve was about his sister.'

Deborah nodded. 'I know. It makes you wonder. What if he was unnaturally possessive of her? If so, is it possible he was in love with her and when he found out about her marriage, he reacted in a jealous rage?'

'And since he couldn't find the husband, took that rage out on Emily?'

Deborah laid down her fork. 'That's a revolting thought. And so hard for me to accept. And yet, he *was* possessive of her. He always acted like

232

he didn't want even me to be around her – visits to her were something private.'

'Maybe he was telling you the truth. Maybe he just didn't want you to be upset by her. After all, look what happened today.'

'And according to Jean, she often showed fear around him. That outburst wasn't unusual.'

'Just because she showed fear around Steve doesn't mean it was directed *at* him. Listen, Deborah, Jean has had a hard life and she definitely has an ax to grind with Steve. She might have the wrong perspective on those outbursts. Maybe Emily is remembering when she was terrified and is begging Steve to help her. Think about the *way* she said what she did. "Steve, hurt".'

'As if she's telling him something hurts.'

'If he'd been strangling her and pounding her on the head with a pipe, I don't think she would have been telling him it hurt. It was more like she was telling him about something that *had* hurt.'

Deborah sighed. 'Oh, lord, now we're trying to take apart her sentences, just like we did with that note that came with the music box, experimenting with inflections to figure out what someone meant. But Jean had her doubts.'

'As I said, she's an unhappy woman with her own agenda.'

'But we can't ignore all the physical evidence. The money missing from the bank account, the *jewelry*, for heaven's sake.' She picked up another shrimp and abruptly dropped it. 'My God, the oleander plant!'

Joe stared at her. 'What are you talking about?'

'Steve had brought Emily an oleander plant. Agent Wylie asked me if Steve grew oleanders! I completely forgot it because it seemed like such a silly question. I thought he was just trying to divert me.'

Joe looked baffled. 'What's the significance of oleanders?'

'I don't know. But Steve took great pride in those plants. He said they weren't easy to grow. He also said they must always be kept on a high shelf, out of the reach of the children and Scarlett, because they're poisonous.'

'So you're making a point out of Steve bringing his sister a poisonous plant? Deborah, hundreds of plants are poisonous. Yew trees are poisonous and lots of people have them. Hell, lilies of the valley are poisonous, too, and they're my mother's favorite flower, but she doesn't eat them.'

Deborah smiled. 'I guess I'm going over the edge. I just wondered what point Agent Wylie was trying to make about oleanders. I'm sure the fact that Steve grew them wasn't a casual observation on his part.'

'Maybe it was, FBI agents *are* human beings, Deborah. They're not all business all the time.'

'I think Wylie is. I wonder if he's married.'

'Got someone you want to fix him up with?' Joe asked.

Deborah pulled a droll face. 'How about Barbara if she and Evan break up?'

'Wylie and Barbara. Now that would be a match made in hell. Then you can arrange something for Jean and Pete.' He frowned. 'I wonder why Pete never mentioned he dated Emily.'

'It was a long time ago. He did make a point of telling me once that he'd been friends with Steve and Emily. Maybe he took her out a few times and Jean made more of the whole thing than there was.'

'That's the puzzling thing. We don't know how seriously to take Jean.'

'You can't deny that she was ill this afternoon. Our visit brought on that sick headache. Seeing us must have really upset her to bring on that reaction.'

'She perjured herself fifteen years ago, Deborah. That's serious, and she probably thought you already knew about it.'

'Maybe. But what if she was right about Steve acting weird and giving her creepy looks?'

'He had to be uncomfortable around her. After all, she did lie for him and he must have known she expected to marry him. How would you feel in Steve's position?'

Deborah shook her head. 'I have no idea. There's so much I didn't know until this week, Joe. I still haven't absorbed it all.'

'Then put it out of your mind for a few hours. Later you can come back to it fresh. Maybe things will make more sense then.'

Deborah decided to take his advice and they relaxed after that. Although she was not a jazz fan, the group was good and she enjoyed drinking another glass of wine while they played their first set. A few people danced. Joe looked at her apologetically. 'Sorry, but all I can do is the two-step.'

'That's okay. I don't want to dance.'

'Feel like singing?'

She smiled. 'I don't even feel like doing that. Actually, I'm afraid tonight's been too hard on me. I'm worn out. Mind if we go back to the motel now?'

'I was just going to suggest the same thing.'

They returned to the motel at ten o'clock. Although she was terribly tired, she wasn't sleepy. She washed her face, brushed her teeth, slipped out of her slacks and sweater and, sitting on the bed in panties and bra, spread out the yearbooks, the album, and the letter she'd found in the Robinson house. She was still amazed by her temerity in breaking into the house, and she knew Lorna Robinson would be furious, but given the woman's fear of publicity, Deborah was certain the matter wouldn't be brought to the attention of the police when she returned the items.

The letter was disappointing. Written on yellowed parchment stationery decorated with little pink flowers, the unfinished letter was to a girlfriend named Martha who lived in Florida. It was full of trivial details about Emily's life in Wheeling, followed by exclamation marks, sometimes two or three in a row. The only interesting part was a paragraph about a young man:

I'm *so* in love!! I'm not going to tell you his name, not now, but he's not a boy. He's *so* different from the guys at school or even Steve and Pete. He's from a whole different world. You wouldn't think we'd have anything in common, but we talk for hours! And he *loves* me!!! I can't believe it! Of course, my parents, and his too, would have a *fit* if they knew how we felt. I guess we're like Romeo and Juliet. It's so ROMANTIC!!!

Good heavens, how young she sounded, Deborah thought. How starry-eyed. But the important thing was her emphasis on how different the mystery lover was, because Deborah was certain he'd become the secret husband. But *what* was so different about him? Simply the fact that he was older than Steve and Pete? Or that her parents would disapprove of him. That would make him forbidden fruit, irresistible to a passionate, headstrong girl like Emily.

The yearbooks were next. They revealed little except how much styles had changed in the past twenty years. Emily had been a sophomore when Steve was a senior and in the yearbook she beamed from a small picture, her dark hair shining under the lights, her teeth perfect from years of braces. Deborah turned to the picture of Steve. He looked so different, the eyes serious, the chin fuller. Then she looked closer. There was a mole beside his right eye. Steve didn't have a mole. 'That's not Steve, it's *Pete*!' she exclaimed aloud. She flipped forward to find Steve's familiar smile beneath thick hair parted on the side and worn longer than he wore it in recent years. She turned back to the picture of Pete. His hair hadn't thinned then. It was thick and styled exactly the same as Steve's. Even their facial structure was similar except for the chins. She laughed. No wonder their pictures had been exchanged. They looked so much alike when they were teenagers, they could have been brothers. But how dismayed they must have been to have had their senior pictures reversed.

She went through two earlier yearbooks, those dating from Steve's sophomore and junior years, scanning the senior section for Emily's mystery husband. The exercise was fruitless. She had no idea who she was looking for.

Frustrated, she turned to the album. The older photographs showed two attractive people, obviously the Robinsons. Then they were joined by a baby that turned into a light-haired little boy. At last came another baby. Dozens of pictures of young Emily followed: Emily grinning in a ballerina outfit; Emily in a swimsuit holding her nose before she plunged into a pool; Emily seated at a piano. 'Not much film wasted on Steve after she came along,' Deborah muttered.

Feeling chilled, she pulled back the covers and climbed into bed. Next door she could hear Joe's television going. Once again the urge for a cigarette assailed her, but she hadn't brought any with her. Just as well, she thought. She fished in her purse for a peppermint, then settled back against the pillows with the album.

There were a couple of pictures of Emily in a pink party dress, determinedly smiling with her mouth shut. She was still wearing the braces, Deborah thought, amused. Another photo showed a more mature Emily in a red dress with a sparkling clip in her long, thick hair. Deborah took the picture from the album and looked at the back. 'Valentine's Day. Queen of the Dance,' was written in large, round script. The next shots revealed an older and lovelier Emily. She obviously loved having her picture taken – she looked completely relaxed, even flirtatious, as if the eye of the camera were the eyes of a man. Deborah thought of the photos taken of herself when she was a teenager. She'd stood self-consciously stiff, squinting and wearing a silly, lop-sided smile. Cindy Crawford had nothing to fear from me, she mused. Emily had been another matter.

Pictures on the next page proved more interesting. In one, Emily sat on a blanket wearing a bikini and sunglasses. She looked almost like a *Playboy* model, lush-figured and deliberately provocative. Is this why Steve had always preferred she dress so simply and look almost plain? Deborah wondered. Was it because of his deliberately tantalizing sister who'd ended up so tragically?

Deborah forced thoughts of her own relationship with Steve aside and continued her study of the pictures. In the next one, Emily wore a different, yet no less sexy, bikini. Beside her was a young Pete, laughing shyly although his eyes were serious. A beautiful German Shepherd lay in front of Emily, and her hand was buried in its hair. Deborah took the photograph out of the album and turned it over to inspect the handwriting on the back. 'I'm sweet sixteen! Me, Pete, & Sax, June 2.' '*Sax*,' Deborah said aloud. She thought of the way Emily had reacted to the picture of Scarlett, who was part German Shepherd. She wasn't saying *sex* at the nursing home. She was saying *Sax*. It was the dog's name. Had Pete given it to her?

She stared at the picture, but it gave no further clues. The date was alarming, though – 2 June. She'd been attacked on 7 June. With a catch in her throat, Deborah realized that the beautiful, insouciant girl in the picture had only five more days of normal life.

There were a few more photos of Emily posing saucily in her bikini. Then Deborah turned the page and gasped as she looked at a copy of the photo she'd seen at The Blue Note. Two young men and two girls sat at a round table. Now that she'd seen what Steve's sister looked like as a teenager, she knew that one of the girls was Emily, gazing rapturously at the handsome young black man on the dais playing the saxophone directly to her.

The saxophone. Sax. 'Oh my God,' Deborah murmured, collapsing back against the pillows. What had Harry Gauge said the saxophone player's name was? Eddie. Eddie Kaye. Emily had said 'Ed' over and over. Jean had said he was an orderly.

Deborah abandoned the album and jerked open the nightstand drawer, looking for the Wheeling phone book. In a moment a young woman was saying, 'The Blue Note.'

'May I speak with Mr Gauge, please?' Deborah said breathlessly.

'Who's calling?'

'Deborah Robinson. I was in earlier this evening. It's *very* important that I speak with him.'

'Just a minute.' Deborah could hear jazz playing in the background. She drummed her fingers nervously on the nightstand until Harry Gauge's deep voice came on the line. 'This is Gauge. How can I help you?'

'This is Deborah Robinson, Mr Gauge.'

'Sorry, ma'am, but I don't believe I know you.'

Fool, Deborah chided herself. She hadn't given him her name earlier in the evening. 'I was in your restaurant a couple of hours ago. I have long black hair. I was with a man and we were asking about the photos on your wall—'

'Oh, yes, I remember. Did you leave something here?'

'No. I wanted to ask you about that saxophone player you told us about. Eddie Kaye.'

'Eddie? What about him?'

'Was his last name K-a-y-e?'

'No. He used the initial *K*. His last name was King. Why?'

'Thank you so much,' Deborah said and hung up, her mind whirling. Finally Deborah knew the truth. Emily's 'husband' was Eddie King, and the provincial Robinsons had treated the whole episode like a shameful secret because he was black.

But she also knew something else. The man who'd rented the O'Donnell house had claimed to be Edward King, but Barbara's friend hadn't described him as black. It could be a common name, but what were the chances of an Edward King moving into a house right across from Steve? 'Very slim,' she muttered, her heart racing. 'Very slim indeed.'

FOUR

'Alfred, Alfred . . .'

A nurse checking the IV needle looked sharply at Mrs Dillman. 'My God, is she waking up?' she muttered.

'Al*fred* . . .'

The nurse leaned over her. 'Honey, can you hear me?' The woman's eyes remained closed but her face twitched. 'Mrs Dillman, *can you hear me*?'

'You be on time for dinner,' the woman mumbled. 'Beef stew, your favorite.'

The nurse took Mrs Dillman's cold hand. 'Honey, I'm here,' she said loudly. 'Can you *hear* me?'

Mrs Dillman's eyes snapped open. 'Of *course* I can hear you. There's no need to shout.'

The nurse drew back. 'I didn't mean to shout. You just surprised me. I'm going for the doctor.'

Mrs Dillman's hand clamped on the nurse's. 'Where am I?'

'The hospital, honey. You got a nasty bump on the head.'

'Stop calling me honey. I don't even know you.'

'I'm sorry, hon – Mrs Dillman.'

'My head . . .'

'Yes, a nasty bump.'

'I hurt my head?'

'Yes, a—'

'Nasty bump. I heard you the first time.'

'I must get the doctor. If you'll just let go of my hand . . .'

Mrs Dillman suddenly glared. '*I* didn't hurt my head. Someone hit me!'

'Oh, I don't think so, honey.'

'Well, *I* think so. And if you don't stop calling me honey, I'm going to—' Mrs Dillman gasped, her eyes widening. 'I remember! I remember who hit me.'

'That's fine. I'll get the doctor and you can tell him all about it.'

'Don't try to humor me!' Mrs Dillman clutched fiercely at the nurse's hand. 'That young woman – Deborah! I must warn Deborah!'

'We'll see what the doctor has to say,' the nurse soothed.

'The doctor, hell!' Mrs Dillman exploded. 'I'm telling you, I'm not rambling! This is important!'

'Now, now, don't get yourself upset.'

'Don't you "*now, now*" me! I want to talk to Deborah.' Frantic pleading showed in Mrs Dillman's faded eyes. '*Please* listen to me. I have to tell Deborah!'

24

The phone jangled. Deborah jerked. She wondered if she would ever react normally again to the ringing of a telephone. She picked it up, certain it was Joe wondering if she'd discovered anything important in her plunder from the Robinson house. 'Deborah?'

'Pete!' she said with a start. 'What's wrong?'

'Nothing with the children. They're fine. Are you alone?'

'Alone? Of course. Joe's in his room.'

'You must promise me you won't call him.'

'Why?' Deborah sat up straighter. 'Pete, you're scaring me.'

'I don't mean to, but you must promise. And I want you to turn on the television for background noise.'

His voice was strained, even slightly quavery. He had bad news to impart, and Deborah wanted him to get it out. She clambered to the foot of the bed, turned on the television, then picked up the receiver again. 'All right. The television is on and I promise I won't call Joe. Now what *is* it?'

'It's Barbara. A couple of hours ago her body was found in the O'Donnell house. The police believe she was killed last night.'

Deborah stared straight ahead. A low roar started in her ears, gained volume, then diminished again. Her body seemed to have gone numb, and her breathing was slow and shallow. Finally Pete said, 'Deborah? Are you there?'

'Yes.' The word came out in a long sigh. 'How was she killed?'

'She was beaten and strangled.'

Deborah choked. 'Oh, God, just like—'

'The Dark Alley Strangler's victims. Deborah, I'm so sorry.'

'She was so curious about that house. She must have sneaked in to investigate.' She drew in a sharp breath. 'Where's Evan?'

'I have no idea. Maybe he knows about her. I haven't seen him.'

'She suspected him, Pete. She thought maybe he was the Strangler.'

'I don't think he is.' She heard Pete breathing heavily in agitation. 'Deborah, you must listen to me very carefully. I was worried about you last night. I had a bad feeling, don't ask me why. Anyway, I drove past your house around 2 a.m. and I saw Joe. He was outside, Deborah, going around the side of your house.'

'The side of the house?'

'He could have been coming back from the O'Donnell house.'

Deborah felt the blood draining from her face. 'No, he couldn't have had anything to do with Barbara's death.'

'We can't *know* that. Deborah, did Barbara express any suspicion of Joe?'

Deborah's mind whirled. She could see Barbara sitting stiffly on her couch. She'd said Evan thought maybe the Strangler was someone Steve worked with, someone who knew his patterns. 'Of course Joe's acting odd . . . He's become your watchdog.' Barbara's words rang in her ears.

'She *was* suspicious, wasn't she?' Pete asked. 'And now you're in Wheeling alone with him. He's probably in the room next door, isn't he?'

'Yes,' Deborah whispered. 'We have adjoining rooms although the doors are locked.'

'I want you to get out of there,' Pete said firmly. 'Let the television run and leave quietly, avoiding his window. Get to a public phone. Call a taxi. Then rent a car, take a bus, anything. Just get back here.'

'Pete, wouldn't it be better if I called the police?'

Joe tapped on the adjoining door and Deborah nearly dropped the phone. 'Deborah? You asleep in there?'

'Answer him!' Pete was hissing over the phone. 'Act natural and answer him.'

'No,' Deborah called thinly. 'I was just going over the yearbooks.'

'Find anything interesting?'

'Not yet.'

'I thought I heard the phone.'

'Oh . . . uh . . . someone called the wrong room.'

'Are you sure you're all right? You sound strange.'

'I'm fine.'

'You don't sound fine. I thought you might like something from the coffee shop next door.'

Deborah had been holding the receiver to her ear through the interchange with Joe. 'Say yes,' Pete ordered 'Say you want something from the coffee shop and get him out of his room.'

'I'll see you as soon as I can,' Deborah whispered into the phone. She hung up. Then she climbed off the bed, slipped on her coat, and opened the door leading into his room. He heard her and opened his own. 'I'd just love some coffee.'

Joe smiled. 'I didn't think you'd been in the mood for sleep.'

'I'm also starving.' Joe looked at her quizzically. 'I don't know what's wrong with me. I feel like I didn't eat any dinner. Could you also get me a doughnut or a Danish? Maybe a piece of pie.'

'Well, sure. What kind of pie?'

'Cherry. Or apple. Or whatever they have that looks good.'

Joe was frowning slightly. 'Anything else?'

'No. Coffee and something sweet would be wonderful.' Her voice was higher-pitched than normal. She couldn't make it sound natural. 'Oh, by the way, Joe, I've lost an earring. It's probably in your car. Would you mind letting me have the keys? I'll look for it while you're gone.'

His forehead creased. 'You have to get the earring tonight? It's really nasty outside.'

'I'm sure to forget about it tomorrow.' She tried to look regretful. 'You see, it's one of a pair Steve gave me, and I'm afraid if I don't get it now, it might fall out of the car or slip down into a seat and I'll never find it.'

'I can look for you.'

'No, you get the coffee,' she said quickly. Then she smiled. 'I'm really dying for coffee and something to eat. I'll look for the earring.'

Joe shrugged and reached in his pocket for his keys. 'Okay. Here you go.'

Puzzlement showed in his gray eyes and she tried a sheepish smile. 'I know this anxiety over an earring seems silly, but at a time like this . . .'

'If it'll make you feel better, look all night,' he said. 'I'll walk next door and get the coffee.'

'Thanks so much, Joe.' Deborah shut the adjoining door. She waited until she heard the front door of his room close and immediately took off the coat, slipped on her slacks, sweater, and shoes, redonned the coat, and stepped out of her room casually. Joe was rounding the side of the motel, his head bent against the snow, his hands buried in his pockets. She made a beeline for the car and slipped the key into the lock.

Just as she turned it, a hand touched her shoulder.

She stifled a scream and whirled round to face a slender, brown-haired man she'd never seen in her life. He was nice-looking in a hard way, but a tic around his eye detracted from what could have been a handsome face. 'What is it?'

'Mrs Robinson, I've got to talk to you.'

'How do you know my name?' Deborah asked, her heart pounding. 'Who are you?'

'My name's not important,' the man said. 'But I know where your husband is.'

Her alarm growing, Deborah stared at him. 'What are you talking about?'

'I'm talkin' about your husband, Steve. I know where he is. You've gotta talk to me.'

Deborah didn't know *how* she knew, but she did and her skin turned icy. 'You're Artie Lieber, aren't you?'

'I've been trying to get to you for days, but someone's always around.' His hand closed more firmly on her shoulder. 'I finally got you alone.'

'Let me go!' Deborah cried.

'You and me, we're gonna get in that Jeep and we're goin' someplace.' 'No!'

She tried to twist out of his grasp. He looked at her coldly, then slapped her across the face. Her head snapped back and her eyes filled with tears, as much from shock as from pain. 'Don't get hysterical on me,' Lieber said. 'All I want is to talk. And you're *gonna* talk to me or—'

'Hey!'

Deborah looked up to see Joe running toward them. Lieber's hand dropped away from her shoulder. Two men, one standing beside her, the other bearing down on her, and one of them was a killer. Without thought, she flung open the door of the Jeep, jumped in, and locked the door. Outside she saw Lieber running across the parking lot. Joe pursued him a few feet. Then he heard the Jeep starting, and turned just as Deborah threw it into reverse and shot out of the parking space. 'Deborah, what are you *doing*?' he yelled as she shifted into drive and shot forward. He ran after her. 'Deborah,' he shouted. 'Deborah, for God's sake!' She shut her ears to his voice and drove as if her life depended on it. For all she knew, it did.

25

All the way home she thought about Barbara. What had possessed her to investigate the O'Donnell house? The irresistible urge to know for certain if Evan was the mysterious renter? If so, how had she gotten inside? Or had she been taken in before she was killed? Or afterward?

The possibilities were too awful to consider. And Joe. All the nights when she'd come downstairs to find him gone, once because he said *he* was investigating the house. And what about the night Mrs Dillman and Kim saw something? He'd been gone an hour and a half just getting Kim cough syrup. Then there was Kim's doll in the freezer. Kim had heard bells, and Joe claimed he hadn't been aware of her leaving the house because he was in such an uncharacteristically deep sleep. And the jewelry. Good heavens, Joe had lived in the house nearly a week. He could have hidden it in the basement at any time. He could also have put the doll in the freezer and rung bells in the back yard to lure Kimberly out. And Sally Yates. Jean said someone had tried to slit her throat. Joe's Lisa in Houston had died of a slashed throat.

Most frightening of all, what had he intended to do to her tonight? Kill her and drag her outside a bar? But why would he want to kill her? She'd never suspected him of anything. And what was Artie Lieber trying to do? Certainly not just tell her something, like he said. None of it made sense. And none of her speculating would bring back Barbara.

She reached Charleston at three in the morning, cold, frightened, and exhausted. A single light burned in the front window of Pete's house. Deborah almost cried when she saw it. Safety. The children were waiting inside.

Pete must have been watching for her. He opened the door as she came up the walk. 'Deborah, thank God you're finally back safely.' He wrapped his arms around her and she noted absently that he was wearing a cashmere sweater that felt good against her cold face. 'You're trembling.'

'This hasn't been the best evening of my life.'

'Did you call the police before you left?'

'No. I just asked to borrow Joe's keys while he went to a coffee shop next door. But as I was getting in the car, Artie Lieber came up to me.'

'Lieber!'

'Yes. He kept saying he wanted me to go somewhere with him to talk. When I said no, he slapped me. Then Joe appeared. I jumped in the car and took off.'

'Good lord! I never expected Lieber . . .' Pete trailed off, looking deeply troubled. 'You had a very close call, Deborah. I didn't want you to go.'

''I know. But I'm back now.'

'Take off your coat and come into the living room. I've made tea.'

Deborah smiled. 'Tea sounds good, but the first thing I want to do is see the children.'

Pete glanced at her in surprise. 'But they're sleeping.'

'I know. I won't wake them – I just want to see them. Which room are they in?'

'Upstairs. The first room on the right. But please be very quiet. They were unhappy that you didn't come home and I had a devil of a time getting them to sleep.'

Deborah hurried up the stairs on light feet, Pete behind her, and opened the bedroom door. Dim light from a hall lamp revealed an empty double bed. She whirled to face Pete, who gaped at the tumbled covers. 'Where are they?' she asked in alarm.

'They were right here half an hour ago. I don't understand . . . My God, you don't suppose they tried to go back home, do you?'

'Home!' Deborah exclaimed, appalled. 'It's freezing outside. Oh my lord, Pete.'

'Calm down,' he said firmly. 'They must have gone out the back way. Let me see if Adam heard anything.' He walked down the hall toward the back of the house and opened another door. He glanced in and stared, his face expressionless. He quietly shut the door. 'He's sound asleep,' he told Deborah. 'I don't know what I was thinking. If he'd heard anything, he would have told me.'

'What should we do?'

'We'll cruise the streets in this area.'

'Shouldn't we call the police first?'

'By the time they get here and collect all the information they need, the children could have spent another half an hour out in the cold when they may be only a few blocks away. If we haven't found them in twenty minutes, we'll call the police.'

'Maybe Scarlett can help us find them.'

'She was sleeping in the room with them, Deborah. They must have taken her with them.'

Of course they wouldn't leave her behind, Deborah thought. 'All right, let's go,' she said, her breath coming in short bursts. She felt as if she might hyperventilate.

They hurried downstairs and Pete pulled a down jacket from the closet. 'I'll drive,' he said as they went outside and rushed back to Joe's Jeep Cherokee. 'You're too nervous.'

'All right.' Deborah handed him the keys. 'I hope they stayed on the streets and didn't go through lawns,' she said, thinking of her own trip through back yards a few hours ago. Guilt stabbed her as they started out, going slowly through the heavy snow. She should have been home with her children. Instead she'd been raiding the Robinson house and dining at The Blue Note. And what had it all been for?

'I think I've discovered who Emily's husband was,' she blurted out, following the train of her thoughts.

'Oh?' Pete drove carefully down a slick residential street. 'Who?'

'A guy called Eddie K. He was a saxophone player at The Blue Note.'

They turned down another street. Deborah peered anxiously through the snow, desperately looking for two small children and a dog. Except for some cars parked along the curb, the street was empty.

'I'm sure you're mistaken about Eddie King,' Pete said, craning his neck to look past her. 'I thought I saw movement behind that tree, but it's nothing. Anyway, Eddie King was black.'

'I think that's why the Robinsons were so adamant about keeping the whole thing quiet. From what I've heard about Steve's parents, they would have been horrified that Emily was involved with a black man.'

'Well, that's certainly true.'

'Pete, here's our street,' Deborah said. 'Slow down.'

'Sorry, I was just thinking about what you said.' He carefully turned into the cul-de-sac. Snow crunched under the tires. There were no tire tracks. No one had driven here for hours. 'It's so dark on this street,' he complained.

'Most of the houses are empty,' Deborah told him. Fred Dillman had left a porch light on. Every other house sat quietly in the night: the Vincent house, her house, the O'Donnell house. The O'Donnell house where Barbara's body had been found just a few hours ago. But there was no tape marking it as a crime scene, no sign of activity, no tracks in the snow. There it sat, lovely, serene, and untouched in the snow.

And it had been rented by a man no one had seen. A man who claimed to be named Edward King. Pete said he'd never been to The Blue Note and hated jazz. He couldn't have been a fan of Eddie K. She'd called Emily's love Eddie K. Yet Pete referred to him as Eddie King, as if he knew him. And Pete had plenty of money to rent a house in which he didn't plan to live.

Deborah's eyes fixed on the house and she stiffened. Pete glanced at her. She swallowed. 'I still don't see the kids,' she said too sharply. 'We'll have to call the police from my house.'

Pete ignored her, sailing around the cul-de-sac and back out on to the main road again. 'Pete, we have to call—'

'Shut up.'

She felt the blood draining from her face. 'Pete, I don't understand.'

'Like hell you don't.'

In the light coming from the instrument panel, Pete's kind, benign face had turned hard, sharp-angled. The day had been full of shocks. Lieber. The flight from Joe. Hearing about Barbara.

'Barbara isn't dead, is she?' Deborah asked numbly.

Pete's tone was conversational. 'Why, no, I don't suppose so.'

'You told me she'd been murdered just to get me back here.'

'To get you back here without Joe. I don't need him in my way.'

Deborah felt dizzy with shock. This was Pete, whom she'd known almost as long as she'd known Steve. Pete, who'd always been gentlemanly, considerate. Pete, who'd brought groceries and spent Christmas Eve with her and the kids.

'Where are my children?'

Pete frowned. 'I hid them somewhere. You'll have to come with me if you want to see them.'

Deborah stared at him. Her rapid heartbeat slowed. She suddenly felt calm, her mind working smoothly. She didn't know where this steadiness was coming from, but she was grateful for it. She couldn't give into nerves now. 'You're lying,' she said coolly. 'You were as shocked as I was to see

247

that empty bed in your house. You don't *know* where they are.'

'I'm as good at feigning surprise as I am at feigning friendship,' Pete returned equably.

'Like your friendship with Steve?'

'Exactly.'

They headed away from Charleston. The road was narrow and they were going too fast. Where in God's name was he taking her? she wondered. She reached for the door handle. Jumping from the Jeep would injure her, but injury was better than staying with Pete, because she knew he was going to kill her. Her hand closed around the cold metal.

'Don't do that,' Pete said. The barrel of a gun touched her temple. She gasped and released the handle. 'That's better,' he said in satisfaction. His driving had become more erratic with only one hand on the steering wheel, but he didn't pull the gun away from her head. 'I *will* shoot you right here if I have to. After all, it's not my car.'

He sounded more concerned about the mess that would result from shooting her in the head than the fact that he was threatening murder. Aghast, Deborah folded her hands in her lap. His voice was so maddeningly gentle, but there was a sing-song quality about it. He didn't sound quite sane.

She took a deep breath. 'Steve's dead, isn't he?'

'Yes.'

Oh, Steve, she thought miserably. My poor Steve. 'Why, Pete? Why did you kill him?'

He smiled eerily in the half-light. 'You must know. I'm a brilliant man, Deborah, but I'm not insane. I'm not one of those egomaniacs who think they can't be caught. I knew eventually the police would get too close, so years ago I started setting up Steve to look guilty.'

'Guilty of all those murders? You mean you're The Dark Alley Strangler?'

Pete grimaced. 'I do so hate that absurd name the newspapers invented. It's tacky and doesn't befit someone who's killed so often and so brilliantly.' He sighed. 'But that's the story of my life. No matter what I accomplish, it's minimized, tainted by the common man's very common touch.'

Headlights fell across the windshield. Another car came toward them, then was gone. What if the people inside knew what was happening? Deborah wondered. Would they try to help her? Or would they only think of escaping with their own lives?

'Did you attack Emily?' she asked, trying to break the awful silence in the Jeep.

'Oh, yes. She was my girlfriend. I wanted to marry her. Of course, the Robinsons didn't think I was good enough for her, including your arrogant Steve, Mr All-American,' he sneered. 'But I wanted her. Then I realized there was someone else. And when I figured out who it was, when I discovered I was only being used as a decoy to hide her relationship with that black *trash*—'

He broke off and, alarmed, Deborah saw saliva collecting at the side of his mouth. Oh my God, she thought. He's a lunatic. She once again felt like reaching for the door handle, but then her eyes fell on the gun which was no longer at her temple, but still clutched firmly in Pete's right hand.

'You must have been furious,' she managed shakily.

'Yes. Furious. You see, I realized she was just like my mother. My mother bedded every man going. She thought when I was young I couldn't hear her in her bedroom when Dad was out on the road, but I did. Thrashing. Moaning. It was disgusting. And I watched my dad declining. He always looked worried, depressed. They fought when he was home, and he drank. He drank so much he didn't have time for me any more, and we'd been so *close*, Deborah. My mother didn't care about me, but he adored me. For a while he seemed to forget me, though, all because of *her*. But finally there was an awful fight when he actually caught her in bed with someone. He threw a whiskey bottle against the wall. He told her he was going to leave her and take me with him. I was *so* happy! I knew everything would be like it used to be, when I was small. Dad and me together. Best buddies.' His voice hardened. 'Then he went out to the car, and that bitch followed him. He wrecked because of her. He'd had too much to drink and I'm sure she was hanging on to him, yelling at him.' His eyes filled with tears. 'The filthy slut took my daddy.'

The filthy slut, Deborah repeated mentally. The woman whose picture Deborah had seen in Violet's living room, the beautiful woman with long dark hair. She was probably tall and slender, too. 'I'm very sorry,' she murmured.

'Oh, what would you know about it?' Pete snarled, the tears running down his face. 'You can't be sorry when you don't know how the hell it feels to be left by the one person in the world you love.'

'No, that's never happened to me,' Deborah said meekly.

'You're damned right. Nobody can know how I felt.'

'But you had your grandmother.'

'That babbling idiot? And my lazy, ineffectual grandfather! He couldn't even earn a decent living. Our house was a disgrace. My clothes were the cheapest thing Grandma could find. I was what Adam would call a geek. I made good grades, though, and when I was in high school, I got on the basketball team. And I was *good* – damned good. But *she* ruined it all by insisting on coming to all the games. Even above all the noise I could hear her up in the stands, rattling on about *Petey*, for God's sake, jumping up and down and screeching whenever I scored, which I did frequently. Everyone was laughing at her, but she never caught on.' Deborah thought about the pride in Violet's voice when she'd talked about 'Petey'. If she only knew how he really felt about her.

'But you and Steve were friends,' she said softly.

'We were classmates. And teammates. He acted friendly, but then he acted that way with everyone. He wanted to be *liked* by everyone. I could tell he didn't approve when I started seeing Emily, though. Oh, he was smart enough not to *say* anything, but I could feel it. I could feel *everyone's* disapproval.'

You imagined it, Deborah thought. Your mother ignored you, your father, whom you thought adored you, forgot about you in his despair over your mother. By the time you were a teenager, you'd become the perpetually rejected child. No matter what anyone did, you thought no one liked you, that you were the butt of everyone's jokes.

Snow poured down and the windshield wipers slapped ceaselessly. They went around a curve too fast and slid, but Pete didn't seem to notice. The tires gripped the road firmly again and they sped on. 'I thought Emily cared for me. Or *would* care for me when she was old enough to have some sense. Then I found out about Eddie. You see, first she suddenly had that damned dirty dog. A Christmas gift from Eddie, although she claimed it had been given to her by a family moving out of town. But she named it Sax. How's *that* for a clue? Emily wasn't too bright, you see. Then, that summer, she started acting different. Dreamy but at the same time more mature. I went over there one day. She was outside in that blue bikini she'd gotten in the spring. The dog was inside. Usually he was right by her side like some sort of guardian.' He laughed roughly. 'Rather like Joe with you lately. I suppose I lost my head that day. She was in the bikini, her long, dark hair hanging halfway down her back. She was tall and slim and graceful. She looked unbelievably beautiful. No one was around that day and I got very . . . physical with her. She started fighting me. When I wouldn't let her go, she screamed that she was married to Eddie.'

Pete closed his eyes and Deborah gasped as they swerved off the road. Snow pounded under the Jeep. A tree loomed about twenty feet ahead of them. 'It was as if she'd stabbed me in the chest. I haven't felt like that since they told me my dad was dead,' he said vaguely, opening his eyes and violently jerking the car back on the road, throwing both of them to the left. 'That *African*!' he went on, seeming unaware that he'd nearly flipped the vehicle on its side. 'I'm a little fuzzy about what happened next. The Robinsons were having some work done on the house and I suddenly had a pipe of some kind in my hand. I hit her on the head, strangled her and . . . well . . . raped her. She wasn't conscious when I did the last, but I know she would have enjoyed it. Sex with me had to be better than it was with *Eddie*. Then, out of nowhere, Lieber came around the house. He was about fifty feet away. My hair was thick and long then. It had fallen over my face from the exertion. Lieber started shouting, 'Steve! What the hell are you doing?' We looked alike in those days, Steve and I did. We still do when I wear my toupee and tighter clothes. We were even both wearing jeans that day. How's that for a stroke of luck? Lieber charged after me, but I was in great shape. I ran like I'd never run before. He didn't stand a chance of catching me.'

'And Steve came home to find Lieber bending over his sister.'

'I think he was trying to give her mouth-to-mouth or something. Maybe he was going to rape her, too. Who knows?'

'But Steve saw Lieber and thought he'd attacked Emily, while Lieber was certain he'd seen Steve attacking her earlier.'

Pete snickered. 'Right. Isn't that hilarious? Like some silly farce. It worked out perfectly for me, although I was a little put-out because no one ever suspected me. I guess they thought I wasn't *man* enough to do such a thing. Ah, here we are.'

They turned on to what Deborah suspected was a dirt road although there was so much undisturbed snow on it she couldn't be certain. Pete shifted into four-wheel drive and they jolted forward. On either side of the road stretched barbed-wire fence laden with snow. After a few moments, a structure loomed ahead. Squinting, Deborah saw that it was a barn.

Pete stopped the Jeep about fifty feet away from it. 'The snow has drifted around the barn. I'm not driving any closer. Get out now, but don't try running away. You can't make any time in this snow, and I have a gun. You won't get ten feet '

With a sinking feeling in her stomach, Deborah knew he was right. Escape at this point was impossible. With Pete's gun on her, she opened the door and stepped down into nearly a foot of snow. She stood very still while he climbed out and circled the car to where she stood. 'Very good,' he said. 'Now walk.'

'To where?'

'The *barn*, of course. I don't want to stand out here in this mess.'

Deborah plodded forward. She was still wearing the cheap shoes she'd bought earlier in the evening and they immediately began leaking. In fact, the snow was well above her ankles, dragging at her as she struggled toward the hulking shape of the barn. 'Where are we?' she asked.

'A piece of property for sale. It's been vacant for years.'

'Just like the O'Donnell house.'

'Yes. I suppose by now you've figured out that I rented it.'

'Why?'

'So I could watch you and Steve. You see, I'd realized the time had come for Steve's charmed life to come to an end,' he shouted, although the wind had settled. The night was now cold and still. 'He still grieved over Emily, but not like he used to. He had you and the children. He told me you even planned to have another child. I didn't want him to be happy. He didn't deserve to be, not after the way he looked down on me all through school, not after the way he disapproved of me seeing his precious sister. And then there was Hope.'

'Hope?'

'Yes, my beloved wife. Did you know that she and Steve had an affair?'

The air went out of Deborah. 'That is not true.'

'Come now, Deborah. I think in your heart you knew all along.'

'I knew no such thing! What on earth are you talking about?'

'Hope didn't just wander off. She was having an affair.'

'But not with Steve!'

'*Yes*, with Steve. She denied it, but I *know*. She'd always liked him. Didn't you ever catch them exchanging looks? Didn't you notice Steve was home less than usual? Wasn't there a little less activity in the bedroom?'

It was crazy. Steve would never have had an affair with Pete's wife. There hadn't been a change in his behavior for so much as a week during their marriage. And even if there had been a one-night drunken dalliance,

Steve could never have acted normal around Pete again. But Pete was convinced. Jealousy, long nurtured in a sick mind, had turned to hatred and paranoia.

'Did you ever talk with Steve about the affair?' she asked, playing along.

'No. I took my revenge another way.'

'By setting him up to look like The Dark Alley Strangler.'

'Right. I was killing two birds with one stone, to use a cliché. I got back at him for all he'd done to me, and I also removed any possibility that I would ever be suspected of being the Strangler. Everyone would think he was still alive, still out there murdering young women.'

'But someone saw Steve's car the night Sally Yates was attacked.'

'Of course. I followed him to Wheeling and took his car in the middle of the night. Hot-wired it, as they say. I went to some bar and found the Yates slut. I made sure I was seen coming out of the alley after I'd attacked her. I waited until I saw someone coming down the street, then I emerged from the alley laughing and gibbering, acting crazy to draw attention to myself. And to the car. It was all part of the plan. For the last three years I'd made sure my attacks coincided with Steve's visits to Emily. I even stuck bits of oleander in the women's mouths, since Steve was so damned proud of his ability to grow the silly plant.'

Oleander in their mouths, Deborah thought. That's why Agent Wylie had been so curious about Steve's interest in the shrub. 'But witnesses say the man had dark hair.'

'My dear, I have a dark toupee, and the rest I took care of with a temporary rinse. I also wore dark glasses and a fake mustache. I couldn't take a chance on anyone identifying *me*. And it still looked as if Steve were making an attempt to disguise himself.'

'And who was it at the school who tried to take Kimberly?'

'Me. I wasn't actually going to take her. I saw the teacher watching me. I just wanted to scare you, make you think perhaps Steve was still around. That fool Lieber followed me that day. The police arrived so soon, they almost got him instead of me.'

'And the bells Kim heard?'

'Me again. That one wasn't sure-fire. I didn't know if she'd actually come outside, although I'd given her a suggestion earlier in the evening that if she heard bells close by, it was Santa. I didn't know if you'd check the freezer, either. But it went perfectly.'

'I still don't understand why you rented the O'Donnell house.'

253

'I told you, I decided it was time for Steve to be caught, so I needed to watch every move. And I wanted to see what was going on after he disappeared. After all, I couldn't camp out at your house like Pierce did. I had a son to raise.'

'And you attacked Mrs Dillman.'

'As I was sneaking out of the house one night, the old crone ambushed me. Can you imagine it? She'd slipped past the surveillance and was *waiting* for me. Waved a knitting needle at me,' he laughed, then he sobered. 'The bad part was that at close range, she recognized me. Well, it didn't take long to put her out of commission, but carrying her back to her yard without being seen was no easy feat, I assure you.'

'But you seem to be losing your touch,' Deborah said acidly. 'You didn't manage to kill Sally *or* Mrs Dillman.'

A hand slammed against the back of her head and she went sprawling into the snow. 'I am *not* losing my touch, you stupid cow. They were just unusually tough. But the Dillman woman is too old to live through this, and I'll get Yates yet. Oh, yes, I'll get Mrs Sally Yates. Now *get up.*'

Deborah had a mouth full of snow. She spat it out, then clambered to her feet, her ears ringing from the blow. She stumbled forward until they reached the barn. Still holding the gun on her, Pete opened one of the big doors and pushed her inside. She fell again, this time on cold, naked earth that still smelled of hay and horses.

It was dark in the barn, but Pete produced a flashlight and shone it in her eyes. 'Well, what do you think?' he asked.

She didn't rise from the ground. She asked tonelessly, 'Is this where you killed Steve?'

'Yes.'

She expected a rush of emotion, an outpouring of grief, but she felt nothing. She realized she'd known all along Steve was dead. Entertaining doubts about his being The Dark Alley Strangler who'd gone into hiding was only a way of keeping him alive in her mind.

'How did you get him out here?' she asked.

'My goodness, you are chatty tonight, aren't you? But I've found that most women can't shut up. Oh well, what the hell.' He laughed again. Deborah couldn't see his face. She could only hear the voice that sounded like a distorted version of Pete's familiar tones. 'He apprised me of the whole FBI thing. I was the sympathetic friend, as always. He was afraid that if he were arrested and indicted, his bank accounts would be frozen and you and the children would be left with nothing. He asked if I'd hide the money if he emptied his savings account. I said I would, of course. I told him I was afraid of his place being watched, or of Adam overhearing us if he came to my house, so we agreed to meet out here.'

So that's why Steve had withdrawn the money. To protect it for her and the kids. And naturally he had no idea that Pete hated him and was setting him up as a murder suspect. He thought he was asking his oldest, closest friend to do him a favor. 'So when he brought it out here to you, you killed him,' she said stonily.

'I killed him, yes, but he didn't bring the money. He said he was rethinking the situation. That even though he'd withdrawn the money, he was afraid hiding it would only make him look guiltier. Besides, it wasn't ethical. *Ethical!* Stupid fool. He'd hidden it in your storeroom. He planned to take it back to the bank on Monday.'

'Then it was *you* in the storeroom that night?'

'Yes. I couldn't have the police searching the house and finding the money. Then they'd know Steve didn't have it and this whole deliberate disappearance angle would fall apart.'

'And did you hide in the evergreens behind our house the night of the party?'

Pete was silent for a moment. 'No. I think that was Lieber. I told you, the creep has been lurking around peeping and spying on me, making a general nuisance of himself.'

Deborah's mind flashed back to Lieber in the parking lot. 'I know where your husband is,' he'd said. Now she understood what he meant. 'Artie Lieber knows you killed Steve, doesn't he?'

'As I said, he's been spying for days,' Pete said resentfully. 'Yes, he followed Steve out here. He knows what happened. I saw him, when it was too late. There's not much he can do about it since he came here to kill Steve himself. That's why he was following Steve around in the first place. But I'm not afraid of him. He can't go to the police with some absurd story about the respectable Peter Griffin killing his best friend.'

'He came to me,' Deborah said.

'And you ran.' Pete started that damnable snickering again and Deborah's skin crawled. 'He had the information that could have saved your life and you ran from him. Oh, it's too rich!'

Rage bloomed in Deborah. She stood up and faced the flashlight. 'You son of a bitch! You killed all those young women and tried to frame my husband. Then you killed *him*. You ruined Emily's life. What happened to Eddie King, Pete?'

'Eddie is resting peacefully on a hillside outside Wheeling,' Pete said matter-of-factly. 'I'm afraid I indulged myself and tortured him for a couple of days before I finally finished him off. Once, when it looked as if Emily might be getting better, I told her exactly how Eddie had died. I described those glorious two days of torture *so* graphically, I sent her into the abyss forever.'

Deborah felt sick. 'And now you're going to kill me.'

'That's right. Steve is buried in this barn. I'll bury you right beside him.'

'He's here?' she faltered. 'He's in here?'

'Where else? You didn't think I'd drag him home and bury him in the yard, did you?'

'I don't know what you might do,' Deborah said in a dead voice. 'I don't even know why you want to kill me.'

'Because you found out too much. I tried to keep you from going to Wheeling,' he said petulantly. 'But you had to have your way. You dumped the kids on me and hit the road with your lover. I wasn't a bit surprised when you called and said you were spending the night. What I didn't expect was that you'd find Jeannie. I never dreamed my old bat of a grandmother would remember her name. I didn't even know Jeannie was back in town. But after talking with her, I was sure you knew too much.'

'I didn't know *anything*,' Deborah said furiously. 'I guessed that Eddie King had been Emily's husband. That's it.'

'Oh well, maybe I jumped the gun,' Pete responded carelessly. 'But you had to be eliminated anyway.'

'Eliminated? *Why?*'

'Because you were just like the rest. Oh, I used to rather admire you. So loyal to Steve, so self-effacing. A good mother. And then Steve disappeared and your true colors showed. You moved Joe Pierce into your house the very night Steve disappeared. He wasn't your husband, but you treated him like *family*. Any fool could see that you were sleeping with him. It made me ill, especially Christmas Eve when you were all decked out in your dangling earrings, acting as if *he* was your husband. But I knew you'd get a nice surprise later that night when the music box came. Do you know that "The Way You Look Tonight" was my mother's favorite song? That music box was hers. My father gave it to her. And then Kim whispered to me that she'd found some pretty rings down in the basement and was going to give them to you Christmas morning. I'd hidden the jewelry there the night of your Christmas party. But Kim finding it and presenting it to you as a present was a delight I hadn't counted on. And then there was the doll. You were so busy fluttering over Joe and your friends you didn't even notice me take it and go out to the kitchen, then into the garage.'

Deborah wanted to scream at him that he was crazy, but something held her in check. She didn't know what because there was no way she was going to leave the barn alive, but she still clung desperately to her last few minutes of life.

'Don't you think anyone is going to suspect what happened to me?' she asked.

'Why should they? They'll simply think Steve got you.'

'What about my children? Where *are* they?'

'I told you. They're . . . hidden.'

For the first time uncertainty had crept into his voice, and Deborah pounced. 'I said it before. You don't *know* where they are. You weren't expecting them to be gone when we went upstairs. What were you going to do if they'd been there?'

'Say that they were sleeping peacefully and send you home. Then I would pay a call and kill you.'

'But they weren't there.' She paused, her memory zeroing in on Pete's expressionless face when he looked into Adam's room. 'Adam wasn't there, either, was he?'

'Of course he was.'

'No, he *wasn't*. He ran away with the children, didn't he?'

'So what?' Pete shouted. 'So what if he did?'

'Pete, what are you going to tell *him*? He must know something is wrong. That's why he took the children.'

'He's my son. He loves me. I'll simply explain things.'

'Explain that you *murdered* me?'

'Explain that things got out of hand. That you were making wild accusations. That you tried to kill me and in trying to get the gun away from you, I accidentally shot you.'

His voice quavered and Deborah knew he was frightened. He didn't *know* what he was going to do. He'd simply started on a course of action and was now following through, willy-nilly, without the faintest idea of how he was going to handle the resulting questions.

257

'Pete, do you want your son to know you're a murderer?' Deborah demanded. 'Do you want him to know you killed all those young women? That you killed *Steve*?'

'Dad?'

With the flashlight shining in her eyes, Deborah hadn't seen Adam, whose voice came from the direction of the open barn door. Pete spun around and croaked, 'Son! How did you get here?'

'I drove the Ram Charger.'

'But you don't have a license,' Pete said inanely.

Deborah took a step forward and Pete swung around again, pointing the gun at her. 'Don't!'

'Dad, what the hell are you *doing*?'

'Get out of here, Adam,' Pete said.

'*No!*' Even though Deborah was glad help of some kind had arrived, she ached for the devastation Adam must be feeling.

Pete spoke in a kindly tone. 'Son, I want you to get in the Jeep and I'll drive you home as soon as I'm done here. It's a very bad night and I'm surprised you didn't wreck getting here.'

He's gone completely over the edge, Deborah thought. He no longer possessed the cunning of The Dark Alley Strangler. But that didn't mean he wasn't still a killer. She stood very still.

'You killed my mother,' Adam said in a voice that sounded as if it were being wrenched from him.

Pete made an attempt to laugh. 'Why would you say something like that?'

'Oh, *God*, Dad,' Adam went on in that agonized voice which shot to the core of Deborah and twisted painfully. 'You told me that whole big story about her and another man.'

'It was true.'

'Maybe. But it's not like you to tell me all those details – finding her in bed, saying you hadn't had sex with her for a long time. That's not the kind of thing you'd tell *me*. You overdid it. You were nervous because I wanted to go find her. For a couple of days I thought about how weird you were acting. I also thought about you telling me a friend of Mom's in Montana was sending me the cards and letters. But I remembered *you* had a friend in Montana. Jim Lowe. I called Jim and he admitted he'd been sending the cards for *three* years, not two, like you said. And I wondered why you told me that for the first year she was in Montana, *she'd* sent the cards, when Jim said she hadn't. And then I realized she'd probably never been there at all.' Adam's words picked up speed as he became more agitated. 'You also said you hired a private investigator to find her. I went through your canceled checks for the year Mom disappeared. There were no checks made out to a PI agency, or even a person I'd never heard of. There was *no* search because there was no one to search *for*, was there?'

'Adam, your imagination is running away with you,' Pete said almost primly. 'I must insist you get in the car now.'

'I saw you take Kim's doll into the kitchen. I couldn't figure out what you were doing. Then I heard you call Deborah in Wheeling earlier this evening,' Adam rushed on. 'I heard you tell that lie about Barbara being murdered. I hadn't been sure about Mom, but after I heard you make that call, I *knew*.' A choking sob escaped him. 'I *knew* you were trying to get Deborah back here to *kill* her. You kept prowling around. I couldn't use the phone to warn her or call the police. Finally, right before Deborah came, I sneaked the kids out the back door.'

'Oh, thank God,' Deborah moaned. 'Are they all right?'

'They're fine.' Adam hesitated. 'Dad, after I got the kids out, I did call the police.'

There was a moment of silence. Then Pete muttered, 'Goddammit!' and fired a shot. Deborah heard the bullet whizzing in the air before pain seared down her arm. She screamed and fell to the ground, clutching her arm. Blood oozed from a spot below her shoulder.

'Dad, stop it!' Adam yelled hysterically.

'Don't lie to me!' Pete blazed back at him. 'You did not call the police.'

'I *did*.'

'Then where are they?' Pete demanded.

'They're coming.'

'No they aren't,' Pete sneered. 'It's my guess you took those children to Barbara's, told her to call, and took off. You probably remembered about this place while you were driving around, but the police don't know about it.' Adam was silent and Deborah knew Pete was right. 'Good try, son,' he said cockily, indulgently. 'But it won't work.'

Suddenly Adam rushed forward. With amazing dexterity Pete dodged him and Adam fell, landing beside Deborah who cried out as his weight came down on her injured arm. Adam pulled himself off, muttering a choked, 'I'm sorry' as he scrambled back to his feet and stood in front of her.

'Adam, stop these ridiculous heroics,' Pete said. 'Get out of the way.'

'I'm not going to let you kill her like you did my mother,' Adam sobbed.

'I *have* to kill her. You can see that. But it will be our secret.'

'Jesus, Dad, are you *nuts*?'

'Don't speak to me that way!'

'You're a murderer!' Adam ranted. 'I loved you so much and you're a filthy rapist and *murderer*! How could you have killed all those women? And Steve? How could you have killed *Mom*?'

'Your mother was a whore and a very bad influence on you. I did what was just, and now I'm getting very tired of this carrying-on from you. *Very* tired.' His voice had taken on a dangerous edge. Could he be pushed to the point of killing his own son? Deborah wondered. She was afraid he could.

'Adam, move away from me,' she said steadily.

'He'll *kill* you.'

'Better just me than both of us.'

'She's right, son.'

'You wouldn't kill *me*, would you?' Adam asked incredulously, his voice throbbing with anguish.

'Move. *Now!*' Pete ordered,

Adam stood motionless for a moment. Then he lunged at his father again. This time he caught Pete around the legs and they both went sprawling. The flashlight rolled away and Deborah could see nothing. She heard only grunts, then Adam crying out in pain. Her heart froze. 'Adam!' she called wildly. 'Adam, are you all right?'

'He's . . . fine,' Pete answered breathlessly.

'Adam?' Deborah persisted. '*Adam?*'

The boy groaned and she felt a wave of relief. At least he was alive.

Against the veil of snow visible through the open barn door she saw a shape rise from the floor. From its height, she knew it was Pete. She didn't dare try to stand – he'd think she was going to run – but she couldn't help scooting backward.

'My dear, you look like a crab scuttling along the beach. And it isn't going to do any good, Deborah,' Pete said. He trained the flashlight on her, then the gun. 'You've disappointed me, and you've for ever tarnished my son's image of me. I can't forgive you.'

'Pete, *please*,' Deborah begged. 'I have two small children.'

'And they have grandparents, just like I did. They will be fine, and hopefully Kimberly will not grow up to be a slut like her mother. Sorry, but you've brought this on yourself.'

He aimed the gun. She'd always been told that before you die, your life flashes in front of you. It didn't. She was aware only of the cold earth, the musky smell, the silhouette of Pete against the snow. He cocked the gun—

A shape appeared behind him and leaped. With a shout Pete went down again. The figures grappled. Light flashed as the gun fired. Then they were still.

Deborah cowered, too stunned to move. At last one of the shapes stood. 'Deborah?' Joe asked anxiously. 'Are you okay?'

'Just dandy,' Deborah breathed before she fainted.

Epilogue

'Does it hurt, Mommy?' Kimberly asked, admiring Deborah's bandaged arm in its sling.

'Not much, sweetie,' she lied.

It was eight in the morning, and sunlight bounced off the snow to shine brightly through the living-room windows. Deborah found it unbelievable that only four hours ago she'd been scrambling around on the floor of the barn, begging for her life. Now she sat on her couch, surrounded by Barbara, Evan, Joe, Scarlett, and the children. Adam was in the hospital with a mild concussion and a sprained wrist. Deborah inwardly cringed to think of Adam's real pain, which would come when he'd recovered enough to assimilate the truth about his father. She only hoped the boy was as strong as he seemed to be. At least Pete wouldn't go on trial for the murders of all those people. In the scuffle between him and Joe, a bullet had gone through his heart.

Back at the barn, police were digging up Steve's body. The thought made Deborah almost dizzy with grief and horror. Poor Steve, who'd been lying under the cold ground since Sunday afternoon. She hadn't really accepted his death yet, but she knew that soon reality would hit her in thundering waves. Right now, however, she felt relatively calm and wildly thankful that the children were safe. She hadn't told them about Steve. That would come later, after they'd settled down from the excitement of their secret flight to Barbara's where they'd stayed until an hour ago. Deborah would tell them about Steve this evening, when she'd figured out how to do it as gently as possible.

After they'd finished studying her arm, Kim and Brian rushed into the kitchen to fix Scarlett her breakfast. 'Barbara doesn't even have *dog* food,' a disapproving Kim had whispered loudly to Deborah. 'That's because she doesn't have a dog,' Brian chimed in with a roll of his expressive eyes.

'I promise to get some,' Barbara laughed, 'just in case I have another unexpected visit from Scarlett.'

With the children gone, the adult conversation turned back to the events of the previous night. 'I still can't believe Lieber brought you back to Charleston,' Barbara told Joe. 'He saved the day.'

'Before you get sentimental over him, remember he was only trying to clear himself of Steve's murder,' Joe said. 'He came to Charleston with the intention of killing Steve himself. He says he couldn't go through with it.' He shrugged. 'Maybe he's telling the truth, or maybe Pete just beat him to it. Anyway, he knew he'd be the number-one suspect, and he didn't stand a chance telling his story to the police, so he was trying to convince Deborah so she'd divert the FBI's attention to Pete. Otherwise, Lieber would most likely have ended up in jail for the rest of his life.'

Deborah looked down. She could barely comprehend the number of malevolent forces surrounding her husband the last few days of his life: Pete and Artie Lieber wanting him dead; the FBI thinking he was a serial killer. And Emily. Always his beautiful sister, irreparably damaged because he'd left her alone for a couple of hours.

As if sensing her falling mood, Barbara said brightly, 'Who would have believed Mrs Dillman could survive this?'

'Fred told me she woke up last night,' Deborah said. She smiled. 'She told the doctors she'd been attacked by Pete Griffin and that the children and I were in danger. They didn't believe her, but she was absolutely right.'

'That's amazing,' Barbara said. 'I hope even if my memory's not quite up to par, I'm as resilient as she is when I'm her age.' She smiled fondly at Evan and looked at the new ring on her left hand. 'Especially since I'll have a young husband to keep up with.'

Evan grinned. 'Honey, when you're Mrs Dillman's age, I'll be eighty-five. I don't think I'll be too hard to keep up with.'

Later, to the children's delight, Barbara and Evan left to pick up breakfast for everyone at McDonald's. As they drove away, Joe threw Deborah a wry look. 'Two days ago I thought those two were finished. Now they're engaged.'

'Barbara said they reached a crisis point. Evan had a choice to make, and luckily he made it in her favor.'

'I think we'd better wait a while before we see whether or not Evan's decision was lucky for Barbara. I don't think he's absolutely sure of *what* he wants.'

'I suppose we'll have to just hope for the best.' Deborah looked out the window. 'The night of the Christmas party Steve said any romantic pairing was a risk.'

'He was right.'

Deborah sighed. 'Joe, I can't believe Pete murdered him. He's gone.' She snapped her fingers. 'Just like that, Steve's gone. I'll never see him smile again, never hear him complain that the children watch too much television, never watch him tending his plants.' She shook her head. 'I'd come to hate our annual Christmas party – it was so much work – but right now I'd give a party every night if he could be with us again.' Her eyes filled with tears. 'Oh, Joe, none of this seems possible, and I feel so awful that I've been sitting here smiling and talking like nothing has happened.'

'You've been through too much to absorb it right now,' he said gently. 'But I know you loved him. *He* knew you loved him. And don't feel guilty because you're functioning in a mild state of mental shock. You have to right now, for the kids' sake Unfortunately, the pain will hit later.'

'I know.' She frowned. 'What I don't know is how to tell the children.'

'Need some help with that chore?'

She looked at his tired face, at the slightly bloodshot eyes and the scar standing out more prominently than usual. 'I think we've imposed on you enough already.'

Joe sat down beside her on the couch and looked earnestly into her eyes. 'Do you remember when you asked if I was happy, and I told you I wasn't happy or unhappy?' She nodded. 'That was a lie. I hope Steve can forgive me, but I've been happy this week, here with you and the children, in spite of the circumstances. I loved playing games with them, the four of us eating dinner together, even skulking through back yards with you in the middle of a snowstorm.'

'Oh, Joe,' Deborah faltered, feeling guilty and sad and pleased all at the same time. 'I don't know what to say.'

'Just say you won't shut me out now that the threat to your life is over.' His voice softened. 'Please, Deborah. I'd like to help if I can.'

She looked down at her hands for a moment. 'We need you. Kim and Brian and I need you.' She met his eyes and smiled. 'I won't shut you out, Joe. Not ever.'